Superhero's Apprentice

Cassandra Morphy

The author attests that the work in its entirety is uncorrupted by genAI and every element is wholly a result of the author's creative practice.

Chapter One
Arrival

Sparks flared up from the console in front of Drilora, hitting zer in the face. Zer fur caught on fire in places, and ze felt it burning. But ze was too busy keeping zer ship from slamming into the krylonian ship next to it. Drilora kept zer eye locked on that other ship, even as ze swatted away at the small fires burning in zer fur. The targeting computer couldn't get a lock on the other ship, with both ships circling around each other. Another rocket launched out of the krylonian ship, and Drilora pulled up on zer controls, desperately trying to get out of the line of fire. Only ze was certain that the krylonian already had a lock on zer ship.

"Screw it," Drilora said. Or, at least, a reasonable facsimile. Drilora didn't speak English. Ze spoke Uvvelian, the only language that ever emerged on zer homeworld of Uvvelia. Drilora was already further from Uvvelia than any other uvvelian had ever gone before. And ze was about to go much further than that.

With the rocket coming closer to Drilora's ship, shown as little more than a blip on the scope in front of zer, Drilora reached over to the controls next to zer. The device those controls were connected to was something that the uvvelians had stolen off of a downed krylonian ship. The scientists were certain that it had to do with how the krylonians got to their sector of space to begin with, some method of faster than light travel. Drilora had been out on a test flight for the device when the krylonian ship attacked zer. So, Drilora figured that it was time to test the device.

The scope was giving off a low beeping sound, the speed of which was increasing as the rocket came closer. There was no time like the present, so Drilora hit the switch, not really knowing what the device would do. All ze knew was that it was zer only chance to get away from the krylonian ship. Away from the rocket that was just seconds away from hitting zer.

Once the switch was flipped, Drilora looked back to the main display, searching for signs of what the device did. At first, it didn't look like it did much of anything. The space in front of zer ship was as dark and empty as it usually was when there wasn't a ship shooting at zer. But then, ze noticed an odd distortion out there. Something that was making the stars behind it fluctuate in a strange way. Drilora didn't have time to wonder at what that was, what could have caused that sight. The beeping was only getting faster.

Before Drilora could do much of anything, though, the rocket slammed into the back of zer ship, knocking it forward and into that distortion. Drilora's stomachs, of which ze had three, all clenched at once, which was the reaction that uvvelians had to sudden, extreme motion. Drilora's ship started to shake, and ze thought for sure that ze was about to die. That the rocket had caused a chain reaction that would soon destroy zer ship. But then, the shaking stopped, and a strange blue planet came into view in front of zer.

Alarms were ringing all over the cockpit, lights flashing to tell Drilora about all the damage that the rocket had done. The rocket, and travel through that strange distortion. Without knowing what the distortion was, or how it worked, Drilora had no idea where ze was. What world that blue planet was, or if ze could even survive down there. After a few seconds of zer just staring at that strange planet, it slid out of view.

Once Drilora was no longer captivated by that sight, ze looked around at the instruments in front of zer. The planet was still on the scope, spinning around the ship. Or, more accurately, the ship was spinning around under the force of the impact from the rocket. The distortion soon came into view again as the ship came back around to point back at it.

Just in time for Drilora to see the krylonian ship coming through it.

"Mud water," Drilora said, an Uvvelian saying that was more akin to "well, crap." Ze shook zer head in defeat, staring at that other ship coming zer way. The damage readout showed that the targeting computer was off. There was no way for zer to lock onto the krylonian ship. All ze could do was fire blindly into the space between them.

So, ze did just that, grabbing onto the stick and pressing the fire button again and again. As the ship spun in space, the laser cannons fired off several shots. Most of them went wide, as expected. But as Drilora's ship continued to spin, ze kept firing.

The krylonian ship turned toward Drilora's ship, and ze had no doubt that it was lining up another shot. That the next rocket would end Drilora. Ze could even see the rocket that ze thought for sure would be the one to hit, right under the left wing of the krylonian ship.

Right where the next rounds from zer laser cannons hit.

The rocket exploded when the laser fire hit it, while it was still connected to the wing. The krylonian ship started its own spin under the force of the blast, and it seemed like it was no longer capable of lining up its next shot. That maybe, just maybe, Drilora might be able to make it out of there alive.

As the krylonian ship slipped out of view once more, Drilora turned to the rest of zer instruments, trying to make sense of all the damage reports that were coming up. It was immediately clear that the control thrusters were damaged, which explained the spin and why ze couldn't stop it. There was no signal from home base anymore, though ze had no idea if that was because of travel through the distortion or if the communication systems were damaged. The computers seemed to think the former, as it wasn't listed among the damaged systems. But what worried Drilora the most was when ze noticed that the main thrusters were offline, perhaps even destroyed.

And that the blue planet was starting to get awfully close on the scope.

Drilora turned off the alarms one by one, as ze acknowledged each of the alerts that they were connected to. There was a blue light that continued to flash in the cockpit, replacing the sounds. It would continue until Drilora repaired the systems, or the ship lost power, whichever came first. As the blue planet came into view again, with flames forming around the main display, Drilora figured that a complete destruction of zer ship would cause that loss of power.

With no control thrusters, and no main thrusters, there wasn't much that Drilora could do as the ship came into the atmosphere of the planet. One system that seemed completely functional is the science system, which Drilora was the least familiar with. Another display came up on the console in front of zer, showing that the atmosphere of the planet would at least be breathable, though uncomfortable. That was little consolation to zer as ze came in for a crash landing.

Ze kept turning off systems as the ship continued to fall through the atmosphere, desperate to get as much power as ze could to the last system that might still save zer. The retrorockets wouldn't be much help if the ship was pointed in the wrong direction when ze fired them off, but the ship was still tumbling as it fell through the atmosphere. As long as the timing was right when ze fired them off, the crash could at least be survivable. That was the best that Drilora could hope for at that point.

However, as the sky came back into view, so too did the krylonian ship. It seemed like the other ship was on the same tragic trajectory, and likely to crash not too far off from where Drilora would.

Just as the krylonian ship fell out of view once more, the proximity sensors sounded. Drilora knew that the ground was too close, that ze needed to fire the retrorockets if ze wanted to survive the crash, no matter which way the ship was pointed. Without being able to control the ship, all that Drilora could do was compensate with the rockets. Ze had to guess, which ze always hated to do.

Drilora hit the aft rockets first, hoping that they would turn the ship so that the retrorockets were pointed down. Zer stomachs clenched once more under the force, but ze ignored it as ze hit the forward rockets. As the ship's fall slowed, Drilora got zer first view of the area that ze was crashing in. There were large trees visible in the distance, but the area around the ship was mostly grass. Strange creatures were standing there, staring up at the ship. The science system quickly classified those creatures, giving them a long, drawn out, purely scientific name. Drilora abbreviated the scientific name automatically, calling them pips. It would be a few days before Drilora heard the word human.

The ship gave an odd lurch as it crashed down. Another round of sparks flew up from the main console as several fires popped up all around the cockpit. But with the krylonian ship coming at zer, Drilora didn't have the time to worry about such things. Ze just grabbed the emergency supplies pack that was stashed beneath the console before punching up at the main display. Three punches had the display popping out, giving Drilora a clear path out to the alien planet.

Drilora quickly jumped down from the ship, landing on the grass. Ze could feel the difference in the gravity between that world and Uvvelia. It was so much lighter there, and Drilora knew that ze would be hopping around more than walking most of the time. But it was solid ground beneath zer feet for the first time since leaving the homeworld, and it would do just fine as a place to stand against the krylonian coming down.

However, before Drilora could pull the blaster out of zer supply pack, the pips jumped up in front of zer, brandishing long, metal weapons that looked like something that the uvvelians had used a few centuries earlier. With how they were pointing them at Drilora, it was clear that they were some kind of weapons. That they meant Drilora harm if ze made any move that they thought of as a threat.

"No, not me," Drilora said. "Them." Ze pointed up at the other ship, but the pips all kept glaring at Drilora. That was one mistake that Drilora hoped that the pips would live to regret. Otherwise, they wouldn't live at all.

The krylonian ship's own retrorockets popped off, bringing the ship down into a much more controlled landing. A few of the pips turned to that other ship, but their weapons stayed locked on Drilora. For a moment, Drilora thought that maybe the weapons had some kind of targeting system on them and that they needed to decouple zer as a target. But then, one of them quickly swung their weapon over to the other ship.

"Yes, finally," Drilora said, pointing toward the krylonian ship. "That's the one you need to be worried about."

Once the krylonian ship landed, the canopy on the cockpit quickly flipped up, and the krylonian hopped out. It already had a blaster in its hand, pointing around at the pips. The krylonians were not much to look at, just as tall as the uvvelians, with long snouts, and a thick carapace instead of fur. Drilora often thought that the krylonians had started the war simply because they were jealous about how much more attractive the uvvelians were than them. But when you're staring down the barrel of a blaster, such things as looks don't matter too much.

At the sight of that blaster, all the pips turned their weapons on the krylonian. But it was already too late. The krylonian opened fire, killing three pips in seconds. Drilora quickly reached into zer bag, pulling out zer own blaster. Three more pips went down before Drilora managed to get a shot off, hitting the krylonian straight in the chest. The krylonian remained standing, turning its blaster toward Drilora. Ze let off three more shots, each one slamming the krylonian's chest, right next to the first shot. Drilora always had excellent aim.

After the fourth shot, the krylonian let out an odd shriek. Its empty hand went to its chest as it dropped to its knees. Its eyes stayed locked on Drilora as the life seemed to fade from it. Drilora got off two more shots at the krylonian as it fell over, lying there on the ground, right next to the bodies of the pips.

And then, of course, the few pips that were still standing turned their weapons back at Drilora.

Chapter Two
Five Years Later

"Come along," Cecilia's father shouted at her, waving her forward. "Let's get this over with."

"Ha," Cecilia scoffed. She knew what her father meant by "get this over with." He was planning to dump her on the doorstep of the tower and leave her there. She had no interest in making it easier on him.

"Come along," Cecilia's father said again.

Cecilia's father kept pushing against the tall grass around them as they came out into the space in front of the tower door. Only once they were there did Cecilia see a similarly trod path back to the parking lot next to theirs, one that they had missed when leaving the lot. A sign was hanging on the door that had some kind of alien script on it. Below the script were the words again in English, as well as Spanish, French, and Cantonese. "Go away." It was a simple message, one that Cecilia wanted nothing more than to follow. Her father had already made it clear that she had no choice in the matter. She hoped that he would let the alien have a say, but she doubted that would happen either.

Cecilia's father stood there in front of the door for a moment, looking around at it. It took Cecilia a moment to realize that he was looking for a doorbell. A doorbell that obviously wasn't there. After all, just how welcome would visitors be at a tower with such a sign? Why have a doorbell at all when you don't want anyone there? He seemed to figure that out himself soon enough, as he started to bang on the door loudly.

"Maybe it won't hear you," Cecilia muttered, low enough that her father might not hear over his banging. But he glared over at her just the same, making it clear that he had.

After a minute of banging on the door, Cecilia's father switched hands, shaking out his tired right one as he continued with his left. As he banged away at the door, Cecilia looked around at the tower. The place had been built soon after the creature arrived there, in the very spot that the ships had crashed down. It had once been a public park, though no one wanted to go there anymore. Not after what had happened.

Some said that over a hundred people died in that very spot, and were buried beneath the tower. Cecilia had been twelve at the time, and everyone in her school insisted that the place was haunted. As she looked around at the tower, this five story structure of brick and glass, the place didn't feel haunted to her. However, the known occupant of the place was said to be scary enough.

"What?" someone finally shouted from the other side of the door.

Despite what everyone in town always said about the alien, that one word came out in perfect English, in a clear alto over the sound of Cecilia's father's pounding. However, he didn't stop in his insistent knocking, only switching back to his right hand as he continued to pound away.

"Oh, for heaven's sake," the voice came again.

There was a loud thud coming from the door, and Cecilia's father finally stopped bashing on it. He took two steps away from the door, coming to stand next to Cecilia. His arm went around her shoulders, pulling her close to his side, as the two of them looked at the huge doors in front of them. The sounds from the doors quickly stopped, though, silence filling the area once more.

"Uh..." Cecilia's father said, before jumping forward, his hand already up to knock on the door once more. Before he could swing the first knock, though, the door let out another thud, slowly turning inward.

"What do you want?" came a voice through the smallest of cracks in the door. The words were repeated, first in Spanish, then French, then Cantonese, then Portuguese, then some language that Cecilia had never heard before.

"Uh, what?" Cecilia's father said, once that steady flow of questions ended. "Oh, right, sorry."

"Yes, you should be sorry," the voice said. "Goodbye."

"Wait, no, I," Cecilia's father called out. He rushed forward before the door could close, sticking his foot in the crack there. "Please, I... I must speak with... with the hero."

"No heroes here," the voice said. "Goodbye."

"Please, it... It is a matter of life and death," Cecilia's father insisted.

Cecilia just rolled her eyes at that, knowing full well that her father was full of crap. That he would say anything to be rid of her, pawning her off on this creature. A creature that no one saw outside of the amazing work that it did for the city. Even as they stood there on its doorstep, with the door open just enough for it to peek out, Cecilia couldn't see anything of it.

An odd sound came from the door before it slipped open further. Cecilia shifted to her right, trying to see through that crack, but there wasn't enough light coming through it for her to make out anything. All she could see was the same darkness as before.

"What is the problem?" the creature asked. There was an odd tone in its voice, making the words come off with something of an accent, though they were still clear enough for her to understand.

"It's... It's my daughter," Cecilia's father said. He waved behind him toward Cecilia. "Her name is Cecilia."

"Hello, Cecilia," the creature said, in that same tone. "You don't look like you're dying."

"Oh, I'm not," Cecilia said, nodding her agreement. "Thank you." She stood there awkwardly, feeling like she should curtsey or something, though she had never curtseyed before in her life.

"Yes, thank you," Cecilia's father said. "You saved her just two days ago. If it weren't for your actions, she would have died in that fire."

"Well, then, you're welcome," the creature said, though the tone of its voice still hadn't changed. "Now, go away."

"No, no, wait, please," Cecilia's father said. "You-you don't understand."

"What don't I understand?" the creature asked. The door opened a bit more, and a single sliver of light passed through. Cecilia could make out a patch of brown in that light, but not much else. "There was a fire. Your daughter was in it. She's safe now, thanks to me. It is my job, nothing more. If she is experiencing continued issues, she should seek medical attention. I am not a doctor."

"No, please," Cecilia's father said. "You don't understand. It's... It's my culture."

Several words streamed out through that crack, none of them familiar to Cecilia. It was then that she realized the creature was talking in its native language. That as its annoyance at her father increased, it resorted to that language to curse at him in a way that he wouldn't understand. Her own father had a habit of doing that, swearing in Catalan.

"Fine, fine," the creature said, eventually. "Explain it like you would a child. Perhaps I could keep up. Then, you can finally go away."

"In our culture, when one saves another's life, they owe you a life debt," Cecilia's father said, slowly. "You saved Cecilia's life, and therefore, she owes you a life debt."

"Ugh, a life debt? Really?" the creature asked. "Fine. You're forgiven of this life debt. Go in peace."

"Oh, I'm afraid it doesn't work like that," Cecilia's father said.

"Ah, if only," Cecilia muttered. But then, she knew very little of this whole life debt stuff. It wasn't something that her father had taught her growing up. The first time that she had heard anything about it was when she was rescued from the fire. She had a feeling that he was only insisting on it because it was a way to get rid of her, something that he had made clear he wanted since long before the fire.

"What would I even want with a life debt?" the creature asked.

"It's not something to give," Cecilia's father said, as if he really thought the creature so stupid. "Cecilia is to stay with you until such time as she has fulfilled the debt."

"And who determines that?" the creature asked, getting to the heart of Cecilia's issue exactly. "You? Cecilia? Some weird god thing that you creatures have made up to explain away the unexplainable? Even though you've already explained most of that stuff anyway."

"She must save your life," Cecilia's father insisted. "Or in some way makes your life better that saving hers is worth it to you."

"Oh, well, in that case," the creature said. The door opened just a bit more, and an eye appeared. The eye was a dark black, against the brown fur around it, but with how high up it was and how it was pointed straight at them, Cecilia was relatively certain that it was an eye. "The two of you leaving me alone would definitely make my life better. I invite you both to do just that."

Cecilia snickered at the comment, her hand going to her mouth to keep a larger laugh from escaping. Her father glanced over his shoulder at her, leveling his glare on her for a moment, before turning back to the door. Slowly, he shook his head at the creature, making it clear that he would not be dismissed so easily.

"I'm sorry, but that's insufficient," he said. "I'm sure there is something that she can do around your tower that could be of help to you."

"Oh?" the creature asked. "Does she know how to recalibrate a plasma cannon? Does she know how to repair an ion drive? Does she know how to program a slip drive navigation system?"

"No," Cecilia said, shaking her head. "I know how to cook, though."

"As do I," the creature said. "I'm not some... human male who thinks such things beneath them."

"She... She could be your apprentice," Cecilia's father said.

"My apprentice?" the creature asked. "In what way? She's already said that she knows nothing about the technology that I need to get off this planet."

"No, not for your ship," Cecilia's father said, waving off its words. "For your superheroing. She has a superpower herself, you know."

"Ha, right," the creature said. "Humans don't have... superpowers." That tone returned to its voice, making it clear just how it felt about that word. About calling what it can do a superpower. It was just what the creature was naturally capable of, as all of its species would be.

"I uh... I do actually have a superpower," Cecilia admitted, reluctantly. "Something that only I can do, rather than what all humans can."

"Oh?" the creature asked. "And what is that?"

"Being underestimated," Cecilia said.

Silence fell between the three of them for a moment, that eye staying locked on Cecilia from behind the door. Slowly, an odd sound started to come from the door, getting louder by the second.

"Being underestimated?" the creature said. "That's.... That's not a superpower."

"It is the way I do it," Cecilia muttered.

Cecilia didn't like being laughed at, but it was clear that that was what the creature was doing. That it was laughing at her, at her thought that her being underestimated could be a superpower. Clearly, it had never thought of such a thing.

"Fine, fine," the creature said, finally. "Impress me with your superpower."

The door opened a bit further, and Cecilia could make out more of the creature's face. It wasn't often that anyone captured the creature in an image or video, and it was never clear. There were more images of Big Foot out there than of that creature. And as Cecilia stared up at it, she realized why.

The creature was close to seven feet, with a single black eye in the center of its face. There was no sign of a nose anywhere, with a mouth just below that eye. Its entire body was covered with brown fur, and it wore no clothes that could be seen over it. Given how they were intruding on the creature's privacy, Cecilia wasn't sure if that was normal for it or if it just hadn't gotten dressed to answer the door. All in all, it was quite ugly by human standards, though Cecilia figured that she shouldn't judge it by them. That its own society would have a different opinion on the matter.

"It... Uh... It doesn't work that way," Cecilia said. She glanced away from the creature and over to her father, hoping that he would change his mind and let her come home. He just stood there, staring up at the creature, his eyes wide and his mouth half open.

"Yeah, that's what I thought," the creature said. "Go away," it shouted, before slamming the door in their face. With Cecilia's father stunned by the appearance of the creature and his foot no longer in the doorway, there was nothing stopping the door from closing.

Chapter Three
On the Tower's Doorstep

"Well, that's that, I guess," Cecilia said. She looked back at her father, trying desperately not to smile. Trying not to show just how happy she was that they couldn't get her inside the tower. But from the look on her father's face, it was clear that he wasn't satisfied. That they weren't done there. That Cecilia wasn't about to head home.

"You could have tried harder back there," Cecilia's father said, pointing back at the door behind her. "You know how important this is to me. To our people. You're not to leave here until you've accomplished what we came here to do. Understood?"

His glare stayed locked on Cecilia, making it clear just how serious he was. But Cecilia already knew that; he was a serious man. He never had any tolerance for joking around or play. Even before Cecilia's mother died seven years earlier, she remembered how gruff the man always was, though it got so much worse when the creature arrived. And there he was, pushing her off on the creature, just to get rid of her.

"Yes, father," Cecilia said. She turned her eyes to the ground between them, not wanting to see that look. Not wanting that glare to bore into her soul like it did so often to others in their community.

"Good," Cecilia's father said. "Now, stay here. I'll go get your bags."

"But..." Cecilia started, her eyes flicking back up to her father. However, he was already heading back to their car.

As Cecilia watched her father heading back through their path in the tall grass, she looked around at the park. Most of it remained intact, though the grass had grown tall throughout it. The park had been tended to in those first few months after the creature arrived there, but that had stopped soon after. From the welcome that she had gotten from the creature, Cecilia figured that was related to it.

The park was at the edge of the city, the looming towers visible over the trees in the distance. Behind Cecilia, behind the tower, the trees hid the ocean beyond them. With the tower looming tall overhead, Cecilia had the sense that it would have a beautiful view of the water out there. And with her father abandoning her there, she wondered if she might soon see that view.

As Cecilia waited there, she looked up at the tower, her eyes tracing the walls as they disappeared overhead. The tower was simple, having been erected over the span of a couple months. The base of it had been built around the initial containment building that had been put up that very first day after the creature arrived. The tower was supposed to be five stories tall, but as Cecilia looked up at it, it looked more like ten to her. However, with the gray stone matching the clouds above, it was hard to tell where the tower ended.

Cecilia's father was back soon enough, depositing the two suitcases next to her. They had once belonged to her mother, some of the few remaining items that they still had of hers. Cecilia's father wasn't one for sentimentality, though Cecilia had managed to rescue the suitcases from the trash. If she had known what she would be using them for, she might not have bothered.

"Is that everything?" Cecilia's father asked, sounding almost like he cared. It was clear to Cecilia that he didn't.

"Everything I brought with me," Cecilia said. There were several things that she had been forced to leave behind, like her friends. Her DVD collection. What books that she couldn't fit in the suitcases around her clothes. From how the creature had been noticeably naked before, she had a feeling that those were going to be the only clothes available to her until her time in that tower was over. A time that had no scheduled end to it, if it ever truly started at all.

"Good, good," Cecilia's father said, nodding. "Then, I'll leave you to it. Goodbye, Cici." Cecilia flinched away from that nickname, never much liking it, but her father seemed oblivious to her reaction. Or, perhaps, he just didn't care.

"Goodbye, father," Cecilia said, simply. Neither of them moved to hug the other; Cecilia knew that her father wouldn't respond even if she tried, slipping out of her grip. With one last nod, Cecilia's father turned around, heading back to the car.

Cecilia stood there quietly, watching as her father drove away from the tower. The road led off to the left, heading around a bend and back out into city traffic. Once the car made it around that bend, it was blocked from view by the trees. Only then did Cecilia turn back around to the door, knocking lightly.

"My father is gone," Cecilia called out, hoping that the creature would be able to hear her through the door. That it even cared about her being stuck there. When the door didn't open for her, she figured that was the only answer that she was going to get from it.

With nothing else for her to do, Cecilia shifted one of her suitcases around so that she could sit on it. She laid the other one down on the ground next to her, opening it so that she could retrieve one of the books that she had brought. Cecilia had read each of them multiple times; they were her favorites after all. So, she just grabbed one at random, flipping through to the first chapter. She figured that she could get halfway through the book before the creature even noticed that she was there.

A low rumble went out. Cecilia glanced back over her shoulder at the door, wondering what the creature could be doing in there. Wondering if it was trying to do any of the things that it had asked Cecilia if she was capable of, which all sounded like trying to fix a spaceship. With the tower built around the crash site, though, Cecilia wasn't sure how the creature expected to get a ship out of there.

Soon after the rumble, a drop of rain hit Cecilia on the head.

"Oh," she whined, looking up at the clouds as she realized that the rumble must have been thunder. That the storm that was about to open up on her would likely run for hours. And with her father already long gone, and the creature seeming to ignore her, she was likely to get soaked through, stuck out there in the rain.

Quickly, Cecilia put her book back into the suitcase, zipping it back up to keep it dry. The suitcases were old, though, and Cecilia wasn't sure if they were waterproof. If they would keep any of her things dry, let alone her books. So, once the suitcase was closed once more, she picked it up, placing it against the tower as close as she could get it. Her hope was that the tower would protect it from the worst of the weather.

As soon as the suitcase was in place, the rain started up, pouring down all at a go. Cecilia was quite drenched within seconds, even before she could get her second suitcase against the wall. She huddled against the doors to the tower, looking out at the rain that seemed everywhere. The doorway gave her little protection from the deluge.

"Hello?" Cecilia called out, knocking on the door again. "It's... It's raining. Not that you care," she mumbled, knowing that the creature wasn't listening.

Another crackle of thunder rang out and Cecilia jumped in startlement. Her hand went to her chest to stay her racing heart as she turned around to look back at the city. Despite her father's words, Cecilia wondered about running away. About heading out into the city to try to find somewhere else to live. Anywhere but in that park, getting rained on. However, the tower was half a mile away from the rest of the city, and she would be out in the open the entire way if she tried to make a run for it. By the time she made it to the city, she would be hopelessly drenched.

But then, she was already hopelessly drenched.

"Can... Can you let me in, please?" Cecilia called out, bashing on the door much like her father had earlier. "Please? Just-just inside. You-you don't have to keep me."

She laughed a little at her choice of words. At the idea that the creature would be keeping her like she was the pet. Whenever the creature was depicted at all, it was usually drawn quite like a dog. What she had seen through the door didn't look anything like a dog, though.

When no answer came from the tower, Cecilia reached for the knob, hoping that it was open. That the creature wasn't as careful with its security. The knob barely rattled at her twisting, proving to be quite as locked as she was expecting it to be. Still, she twisted it back and forth, hoping that it would give way. That the door might underestimate her, much like people had been doing her whole life.

After turning it a dozen times, the door seemed to do just that, the handle finally turning.

"What?" Cecilia asked, staring down at the knob in shock. However, just seconds after the knob turned, it was pulled out of her grip. The door spun open, revealing the creature standing there once more.

"Go away," the creature said again, staring down at Cecilia there, soaked and alone.

"I'd love to," Cecilia said. She raised her arms to either side, drawing attention to the weather behind her. "It's raining. The city is half a mile away, and I'd still have to find somewhere that would let me in there. Or you could let me in here. I won't go far. Just inside. Please?"

"Where's your father?" the creature asked, glancing up from Cecilia to look around the parking lot behind her.

"Gone," Cecilia said. "He left me here."

"I'm not equipped to raise a human child," the creature said. "I'm barely equipped to raise an uvvelian child."

"I'm no child," Cecilia said, bristling at the word. "I'm plenty raised, thank you very much. No one is asking you to raise me. Just... Just to train me so that I can do what you do."

"Ha," the creature laughed, a purely human laugh that contained no real humor. "None of you puny humans can do what I do. You're not built for it."

"I'm not talking about your powers," Cecilia said. "I'm talking about teaching me to help people. To use my gift to help those that need help. That's all."

The creature stood there silently for a moment, staring down at Cecilia. Cecilia just stood there in the rain, looking the creature in the eye. Trying not to look disgusted by the sight of the thing, which was quite hard for her. After what felt like a small eternity, the creature looked back at the parking lot behind her before looking down at her once more.

"That's all?" the creature asked. "I teach you how to be a superhero and you leave me alone?"

"If you want," Cecilia said, nodding her agreement. "I would like nothing more than to just go home, but Father made it clear that I wasn't to leave here until my work is done."

The creature just stood there for a moment longer, staring down at Cecilia, before finally stepping to the side, opening the way for her to head inside. Cecilia quickly scooped up her bags once more, pulling them with her into the dry interior of the tower.

Chapter Four
Inside the Tower

The grass of the park stayed beneath Cecilia's feet as she headed inside the tower. However, instead of the tall, overgrown grass that was outside, it was brown, mostly dead, and trampled flat. The far wall was several yards away, almost the same distance as the parking lot was behind her, with no other walls blocking off the space. There were tables off to the side, with several metal bits and pieces cluttering it. With the creature's earlier comments, Cecilia figured that those bits were what was left of the parts that it was trying to repair. And in the center of the room was what was unmistakably a spaceship.

"Whoa," Cecilia said, as she stared at that spaceship.

The craft wasn't as big as many claimed it to be, from the stories of the crash from years earlier. However, it was large enough to fit a couple dozen people on it. Or, at least, a couple dozen humans. With the creature looming tall over Cecilia, she thought that the spaceship wouldn't be able to fit more than six or seven of them. There was a huge hole in the top of the ship on the side facing her, with a large chair visible through the hole. The rest of it was solid metal, though there were scorch marks in several locations and holes in several places along the bottom.

"Is that your spaceship?" Cecilia asked, pointing at the craft.

"No," the creature said. There was a bitter tone to its voice, making Cecilia think it was offended by the suggestion. "Mine is the one behind it." The creature pointed off to the side, to another craft just visible around the first one. "This belongs to the krylonian that shot me down onto this mudball. I've been stripping it for parts, but they're not exactly compatible. It's almost like taking apart one of your cars to fix my spaceship, though the parts from the krylonian ship are more useful. This ship at least used to fly before I shot it down."

"Wait, I thought you said the crayons shot you down," Cecilia said, glancing back over her shoulder to the creature.

The creature let out a light snicker at the comment. "The krylonian," it corrected. "We shot each other down. But, since the krylonians started the war, I usually blame it for the misery that I've had to put up with." Its eye was locked on Cecilia, making her think that she was part of that misery that it was talking about.

"Right," Cecilia said, nodding her understanding. She figured that it was best to drop the subject at that point, not wanting to anger the creature further. "So, where will I be staying?" She looked around the room, wondering if she would be stuck sleeping on the ground down there somewhere.

"If it were up to me, you wouldn't be," the creature said, making it clear just how unwelcome she was. "But, as usual, this planet of yours has made it clear that nothing is up to me. Can't go home. Can't fight in the war. Can't save my people. Stuck here, in the mud. Stuck with... Well... You..."

"Cecilia," Cecilia said, reminding the creature of her name.

"Right," the creature said, nodding. "Come with me, Cecilia."

The creature started away from Cecilia, keeping to the outer wall of the tower as it headed over to a set of stairs leading up. It kept hopping up and down as it went, like it was enjoying itself. It reminded Cecilia of her more innocent years, when she would skip up and down the road in front of her apartment building. Between how large the creature was and how quickly it could move, Cecilia had to run to keep up with it. She needed to take three steps for each of the creature's bounds, her suitcases rattling as she ran.

"Uh... What-what do I call you?" Cecilia asked. She was already starting to pant from the exertion of running along behind the creature.

"My name is Drilora," the creature said, not bothering to look back at her as they headed up the stairs. "My pronouns, as you humans have started to say, are ze/zer. Not it. Not he. Not she. Not they, which makes no sense to me. How can a single creature be a they? Ze/zer is the closest pronoun to the ones we use in our own language."

"Uh... Okay..." Cecilia said. She had never heard anyone using those pronouns before, though she had heard of them at times.

It was difficult running behind the creature as they headed up the stairs, her suitcases hitting the railing next to her as she went. The stairs ran along the outer wall of the tower, turning with its curvature. When they came out into the first floor above, the space opened up on the right. Much like the ground floor, this one was a huge, open room, with a few pillars scattered around it for support. However, instead of the spaceships like below, the room was outfitted as a gym, complete with several machines and weights. Many of the machines looked broken, their frames bent and their wires frayed. The closest of the machines was set at the highest weight possible, with several more weights placed on top of the pile.

"This is the gym, obviously," Drilora said, pointing at it. "Please don't touch anything in here. It's hard enough to keep up my muscle and bone mass in this low gravity. I'm in here for several hours of the day. When I'm in here, don't be."

"Sure," Cecilia said, nodding. She never bothered with such things herself.

Drilora quickly continued up the stairs, heading for the next floor up. Cecilia lingered there just a moment longer, more to catch her breath than to see more of the gym, before following zer. Ze stopped at the top of the next flight of stairs, pointing out to another open floor. This one was just as recognizable as the last, only much more of a draw to Cecilia. She stood there, three steps below the floor, staring out at the room in wonder.

"This is the library," Drilora said, waving a hand at it.

The place was packed with shelves full of books, with several more stacks of books next to three big, comfortable looking chairs, and a table in the center that looked to be piled high with comic books. As Cecilia slowly came up the remaining stairs, she got a glimpse at the comics on top, surprised to see that most of them featured Superman.

"Please, don't take any of the books off this floor, and treat them all with the respect that they deserve," Drilora said.

"Of-of course," Cecilia said. "Do... Do you read a lot?"

"It is how I learned your language, and several others," Drilora said, simply. "Come."

Ze continued up the stairs, but Cecilia didn't want to leave that floor. She lingered there, staring around at the wonder before her, wishing that she could read all the books inside just from standing there. That was one superpower that she would have loved to have gotten, rather than the one that she was born with. Long before she got her fill of that floor, Cecilia managed to pull her eyes from that sight, following Drilora up.

Unlike those below it, the next floor up wasn't open. A hallway led off from the stairs, with two doors on either side of it. Cecilia figured that these were the bedrooms, and she looked around at the doors, trying to figure out which one was open.

"The kitchen and dining room are on this floor," Drilora explained, pointing around at the doors. "Most of the food here is not suitable for human consumption, so be careful. Or don't. No fur off my nose."

"Wait, nose?" Cecilia asked. She looked up at Drilora with a confused expression. Drilora rolled zer eye back at her, shaking zer head.

"Yes, I have a nose," Drilora said. "It's not plain on my face like with you humans. A nose is a pretty important organ, one that should be protected. Not decorated or pierced." Drilora shook out zer fur at the thought of it.

"Sorry," Cecilia said.

"As I was saying, most of the food in there isn't suitable for human consumption. If you insist on staying longer than the storm, we may look into getting more human food. Personally, I doubt you'll make it past our first call. If you get in my way on a call, you'll be put out. Understand?"

"Yes, of course," Cecilia said, nodding feverishly. "I-I won't get in the way. I promise. I'm good at staying out of people's way."

"I thought your skill was being underestimated," Drilora said. Ze blinked zer eye several times in a weird way, with it flipping all over. "The thought of that being a superpower. Ugh, I need a good laugh now and again."

Cecilia blushed deeply, her glare set on Drilora, when she realized that ze was laughing at her. That that was how zer species laughed. It was quite insulting, but nothing that she hadn't had to put up with before.

"Alright, alright, come along," Drilora said, waving Cecilia further up the tower.

Cecilia pulled her suitcases up as she followed along behind Drilora, though they fell back down soon enough. The suitcases were quite heavy, making her wonder if maybe she should spend a little time in the gym after all. It might make helping out on the calls easier for her.

Rather than continuing past the next floor, the stairs simply stopped there. There was a wall at the end of the stairwell, lined up with the wall leading out into another hallway. The doors off that hallway seemed to match the ones below, though the stairs hadn't run the entire perimeter of the tower between the two floors. At the far end of the hall was a ladder, leading up to a hatch in the ceiling. Drilora led the way down the hall, coming up to the first pair of doors.

"My room is over here," Drilora said, pointing to the door on the left. "Do not go in there, or you will be put out of this tower. Understood?"

"Yes, Drilora," Cecilia said, quickly, nodding her head.

"This room will be yours until I can be rid of you," Drilora said, zer voice softening a little as ze pointed to the door on the right, across from zers. "The room has never been used. It might be a bit dusty, but everything is new. I expect it to still be like new by the time you're put out of this tower. Understood?"

"Uh... Yes-yes, Drilora," Cecilia said.

At least, she thought she understood zer. Understood that she wasn't to put in too much wear, rather than that she wasn't to use anything inside of it. She wondered at how she would be able to use the room without using anything. But since she had long since grown out of jumping on the bed, she figured that everything would be more or less in the same state that it was when she arrived in the tower. Though maybe a bit cleaner, if the room really was dusty.

"Fine, fine," Drilora said. "I'll leave you to get settled in. When a call comes in, I expect you to be ready."

"Ready?" Cecilia asked.

"Wear something... appropriate for such activities," Drilora said. Ze pointed at Cecilia's dress, which was still damp from the downpour outside. Cecilia wanted nothing more than to change into something dry, but she wasn't sure what ze meant by "appropriate for such activities."

"Uh..." Cecilia said, hesitantly.

"Ugh, something you can run in that you don't care if it gets destroyed," Drilora said.

"Oh, yes, alright," Cecilia said, nodding her understanding. "Are we expecting a call today?"

"I'm always expecting a call," Drilora said. "It helps to be prepared for the worst, like a chemical fire in the middle of a thunderstorm." Just as ze said that, another rumble of thunder came through the tower. It sounded a lot louder than the low rumbles that she had been hearing during the tour. "Now, please, for the love of your imaginary divine, please leave me alone."

Cecilia stood there by the door, watching as Drilora headed back through the tower, down the stairs. While she got the sense that she would never quite be considered welcome there in that tower, she was already more welcome there than she was at home. Moreover, she had finally accomplished the first step in the task that her father had brought her there for.

Chapter Five
The Spare Bedroom

The door to the bedroom opened silently. Cecilia stayed in the hallway for a moment, sticking her head through the crack to look around the room. Just as Drilora had said, the place looked unused, with just a fine layer of dust over the furniture. The bed wasn't made, but there was a pile of sheets at the foot. If Cecilia didn't know better, she would have thought that Drilora had placed them there while she was standing out in the rain. However, the fine layer of dust that was in the rest of the room was visible on top of the pile of sheets as well. The sheets must have been there a while, waiting for someone to visit.

"Well, I've certainly done with worse," Cecilia said to herself, as she slipped inside the room. Inside her room.

Cecilia slammed her suitcases onto the bed, sending the dust back up in the air. She waved her hand at it, clearing it away from her nose before she could inhale it. The lights were off in the room, but there was enough sunlight coming through the storm clouds and the windows to see by. She could see the curve of the tower in the far wall, though the furniture seemed well suited to fill the space. There was a small, low dresser below the window, and a tall, narrow wardrobe next to it; both seemed perfect for Cecilia's needs. Against the wall on her left was a desk, tucked away in the corner, that looked made for reading at. Already, the place was feeling more like home to Cecilia than her own home had felt in years. Not since her mother passed.

"Alright, time to get started, eh?" she asked herself, clapping her hands as she looked around the place.

Cecilia grabbed one of her suitcases at random, pulling it around her bed to the dresser. When she flipped it open, she noticed that her clothes were already wet. A light whimper escaped from Cecilia's lips when she realized what that might mean, and she quickly dashed back around the bed, over to the other suitcase. She held her breath as she reached out to that suitcase, slowly opening it. The top of the case slammed into the bed, jarring loose another spray of the dust, but Cecilia paid it no mind. She just stared down at the contents of that suitcase, and at the three books tucked inside.

Just like with the first suitcase, the contents of the second suitcase were damp from the rain. The books were already showing water damage, their covers bent and their pages wrinkled. Slowly, carefully, Cecilia reached out, pulling the books out one by one. There was no sign of the cover peeling away onto her clothes, so she hoped that the damage would be limited to what she was already seeing. She placed the books down onto the small table next to her bed, leaving them there to dry. Short of bringing them to a book conservator, there wasn't much else that she could do for them. Still, seeing them sitting there like that, so damaged from the weather, felt like a wound in the memory of her mother.

A slight sniffle came out of Cecilia before she could stop it. The tears wouldn't be far behind. Cecilia shook her head, trying to jar those tears away. Trying to block out the hurt that she was feeling, not just by the loss of her mother, but by her father so heartlessly throwing her away like that. Despite everything that had played out between her and her father, she still loved him, and knew that he loved her too. At least, in his way. That had always been what her mother said about it.

"I miss you, Mom," Cecilia said, and the tears started coming. She wiped away at them, trying to put on a brave face. Trying to get past the hurt that still hung over her, even after all those years.

Cecilia quickly turned away from those books, looking back at her clothes. Unlike the books, the clothes would take better to the water, but they still needed to dry. She took her time in unpacking them, more to allow herself the time to grieve the loss of her mother, of her life, than that the clothes needed it. However, as she slowly put them away, she was searching through what clothes she had brought, looking for something that would work for what Drilora had asked her to wear. Most of her clothes, both the ones that she brought and the ones that she had left behind, had always been dresses. The best she found were a pair of sturdy jeans at the bottom of her first suitcase, though she doubted they would be acceptable to the creature. Fortunately, she remembered to bring a pair of sneakers; she doubted her heels would be appropriate footwear for anything that the creature usually did out in the city.

Once her clothes were stowed, Cecilia quickly made the bed. None of the sheets proved to be a fitted sheet for the mattress, but she figured something out, folding one of the sheets around it. The bed was longer than her bed at home, like it was designed to fit the creature, and the headboard and footboard kept getting in the way of her efforts. She wasn't sure how well it would hold up to her first night there, if she even made it that far. However, the work helped distract her from her life ending in the way that it had. By the time the bed was made, her tears were dry once more.

With her bed made and her clothes stowed, Cecilia just stood there in the silence of the room. The only sound she heard was the rattling of the rain against the window, making her feel more alone than ever. There was no sign of anything from the creature, though she knew that it, that ze was still out there somewhere in the tower. But as she looked around the room, she noticed another door that she had missed before. Drilora hadn't said anything about the door, whether it was off limits or not, but it was inside her room. She figured that it was a closet or something, despite the wardrobe.

Cecilia glanced toward her still open door, almost expecting the creature to be watching her from the hallway. Waiting for when she did something that ze didn't like. However, the hallway was just as empty as it had been when she came in there. With no sign of the creature, Cecilia slipped over to the door. She grabbed onto the knob, turning it slowly and softly, bracing herself for the door to whine at her opening it. But the door was as silent as the one from the hallway.

And as she looked through the doorway, she realized that it led to the bathroom. There was another door opposite from her that seemed to lead into another bedroom next door. But with the creature sleeping in the room across the hall, that meant that they wouldn't need to share a bathroom.

"Few," Cecilia said, letting off a sigh of relief, even as she started laughing at herself.

Of course, the door would lead to something simple like a bathroom, rather than some secret room that the creature was trying to hide from her. From what she had seen of the tower so far, the place seemed pretty simple, built only for the creature's use while ze was stuck there on Earth.

With the mystery of the door solved, Cecilia started moving her toiletries into the bathroom. They were the last things that she needed to unpack, and she found plenty of room for them. Once she was fully unpacked, she glanced at the shower next to her, thinking that she could use one. That she needed to get warm after being stuck outside in the rain. But with most of her clothes wet, she would be stuck in a towel waiting for them to dry. Instead, she opted for changing into her jeans, which were at least drier than her dress, and an old t-shirt that she didn't remember packing. She hung her dress up with the rest of her clothes, wondering if the tower had laundry facilities hidden somewhere, perhaps in the floor below.

Once she was dressed, Cecilia stood there at the foot of her bed, looking around her room. She felt a bit lost, like she was forgetting something. If she had forgotten anything, it would have been left behind at her father's apartment. While the apartment was only on the other side of the city, rather than the other side of the world, it might as well be that far away for how welcome she would be there. At least, until she accomplished what she came there for.

"Speaking of which, I guess there's no time like the present," she muttered to herself. "Time to go find the creature and... see my training started, eh?" She glanced over at the three books as she said that, all but talking to her dead mother as she asked the question.

Cecilia let out another sigh, shaking her head as she looked at those books, before turning to the door next to her. The hallway outside was just as empty as it had been before, with no sign of the creature anywhere. Slowly, Cecilia walked back through the hallway toward the stairs, trying to make as little sound in her sneakers as possible. She wasn't trying to sneak up on the creature; only making it so that she didn't disturb zer, wherever ze was in the tower. However, she didn't get that far before hearing zer footsteps storming back up the stairs toward her.

"Good, you're..." Drilora said. Ze paused, zer eye flicking up and down Cecilia's body, examining her outfit. "Is that the best you have?"

"Yes, sorry," Cecilia said, looking down at her outfit.

"Fine, fine," Drilora said, waving off her apology. "It's not like you'll be doing much running on this one anyway. You'll need to put your hair up, though. That's likely to catch on something, or someone might grab it. That would not be pleasant."

"Right," Cecilia said, nodding. She glanced back at her bedroom door, just behind her, as she tried to remember if she brought any hair ties. There might have been one among her toiletries. But then, Drilora's words registered to her. "Wait, we have a call?" she asked, turning back to zer.

"I have a call," Drilora corrected. "It's a dangerous one, so it might be better if you just stayed here. But we have to start somewhere. The sooner that I see how horrible you are on these calls, the sooner I can send you home to that father of yours. Come along, human. You'll soon find out that I don't have much patience. Not when it comes to your kind."

"Yes, of-of course, Drilora," Cecilia said, nodding her understanding. And yet, she still stood there, staring up at the creature.

"Go," Drilora barked, waving Cecilia back to her room. Zer voice echoed around the enclosed space of the hallway, hurting Cecilia's ears. She flinched away from zer, her hands going to her ears. The creature didn't show signs of caring. "Meet me up on the roof once you've tamed that hair of yours."

"Right," Cecilia said, before rushing back into her room. With only the one place to search for a hair tie, it didn't take her long to find it. Even as she was putting her hair up, she was racing back into the hallway. Drilora was climbing up the ladder at the end of the hall, heading for the roof above. Cecilia was quick to follow after zer.

Chapter Six
The First Call

Cecilia wasn't sure what to expect on the roof of the tower. A helicopter. A working spaceship. She hadn't seen anything from the ground. But with Drilora scrambling to get up there, she figured that there had to be something up there. Something to get them into the city quickly, and over to wherever it was that they were going.

However, as she climbed up the ladder after Drilora, poking her head up through the trap door, she found... nothing.

"Did I miss something?" Cecilia asked, as she climbed out onto the roof.

The rain was still coming down in torrents, and her previously damp outfit was soaked within seconds. She was just glad that she hadn't bothered with that shower, knowing that she would need another one by the time she got back to her room. If she got back.

"Was this some kind of test?" Cecilia asked, glaring over at Drilora. Ze was standing just next to the trap door, looking over at her.

"If it was a test, you would have failed it," Drilora said. "Next time that I have a call, if you're still here, I expect you up here faster. Now, come on. We need to get to the bank."

"Which bank?" Cecilia asked.

"Oh, right," Drilora said, shaking zer head. "Your city has several banks, doesn't it. You humans and your fascination with useless metals and paper. The uvvelians evolved past needing such things to incentivize work centuries ago. Now, let's go."

"Go where?" Cecilia asked. "How are we getting there?"

"Less questions, more action," Drilora said.

Without another word of warning, Drilora came back those three steps between them. Ze reached down, grabbing onto Cecilia by her arms and pulling her up. Before Cecilia knew what was happening, she was on Drilora's back, desperately clinging to zer shoulders. Her feet were several feet off the ground, and she tried to wrap them around Drilora's hips. However, the creature's hips were way too wide for the effort, and Cecilia's legs just dangled down, hitting the creature in the rear.

Or, at least, what the creature had instead of a rear. All that Cecilia could see back there was more fur.

"Hold on tightly," Drilora said, before running forward.

Cecilia could just see over Drilora's shoulder. But as the creature ran for the other side of the roof, she wished that she couldn't. They were five stories up, and it looked like the creature meant to just jump off the roof. It made Cecilia wonder why they hadn't gone through the front door. She wondered if they were jumping off the roof like that simply because that door was closer to her bedroom.

But then, Drilora jumped. The tower's roof, the park, it all fell beneath them as they soared up through the air. Everyone always said that the creature could somehow fly like gravity had no hold over it. Fly like Superman. However, the creature kept zer feet under zer, zer head pointed upwards, as they headed out over the park.

At the edge of the park, there was another tower, this one smaller, barely a few feet across, and made of wood. It was built soon after the main tower was built, though no one in the city knew what it was for. As the two of them fell back toward the ground, Cecilia suddenly knew exactly what that tower was for, as they were heading straight for it.

Cecilia closed her eyes, holding tighter to Drilora's shoulder, as they came in for a landing. That didn't stop her from hearing the odd, wooden, groaning sound coming from beneath them. She thought for sure that the tower would break from the impact, that it would fall out from beneath them and they would fall to their deaths. But then, she felt them soaring upward once more, with Drilora jumping back off that tower.

As they headed past the road at the edge of the city, they rose above the rooftop of the first set of buildings. Drilora came in for a landing on the first roof, zer feet kicking up the gravel that was up there. Rather than slowing, Drilora ran faster, heading for the far side of the roof. There was a set of stone steps over there, leading up to the ledge. Drilora ran up the steps, jumping once again on the top of them, soaring further up into the air and over the buildings beyond.

"Well, I'll give you one thing," Drilora said. "You're not messing up my travel nearly as much as I was expecting you to."

"What?" Cecilia shouted, her eyes flying open as she looked around them once more. They were already soaring over the city, with the first buildings coming on quickly. Far faster than she was expecting it to. "What would have happened back there if I had?"

"Oh, nothing," Drilora said, shaking zer head. "Well, not much anyway. I might have broken the tower if I hit it straight on. But, no, I would have been able to land just fine. Your planet's gravity is too low for me to get hurt from falling like that."

"Well, what about me?" Cecilia asked. Drilora didn't respond to the question, though. "Do you even know where you're going?" Cecilia asked, as they all but flew over the buildings of the city.

"Yeah, the bank," Drilora said.

"But which bank?" Cecilia asked.

"The one with the flashing lights in front of it," Drilora said, as if that were the obvious answer to the question.

Cecilia looked out around the city beneath them, though it made her stomach queasy to see that. To see how high up they were, with nothing but Drilora's abilities keeping her from dying on the pavement below. A quick way for the creature to get rid of her would have been to simply toss her off anywhere along there, probably just explaining it away like she had slipped or something. Cecilia only squeezed tighter onto zer fur, making sure that didn't happen. But with the rain soaking zer fur through, just as much as Cecilia's clothes, her purchase wasn't as secure as she would have liked.

It took Cecilia some time to spot the flashing lights in the distance, though Drilora seemed to know exactly where they were going before then. They were already angled along that path, heading straight over there. Cecilia wasn't sure on which jump that Drilora had shifted course as they made their way through the city, or if ze always knew that that was the bank where they were heading. But as they approached those lights, Cecilia had a bigger concern to think about.

How they were going to get back down to the street.

Drilora didn't say anything about it as ze landed perfectly on the roof of the building in front of the lights. Ze kept running forward, making for the far edge of the roof. At first, Cecilia thought that Drilora would just keep going. That ze would make another jump at the end of the roof and head further into the city. There was another set of stairs on that roof, much like every roof that they had landed on along the way, and Drilora was running for them just the same. Cecilia closed her eyes tightly as they came up to the edge, not wanting to see what was about to happen.

So, Cecilia didn't see it when Drilora jumped off the edge of the roof, but she felt it in her stomach as they fell back to the ground.

The landing on the pavement below was just as light as the landings that Drilora had made on the roofs above. Cecilia only knew that they had stopped by the lack of motion. Still, she hung there, clinging to Drilora's shoulders, much longer than she needed to. Slowly, she opened her eyes again, looking around at several cops staring her way.

"Anything we need to know?" one of the cops asked, pointing toward Cecilia, still hanging onto Drilora's shoulders.

"No," Drilora said, simply. "What do we have?"

"Five hostages behind the teller desk, plus three robbers," the cop said, with no further mention of Cecilia.

He turned to face the bank in front of them, pointing through the windows like he could see the inside through them. When Cecilia glanced over Drilora's shoulder, though, all she could see was her own reflection. Her face looked stark white against the brown of Drilora's fur, making her look like a ghost that was haunting the creature, rather than a human.

Off to the side of the doors to the bank was a rain-soaked flyer taped to the wall. It was flapping in the wind, which was what drew Cecilia's eyes to it. As she stared at it, the flyer fell away from the wall, flipping around in the wind as it disappeared into the distance. The storm seemed like the worst possible thing to be out in at that point.

"The robbers all have semi-automatic rifles," the cop continued. "You... You know--"

"Yes, I know what those are," Drilora said. Cecilia could sense zer anger, carefully kept in check. "They won't be a problem. Well... At least, not for me. My apprentice might have a problem with them, if she's shot."

"Apprentice?" the cop asked, looking back at Cecilia.

"Hi," Cecilia said, simply, waving at the cop.

Once her hand came away from Drilora's shoulder to wave at the cop, her grip became more tentative, and she slipped down along the wet fur of the creature. Before she could grab back onto that fur, she found herself landing heavily on the street behind zer. Drilora quickly stepped away from Cecilia, turning around to look back at both the cop and Cecilia. Without a word, ze made it clear that Cecilia wasn't going to be riding zer into the fray.

"Are you sure you should be bringing your... apprentice in there?" the cop asked, nodding toward the doors.

"No," Drilora said, shaking zer head. "But she has to start somewhere. I need to know just how useless she is, so I can get rid of her. The sooner the better. And, if she gets herself killed in there, that's not my fault." Ze glared over at Cecilia as ze said that, making it clear that ze meant it.

"I won't get myself killed," Cecilia said. "No one is going to be shooting at me. What about you?"

"Don't worry about me," Drilora said. "Let me be absolutely clear with you. Do not worry about me in there. I have dealt with far worse than this. If you stay with me past this incident, you will too. Best get used to it. If it looks like I'm in danger, I'm not. Just keep yourself safe, keep your head down, and try not to get killed. Understood?"

"Yes, Drilora," Cecilia said, nodding.

"That's it?" the cop asked. "Try not to get killed? Aren't you going to... I don't know, instruct her? What is she going to be doing in there?"

"I don't much care," Drilora said. "All she needs to do is not die. That's probably more than she's capable of doing on her own, so having her in there is only going to make my job harder."

"No, it's not," Cecilia said. She stood tall, smiling up at the creature in front of her, as she tried to put more confidence in her voice than she felt. "Just as I shouldn't worry about you, you shouldn't worry about me in there. Trust me. I have this."

"Said the girl that needed to be rescued from a fire not three days ago," Drilora said.

"Uh, yeah, that was a fire," Cecilia said. "Fire can't underestimate me. Fire is fire. My power doesn't work against fire, but it'll work against three robbers with semi-automatic rifles. Trust me. I've got this."

"Well, then, maybe I should just be sending you in there on your own," Drilora said, smiling down at Cecilia as ze waved zer hand at the doors. "Go on."

Cecilia just stood there, looking between Drilora and the doors for a moment. She wasn't sure if the creature was serious about that, but she hoped that ze wasn't.

"Uh, why don't you go first?" Cecilia asked. "I'll stay close, but not too close to be in your way."

"That's what I thought," Drilora said. "Alright, come along, apprentice." The tone of zer voice shifted under that word, making Cecilia think it was zer way of scoffing.

Chapter Seven
The First Mission

Cecilia stayed close behind Drilora as ze headed for the doors to the bank. As they came up in front of the building, she could make out the three bank robbers through the revolving door. One of them was behind the counter, their gun pointed down at the ground at an odd angle, like he was about to shoot the floor. The other two were out in the middle of the room, pointing their guns at the doors. All three of them were wearing black clothing, with hoods that hid their faces; only their eyes were visible.

Drilora stopped short of the revolving doors, and Cecilia bumped into zer. She fell back a step, looking up at Drilora's face as ze glanced back at her over zer shoulder. "Sorry," Cecilia said, raising her hands up in front of her. Drilora just shook zer head before turning back to the doors in front of zer. However, instead of heading through the revolving door in the middle, ze went over to the regular doors next to it. Ze headed in slowly, coming just inside the doors before taking a step to the side. As Cecilia came in behind zer, she almost expected zer to shake off the rain like a dog. The water was dripping off zer fur onto the floor, but ze seemed oblivious to it as ze stared toward the robbers.

Off to the side of the door was a bulletin board with several postings on it. One of the flyers looked like the one that had been taped on the wall outside. Cecilia glanced at it for a moment, noticing that it was one of several anti-creature flyers that she had been seeing around the city for years. There was a grainy picture of Drilora, that looked nothing like zer with zer standing right next to it, with the name of the anti-creature group. She didn't pay it much attention as she focused on the situation in front of her.

"Don't try anything, monster," one of the robbers said, his gun aimed at Drilora. The gun was shaking a little in his hand, rattling as it did so. "You don't get paid if the hostages get killed, now, do you?"

"Paid?" Cecilia muttered.

Of course, she knew that was how it worked. Drilora was paid to do zer superheroing out in the city. That was how ze paid for the tower, everything in it, and the equipment that ze needed to repair zer ship. Still, it confused Cecilia for a moment before she remembered that.

Cecilia's knees were already shaking, even without the gun pointed at her. She turned her head to the side, trying to flick her hair over her face to hide from the situation in front of her. When nothing happened, she remembered that her hair was up. That the move wouldn't work in situations like that. Cecilia worried that it would somehow impact her ability to be underestimated. That the robbers would see her as a threat, just as they saw the creature. She stood next to Drilora, looking up at the creature, waiting for some orders. Waiting for zer to tell her what to do there. All she knew was to stay out of Drilora's way. So, she stayed near the doors, watching the professional do zer job.

The robber's eyes seemed to flick over at Cecilia when she spoke, though the gun stayed pointed at Drilora. Ze was the danger there, the one coming to stop the robbers and save the hostages. Even if Cecilia were coming in there on her own, they wouldn't have paid much attention to her. After all, that was how her power worked. At most, they might have tried to add her to the hostages behind the counter. With none of them staring her way, it seemed like her hair wasn't that important to her power.

"How about you just let the hostages go and we can walk out of here together?" Drilora said. Zer hands were up in front of zer, showing that ze was quite unarmed. Seemingly unprepared to meet the might of these robbers. However, everyone there knew that that was far from the truth. That the creature would be able to disable the robbers with nothing more than zer brute strength.

Drilora took a step closer to the robbers, and both robbers took a step back away from zer. However, with how tall Drilora was, that one step still brought zer closer to the robbers. And with the counter right behind them, they were just two steps away from bumping against it.

"Don't move," the robber said. It seemed like he sensed how close the counter was as well. Sensed that they were cornered there, unlikely to make it out of there before Drilora was on them.

"Alright, alright," Drilora said. "Let's think this through, shall we? I'm here. There's plenty of cops out there already. The building is surrounded. There's no escape. Either you surrender, or I make you surrender. Those are the options."

"Or, maybe I shoot you in that big, beady eye of yours and I get my helicopter like I demanded twenty minutes ago," the robber shouted. He motioned the gun forward, jabbing it through the air between them, though he didn't fire it. Cecilia had a feeling that he was about to. That at any moment, he would shoot, and it wouldn't go well for anyone there.

Drilora stood up taller at the mention of zer eye, zer hands falling back down to zer side. Cecilia looked up at zer face, but she couldn't see much of it from her place by the door. The robbers' guns were both starting to shake faster, their rattling getting louder. From that, she figured that the glare ze was giving them could have stopped hearts.

"Go ahead," Drilora said. Ze took another step closer to the robbers, waving zer hand at zer eye. "Give it a shot. Shoot me in my 'big, beady eye', as you call it. It's a perfectly normal eye for my people. Some might even call it attractive."

"Ha, maybe in hell," the robber said. "How about I send you back there."

Before Drilora could say or do anything else, the robber fired the gun. It was loud, the sound of it echoing around the room. Cecilia ducked down, her hands going to her ears as she closed her eyes, shielding her sight from the devastation that was about to happen. The gunfire sounded like it went on for forever, though Cecilia knew that it couldn't have been more than a few seconds. Even after it ended, the sound of it echoed around the room, slowly dying. Only then did Cecilia open her eyes once more.

Opening them to see what had happened.

The robber that had been talking to Drilora was on the ground, with Drilora holding his gun. The other robber on their side of the desk was backing away from Drilora, their gun still pointed at the creature. Drilora just stared back at them, not bothering to turn the gun in zer hands on them.

"No more of that," the robber behind the desk called out. It was the first time that the robber spoke, and Cecilia could tell from her voice that it was a woman, though she couldn't see much of her body through the protective glass. Her gun was still pointed at the hostages, keeping Drilora from finishing the job. Her eyes were pointed in Drilora's direction, but downward to the robber at zer feet. It didn't seem like she would be able to see his body down there, though, blocked by the counter between them.

"Y-yeah," the other robber said, his voice shaking. "You-you need to go, or... Or we start shooting the hostages."

The woman's eyes flicked between Drilora and the other robber for a second, her hand starting to shake at the comment. Cecilia figured that she wasn't ready to do that. That she didn't want to hurt anyone, and had expected that they would be out of there by then. However, it all felt like a huge mess to Cecilia.

Slowly, Cecilia stood back up, staying by the doors. She looked around at the three of them, at a loss for what to do. And with all three of them ignoring her, she figured it was best to just stay where she was and wait for some sign as to what she should be doing. It was the best way for her to stay out of Drilora's way and not get killed, the only instructions that she was given.

"Alright," Drilora said. Ze raised zer hands again, this time with the first robber's gun in them. "We'll be leaving."

"No," the other robber said. "She stays. You go. We could use another hostage. A penalty for killing Kenny."

"But..." the woman said, her eyes darting over to the other robber.

"Oh, he's not dead," Drilora said. "Not yet, anyway."

"What?" the woman said, looking back at Drilora. There was a noticeable amount of hope in that one word, though she kept the gun pointed at the hostages behind the desk.

"Do you want me to bring him out with me?" Drilora asked. "I'm sure we can get him some help."

"Yeah, and have him arrested while you're at it," the other robber said.

"Wait, no," the woman said. "Please, he--"

"No," the other robber shouted, shaking his head. "He'd rather die than go back to prison."

"Or, we could do this," Drilora said, though ze didn't say anything further. Both of the robbers looked at zer, seeming to wait for zer suggestion. Instead of saying anything,

Drilora whipped the gun off to the side. It sailed over the protective glass of the teller desk, bumping against the ceiling before tumbling down on the other side. It slammed into the woman's head, and she was knocked backward, falling beneath the desk.

"What?" the other robber asked, his eyes turning toward the woman. That was the last mistake the man made there.

With the other robber distracted, Drilora rushed forward, grabbing onto his gun before he could try to shoot zer. A single flick of zer wrist had the gun pulled out of the man's hand, tumbling off toward the doors. Then, Drilora rose up tall once more, looming over him, making it clear that there was no escape. That he wasn't going to get far before he was captured by the creature.

"Damn it," the man shouted, before turning around, trying to run anyway. He barely got three steps away from Drilora before ze punched out, knocking him to the ground. Even with him prone on the floor, Drilora loomed over him, seeming like ze wanted to continue the fight.

Instantly, the doors opened behind Cecilia. She jumped to the side, desperate to get out of the way, as the cops from outside stormed in. Their guns were all pointed at the robber as they swarmed around the room. Five of them headed for the door to the side of the desk, sweeping around to the hostages behind it. In seconds, they had the three robbers contained.

"Thank-thank you, uh..." the cop from earlier said, as he came up next to Drilora. He stood next to the creature, looking up at zer eye as he stepped between zer and the other robber, who was still lying on the floor next to zer. It took Drilora a moment to turn away from that other robber, looking at the cop next to zer. "We-we have it from here," he said, his voice shaking as he stared down the creature.

"Right," Drilora said, before finally turning away from the robber next to zer. Ze turned back toward Cecilia before looking all around the room, seeming to be searching for something. Whatever it was, though, Cecilia had no idea what that would be. It wasn't like they brought anything in with them, and they wouldn't be leaving there with anything either.

"That was amazing," one of the cops said. There was a group of three of them standing by the revolving door, all staring up at Drilora in wonder. It seemed like this was the first time that group had seen the creature in action.

Drilora ignored zer fans as ze made zer way through the throng of the collected cops in the bank, heading back over to Cecilia. Ze just shook zer head as ze stared over at Cecilia, not slowing in zer pace as ze headed for the door next to her.

"Come along, Cecilia," Drilora said, as ze headed back out into the day.

Cecilia stood there a moment longer, looking around the room expectantly. Part of her wanted to stay there, to ask the cops if there was somewhere that she could go other than back to the creature's tower. But she knew that her father wouldn't stand for it. That if he heard she left just hours after getting inside the tower, he would be furious with her. So, reluctantly, Cecilia headed out the door after the creature.

Chapter Eight
The Useless Human

Drilora was standing just outside the doors to the bank, staring back at Cecilia as she followed behind zer. Zer arms were folded over zer chest in a purely human expression, and ze was glaring at her with zer one eye. There was an odd expression on zer face, zer mouth stretched out away from zer eye, which Cecilia figured was something like a scowl. Without zer having to say a word, Cecilia knew that ze was frustrated with her. That ze was disappointed with what she had managed to do in there.

"I didn't get shot," Cecilia said, shrugging.

"Get on," Drilora said, simply, zer words strained. Ze quickly turned zer back to Cecilia, ducking down to give the girl an easier time up.

The rain had slowed during their time in the bank, but it was still coming down and Drilora's fur was already wet. Cecilia hadn't dried off much during their time inside, so she tried to put it out of her thoughts as she came up behind the creature. She grabbed onto zer shoulders in the same place that she had before, though zer fur seemed thicker than she remembered. Cecilia figured that had something to do with the rain, the fur acting like some kind of sponge to soak it all up like that. However, the fur didn't let out any water as she squeezed on it.

Once Cecilia had solidly grabbed onto Drilora's shoulders, ze stood up again, pulling Cecilia up off her feet once more. Drilora shook zer shoulders back and forth for a moment, seeming to test how secure she was on zer back. Cecilia looked out over Drilora's shoulders, looking around at the street, wondering just how they were going to get back up to the top of the buildings. With how they had arrived, she knew that they would be heading home the same way. Drilora didn't say anything about it, didn't give Cecilia any warning, before crouching down. This time, when ze came back up, ze jumped straight up into the air, leaving the street far beneath them.

Cecilia closed her eyes once more as they came at the wall of the building in front of them. They had barely cleared five stories, and there were several more stories to go. She didn't see it when the creature came at the wall, but she felt it when ze jumped back off of it, heading further up. Three more jumps like that had them soaring up over the rooftop, and the trip back to the tower could truly start.

The trip across the city was the same as the one out. Cecilia was growing in her confidence in Drilora's ability to keep her safe on the trip, and she managed to keep her eyes open for more of it. The storm was starting to move out of the area, and Cecilia managed to catch a few rays of sunlight streaming through the clouds on their right.

By the time Drilora landed on the wooden tower at the edge of the park, the rain had stopped, though the clouds lingered overhead. Ze landed in the middle of that small tower perfectly, seeming just as in control of zer jumps as ze would have been if ze could fly. That one last jump off the tower brought them over the rest of the park to land at the edge of the tower roof. Drilora skidded to a halt there, zer body perfectly balanced the whole time. Once they had stopped, Drilora just stood there, looking out at the few rays of sunlight streaming through the clouds in the distance. As Cecilia looked over Drilora's shoulder, out at that sunlight, she could see the water stretching out into the distance over the top of those trees. The storm still seemed thick out there, and she was glad that she was on the solid roof of the tower.

Or, at least, that Drilora was.

"You can get down now," Drilora said, after a few seconds of them just standing there like that.

"What?" Cecilia asked. She looked at Drilora's back, then the ground beneath her, before she finally realized that she was still clinging to Drilora's back and that it was safe to let go. "Oh, sorry," she said, but she stayed there a moment longer before slowly opening her hands. Her fingers seemed to cling to zer fur a bit longer before she slid free, landing lightly on her feet.

Drilora took a pointed step away from Cecilia before turning back to glare at her once more. Zer arms went back across zer chest as ze slowly shook zer head in disappointment.

"I already had low expectations for what you would be able to manage out there, but that? That was absolutely horrible."

"What?" Cecilia asked, flinching away from zer words.

"Not only did you contribute nothing to the job, but you almost got yourself captured in the process. If we had been outnumbered, things would have been very different in that bank."

"Uh... Weren't we outnumbered?" Cecilia asked. "It was three to two."

"No, it was three to one," Drilora said. "Or, perhaps, I should count you on the robber's side of that whole mess. You were worse than useless. You were a liability, just as I thought you would be." Drilora's words gradually got louder as zer anger came out in full force.

"Well, what did you expect me to do?" Cecilia asked. Rather than yelling back at Drilora, rising to meet zer anger, Cecilia shrank away from zer. Her voice was barely audible even to herself, but Drilora didn't seem to have any trouble hearing her. She shifted her head to the side, trying to hide behind her hair. With it still tied up, the move didn't work like it usually did.

"Anything," Drilora said. "Something. Make yourself useful. Use this so-called power of yours. How exactly do you expect to be a... a superhero if you don't act?"

"I did use my power," Cecilia said. She shook her head as she lowered her eyes to the roof between them. Her eyes traced the cracks between the stones as she continued. As she explained what she did back there. "If they saw me as a threat, as anything but some other human that came in with you, don't you think they would have tried to shoot me? Tried to use me against you?"

"They did try to use you against me," Drilora shouted. "Weren't you there? Didn't you understand what was going on? They were threatening to take you hostage. To use you against not only me, but the cops that were only trying to keep people safe. If you had gone in there alone, you would have joined the hostages behind that counter. I would have had to save you as well. What use are you at all? No. No, you're clearly useless."

"So, teach me," Cecilia said. She looked up at Drilora's eye, hoping to see something there to hint that zer anger would let up. That her mission there wasn't as hopeless as it was starting to feel.

"Teach you?" Drilora asked. "Teach you what? How to be a superhero? How to not be terrible in a fight? How to... not be a... a useless human? That isn't something that you can unlearn, little one. You are a human. You'll always be a human. Being underestimated isn't a superpower. Humans don't have superpowers. Hell, I don't have superpowers. What I can do is perfectly normal for uvvelians, as I told you from the start. Any uvvelian that came to this planet would be able to do what I did back there. What I have been doing on this mudball since I got here. And yet, the one thing I want to do, the one thing I've been trying to do all these years, is to leave. That is the only way that you could ever be of any use to me, and you can't even do that. No, because you're only a human."

Cecilia wanted to run from Drilora's anger and hide in her room. No, she wanted to run back home to her father's apartment and forget ever trying to do anything again. It was clear how little Drilora thought of her, of any human. But Cecilia just reminded herself of why she was there, what her mission was. The very reason why her father had dumped her at that tower to begin with.

"I'm not asking you to teach me not to be a human," Cecilia said. "I'm asking you to teach me to be a better human. To do... what those cops were trying to do back at the bank, only better."

"If you want to be a cop, go be a cop," Drilora said.

Ze waved zer hand back at the city, like the police academy was visible over there. Cecilia glanced that way, already knowing that it wasn't. That the buildings on that end of the city were mostly apartments overlooking the park. They used to be the most expensive apartments in the city before Drilora arrived there. Before people stopped using the park.

"I don't want to be a cop," Cecilia said, pulling her eyes away from the city to look back at Drilora. When she saw that the glare was still there, Cecilia looked back at the floor at her feet. "Even if I wanted to be a cop, they wouldn't take me. No one will teach me to be anything, because--"

"Because they all underestimate you," Drilora finished. "Yeah, so you say. Well, guess what. I don't think people are underestimating you. I think you're just useless. Not even a useless human, but useless for a human. I'd say you should go home to your father, but it's clear that he doesn't want you any more than I do. That he dumped you on my doorstep simply because he couldn't deal with you anymore. I have half a mind to send you back to the city on your own. There are plenty of worthless humans back there, living on the streets."

Cecilia didn't think that was fair; not the comparison between her and the homeless of the city, but referring to the unhoused as worthless. Most of them were just down on their luck or dealing with problems that were beyond their abilities to handle. If the city took care of them as well as it was taking care of the creature, the world would be a less scary place. Not to mention her place in the world.

However, standing under Drilora's anger, Cecilia had no words to counter it. No words to get Drilora to change zer opinion of her. She knew that ze was just as likely to kick her out if she spoke or if she kept quiet. So, Cecilia just stood there, waiting for Drilora's anger to fade. Waiting for some sign that she would be allowed to stay there.

"Just... Just get out of my sight," Drilora snapped, waving zer hand at Cecilia.

Cecilia nodded before slowly turning away from Drilora. She stood there quietly, her eyes scanning around the roof, searching for the way down. It took her a moment to remember the trap door that had let them up there, and another moment for her to find it. There was water collecting all around the hatch, and Cecilia was worried that she would end up flooding the hallway below if she opened it. Worried that Drilora would use that as an excuse to get rid of her. It was only the fact that Drilora wasn't telling Cecilia to leave the tower, that ze just told her to leave zer, that had Cecilia slipping along the roof, heading over to that hatch.

The hatch let out an odd sucking sound as Cecilia pulled it out of the puddle. As expected, the water slipped back through the hole, falling to the hallway below. However, as Cecilia descended the ladder, she noticed that the water didn't collect there. That it flowed through a small grate against the wall, and down through the floors below.

Cecilia stayed on the ladder for a moment, looking back out at the roof at Drilora. The creature just stood there on the roof, looking out over the park at the sunlight in the distance. Cecilia figured that the creature wanted to be left alone, so she did just that.

Chapter Nine
Hiding

Cecilia rushed down the ladder and along the hallway, slipping into her room the moment that she got there. However, she didn't go far, staying against the inner wall by her door. She kept the door open a sliver, just enough for her to look through it. The hallway stayed empty for a moment longer before Drilora finally came down from the roof. Cecilia watched zer from the safety of her room. She held her breath, waiting for signs that Drilora was about to kick her out of the tower. For zer to send her home.

For her mission there in the tower to fail.

Drilora paused just outside Cecilia's door, too close to the crack for her to see anything of what ze was doing out there. She thought for sure that ze was staring at her door. That ze could see her through the crack, just like she could see zer. It felt like her heart was pounding in her ears as she waited for the worst to happen. Waited for Drilora to barge into her room, dragging her out of the tower. After what felt like an eternity of them standing there like that, Drilora finally shifted to the side, heading away from Cecilia's room.

Once Cecilia knew that Drilora was gone, she turned away from the door, pressing her back into the wall. She finally let out her breath, worried that even that sound would summon the creature back. That it would remind zer that she was still there. Only when no further sounds came from the hallway did Cecilia start to relax. She slid down along the wall, sitting on the floor next to her door, hugging her knees to her chest.

When a sob ran through Cecilia, she realized that the water on her face wasn't entirely the rain. That she was crying.

Crying about her failure. Crying about her almost ruining everything. She always ruined everything. Nothing that she had ever done growing up seemed enough for her father, and it seemed like the same would be true with the creature.

"Stop crying, Cecilia," she said to herself, keeping her voice low so it wouldn't be heard in the hallway. "Stop crying and do something about it." They were her father's words, the same words he always said to her, every time he found her crying like that. But just like when he said it, they were of no use to her. They did nothing to stymie the tears, or to lead her to figure out what she should be doing next.

With nothing better to do, no ideas on how to fix things with the creature, Cecilia slowly got up from the floor, heading into the bathroom. She peeled her soaked outfit off of her, tossing it on the floor, before stepping into the shower. The hot water felt good on her cold body, refreshing her in a way. Her tears merged with that water, which swept them away down the drain. But the tears lingered. Tears of loss, of frustration. Nothing came to her on how to fix things, but she figured, she hoped, that an answer would come in time.

Cecilia stayed in the shower until she thought that her tears were under control once more. That she could leave the pain and fear behind her. Only then did she turn off the water, but she stayed in the shower as she dried off. As she stood there, naked save the towel, she started to feel like she was being watched. Like the creature had rigged the bathroom with cameras and was watching her in there.

She kept the towel wrapped tightly around her body as she stepped out of the shower, heading back into her bedroom. Her dresses had all been hanging while they were out at the bank, but they were still wet when she checked them. She grabbed the driest of them, a light blue sweater dress. It was difficult trying to put on the dress while still having her towel around her, but she managed it. Only then did she pull the towel away, hanging it up in the bathroom.

Once dressed, Cecilia headed back over to the hallway, peeking out through the door to check for the creature out there. There was no sign of zer, though Cecilia knew that didn't mean much. That ze could be anywhere in the tower and still be watching her. She opened the door further, just wide enough for her to poke her head out through it, before looking up and down the hallway.

Only after making sure that she was alone up there did she slip forward, heading out into the hall. As much as Cecilia wanted to hide in her room until the creature forgot about her, she had a mission that she needed to accomplish while she was there in the tower. A mission that she couldn't do while hiding. So, she crept forward, heading back down through the tower in search of the creature. Trying to find zer before ze found her.

Cecilia paused at the next landing down, looking along the hallway there. The doors were all closed, but that didn't mean much. That didn't mean that the creature wasn't hiding somewhere on that floor. She slipped forward into the hallway, looking at the closest of the doors. Just before she came up to it, though, she heard something behind her. It sounded like a metal tool falling onto a stone floor. From her earlier tour of the tower, she knew that the only place that could have come from would be the gym.

She lingered by the door for just a second longer before turning back toward the stairs. As she made her way back along that hallway, she got the sense that they weren't alone there in the tower. Like the tower itself might be alive, or maybe someone was hiding in there. Hiding like she was, or perhaps even better than that. She wondered if they would be on her side, or on the creature's.

Cecilia came to a stop when she got to the library. Despite the draw that the library had to her when she first headed through there, Cecilia barely glanced that way. Instead, she slipped off to the side. She paused there, holding her breath, waiting for another sound to come from the gym. Waiting for a sign that the creature really was down there. When none came, she slipped down onto her stomach, slowly slinking closer to the gap in the stairs. She peeked down through the crack there, expecting to find the creature working out in the gym.

And yet, there was no sign of zer down there. That floor was dark, with just the sunlight coming in through the windows next to her. The place looked exactly like how she had last seen it, with no hint of change for the intervening hours.

Cecilia lingered there on the floor for a bit longer, watching for signs of something down there. Perhaps something hiding out among the machines. The creature, invisible in the low light of the floor. Or maybe something else, some pest that had come into the tower and simply knocked something over in there. Something to make the sound that she had heard before. But the place stayed stagnant, with nothing moving, nothing making a sound.

Lying there on the floor like that, staring at an empty room, Cecilia started to feel quite silly. Like the silly, useless, little girl that the creature thought of her as. Again, she felt like her father brought her there simply to get rid of her, rather than for the purpose that he told her. It all seemed so impossible, so beyond her.

With nothing coming from that lower floor, Cecilia slowly got back up to her feet. She glanced up the stairs behind her, wondering if the creature had been on the floor above. The sound had been below her, though, and she still thought that it had come from the creature. The only place below her was the ground floor, the garage of sorts. That seemed like the perfect place for someone to hang out and get some work done after yelling at a girl.

Cecilia slipped down another floor, again lying down on the landing to look through the crack in the stairs. This time, she saw what she was looking for. The creature was standing across from her, in front of one of the tables down there. As expected, there was a screen in front of zer. Only, instead of seeing scenes from her room, she could make out a scene from the bank. She could see the creature, standing there in full view.

Growing up in that city, Cecilia had heard all about the creature hiding out in that tower. But she had never seen zer until she met zer in person. There were barely any images, and no video, of zer online, even with how often ze went out into the city, and all around the world. And seeing the creature on the video there made no more sense than anything else that had been happening there since Cecilia arrived.

As Cecilia watched Drilora working on the computer from the safety of the stairs, she saw the video playing out. She saw the creature throwing the rifle over the protective glass, hitting the robber in the head. But then, the video suddenly went dark. Cecilia could see words in the center of that blackness, but she had to squint, to strain her eyes to see what they said.

"Video deleted," they said.

Realization ran through Cecilia when she saw that. The creature had hacked into the surveillance system of the bank and deleted the videos of the mission. Deleted the images of zer in the bank like that. That must have been why there were so few images and videos of zer online, with zer deleting them all. All signs of zer work, all proof that ze even existed outside of that tower.

Suddenly, Cecilia felt quite silly about the whole thing. The idea that the creature would be watching her in the shower like that, when it was clear that ze had more important things to do. Plenty of things for a superhero to be doing after a mission. Things that she was probably meant to be doing as well.

With that mystery solved, Cecilia slowly slipped back up from the floor, trying not to make a sound as she headed away from the creature. As she left zer to zer own hiding there in the tower. Only the creature was hiding from the world, from the humans that surrounded zer. Much like Cecilia was with the creature.

Only Cecilia was encroaching on zer solitude there in the tower, in what should have been zer safe space from the gawking humans outside. For Cecilia knew exactly why Drilora would be removing all traces of zer from the world online. All the name calling, the derision, the scapegoating that ze would have to suffer through. The anti-creature propaganda flyer from the bank flashed through her mind at that moment, a frequent sight growing up that she hadn't put much thought into before meeting the creature herself. It was all so similar to what Cecilia had lived through herself, growing up with her superpower.

Chapter Ten
The Lights of Home
Drilora

Drilora stayed on the roof as ze tried to calm down. Ze didn't used to get so angry, growing up on Uvvelia. It had more to do with the krylonian invasion than being stranded there on Earth like that, though that didn't help much either. However, ze already knew, even as ze was yelling at Cecilia, that it wasn't the girl's fault. While she was completely useless in the bank, ze knew that she would be when going into the situation. There was a reason why ze had stepped up, taking on so much and trying to help the humans while ze was stuck there. It wasn't just to earn the funds to build and keep the tower; ze had been raised to help society in any way that ze could. And yet, the humans seemed to have been raised to do the exact opposite.

Once Drilora had managed to calm down, ze took a deep breath in, trying to steady zer nerves. The stink of the Terran air caught zer all over again, reminding zer of the constant smell that ze had to put up with. In the years since ze had been on Earth, ze had never grown nose blind to it. That wasn't something that happened in uvvelians. Ze had just learned to ignore it, knowing that it would do zer no good to constantly be thinking about that. Another reason to be angry at zer situation.

Drilora turned away from that sun to look out over the ocean. Before coming to Earth, Drilora had never seen such a huge body of water. Uvvelia was more land than water, with thick rainforests covering much of the land. That was such a beautiful sight to zer, something that almost made zer time there on Earth worthwhile. Almost. But staring out at that sight only reminded zer of how alone ze felt there on that mudball of a planet.

Ze had seen the anti-alien flyers back at the bank. The reminder of how much the humans hated zer without even knowing zer. Without zer doing anything but try to help them. Drilora was surrounded by reminders of how ze didn't belong there. How much ze wanted to leave. To head back to Uvvelia, not just because it was zer home, but because ze knew that the war was still raging there. That zer home might be destroyed while ze was stuck there in that mud.

With a shake of zer head, Drilora turned away from the ocean, heading back over to the trap door and down into the tower. The hallway was empty as always, and it was easy to forget the interloper in zer tower. But as ze came up in front of Cecilia's door, ze paused there, looking at it. Part of zer wanted to kick the girl out of the tower then and there. She had no right to infringe on zer solitude. However, with thoughts of just how alone ze felt there on that planet still fresh on zer mind, ze figured that it was better to just leave the girl be.

After how Cecilia's father had treated her earlier, it felt to Drilora like she was just as alone there. Just as lost and abandoned on that world. Why couldn't they be lost and abandoned together? That way, ze didn't have to be so alone. But Drilora didn't think for one moment that Cecilia would be anything more than some girl that ze had been stuck with. A pet if anything, rather than a partner or friend. Never someone that could actually help in any way. Drilora just stood there, staring at the door for a moment, before moving on. Heading back down through the tower, to the garage below.

Whenever Drilora was feeling sorry for zerself, or overly annoyed at the humans, like ze was that day, ze would lose zerself in trying to get the ships working again. Ze had spent days down in the garage, just taking apart those broken components and trying to put them back together. Both ships had their own collection of broken components, things that would make it impossible for either ship to fly again. Even getting the retrorockets to fire would be too much. Not all of the damage had happened in the battle, though most of it had. The humans had gotten to both of the ships, long before Drilora had managed to escape the holding facility. Getting them back from the humans had been harder, but it wasn't like the humans would understand the technology contained within them.

Drilora had enough trouble understanding the technology on the krylonian ship. While ze knew every component in zer ship, how to take it apart and put it back together, the only component in the krylonian ship that ze knew on that level was the slip stream generator. The same generator that was in zer own ship, stolen from the krylonians. It had been quite the struggle to figure out anything in that other ship, and ze was convinced zer lack of knowledge in that technology was the main reason why ze couldn't get the krylonian ship flying again. It was the lack of proper support, proper supplies, that kept zer from getting zer own ship flying.

After a few minutes of puttering around with the parts, Drilora only found zerself getting more frustrated by it all. Ze picked up the repositator of the ion drive from zer ship, throwing it hard against the far wall. The sound of metal hitting stone rang out around the room, loud enough that ze knew it would be heard all the way upstairs. That it was likely to draw Cecilia's attention. When ze realized that, ze glanced over toward the stairs, almost expecting the human to already be peeking out from up there. However, there was no sign of the human, no sign that ze wasn't alone there like always.

"Good," Drilora muttered to zerself, using zer native language. Ze hated using the languages of the humans, how sloppy and choppy it all was, and ze usually spoke in Uvvelian whenever ze was alone. Not that ze had much of a habit of talking to zerself, but there weren't many options when it came to getting intelligent conversations.

With another shake of zer head and a sigh, ze headed over to pick the repositator back up off the floor where it fell. Ze was about to head back over to the destroyed components when ze noticed the computer on the desk there. The computer was purely human, something that zer assistant had bought zer to help zer feel connected to the world. That had helped in a way, though probably not in the way that they had expected. And seeing it there, ze remembered something that ze usually did after missions like that.

Rather than heading back to the components, Drilora placed the repositator next to the computer as ze settled down in the chair in front of it. The chair let out a light groan at zer sitting in it; the thing wasn't designed to hold the weight of an uvvelian. Fortunately, it held up for the moment, though ze knew that it wouldn't stay that way for long. The computer let out a few wheezes as ze turned it on, not from anything ze did. It was just old. However, even an old computer like that would work for what Drilora needed from it.

The human's technology was woefully primitive, and it didn't take long for Drilora to hack into the surveillance system of the bank. With those anti-alien flyers so blatantly out in the open, and no one taking them down, ze knew that it wouldn't be a good idea for the mission to still be saved in their system. The hate groups would no doubt use it as some kind of propaganda against zer, making it seem like ze was attacking the bank robbers instead of trying to save the hostages. Ze quickly downloaded the video of the mission, saving it on a small thumb drive, before deleting it off the bank's system.

Once that was done, Drilora thought ze heard something behind zer. Ze glanced over zer shoulder back at the stairs, but there was no sign of anything over there. No hint that Cecilia was watching zer. However, it still reminded zer that the human was in the tower with zer. That ze didn't have anything in the way of food that wouldn't kill her. While ze figured that might be an easier way to get rid of the human, ze figured that wasn't a good idea. Ze would only get blamed for it, something that ze had actually done rather than propaganda from the hate groups.

With a shake of zer head, Drilora turned back to the computer in front of zer, pulling up a search engine. Ze had never tried to order food, never needing anything that the human restaurants in the area would have. But from the comic books that ze had read over the years, ze knew all about that strange thing called takeout. However, ze soon got overwhelmed by all the options available, not to mention getting someone that would deliver to the tower. And then, there was the issue about paying for it.

So, after a few minutes of zer getting lost online, ze reluctantly had to message zer assistant, letting them take care of the whole thing. Ze never liked relying on them for the more basic things that life threw at zer, but they were essential for things like tracking zer missions, interacting with the city and those around there that would ask for help, and all things monetary. Money hadn't been a thing on Uvvelia for centuries, and that always got in the way. Ze was convinced that, if the humans didn't insist on getting paid for everything, ze would have been out of there years ago. That even with the terrible level of technology the humans had, if ze had access to all the best systems they had available, ze could have reverse engineered the krylonian technology, repaired zer own ship, and sailed out of there. Ze probably wouldn't have been worrying about giving the humans too much technology either.

"I'll handle it," the assistant messaged, even as Drilora sat there, grumbling over the horrible situation that ze had found zerself in.

Chapter Eleven
Dinner
Cecilia

Cecilia hid out in her room for the rest of the afternoon. She spent most of the time trying to salvage the books that she had brought. At first, she used her hair drier on them, hoping that would dry them out better than having them sit on the table next to her bed. But after a minute or so of doing that, she worried that it would only draw Drilora's attention. Draw zer ire back onto her. So, instead, she ended up wrapping them in her towel from the bathroom, not knowing if it was doing more harm than good.

As the sun started to set in Cecilia's window, she heard a light knock on the door. She stood still, staring over at her door from just outside the bathroom. Her main thought, her main worry, was that this would be it. That Drilora had finally come to kick her out of the tower properly. But she figured, she hoped, that if she didn't respond to the knock then maybe Drilora wouldn't kick her out. That she could just hide out in that room until she could figure out something better. Some plan to get back on zer good side.

Not that Cecilia had ever been on Drilora's good side, if the creature even had a good side.

"Cecilia?" Drilora's voice came through the door, just a few seconds after the knock. "Dinner."

"Oh," Cecilia said, more to herself than to Drilora.

A sigh of relief ran through her, though it was short-lived. While it seemed like the creature was inviting her down to a meal, she suddenly thought that maybe it was a trick. A way to get her out of her room, only to kick her out in the end. Besides, with how worried she was, her stomach was nothing but a nest of knots. The last thing she wanted at that moment was to eat.

"I, uh... I'm not hungry," she called out to Drilora.

"Well, fine," Drilora said. "Not like you did much to work up an appetite out on the call anyway. Don't come blaming me if you starve to death tonight, though."

Cecilia had gone to bed without dinner plenty of times; she knew that it didn't work like that. That she would be able to go at least a day or two before she would starve to death. However, with how big the creature was, with the differences in their physiology, Cecilia figured that might be how it worked for the creature's people.

She stayed there, silently listening to Drilora out in the hall. There was no sound of the creature heading off again. She pictured zer outside in the hall, just standing there, staring at the door like ze had done after the mission. For all she knew, Drilora would stand there all night, just waiting for her to open the door. Waiting for a chance to pull her out of the tower.

Only the creature didn't need to wait for her to open the door. It wasn't like the door was locked. Drilora could come in there at any moment to kick her out of the tower. More than that, Cecilia suddenly realized that sitting down with the creature for dinner might be the perfect time for her to talk with zer. For her to get back on zer good side and figure out a way forward.

Once that thought came to her, Cecilia rushed forward, coming over to the door. She slowed just in front of it, making sure that her dress was squared away and that she didn't look flushed, before opening the door. However, when she peeked out into the hall, there was once again no sign of the creature at all. It seemed like Drilora had managed to sneak off without her hearing anything from inside the room. Despite how big the creature was, ze was light on zer feet.

With no sign of the creature in the hall, Cecilia headed back over to the stairs, rushing down to the kitchen below. That hallway looked just as empty and abandoned as the last time that she had gone through there, but Cecilia knew that Drilora would have gone in there somewhere. She slipped forward, heading for the first door on the left. The door opened smoothly and quietly, revealing the kitchen.

But there was no sign of Drilora. Nor dinner, for that matter.

Cecilia quickly backed out of the room, heading over to the next door down the hall. When she opened it, she expected to see the dining room. Instead, it looked more like a lounge, with a couch and a huge TV on the far wall. There was a noticeable layer of dust on the TV that looked worse than had been in her bedroom when she was moving in earlier. Cecilia figured that Drilora never went in there. So, she quickly backed away from that door, heading across the hall.

The third door proved to lead to a laundry room, which was a huge relief to Cecilia. Unsurprisingly, it seemed as unused as the lounge. What was surprising was the fact that the dining room behind the fourth door looked just as empty and unused.

"What?" Cecilia muttered, staring around at those four doors in confusion. She knew that Drilora had been at her door not more than a few minutes earlier talking about dinner. Suddenly, that seemed more like the trap that she had worried about earlier. That it was all a trick to get her out of her room.

And she had fallen for it.

Cecilia kept her footsteps light as she rushed back over to the stairs, meaning to head back up to her room. But then, she heard that sound again; the sound of metal hitting stone. She turned at that sound, looking down the stairs, back toward the ground floor. Every part of her was warning her against going down, wanting to rush back to hide out in her room where she was safe. But instead, she turned down, slowly slipping along the stairs.

Just like before, she stopped at the library, peeking through to the gym floor from there. When she saw that Drilora wasn't in there, she slipped forward once more, coming down to the gym to peek down into the garage. Once again, Drilora was down there, alone. However, instead of sitting in front of the screen on the table against the wall, Drilora was sitting in one of the ships.

Cecilia could see Drilora sitting there in the open cockpit, in the chair there. Ze was holding a large, metal bowl in zer hands, a spoon halfway between it and zer mouth. She stood there for a moment, just watching the creature eating. When Drilora stuck the spoon back into the bowl, that sound rang out again. Only this time, it was easier for Cecilia to hear what it really was. Not the sound of metal hitting stone, but of metal hitting metal.

With that truth revealed to her, Cecilia just laid there for a bit longer, watching the creature eat alone in zer ship. If she didn't know better, she would have thought that the creature almost looked lonely. Like ze had wanted to eat dinner with Cecilia not to get the chance to kick her out of the tower, but simply to have someone to eat with. But she knew that couldn't be the case. The creature had already shown what ze thought of Cecilia. Of how little ze thought of her, how little ze wanted her in the tower.

After watching Drilora eat for a minute, Cecilia slowly stood back up, trying not to make a sound as she slipped back up the stairs. Her eyes kept darting behind her as she went, trying to see Drilora down there, even after ze was out of her view. Since she was no longer worried that the creature was looking to kick her out of the tower, she slipped back into the kitchen, taking a closer look at what was in there.

As she had seen earlier, the stove was empty, the burners off and the place already cleaned up. There was no sign of food set out on the counter, and Drilora had already warned her off eating the food in there. But as Cecilia came into the kitchen, her stomach rumbled, and she very much did want something to eat. So, she headed over to check out the fridge, hoping that there was something in there that she recognized. Something that she knew she could eat without it killing her.

Or without the food eating her. Given the alien that was downstairs, Cecilia worried that anything was possible.

The fridge was a normal looking fridge, much like the rest of the appliances and furniture in the tower. When she opened it, though, everything inside looked anything but normal. Everything, other than a normal looking takeout container from some Chinese restaurant. The symbols on the side looked familiar, but Cecilia had eaten at several such restaurants over the years. There was no note on it saying that it was safe, no hint that the container hadn't been in there for days, if not weeks. However, as strange as some of the dishes at such restaurants had seemed to her, she doubted that any of them would be bad for a human, let alone be edible to the creature.

Carefully, Cecilia reached inside the fridge, pulling that container out. The container was lighter than she was expecting, though obviously full of something. She placed it on the counter next to the fridge, worried that it would explode if she opened it the wrong way, before popping open the flaps. A waft of steam hit her the moment that the flaps were open, and she could feel the heat of the food flowing up into her face. With it came the unmistakable smell of sweet and sour chicken, complete with rice.

Cecilia glanced back toward the door to the hall, almost expecting Drilora to be standing there, glaring over at her. Demanding that she put the chicken back into the fridge. Insisting that she didn't deserve the food. But with no sign of the creature anywhere, Cecilia quickly searched the cupboards for chopsticks or a fork. Rather than taking the entire container, she poured some of the food into a bowl. She barely worried about the creature noticing that the food was gone, or if ze would care, as she put the rest of the container back into the fridge.

With the pilfered takeout in hand, Cecilia made her way back over to the door. She peeked out through it, making sure that the creature was still nowhere in sight, before slipping back out and making her way back up to her room. Once she was safely tucked away in there, she stuck the chair from the desk against the door, the back of it under the knob to keep it closed.

"Yeah, try to sneak in through that," she mumbled to herself, shaking her head at the door as she thought of how much she was trusting the creature. A creature that had already shown just how much ze wanted her gone. Cecilia wouldn't put it past zer to sneak into the room in the middle of the night, pulling her out of the tower in her night clothes. Only after the door was secured did she head back over to her desk, sitting on the edge of her bed as she ate.

Never once did she consider that the food might have been poisoned. It tasted like normal sweet and sour chicken to her.

Chapter Twelve
First Morning

Cecilia didn't get much sleep that night. She spent much of the night tossing and turning and generally wishing that she was back in her bed at home. As the night grew dark around her, she could almost convince herself that she was back there. She kept staring off into the darkness of her room, trying to make the shadows look like they had in her old room. To see the old poster on the back of her door, despite it not being there. But when the first light of dawn made it into her bedroom, she could no longer pretend that she wasn't still stuck in that tower.

Though she knew that might not be the case for much longer.

She took her time getting ready for the day. Her clothes were all dry once more, and she had cleaned her jeans and t-shirt from her one mission. However, she opted for another dress, a pink floral print which she always felt made her look younger than she was. She was hoping to play on the creature's guilt to let her stay longer. To perhaps see her as more than just a normal human. But she hadn't brought the ballet flats that completed the look, so she went with her sneakers instead.

As Cecilia was just heading outside of her room, the door to Drilora's room opened. Cecilia came up short, her hand still on the knob behind her, as she stared over at that door. Her eyes went wide with a fright that she wasn't expecting as Drilora appeared.

"Oh, hello," Drilora said, after a moment. There was no sign of startlement on the creature's face, though it was clear that ze wasn't expecting to see Cecilia there.

"Uh, hi," Cecilia said, waving at the creature. She felt quite stupid for the simplicity of it all and wished that she had said something more. That she could have come up with something to say in that first interaction of the day. Something that would change the creature's opinion of her. Instead, all she could come up with was, "Good morning." It felt so stupid to her, and she flicked her head back and forth, letting her hair fall in front of her face again to hide behind it. She couldn't see the look on the creature's face as ze spoke to her.

"Yes, quite," Drilora said. Ze stood up straighter, stepping forward into the hall as ze closed the door behind zer. "Come along. We'll have none of that nonsense from yesterday, then."

Cecilia wasn't quite sure what nonsense Drilora was talking about. If ze was referring to the mission, Cecilia's desire to be a superhero, or simply her refusal to come out for dinner. Cecilia got the sense that ze didn't know that she had come out after that, so she didn't mention it.

Drilora quickly headed down the stairwell. Cecilia followed closely, wondering if the creature would head for the kitchen or continue down to the gym. While she was used to having breakfast first thing in the morning, she was hoping that ze would train her. Even if she had to do the training in that dress, it would at least mean that she was closer to her goals. But she wasn't disappointed when Drilora turned off on the next floor down, slipping into the kitchen even as she followed along behind zer.

As Cecilia came into the room, Drilora was standing by the fridge, staring into the takeout container. Zer eye flicked back toward Cecilia, but ze didn't say anything about it. Didn't hint at what ze was feeling about the missing food. Cecilia figured that ze was only then noticing that she had eaten the night before. That she had snuck out of the room when ze wasn't looking. After a moment, Drilora closed the fridge before sticking the leftovers into the microwave to heat up.

"As I said, there isn't much human food in the tower at the moment," Drilora said.

As the microwave ran, ze headed over to the stove, quickly turning it on with one hand even as ze was fishing a pan out of one of the cabinets overhead. Cecilia stood back, staying next to the doors, as she watched the creature cook. And with ze practically bouncing all over the kitchen as ze cooked, that was probably a good thing. As the pan warmed up, ze headed to the fridge, pulling out what looked like a large potato and a normal looking stick of butter, complete with the label still on it. Ze broke a huge piece of the butter off, tossing it into the pan, before starting to chop the potato.

"I've been told that this looks like a potato, but it's not," ze said, nodding down at the potato. "It doesn't have a direct translation into any of your languages, but we call it a ghundernator. I guess the closest translation would be thunder potato. But, unlike your potatoes, it isn't full of carbohydrates. It's... Well, it's similar to your protein, though it has a completely different composition. I'm basically having eggs for breakfast, and a lot of them."

Ze laughed a little at zer comparison as ze dumped the diced thunder potatoes into the pan. They let out an odd sizzling sound that reminded Cecilia of eggs cooking. Just seconds after that, the microwave started to beep, showing that her breakfast was ready. Cecilia headed over to grab it, slipping between Drilora and the counter just enough to grab another fork. Drilora made no mention of Cecilia knowing where the silverware was.

As she stood there, watching the thunder potatoes cook around Drilora's side, Cecilia wondered at why she wouldn't be able to eat them herself. They still looked like normal potatoes to her, just turning brown as they cooked. She gestured to the potatoes with her fork.

"And those are poisonous to humans?" she asked. "Are you sure? I couldn't become just as strong as you are if I ate them like you did?"

"You still seem under the impression that I somehow have superpowers," Drilora said, glancing over zer shoulder back at Cecilia. "That there's something that I'm doing, hidden away here in the tower, that makes me more than what I was born as. All uvvelians eat thunder potatoes. It's as normal to us as eating eggs or bacon or any other breakfast meats that your people eat. If we ate something else, we would be just as strong, as long as we get enough of our protein in our diet. If we started eating human protein, well... If we could survive off of it, we would still be as strong."

"Oh," Cecilia said, only slightly disappointed. She knew that it wouldn't be that easy to become a superhero like zer. "Do you grow those thunder potatoes here in the tower?" She waved her spoon around to gesture at the tower, but Drilora didn't look back to see it.

"Oh, no," Drilora said, shaking zer head. "That would be quite impossible. They only grow on Uvvelia. Between the low gravity, and your horrid soil, even if I planted one of these it would never sprout. It would be harder than, say, growing potatoes on Mars." Ze glanced back over zer shoulder at Cecilia, blinking zer eye with it flipping all around. Cecilia remembered seeing that before, remembered that was Drilora's way of laughing. A real laugh for the creature, rather than the fake ones that ze would make sometimes.

"Then how do you get them?" Cecilia asked. She leaned against the fridge, slowly picking at her leftovers with the fork.

"Oh, well, that's... a delicate question," Drilora said, turning back to the pan. The thunder potato was turning an odd shade of black, making Cecilia think that ze had burned it. But Drilora moved them around a little with a spatula before reaching over to grab a plate. As ze plated zer breakfast, ze continued. "I brought something with me that has kept me fed, something that goes beyond the limited science you humans understand."

"Oh," Cecilia said. She tried to keep her curiosity out of her voice, focusing on the food in her hands, as she asked the obvious follow-up question. "This is something in the tower here?"

"Of course," Drilora said. Ze stood next to the stove, looking over at Cecilia with zer breakfast in hand. Cecilia tried not to look up at zer, but as the quiet continued, she finally did, peeking up through her hair that was once again draped in front of her face. The look on zer face was a complete mystery to Cecilia, though. "Part of my deal for staying here was that I didn't provide access to my technology to the humans. To your people. You're not ready for it, and you would only use it to make war, even if you could understand it. So, yes, it is in the tower. Somewhere. Don't go looking for it. Even if you found it, you wouldn't be able to understand how to use it."

Cecilia just nodded to the comment, not rising to the bait. She wanted to defend her abilities, to say that her people were ready for anything that came to them, but it was nothing that she hadn't heard often enough growing up. Not about humans in general, but about herself. After all, that was how her power worked, and it clearly had worked on the creature just like everyone else she had ever met.

"Would this device of yours not work with human food?" Cecilia asked, gesturing to the almost empty takeout container with her spoon. "Or is it a limited resources thing?"

"I don't make it a habit of feeding humans," Drilora said, zer eye squinting in a half-hearted glare. "But don't worry. I won't let you starve while I'm stuck with you. Hopefully, that won't be for much longer."

"Oh?" Cecilia asked. She glanced back at her food, only to realize that she had already finished it. That she didn't have that excuse anymore not to broach the sensitive subject. "And, uh... What-what are you expecting to do with me?"

"Why, get rid of you, of course," Drilora said. "I would have thought that obvious at this point. No matter what your father thinks, or what you seem to think, you're no superhero. I don't see any real talent that would help you save people. You're not strong, even by human standards, let alone by uvvelian. You're not fast. You're not bulletproof. Or fireproof, which we know from how we met in the first place. The only thing you've claimed to have that other humans don't is... Well, it's not anything useful."

"Ha," Cecilia said, a single bark of laughter with no real humor in it. She kept her eyes locked on her empty container, her fork bashing away at the bottom of it, as she thought of all that she had put up with growing up because of it. "Don't I know it," she said, shaking her head. "It's really more of a detriment than anything else. I still think that it can be made into something useful, though. With the right training."

"And then, there's that," Drilora said. Ze pointed at Cecilia with zer fork, a bit of thunder potato on it, before sticking it in zer mouth. After a moment of chewing, ze continued. "You show signs of delusions of grandeur. If you were to become serious about all of this, about using this so-called power in life-or-death situations... Well, the situation yesterday... If you were a superhero, you'd be expected to be able to handle something like that on your own. You just wouldn't be able to."

"I'm not too sure about that," Cecilia muttered, but she didn't go into detail.

It was the first time that she had thought about that. The first time she had heard it put in that way. Of course, if she were to step up, to become a superhero like Drilora was, she would be expected to handle situations like that. She would be expected to charge into that bank and disarm the robbers. No one would think of her as a superhero until she could do just that. But even as she thought about it, she thought of a few ideas on how to manage it. On what she could have done just the day before if she wasn't focused on staying out of Drilora's way.

Drilora seemed to sense something different from her silence, as ze left her to her thoughts. A smile slowly played across zer strange face as ze picked at zer thunder potatoes. Before they could pick up the conversation again, an odd jingling sound ran through the room. Cecilia glanced back at the microwave, then the stove behind Drilora, but neither seemed to be making that sound.

"Ah, finally," Drilora said, looking at the clock on the microwave. "Come along, human. Let's see if I can pawn you off this morning. We'll see what Leanne makes of the situation."

"Wait, who's Leanne?" Cecilia asked.

Chapter Thirteen
The Assistant

Drilora quickly finished zer thunder potatoes, shoveling them into zer mouth in a way that Cecilia's father would often do when he was rushing off to work. Ze slipped zer plate in the sink as ze rushed out of the kitchen. Cecilia lingered there a moment longer, staring at her already empty container, before tossing the container in the trash and following zer out. By the time Cecilia made the hallway, Drilora was already out of view. However, Cecilia figured that the jingling sound had been some doorbell that she hadn't found the day before. So, she quickly rushed after Drilora, down the hall and the stairs toward the garage.

"Hey, Leanne," Drilora said, zer voice coming up through the stairs just as Cecilia made it to the gym.

"Please, tell me I didn't hear correctly," someone said.

The new voice was low, but still feminine, and completely unrecognizable to Cecilia. As she came past the gym, she could just see someone standing inside the door to the tower. With Drilora standing right next to her, Leanne looked short, though the door behind her made her look taller than Cecilia. She was wearing a suit with a large bag hanging on her arm as she looked up at Cecilia.

"Please, tell me you didn't abduct a human," Leanne said.

"I didn't abduct a human," Drilora said.

"And yet..." Leanne said, waving toward Cecilia as she came down to join them.

"Hi," Cecilia said, waving at Leanne. "I'm Cecilia."

"I didn't abduct a human," Drilora said, again. "More like the human abducted herself." Drilora waved zer hands up and down, like ze was simulating someone being abducted by aliens. Given ze was the alien there, it seemed almost appropriate.

"Uh huh," Leanne said, a disbelieving tone in her voice.

"I wasn't abducted," Cecilia said, laughing lightly. "I'm Drilora's apprentice. Ze is going to be training me to be a superhero like ze is."

"Is that true?" Leanne said. There was a hint of a smile on her face, though Cecilia wasn't sure if that was hopeful optimism at Drilora not having abducted Cecilia or outright humor that a human could be a superhero.

"Well, I wouldn't go that far," Drilora said.

"Dril," Leanne said, her voice scolding. "What is going on?"

"Her father threw the girl at me, left her on my doorstep in the rain. What was I supposed to do? Leave her out there to catch a cold? You humans are so... breakable."

"Uh huh," Leanne said. "So, you let her in to weather out the storm. You don't bring her out on a mission."

"I'm not leaving a human alone in my tower," Drilora said. "Not with the Uvvelian technology that is stored here. Besides, she claims to have a superpower and that she wanted to be trained as a superhero. I figured that I'd take her out on the mission, see just how useless she was, and then have the cops take her on from there. Let the humans deal with the human."

Cecilia hadn't been expecting that last part. The idea that ze meant to just leave her there at the bank. For a moment, she thought that maybe Drilora had never meant to bring her back to the tower. That Cecilia had jumped onto Drilora's back as ze was leaving, rather than having the creature duck down to let her on there. But she remembered that departure rather plainly, including the part where she squeezed her eyes closed to not need to see the actual departure itself. There was no way that she would have been able to hold on to Drilora's back if ze didn't want her there.

"And why didn't you leave her behind?" Leanne asked. She crossed her arms over her chest as she glared over at Drilora.

"You do know I'm right here, right?" Cecilia asked, annoyed at them talking about her like she wasn't there.

"And that's the problem," Drilora said, glaring over at her. "She was too soft. Too useless. Too hopeless. I was worried that she wouldn't be able to survive on her own, and it was clear that her father was having nothing with her. By the time I was bringing the human back to the tower, I knew that her father only wanted to be rid of her."

"Oh, honey," Leanne said, finally turning to Cecilia with a level of sympathy. Only the slightest sniffle played through Cecilia at that comforting look. Cecilia was already done crying about the situation that she had found herself in. "That's just horrible. I am so sorry. My parents threw me out too, though I was a bit older than you at the time. I made my way in the world, and I'm sure that you'll make yours."

"Yes, exactly," Drilora said. "So, why don't you take Cecilia here off my hands? Find somewhere that can better deal with her."

"Deal with me?" Cecilia asked, bristling at zer choice of words. That sounded worse than her failing at her mission, failing to become the superhero that she wanted to be. It sounded like they were going to pawn her off into a situation worse than the one that she grew up in.

"It's not as simple as all of that," Leanne said. "First, well, how old are you, sweetie?"

"I just turned seventeen a few months ago," Cecilia said.

"Old enough that the best that I can get her is a bed somewhere," Leanne said, shrugging. "And with her father still in the picture, even that is... complicated. I'll look into it, but for now, the best situation might just be right here, in this tower."

"Out of the question," Drilora said, shaking zer head. "I can't have her getting in the way of everything."

"Yes," Leanne said, her smile getting broader as she looked around the room. "I can see that you're very busy. You've made so much progress since the last time I was here."

"Well, get her out of my fur for a few hours today at least," Drilora said, waving zer hand dismissively at Cecilia. "I need to get my workout in if I'm going to avoid losing more muscle and bone mass to this horrible gravity."

"Alright, alright," Leanne said, nodding at Drilora before turning back to Cecilia. "Why don't you grab your things. We can head out for a few hours. I do have some work to do for this one today."

"My things?" Cecilia asked, suddenly worried. Did she mean for Cecilia to pack up her stuff? To move out of the tower? That wasn't what it had sounded like.

"Your purse, phone, whatever," Leanne said, waving her hands. "Your house keys, if you still have them. We can possibly swing by to visit your father while we're out."

"Oh, uh..." Cecilia said, hesitantly, before looking down at herself. "I-I don't have anything. I never had a phone, and Dad took my allowance card and keys away when he brought me here."

"Well, alright then," Leanne said, shrugging. "Come along. We'll see what we can do with you. In the meantime, Dril, do your workout and all that. I'll be back with her in a few hours, either way." She turned back to Cecilia, flicking a finger at her. "I imagine you brought something here. That dress doesn't seem to be Dril's style."

"She brought luggage," Drilora said. "Very presumptuous, given what she has to offer. Which is nothing, by the way." Cecilia just rolled her eyes at the comment, expecting it. Leanne snickered at the whole exchange before shaking her head and waving Cecilia toward the door.

Cecilia lingered near the stairs for a moment longer as Leanne headed outside. Despite what she was telling her, Cecilia still felt like she should go up and pack. She had been dreading being kicked out of the tower ever since they got back from the bank, and it seemed like it was happening. Going home empty-handed wouldn't be nearly as bad as going home worse off than she had left, with her things being held hostage by the creature. But as Leanne headed out into the day, Drilora just glared at her, silently making it clear that ze expected her to follow.

Leanne was waiting for Cecilia just outside the tower as she came out. Once Cecilia was clear of the door, it slammed loudly and resoundingly behind her. Cecilia jumped a little at the sound before heading toward Leanne.

"Don't worry about it," Leanne said, as she started down the more well-worn path through the tall grass, heading for the parking lot. "Dril is always a bit grumpy in the morning. Well... I think ze's pretty grumpy all the time."

"How long have you known the creature?" Cecilia asked, as the two of them headed for the parking lot.

"Oh, I hope Dril didn't hear you call zer that," she said. "It might explain some of the animosity between you. Drilora isn't some creature or monster out of a storybook. Ze is an uvvelian, a proud member of a proud people. Warriors and scientists, the lot of them, by how ze tells it. Ze prefers alien to creature; it's at least accurate."

"Okay... How long have you known the alien?" Cecilia corrected.

"A while," Leanne said, simply. "Now, come on. We need to get going. I have more on my to-do list today than getting you out of Dril's fur for a few hours. Do you have anything you need to get done out in the city while we're at it?"

"Uh, I guess I need something to go on missions in," Cecilia said, looking down at her dress. "Drilora wasn't thrilled about my jeans and t-shirt outfit yesterday, and I don't have any workout clothes. Exercise wasn't something I did regularly outside of gym class."

"Boom, done," Leanne said, pointing to Cecilia as she smiled at her. "We'll get you something that is Drilora approved. Maybe then, ze'll let you have a chance at... whatever training ze can come up with. I think it might do zer good to have someone like you. Someone to train; someone that could take up the mantle once ze gets those ships working in there."

"And when is that going to be exactly?" Cecilia asked. "It didn't look like ze has been making much progress."

"Oh, ze hasn't," Leanne said, laughing. "Between shooting each other out of the sky, the crash, and whatever the military managed to do with them before Drilora broke out of containment, those ships were pretty destroyed. That doesn't stop zer from trying. By the way ze tells it, there's only about five pieces that ze needs to get one of them flying. The problem is that none of them are within human technological levels, and ze has no idea how to make them from parts that are."

"It sounded like more than just a few parts to me," Cecilia said, as they came up next to Leanne's car. "Ze listed off all the issues ze has with the ships when I got here, showing how little of use I could be to zer. But I didn't come here to help zer leave the planet. I came to be a superhero."

"And what, pray tell, is this superpower that you're so confident in?" Leanne said. "I don't think that came up back there."

"I'm constantly being underestimated," Cecilia said.

"That's not a superpower," Leanne said, shaking her head.

"That's what Drilora said," Cecilia said, shrugging. "But I think I could have used it at the bank if I had to go in there on my own. I just... I didn't know how before going in there, and Drilora told me to stay out of zer way. That's why I need training, so I'd know what I need to do if I'm in that situation again."

"Well, hopefully, you won't be in that situation again," Leanne said. "But if you're so insistent on being of use with this so-called superpower of yours, let's see about getting you settled somewhere. Even if it isn't in the tower."

Chapter Fourteen
A Trip Out

The buildings of the city zoomed past them as Leanne drove Cecilia away from the park. Cecilia kept looking around them, trying to figure out where Leanne was driving her. The same flyers that were over by the bank were everywhere around there, with the grainy pictures of the creature blurred by the speeding car. As they came up to the first red light, Leanne turned to look over at Cecilia.

"Where am I taking you?" she asked.

"What?" Cecilia asked, her face going white at the question. At the idea that it was all just a trick to get her into the car so that Leanne could drive her home and leave her there. And the follow-up question seemed to only prove that.

"Your address," Leanne said. "We need to swing by your house, at least talk to your father about everything. He can't just abandon you like this."

"He didn't abandon me," Cecilia said, feeling defensive of her father. "He was only trying to do what's best for me. A-and having me fulfill the life debt that I owe Drilora," she added, when she remembered that part of what her father had said the day before. "Ze did save me from that fire." Cecilia glanced out of the window next to her as she said that.

She stared at one of those flyers that was pasted on the crosswalk signal next to them. That felt like a slap in the face compared to what Drilora had already done for her, saving her from that fire and taking her in like that, even if it would only end up being that one night.

"That's all well and good, but he could have approached this differently," Leanne said. "There are ways to fulfill this life debt you owe zer that doesn't require zer to take care of you like this."

"Hey, I can take care of myself," Cecilia said, defensively. And yet, she knew that she couldn't. Without a job or money to put a roof over her own head, she was stuck relying on Drilora, much like Leanne was saying.

"I'm sure you can," Leanne said, as she pulled through the intersection, heading deeper into the city. "With the right set up, the right support. Even Drilora needs help from time to time."

"And that's what you do for zer," Cecilia said.

"Exactly," Leanne said, nodding. "Now, your address?"

"Oh, uh..." Cecilia said, reluctantly, before finally giving in and telling her. Leanne just nodded as they continued deeper into the city.

The flyers seemed to drop off as they came to the more familiar section of the city. Once they headed past Cecilia's usual supermarket, she counted off the remaining blocks until they were at her apartment. Until she was back home. She was dreading seeing her father again, even just after that one day. Dreading his reaction to her coming home so soon. Far too soon for her to have accomplished anything.

The city seemed to conspire against her, as there was a parking spot right in front of the front door. Leanne slid into the spot easily, quickly shutting off the engine the moment that they were in. Cecilia glanced around the block, wondering if she would see people from her old life, and not just her father. Her friends would be at school already, though, and she didn't make it a habit of being in her neighborhood during school hours.

"Come along," Leanne said, not looking at Cecilia before she turned to the car door next to her.

Cecilia lingered in the car for just a moment longer, watching Leanne head around it and over to the doors. Her stomach was in knots, and all she wanted to do was drive away from there. To climb over the console and drive away with Leanne's car, even leaving the woman behind if needed. But she knew that was childish. That she needed to face her father, no matter what happened there. So, by the time Leanne was coming up to the building, Cecilia was climbing out of the car, rushing to catch up with her.

"Which apartment was it?" Leanne asked, not bothering to look back at Cecilia as she came up behind her.

"Oh, uh, eleven oh five," Cecilia said. She didn't think she told Leanne the apartment before, but Leanne just nodded to the number like she remembered it.

Leanne grabbed the phone next to the door, dialing in the apartment number. Cecilia could hear the phone ringing, even with it pressed against Leanne's ear. She held her breath, waiting for something to come. Waiting for the sound of her father's voice. After a few seconds of that ringing, Leanne glanced at her watch.

"Could he have gone to work already?" she asked.

"I don't think so," Cecilia said. It was barely eight o'clock by Leanne's watch, and Cecilia's father worked just a few blocks away from there. He usually walked it, leaving at the half hour. It gave him plenty of time to walk Cecilia to school growing up, before she had decided that she was too old for that sort of thing.

With the phone still ringing against Leanne's ear, Cecilia spotted Mrs. Vaughn coming out through the main doors, heading out into the day. Mrs. Vaughn waved at Cecilia as she passed them, but neither said anything to the other. While Cecilia knew Mrs. Vaughn, they weren't close, not quite friends. But then, that was how it was in that building. Leanne kept hold of the phone until the woman headed past them, but she grabbed the door before it could close once more.

"Come along," Leanne said again, putting down the phone even as she flitted through the door and into the building.

The elevator doors opened at the first press of the button. Another one of those flyers was hanging against the far wall. Leanne pulled it off the wall, crumpling it into a ball even as she hit the button for the eleventh floor. She just shook her head, squeezing the crumpled ball as tightly as she could, as they headed up.

"These stupid flyers are all over the place these days," Leanne said, shaking her fist, the ball of paper barely visible. "If I ever find out who's behind them..."

"It's just some alien hate group," Cecilia said. "Not really worth worrying about, right?"

"Well, these kinds of groups are never something to worry about until they are," Leanne said. "They can do a lot of damage if they ever turn to violence."

"Violence?" Cecilia asked, laughing as if the very idea of such a thing were impossible. "Against Drilora? Ze would take out any group coming after zer."

"Even Drilora has zer weaknesses," Leanne said. She glanced over at Cecilia, as if waiting for the obvious follow-up question. Cecilia didn't ask it, though, too worried that it would get her in trouble.

The elevator let out a little ding before the doors opened, revealing the eleventh floor. Cecilia jumped off the elevator as soon as the doors were open, heading over to her door out of habit. She was just reaching around to her purse before remembering that it wasn't there. That her father had her leave it behind, along with the other stuff that he hadn't wanted her to bring with her. Her father hadn't wanted her coming home like that. It was a heavy reminder of the changes that had happened in her life those past few days, ever since the fire.

Even as Cecilia came to terms with those changes, Leanne knocked lightly on the door. The door turned at her knock, opening just enough to reveal the entryway. When Cecilia noticed that the small table that was always by the door was no longer there, she reached her hand out, pushing the door the rest of the way open.

"What?" she asked, as she stared through the door in shock.

"Well, that certainly complicates things," Leanne said. She slowly headed into the apartment, looking around at the empty space.

It wasn't just that her father was missing, but that everything was. It looked like everything had been moved out in the few hours since Cecilia left there the day before. If she didn't know better, Cecilia might have thought that it was the wrong apartment. Like she had somehow forgotten her own apartment number, after living there her whole life. But as she came in behind Leanne, she noticed the height notches on the corner by the entryway. Her mother had insisted on doing that every year, right up to the point when she died. That was one of many things that her father had made a stop to the moment that they were on their own.

Leanne stood there silently, watching Cecilia as she looked around at her empty apartment. Cecilia wasn't sure what she was thinking at first, but when she looked over at Leanne, she noticed a familiar look on her face. The same look she always got from everyone around her. Pity. Pity at the loss of her life. Pity at the loss of her mother. Pity that she couldn't do anything right. That she wasn't worth anything. Not even worth keeping around anymore. Of course, it made perfect sense that her father would want to get rid of her like that, so that he wouldn't need to pity her anymore.

"Alright, come along," Leanne said. "We still have some shopping to do."

"Shopping?" Cecilia asked. It felt weird that they would be doing something so normal as shopping with her whole life stripped away from her like that. "But..."

"Well, we can't really do anything about your father today," Leanne said, waving around at the empty apartment. "I have some connections, people that I can put on tracking your father down for you. But that's not going to be happening today. For now, I think it's best to get you set up back at the tower, until we can come up with something better for you."

"Right," Cecilia said. But she just nodded as she stood there, staring around at the apartment that was no longer hers. Her bedroom door was open, showing that her room was just as cleared out as the rest of the place. It felt like someone had come and stolen everything from her, including her father. She wanted to track them down and get revenge, or at the very least bring them to justice. But she knew that it was her father that had done the stealing. That he had abandoned her at that tower just to get rid of her. It had never been about her becoming a superhero or the so-called life debt that he had made up as an excuse.

"Come on," Leanne said again, her hand touching Cecilia's shoulder. Cecilia jumped a little at that touch, not having noticed it when the woman came up next to her. As she turned toward Leanne, Cecilia's hands came up defensively, swatting Leanne's hand away.

"Oops, sorry," Cecilia said, once she noticed what had happened.

"It's fine," Leanne said. She raised her hand up in front of her, flexing the fingers in a weird pattern. "No harm done, see? But at least we know you have decent reflexes. Maybe you wouldn't be so hopeless after all. Not as a superhero, obviously, but as a sidekick at least. Sometimes, I feel like Drilora could use one of those."

"Ha," Cecilia said, though there was no humor behind it. She just shook her head as she turned back to her empty apartment. "Tell Drilora that."

"I will," Leanne said. "Now, come on. No sense stewing over a life that is no longer ours. We need to pull ourselves up by our bootstraps, as they say."

"And what if we can't?" Cecilia asked. While she had heard that phrase often enough growing up, usually from her father, it never made much sense to her.

"Then you ask for better boots," Leanne said.

Chapter Fifteen
Returning

On the way back to the tower, Leanne brought Cecilia into a sporting goods store not too far from the park and bought her enough workout outfits to last her the week. Cecilia felt weird about accepting the clothes from the stranger, but she had no money to her name. Without Drilora and Leanne, Cecilia would be all on her own. And with her father just disappearing on her like that, taking everything that she hadn't brought with her to the tower, she'd be on the streets with nothing.

"Are you alright?" Leanne asked, as they drove up the main road of the park. "I don't think I've seen you cry all day."

"Huh?" Cecilia asked. She looked over at Leanne for a moment, confused by the woman still being there. It took her a moment to realize that she still expected for her father to be in that seat. For it to be the day before, when her father was dropping her off at the tower. That none of what had transpired those past few hours really happened outside of her own head. Once she got over that shock, she just shook her head at Leanne. "I'm... I'm fine. I don't think it's really hit me just yet. It was the same when my mother died. I cried for weeks, but only after the funeral. Before then, I... I don't know. I don't really remember those days all that well."

"Well, your father is still out there, I'm sure," Leanne said, as she pulled into the same spot that she had parked in earlier. It was the spot closest to the tower. With the rest of the parking lot empty, she had her choice there. "I should hear back by the end of the day on the progress of the search.

If there's something useful, I'll stop by again to look in on you."

Cecilia just sat there quietly, nodding her understanding. She wanted to tell Leanne not to worry about it, that she didn't think anyone would find anything about what happened to her father. If her father didn't want to be found, then he wouldn't be. But Cecilia really did want to find her father. She wanted to be able to tell him the progress that she might manage to make there in the tower. If she made any progress at all.

"What about Drilora?" Cecilia asked. "What do we tell zer? Ze's probably going to look at me as more of a charity case than ze already does."

"We don't have to tell zer anything yet," Leanne said, shaking her head. "I'll talk it over with zer when we get in there, but... Well, I've been dealing with Dril a lot longer than you have. I know how to handle zer. What to tell zer and what not to. Don't worry. I'll make it clear that you can't be thrown out of the tower. Not until we figure out something better. Alright?"

"Okay," Cecilia said. She gave Leanne a strained smile before turning to the door next to her, heading out into the park.

Cecilia pulled out the two large bags of her clothes from the back seat as Leanne grabbed a third bag. She hadn't noticed what was in that bag, or when Leanne had gotten it, though she figured it had been at some point while she was trying on her workout clothes. However, she figured that it was supplies for Drilora, rather than anything for her, so she decided not to ask questions. With her father's disappearance, she couldn't risk rocking the boat any more than she already was.

Drilora opened the door to the tower before they came up to knock on it. Ze stood there in the doorway, zer arms crossed over zer chest, as ze glared out at Cecilia. Even with the alien expression on the alien's face, Cecilia knew that ze didn't want her coming back into the tower. That if ze wanted to be stubborn, there was nothing that Leanne could do to get her back inside.

"She's staying," Leanne said, simply, glaring right back at Drilora as they came up in front of zer.

"For how long?" Drilora asked. Cecilia was surprised that the creature wasn't contesting it. That ze wasn't demanding that they turn right back around and head out of there together. For Leanne to take Cecilia home with her, if she was so worried about the girl.

"A week to start," Leanne said. "You can put up with a human being here for a week, can't you?"

"Barely," Drilora muttered. "If I have to."

"Well... You have to," Leanne said.

The banter between them felt almost familiar to Cecilia. It took her a moment of them standing there, their path into the tower blocked by Drilora's looming form, to realize why. Her own parents had been exactly like that, back when her mother was still alive. Her father could be just as stubborn as Drilora was, only bending to her mother's will. While Drilora seemed so strong, confident, and demanding, Leanne had just as much control over zer as her mother had over her father.

"Now, let us in," Leanne said, waving her bag toward the door. "I need to get this into the kitchen."

Drilora stood there for a moment longer, looking between Leanne and Cecilia, before finally taking a step back and to the side, coming out of the doorway. Leanne quickly headed inside, with Cecilia right behind her. Cecilia woried that Drilora would try to step between them, to block her heading inside after letting Leanne in. But once they were both in, Drilora headed deeper into the garage, back over to zer spaceships.

Cecilia almost expected the ships to look different from her time out of the tower. For one or both of the ships to be broken down again, pieces lying all over the dead grass. But nothing seemed to have changed while they were out. She could almost see the gaping holes in the closer ship where the five missing pieces were meant to go in. The clutter on the table against the wall no longer looked like clutter, but the destroyed remnants of the parts that ze needed to replace.

Once Drilora was out of the way, Cecilia rushed up the stairs, heading for her room. She figured that she should change into one of her new outfits, to at least show that she was ready to take on the training that she would need in order to become the superhero that she was meant to be. However, when she noticed Drilora following Leanne up the stairs, Cecilia wanted to hear what they would say about her more. So, once she was past the bend in the stairs, heading past the fourth floor, she lingered there, straining her ears to hear them in the kitchen below.

"Couldn't get the father to listen to reason then?" Drilora asked. "He was pretty stubborn when I dealt with him earlier."

"Oh, come now," Leanne said. "You know me better than that."

"At least, I thought I did. I would have expected you to come back alone to pack up the girl. Are you losing your touch? Should I be looking for a new assistant?"

"It's a work in progress," Leanne said. "I'm hoping to resolve everything by the end of the week. If things become untenable by then, I'll put together some other arrangements. Like I said, there are better options than dumping the girl on you. But, in the meantime... I mean, she does seem eager to learn."

"Eager is one thing," Drilora said. "Capable is something else entirely. I have yet to meet a human that is capable of being a real superhero. As amazing as you are, Leanne, even you are just a human."

Silence settled on the conversation for a moment, and Cecilia worried that they noticed her there on the stairs. She slipped down two more stairs, trying to see around the corner into the hallway on the fourth floor. Trying to see if they were standing there, staring up at her. But there was no sign of them in the hall, and before she got much closer, they were talking again.

"I'm not saying that she can be a superhero," Leanne said. "Obviously, only an uvvelian is capable of that."

"I'm no superhero either," Drilora said. "I'm just... more capable than humans. It's the closest that anyone will ever come to having superpowers. There just is no science behind the whole thing. It's why the uvvelians never came up with the idea. We never had superheroes in our own fiction. I had never heard of such a thing before coming here, and only after the military stopped seeing me as a threat."

"Either way, she might be able to help you in ways that you might not have thought of," Leanne said. "I sometimes worry about you being out in those dangerous situations by yourself. Sometimes, it helps to have someone there in case something goes wrong. In case your strength fails you or there's another bomb you're not expecting. She could make a good sidekick, if you give her a chance."

"A sidekick?" Drilora asked. "That's what they called the smaller ones, right? The ones that have weaker powers, or no powers at all."

"Exactly," Leanne said. "She doesn't have your strength or invulnerability, but she can deal with the humans that are... more reluctant to work with you. There have been plenty of calls that I've had to turn down because of the neighborhoods they happen in. If she's there to watch your back, things don't have to go wrong."

"Fine, fine," Drilora said. "I'll... I'll train her. But I'm not bringing her out on calls unless she proves to me that she's ready."

"Perfect," Leanne said. "I knew that you'd understand. I know you better than you probably think I do. Better than most people do, I imagine. And, yes, I'm not saying you should throw her into situations that she's not ready for. But at least consider bringing her out to the perimeter. Let her see what you're doing there, learn from you. She seemed to think that she could have taken the situation at the bank on her own if she had figured out how beforehand."

"Ha," Drilora said. Another silence followed that one word, lingering for a few moments. Before Cecilia could wonder at the silence, though, Drilora continued. "I think I'd like to see her take on three armed robbers. But then, you already said not to send her into dangerous situations."

"By some standards, all situations are dangerous," Leanne said. "Maybe don't worry too much. In the meantime, I'd better go. Plenty of things to do, and not just for you and your new sidekick."

Cecilia quickly rushed the rest of the way up the stairs, not wanting them to notice that she had been eavesdropping on them. The moment that she came into her room, she grabbed one of the outfits out of the bags. She tossed the rest of them under the bed to hide the fact that she hadn't been putting them away properly while the adults were talking. By the time a knock came on the door, she was halfway changed into the outfit.

"Are you decent?" Drilora asked.

"Uh, just a moment," Cecilia called out, hastily pulling her dress off before pulling on the new sports bra. Even as she was pulling on the sweatshirt over it, she turned back to the door. "Yup, I'm ready," she said.

"Good," Drilora said. Ze pushed open the door, still nodding zer head as ze looked in on her. "Then come down to the gym. If I'm going to be stuck with you, if you're going to have any hope at being my sidekick, let alone a real superhero, then we're going to do this right. That means training. A lot of it. By the time I'm done with you today, you're going to wish that you had left with your father while you still had the chance."

"Yeah," Cecilia said, nodding her understanding. A tear tickled the edge of her eye, but she quickly chased it away before it could fully form. Drilora didn't mention it before turning around, heading back down the stairs. Cecilia was quick to follow zer, hoping that the promises of training were real. That she was finally going to be training to be a superhero.

Chapter Sixteen
Training

Cecilia wasn't sure what to expect from superhero training. Maybe learning to dodge bullets or fireballs. Dummies or robots to fight. Perhaps even sparring with Drilora zerself. So, when Cecilia came down to the gym, she tried to be ready for anything to come her way.

Drilora was standing against the far wall, zer back to Cecilia, as she came out onto the floor. Her sneakers barely made a sound as she walked over to zer; the padding on the floor muted it further than her normally light steps did. Cecilia kept her eyes locked on the back of Drilora's head, watching for signs that ze knew that she was there. Waiting for some hint at what she was supposed to be doing. However, trying to sneak up on the creature seemed like a perfect start to her training.

"We won't be starting on anything too strenuous," Drilora said, when Cecilia was still a few paces away from zer. Zer voice was low, making it clear that ze knew that she was close. That Cecilia hadn't managed to sneak up on zer at all. "And there's going to be plenty of homework for you to do."

"Homework?" Cecilia asked. She had thought that she had left homework behind when her father told her about his plan. It seemed like the one advantage of being stuck there at the tower. "Can it really be called homework if you're living in the school?"

"This is not a school," Drilora said. Ze turned around to look back at Cecilia for the first time since she got there. When ze did, ze pulled zer hands behind zer back, keeping whatever ze was holding hidden there. But Cecilia was too focused on zer face to notice. The look on Drilora's face was firm, though nothing all that different from what she had seen from zer since arriving there at the tower. "This is my home. You are a guest here. Please, remember that. As for the term, I'm referring to additional work that you will be taking up on your own. Call it what you will. The Uvvelian word for it is nothing like 'homework'."

Cecilia just nodded her understanding. She didn't know what else to say to that. Perhaps to apologize for her trying to make light of the situation. She just stood there quietly, patiently waiting for Drilora to continue.

"When I first came to your world, after the military tried to make me into something that I wasn't, they gave me a large collection of comic books," Drilora said.

Ze finally pulled zer hands out from behind zer back, showing what ze had been holding. It was an issue of a comic book. The cover showed a woman dressed in all black, falling through a city skyline. Cecilia had never been one for comic books, but the name on the cover was recognizable enough for her.

"There aren't many so-called superheroes without superpowers," Drilora said. "Fewer still are powerless female superheroes. From my own studying of the subject, it is clear that the differences between genders in humans make this an issue, specifically around testosterone levels. Those with lower testosterone levels, commonly found mostly among women, are less likely to be able to build muscle and develop upper-body strength, which is quite important in most methods of fighting. If you insist on being a real superhero, or as close to one as you can be, you'll need to learn to fight. Specifically, fight in a manner that doesn't rely on strength."

"Okay," Cecilia said. "So, does this mean we'll start with sparring?"

"Of course, not," Drilora said. Ze backed a step away from Cecilia, raising the comic up to zer chest, almost protectively. "If I were to spar with you, you would get hurt. Likely killed. There are reasons why I avoid fighting in my missions. Even the strongest fighter among you humans would be no match for me on even ground."

"Yeah, because you're a superhero," Cecilia said, snickering at the comment.

"If you're not going to take this seriously," Drilora started.

"No, sorry, sorry," Cecilia said. She reached out a hand toward Drilora, but didn't quite touch zer. "Sorry, I am taking this seriously. I know this is important. This is why I came here. For you to train me to become a superhero."

"Let me be absolutely clear here," Drilora said. Ze glared down at Cecilia, zer serious face still in place. "You will not become some great superhero by the time you leave here, hopefully at the end of the week. This is not some instant process. There are no radioactive spiders or potions or anything like that that will suddenly make you a superhero. Even if I believed this claim that you already have a superpower, it is not one that will help you in a fight. When you're surrounded by criminals looking to hurt you, being underestimated might help you escape, but it won't help you stop them. Understood?"

"Yes, Drilora," Cecilia said, nodding.

"Now, there are several ways of fighting, even among those that don't require strength. We'll start by putting you through some of the basics of several of them. They're all purely human methods, so, once you leave here, you'll be able to find a more suitable trainer. One that specializes in whatever method works best for you. Many of them are in the city. I will not be training you once you leave here."

"Why not?" Cecilia asked. "Sorry, I don't mean to be difficult, but... Well, I came here for you to train me."

"And I will, but not in fighting," Drilora said.

"But, I thought..."

"Fighting is important, but it is not the only thing. That is where the homework comes in, and I will get to that later. First, let's start with something simple: learning how to punch."

"Oh, I know how to punch already," Cecilia said. She found the suggestion a bit insulting, the idea that she might not know how to punch. But she was used to that sort of thing. It was how her power worked. "My father taught me how to punch when I turned twelve and I broke my hand on Eric Sexton's face."

"Well, then, let's see it," Drilora said, waving toward Cecilia. Ze backed up a little, standing against the wall.

When Cecilia looked around them, she noticed that that portion of the floor was empty of the machines and weights. It seemed the perfect spot to spar, or at least practice fighting moves. She backed up a few steps, not wanting to come anywhere near Drilora when she punched out. Once she was situated, she simply balled up her fist before punching out as hard as she could. It felt weird punching into the air like that, rather than striking at something. But then, she hadn't punched in a few years either. She hadn't needed to.

"That... wasn't half bad," Drilora said.

"For a girl," Cecilia added, knowing that it was coming.

"For a human," Drilora said. "While I understand the differences in the genders in your species, I don't feel the need to denigrate one over the other. The differences aren't so great."

"How big are the differences in the genders of your people?" Cecilia asked. After Drilora had mentioned the genders in humans, it got her curious about Drilora's own people. After all, Drilora was the only uvvelian that she had met. The only uvvelian on Earth.

"Uvvelians don't have genders," Drilora said, bristling a little like the very question was insulting to zer.

"Wait, what?" Cecilia asked, confused. "How does that even work? I-I mean with reproduction and all that. Doesn't that make it... difficult?"

"On the contrary, it makes it easier," Drilora said. "In humans, if a woman falls in love with another woman, or a man with another man, they don't have all the ingredients that they need. They need to... outsource the other half of the equation. In uvvelians, we all have both sides of the equation, we just can't reproduce with ourselves."

Cecilia looked down along Drilora's body. As usual, Drilora was quite naked, zer fur exposed all over. She wondered about how that worked with these aliens, and she only just then realized that she had been thinking of Drilora as a woman, despite zer choice in pronouns. That ze had some kind of internal reproduction organs like in human women. Drilora seemed to sense her confusion, as ze explained.

"Our reproduction system is entirely internal, and the act is completely different from the one performed by your species," ze said.

"So... I mean, you couldn't... mate with a human, then?" Cecilia asked.

Drilora just stood there, silently glaring at Cecilia for a moment. Cecilia had no idea what ze was thinking, but it was clearly not complementary. Only, when ze finally spoke, it seemed so much worse to Cecilia.

"I am to teach you how to be a superhero, not explain reproduction, in either species. If you don't know how impossible breeding between unrelated species is--"

"Oh, no," Cecilia said, shaking her head. "I didn't mean... I just meant... I mean, you've been alone on this planet for five years now. Don't you get... lonely? In-in that way."

"Oh," Drilora said, finally catching on to what Cecilia was really asking. "Again, that is neither here nor there. Let's get back to your training. I've seen how you punch; now I want to see how you kick."

Cecilia didn't mention the fact that Drilora still hadn't answered the question. The same expression was on zer face, hiding any emotions that might be playing through the creature. Cecilia just let the subject drop as she tried to kick as instructed. Only, unlike with punching, she had never tried to kick someone.

"Well, that was..." Drilora said.

"Horrible," Cecilia finished, before ze could.

"Quite," ze said, zer eye flicking around in laughter. Cecilia laughed as well, knowing just how hopeless she was in fighting.

"Do all the fighting styles require kicking?" Cecilia asked.

"No, but many of them do. Kicks have the added benefit of keeping you away from your target, as your legs are longer than your arms. However, it is at the cost of a stable footing. There are some fighting methods that rely on your opponent attacking you. Women tend to excel over men at these types of fighting, but..."

"But when my opponent is already underestimating me, they're not likely to fight me in a way that that would help,"

Cecilia said, already seeing the issue with that. "Eric Sexton never threw a punch at me."

"Then why did you punch him?" Drilora asked. "I hope you don't make a habit of starting fights. That does not align well with the whole superhero genre. More the anti-hero, which is another thing that the uvvelians didn't come up with."

"He was pulling my hair and trying to look up my skirt," Cecilia said. "I didn't tell my father that part. He might have done something far worse than punch him."

"Well, I want you to try to kick again," Drilora said. "This time, I want you to picture Eric Sexton's head right here." Ze raised a hand up just higher than Cecilia's own head, about at the spot where Eric's head would be if he was there.

When Cecilia kicked again, she tried to aim for that higher point. It was odd, weird, and awkward and she didn't come close to the mark, but it was a big improvement over the first attempt.

"Yes, let's skip the kicking," Drilora said, making it clear just what ze thought about all of that. "I think that's enough fighting for now."

"Meaning I'm hopeless?" Cecilia asked.

"Not entirely. But there's also one other item that is important in the superhero gig that might be a better place to start for today."

"Uh oh," Cecilia said. "I'm almost afraid to ask what it is."

"Why, running, of course," Drilora said, with no sign of humor in zer voice. Cecilia wasn't sure if ze was being completely serious or if that was just because ze was an alien. "Let's start with running around the tower. Twenty laps should do nicely. Then up and down the stairs. Depending on how well you manage that today, we'll look into adding patterns to it."

Chapter Seventeen
Tracking Hate
Drilora

Cecilia was completely useless during training. Drilora hadn't thought that zer opinion of the girl could have gone down until ze saw her trying to run. At least, ze thought that she was trying, for most of the laps around the tower. Ze watched her carefully on the surveillance system that surrounded the tower, watching the feed on a screen next to zer as ze did zer own workout. By the time Cecilia finished the laps around the tower and moved inside for the run up the stairs, ze thought for sure that she would collapse at some point, falling down the stone stairs and breaking her neck in the process. It would get her off zer back, but ze had a feeling that ze would be blamed for it. Unfortunately, there were no cameras in the stairwell, so ze focused on zer quieter exercises, listening for the sound of her body hitting the stone. It was much better when Cecilia moved on to the fighting training.

Well... Not for Cecilia's performance. Just that Drilora could watch her more closely, waiting for signs of her hurting herself.

While Cecilia at least knew how to throw a punch, which surprised Drilora, her form was all over the place. She didn't know how to put her weight behind the punch, which meant that the punches had no real power behind them. The human saying "punch like a girl" made a whole lot more sense to Drilora from watching Cecilia try to accomplish something. By the end of the exercise, Drilora thought for sure that the girl was completely hopeless.

"Just... Just forget it," Drilora said, shaking zer head. "That's enough for tonight. Go get cleaned up." Ze waved dismissively at the girl, not wanting to see her anymore.

"Yes, Drilora," Cecilia muttered. There was no real strength in her voice, like she had worn out that as well as the rest of her body. She was practically dragging her feet as she headed out of the gym and up the stairs.

Drilora stood there silently, watching Cecilia head off and listening for her falling down the stairs again. Only after ze heard her door closing in the distance did Drilora finally relax.

"I'm starting to fear that that girl is going to be the death of me," Drilora muttered to zerself, in Uvvelian. Not that ze thought that Cecilia might be listening in, or care about zer assessment of her.

With Cecilia safely tucked away in her room, and Drilora's own workout done for the day, ze headed back downstairs to the garage. At first, ze thought about trying to work on the ships again, but when ze spotted zer computer, ze remembered that ze needed to feed the human. That Cecilia would probably need plenty of food that evening to make up for the workout. Fortunately, Leanne and Cecilia had gotten lunch while out in the city, and Leanne had bought enough food to tide the human over for a day or two. However, Drilora had no interest in cooking anything for Cecilia, and ze doubted she would be up to cooking for herself. Instead, ze ordered another round of takeout from the same restaurant as the day before. Cecilia seemed to like that well enough.

Once Drilora had placed the order, a banner ad popped up on the restaurant's website. Usually, Drilora just ignored those things, knowing that they were just some way to get humans to spend more money that they didn't have.

However, this one caught zer eye, because a grainy, horrible picture of zer was on it. It took zer a moment to recognize it as the same flyer that ze had seen back at the bank the day before. Seeing it randomly posted around the city was one thing, but this seemed like the group was trying to throw sand in zer eye.

Drilora tried not to break zer mouse as ze clicked on the ad, bringing up the hate group's website. There were often meetings for these groups, gatherings of the haters as they talked about how much they hated zer. It always seemed like a waste of time to zer, not something that they would bother with back on Uvvelia. The website seemed to agree with Drilora, as there wasn't much on there, besides a few grainy photos of Drilora and some random conspiracy theories about how ze was trying to take over the world.

"Like I would ever bother running this horrid world," Drilora muttered to zerself.

Ze was still flipping around the website when there was a knock on the door. Ze glanced over at the door behind zer, like ze could see through it to whoever was out there. A few clicks on zer computer brought up the surveillance feed, showing the same delivery guy as the day before. He was already placing the order on the ground outside the door before running back to his car. Drilora chuckled to zerself a little at the sight of that, but it didn't sit well with zer that even the delivery guy that was paid to bring the food there was too scared of zer.

Rather than falling back into the rabbit hole of the hate group's website, Drilora headed over to the door to grab the food. On the way up, ze grabbed a stack of comic books, the promised homework assignment for Cecilia. Ze knocked lightly on the door, but ze could hear the shower running and figured that Cecilia was in the bathroom and safely out of view. Drilora slowly opened the door, waiting for signs of outrage coming from the girl. Only when nothing came did ze slip inside.

Ze quickly stuck the food inside the door, right where Cecilia would be able to find it. Before placing the comics next to it, though, ze looked down at the pile. The comic books had been Drilora's main connection to the humans' society over the last few years, much more useful and understandable while ze was trying to learn their language than the books that were in the library. The comics were precious to zer, and ze didn't want to just place them on the floor. Instead, ze placed them on the table next to Cecilia's bed, figuring that was a better place for them.

Once everything was in place, ze looked around Cecilia's room for a moment, making sure that there was nothing to hint that anything was amiss. Ze wondered if ze should have just stuck all of that in the kitchen instead of Cecilia's room, but it was more to keep the human tucked away in there than anything else. Drilora didn't want her snooping around the tower.

Not when ze already knew that ze was going to be heading out that night.

The sound of the shower running stopped while Drilora was still standing there. Zer eye snapped over toward the door and ze was worried that ze was going to be caught in there. Ze quickly slipped back out of the room, staying just outside of the door to listen for shouts of outrage. Only after ze heard nothing but quiet from there did ze head across the hall to zer own room.

There wasn't much of substance in Drilora's room. The same furniture was in there as in Cecilia's room, though with a lot less on it and in it. The sheets on the bed were disheveled as always; Drilora had more important things to do in the day than to make that bed. As Drilora didn't bother with clothes, there weren't many in the wardrobe. However, there was one thing: a huge trench coat with a hood that could easily hide the uvvelian once it was dark out.

Much like it would be in an hour or so.

Drilora scooped the trench coat out of zer wardrobe before slipping back down to the garage. Ze spent the hour waiting for dark delving back into the website for the hate group. It was easy enough to find the time and location for their meeting that night, especially since the group seemed to be actively recruiting members. By the time ze had finished looking through the site, ze was convinced that this group was just evil. Beyond the normal level of evil that ze had seen from some of the humans out there. More so than the hostage takers from the day before. All ze wanted to do was to track them down and deal with them zerself. And once it was dark enough out, ze figured that ze could do just that.

Ze didn't put much thought into it when ze slipped out of the tower into the night. It wasn't often that Drilora headed into the city when not going on a mission, but ze knew that there were plenty of people that tracked zer movements when ze jumped across the rooftops. There was a link to one of those sites on the hate group's website, making it clear to zer that they knew about it. That it would likely get back to the hate group that ze was coming if ze used zer usual method of travel, and they would likely go to ground. It had happened the first time ze had stalked one of those groups.

It was awkward and complicated to walk in the Terran gravity without hopping with every step. Drilora had to focus on not putting too much force into zer steps, keeping zer feet low to the ground and zer pace slow. With how focused ze was on that, ze didn't notice much of the city around zer or the crowd that ze was suddenly surrounded by. Not that there was much to see in the ugly, human city. Any danger that might come zer way would stand no chance against zer, so ze was more concerned about being recognized than attacked.

Drilora quickly got frustrated by zer slow progress through the city, but as far as ze could tell no one knew that ze was out there. Something caught zer eye at one point, a flash of white on the otherwise brown of the bricks of the buildings around zer. It was another one of those stupid flyers, sticking out in plain view. Before ze could think better of it, ze reached out, pulling the flyer off the wall and crumpling it into a ball. Once ze realized what ze was doing, though, ze looked around zer, searching for signs that there was someone in the crowd who noticed zer doing that. To see if just pulling that flyer off the wall was enough to give zer presence away to the humans. However, the crowd surrounding zer seemed as oblivious to zer as they were to everyone else there. With a shake of zer head, ze continued down the street, tossing the flyer away into the first trash can that ze came next to.

After what felt like an hour of walking through that crowd, surrounded by the humans, Drilora finally found the address that ze was looking for. Ze stood in front of the building for a moment, just staring at the doors. All ze wanted was to rush in there and up to the hate group's meeting. Perhaps scare the ever-living daylights out of those filthy humans. But the building had one of those revolving doors, just like at the bank. Those things weren't built for someone as big as Drilora, and there wasn't a normal door on this building.

With a heavy sigh, Drilora slipped into the alley next to the building. Once ze was out of view of the public walking past, ze crouched down, jumping straight up into the air. Ze cleared the first five floors before hitting the apex of zer jump, and ze grabbed onto a passing window, kicking off the frame to head higher. On zer third jump, ze made it onto the roof of the building next door. From there, ze could make out the windows to the apartment in question.

There were already several people in that apartment, far more than the space should have allowed. It reminded zer of the first fire that ze was called to help out with, at what was supposed to be an abandoned warehouse. Someone had held a rave there, and an electrical fire started up, engulfing the entire building before any of them could get out. A fire would certainly solve the issue of the hate group, but ze wasn't about to start one.

However, ze wouldn't have worked to save any of them if one started.

Ze sat on the rooftop of the building, zer arms folded over the small lip that ran around the edge, as ze settled in to wait for the meeting to begin. The windows were all closed, but ze could make out the low murmurs of the humans inside. Nothing solid enough for zer to listen in, though ze hoped that would change once the meeting started.

But then, as ze sat there, ze spotted several people that ze recognized. Humans that had come up again and again with these hate groups. What really surprised Drilora, though, was when Cecilia came in right behind them.

Chapter Eighteen
Caught
Cecilia

The window shattered, with glass raining down all around Cecilia. Drilora's arms reached through the hole where the window had been a moment before, blocking most of the shards from hitting Cecilia. But that wasn't zer intention. No, ze was far too angry to be protecting the human like that.

Before Cecilia knew what was happening, she was pulled out through the window. It felt like she had left her stomach behind her. And when she saw the ground far below her, with nothing keeping her from falling besides Drilora's grip on her, her dinner threatened to come back up on her. Rather than standing on some kind of fire escape, Drilora was just holding onto the side of the building with one hand, and Cecilia with the other.

With one strong pull, Drilora leapt upwards, sailing away from the window before anyone inside there could see what had happened. The sound of the window breaking should have pulled the attention of everyone at the meeting, but the voices of that crowd had been loud enough to drown out the sound. No one was going to be coming to Cecilia's rescue. And with Eddie's words still in her ear, she worried that he had been right. That this was Drilora showing zer true colors. The colors of a monster.

Just seconds after Drilora pulled Cecilia through the window, they were up on the roof. With the world spinning around Cecilia, she was no longer certain that it was the same building. Drilora could have jumped across the street to the next building over, or perhaps several buildings away. All Cecilia knew as she came back down to her feet was that she was on a roof, with only Drilora there. Moreover, that Drilora was furious with her.

"Ah ha," Drilora shouted, zer voice echoing around them. "The truth finally revealed."

"Indeed," Cecilia shouted.

Her hands went to the hand that was still holding her, keeping her connected to Drilora. All she wanted was to get away from zer. To escape. Perhaps to head back to the meeting and tell that group everything that she had learned during her time living at the tower. But as hard as she pulled at that hand, she could do nothing against Drilora's grip on her.

"The monster shows zer true colors," Cecilia said, before giving up on escaping from Drilora.

"Zer true colors?" Drilora asked. "I'm not the monster here, human."

"Says the alien that pulled me through a glass window," Cecilia shouted. "Just put me down before I scream."

"Scream all you want," Drilora said. "It won't help you any. No one is coming to rescue you. Your terrorist friends don't know where you went."

"Terrorist friends?" Cecilia asked. "What are you even talking about?"

"Don't play dumb with me, human," Drilora said. "You're whole 'everyone underestimates you' ploy is over. I'll never underestimate you again. Not now that I've seen the people you hang around with."

"Who I hang around with?" Cecilia asked. "What are you... You mean the whole Earth for Humans thing?"

"The Earth for Humans thing," Drilora muttered, like the words were a curse. Proof that Cecilia was exactly who ze said she was. "I saw you in that meeting, sitting next to one of their most ardent followers. Cheering along with their calls for my death."

"Whoa, whoa, whoa," Cecilia said, waving her hands at Drilora. "No one said anything about your death. They just want you gone."

"Gone. Dead. They don't much care which. And with my ship permanently grounded, dead is the only way they're getting rid of me. It's also their preferred method. Your preferred method." Ze shook zer head when ze said that. An alien look of disgust played across zer face. "Even with the proof right before my eyes, I still have a hard time believing that you're one of them. That I let you into my tower when you wanted me gone that whole time. Boy, was I blind to your... your humanness."

"My humanness?" Cecilia asked. "I've never pretended to be something other than a human. Other than what I was born as. You, on the other hand, have been pretending to be a superhero this whole time. You're no hero."

"I never claimed to be a superhero," Drilora shouted. Ze pulled Cecilia closer to zer mouth, shouting it straight into her face. "That's just some nonsense that you humans put on me. All I've ever tried to do since arriving on this mudball of a planet was try to help. Try to help and leave, so that you can have your precious planet back. Not that I've taken it from you. Not that I even wanted it. Even wanted to be on it."

"No, you just want to destroy it," Cecilia shouted. "I'll bet those ships of yours aren't even ships, but bombs. That you're just looking for the right explosives to use in them."

"What?" Drilora asked. Shock replaced anger in zer voice, and ze squinted zer eye at Cecilia. "What are you even talking about? What kind of bomb would I be able to make that could destroy a planet?"

"What?" Cecilia asked, stunned. "What are you... No, that... But..."

She tried to think about what was going on there. What she knew, and not what Eddie's words had led her to believe. All she knew was that Drilora had pulled her out of that window, carrying her up to the roof. It seemed to match with exactly what the monster that Eddie had described would do. But nothing that Drilora had said seemed to match with that.

"What-what's going on here?" Cecilia asked.

"What's going on is that I saw you at a terrorist meeting," Drilora said, zer anger returning.

"They're not terrorists," Cecilia said. She couldn't believe that a terrorist group would be meeting there in her city. That was something that happened in third world countries, not there in hers. "They're..." she started, as she struggled to come up with a better word for the group. A word that she could allow to exist so close to home. The best that she could come up with, though, was, "... a hate group."

"And that's better?" Drilora asked, zer voice rising back up into a shout. "I found you at a hate group. A hate group that is targeting me. And you were sitting there like you belonged with them."

"I... I don't... I didn't... I was following you," Cecilia finally managed to get out.

"What?" Drilora asked. "No, that..." Ze went quiet, seeming to think about that.

"I was in my room when you left the tower," Cecilia said. "I heard a noise and thought that someone was breaking in. Then I saw you heading into the city. I thought you were going on a mission and leaving me behind. So, I followed you to this building... Or... Or the building where the meeting took place." She looked around them, trying to figure out if they were still at that building. But all she could see was the city skyline around her. The rooftops all around, none of which had labels for the streets running below them.

"But... What..." Drilora started.

"What were you doing there?" Cecilia asked, throwing the accusation right back at Drilora. "Were you coming to kill the leaders of the group? Or everyone in it? Did I manage to get out of there just in time so as not to die with everyone else?"

"No," Drilora said, zer anger back in place, quickly chasing away zer confusion. "I wasn't here to hurt anyone. I was here to make sure they don't try to hurt me. To make sure that I didn't have to kill them to defend myself."

"Oh, right, you'll have to self-defense them to death," Cecilia said, her own anger rising up to meet with zers. "You're super strong, huge, invulnerable to bullets. What do you have to be afraid of?"

"Ha," Drilora said. "Wouldn't you like to know? I'm sure you want to report that to your terrorist friends downstairs."

"I already told you, I don't know them," Cecilia shouted. "I've never been to one of those meetings before, and I have no intention of going to another one."

"So you say," Drilora said. "So you say. But you looked awfully chummy with them in there. Sitting next to Janine that whole time."

"Who?" Cecilia asked. "The... The woman? I met her on the elevator on the way up. By the time I realized what was going on there, it was too late to leave without everyone noticing me. I left as soon as I could. Then, you broke open a window and pulled me out of it. Now, you're holding me like you're still trying to decide if you want to crush me or toss me out over the city to see if you can skip me across the rooftops like a stone on a pond."

Drilora's eye flicked between the hand that was still holding Cecilia aloft and the ground beneath her feet. It seemed like ze only just noticed that ze was holding her up. That Cecilia wasn't tall enough for zer to be holding her like that while she was still standing on the roof next to zer. Slowly, ze lowered her down, her feet lightly touching the rooftop, but ze kept a strong hand on her, not letting her go just yet.

"Better?" Drilora asked.

"What exactly do you think I'm guilty of?" Cecilia asked, not answering the question. "Consorting with a hate group? Sure. Fine. I didn't know they were a hate group. And I would have thought that my time in the tower would have been enough for you to trust me by now. I could have tried to kill you in your sleep, even if it would have failed. I didn't, now, did I?"

"Not yet," Drilora said.

"Did... Did Leanne tell you about... about my father? About how he..." Cecilia couldn't put words to what her father had done, what had happened to him. What had happened to her life.

"Yes," Drilora said, zer voice dropping to barely a whisper. "You've been quite abandoned, just like... Or so it seems, anyway. But even you have admitted that there's more to you than most people can see."

"Yes," Cecilia said, laughing a little at herself as she shook her head. "My superpower gets in the way more often than it helps. I had been hoping that my time with you would change that, but... Well, clearly that hasn't gone over all that well."

Drilora nodded zer agreement to that sentiment as ze slowly released Cecilia, dropping zer hand back down at zer side. Ze turned around, looking back at the door off the roof and giving Cecilia zer back. If Cecilia had been looking to hurt zer, that would be the perfect time. Only Cecilia knew that Drilora would be expecting it. That it was another test, just like the mission the day before. Unlike the mission, she could easily pass this test.

"I'm not--" Cecilia started.

Before she got more than that out, the door to the roof blew open. It flew a few feet away from the stairwell, slamming onto the gravel there just in front of Drilora. The rooftop shook beneath Cecilia's feet, and her legs felt wobbly from it. There was suddenly someone standing in the doorway, a large gun in their hands. For one moment, Cecilia thought that they were about to shoot her. But when the gun went off, shooting something across the space between them, it slammed straight into Drilora's chest.

Chapter Nineteen
Fighting Hatred
Drilora

Drilora let out a loud roar, zer arms going high over zer head and zer back arching in pain. More pain than Drilora had felt since arriving on that mudball of a planet. Zer mind struggled to figure out what was happening to zer, how the humans could have come up with a weapon that would do that to zer. The only weapons that Drilora had seen that could get through zer fur were invented by the krylonians. But when ze looked down at zer chest, where the pain was at the worst, ze saw what appeared to be a normal looking, very human, harpoon sticking out of zer fur.

"What are you doing?" Cecilia asked. She rushed forward, coming around Drilora to stand between zer and the door. The three humans, Eddie, Janine, and Matt, were standing over there, with Eddie holding a strange looking gun, a long cable flowing out of it. Cecilia turned around, looking back at Drilora in shock.

"Oh, hello," Janine said, smiling over at Cecilia like nothing was happening. Like it was just a normal day, and the three of them weren't attacking someone. "Nice of you to join us. Were you looking to take your own crack at the alien?"

"No, I don't think that's it," Eddie said. He shook his head as he pulled on the gun. Drilora let out another roar of pain at the pull, zer hands going to the harpoon in zer chest. "I think she was up here talking with the thing."

"No, no," Matt said, shaking his head. "We saw the broken window down there. I think the alien abducted the girl. Well, we're here to rescue you. You don't have to worry anymore."

"I wasn't worried," Cecilia said. "Let-let zer go."

"Zer?" all three of them asked as one.

"Don't you mean 'it'?" Janine asked. Drilora would have flinched away from that word, but the pain flowing through zer made it hard to react to anything else. Hard for zer to even think of how to get out of the trouble ze was in.

"Why would we let it go?" Eddie asked at the same time.

"Is it doing some kind of mind control on her?" Matt asked.

"Let zer go," Cecilia said again. She reached over, grabbing onto the cable. The moment that her skin touched the metal, she pulled her hand away from the cable, clutching it to her chest like she was in pain. At the same time, the pain running through Drilora lessened. It lessened enough for zer to move once more.

"What did she do?" Eddie asked, looking between Cecilia and the cable. A look of concern played across his face as he stared at the cable. He seemed to think that her just touching the cable would be enough to save Drilora.

Drilora's roar shifted from pain to anger. With a swift pull, the harpoon came away from zer chest. Cecilia turned back that way, surprise on her face.

Just after ripping the harpoon out of zer fur, Drilora raised it over zer shoulder, throwing it like a javelin back at the three humans. The humans scrambled out of the way, desperate to avoid being hit by the projectile. The harpoon hit the cement of the stairwell behind them, dancing around a little like it was still electrified. Eddie looked between the gun in his hands and the harpoon for a moment before turning it off, the harpoon immediately settling on the ground.

Drilora took just a moment to look down at the gap in zer fur. Zer hand felt around inside of that hole, making sure that the harpoon hadn't penetrated too deeply. There was no sign of blood when ze pulled zer hand away, and all ze could see in the hole itself was more fur. As usual, zer fur was enough to keep zer safe from the weapons of the humans, though ze feared that that wouldn't hold true for much longer. Not with this new weapon out there.

"Go out there," Eddie said. "Distract it. I need to reload."

"Are you kidding me?" Matt asked. "I'm not going out there. That thing will kill me."

"I can still kill you without you coming out here," Drilora said.

Cecilia stood there in stunned silence, her eyes locked on the three humans in the stairwell. It was clear that she had no idea what to do, how to help Drilora. But she had already helped in the only way that she could, disrupting whatever current had been flowing through that harpoon. Even Drilora had to admit that she made a halfway decent sidekick.

Eddie was already reaching down to the harpoon behind him as Drilora rushed toward the three humans. Janine grabbed Matt's arm, pulling him out in front of Eddie to block Drilora's charge. Matt clearly wanted nothing with that, and he turned away from Drilora, desperately trying to get past Eddie. However, the leader of the group was blocking easy access to the stairs behind him. The three of them were stuck there, in the path of Drilora's charge.

Drilora reached out once ze got close enough, grabbing onto Matt's shoulder, pulling him out onto the roof. Janine's hand was still on his arm, and the two of them were pulling the man apart. If the woman had been stronger, that would have been the end of Matt. However, her grip quickly slipped off the man's arm, and he was pulled away from them by Drilora. Ze raised the man up in front of zer face, much like ze had done to Cecilia earlier. All ze was at that point was blind rage, and ze had to resist the urge to throw the man from the roof.

"Why?" he shouted in his face.

"Ah," the man shouted back, too scared to form words. His pants quickly gained a darker tone in the light coming from the stairwell behind him, with the smell of urine filling the air around them.

Drilora raised Matt up higher over zer head as ze looked around the rest of the roof, searching for somewhere to throw him. With how close the stairwell was to the edge of the building, many directions would likely result in the man falling off the edge and landing hard on the pavement below. Instead, ze tossed him backwards, behind zer.

Matt continued to scream as he flew through the air, landing hard on the roof and skidding along the gravel. His screaming only stopped when he did, landing in the middle of the roof. Cecilia looked back at him, staring at the man like she was concerned for him. Like she actually cared if the man died. For one moment, Drilora thought that maybe ze had been right about Cecilia after all. That she had some connection to the group.

"Now," Eddie shouted, pulling Drilora's attention back to him.

Janine quickly jumped aside, heading out onto the roof, closer to Drilora. Ze looked over at her, advancing a step in her direction. But before ze could reach out to grab her, the gun went off again. The harpoon sailed out of the gun, this time slamming Drilora in the neck. Drilora backed up several steps under the impact, zer hands going up to the harpoon. Zer fur wasn't enough to stop the momentum of the harpoon, and it kept moving, the point of it coming out from behind Drilora's neck with the shaft stuck in zer fur.

Drilora let out another roar of pain as the electricity started to run through zer again. However, this time, ze was prepared for it. Ze powered through the pain, turning back to look at Eddie in front of zer. Drilora managed to take a step forward, closing the distance between them further. Zer hands reached out, desperate to grab onto that gun. To get it away from the human.

"Oh, no, you don't," Janine shouted. She rushed forward, stepping between Drilora and Eddie, defending the leader of the group. Drilora's hand swatted through the air between them, slamming into the woman's shoulder.

Janine let out a scream of pain at the impact of Drilora's swing, though ze hadn't put zer full strength into it. Gravel flew everywhere as the woman was knocked aside, sliding across the roof and dangerously close to the edge. Her foot slammed into the small wall that ran around the edge of the rooftop, stopping her from moving further. But she just laid there, looking just as dead as Mark had.

Drilora quickly turned back to Eddie, but the pain running through zer from the electricity became too much. Ze could barely move zer muscles from how they were all clamped down from the pain. Spasms were starting to run through zer back, and zer fur was standing up on end. All ze could do was grip the cable in front of zer, squeezing onto the metal. But as strong as Drilora was, ze wasn't strong enough to crush the metal. To break the cable.

"Let go of zer," Cecilia shouted. That shout seemed to thaw her, and she finally moved forward, heading over to the stairwell door. With how close Drilora was to it, though, she couldn't get through. She couldn't get at Eddie in there. She couldn't attack Eddie or get the weapon away from him. But that wasn't what Drilora needed from her.

Cecilia looked between Eddie and the cable for a moment before reaching out, touching the cable. Electricity flowed through her once more, but this time her hand clamped down on the cable instead of being knocked off of it. Her jaw locked down under the pain, seeming to keep a scream from escaping her.

With one last roar from Drilora, ze managed to pull on the harpoon once more. The harpoon tore free of zer fur, pulling some of it out along with it. The cable shifted to the side, knocking Cecilia away. She fell to the ground, her hand still locked around the metal. But once the metal touched the gravel of the rooftop, the shock flowing through her lessened. Drilora watched that just long enough to see Cecilia releasing her grip on the cable, though ze feared that the metal was too close to her and that it would continue to send electricity through her.

"Big mistake," Drilora said, turning back to glare at Eddie. With Janine and Matt behind zer, there was nothing standing between Drilora and Eddie.

"Ah," Eddie screamed, before turning around, running down the stairs. Running away from Drilora before ze could close the distance between them.

Drilora just stood there for a moment before turning around to look back at Cecilia on the ground. Ze reached down, grabbing onto the harpoon just long enough to knock it away from Cecilia. Her body continued to jerk and spasm under the effects as she laid there.

"Come along, little one," Drilora said, looming over Cecilia and looking down at her. "You did well for a sidekick today. Let's get you home and patched up."

Drilora reached down, gently lifting Cecilia into zer arms. Ze looked around at the other humans, both unconscious on the roof there. Neither posed a threat to them anymore, though ze knew that they would come after them again soon enough. That this wouldn't be the last that they heard of the Earth for Humans movement, and half a dozen other hate groups that seemed aligned against zer. However, with Cecilia hurt, lying in zer arms, for the first time Drilora worried that they could hurt zer in a way that ze wasn't expecting.

Chapter Twenty
Exhaustion
Cecilia

Cecilia stood in her shower for half an hour after training, just letting the hot water flow over her. The heat was wonderful on her skin. She was exhausted and could barely keep her feet under her. Her hand was holding onto the handle of the shower door, but even her arm felt too weak to hold her up.

After the running, Drilora had Cecilia doing more punches. Her arms felt sore and weak and she worried that she wouldn't be able to raise them up at all soon. It all seemed counter-intuitive to her, having her exhaust herself on training like that when another mission could come up at any moment.

"How does Drilora expect me to be able to participate in a mission if I can barely stand?" Cecilia asked herself. But then, she realized the obvious answer. Realized that Drilora might just be tiring her out so that she couldn't go on the next mission. So that she would be too tired to complain about it.

And yet, the entire time that Cecilia had been running around the tower, Drilora had been working out in the gym. Ze seemed to put in just as much work as she did with zer workout, though ze didn't show it in the end. While Cecilia could barely stand on her own, Drilora seemed ready to take on the world as always.

With Drilora busy with zer own workout as Cecilia did hers, it was clear that ze was simply expecting Cecilia to be honest about running the laps, rather than making sure that she did them. However, with this training helping Cecilia become the superhero that she was meant to be, she really did put in the work as assigned.

At least, she did the laps, though not all of them were at a run. With how big the tower was, running around it twenty times amounted to several miles. Cecilia had never run so much as a single mile at a go, so she only ran about half the laps, with walking the other half. By the time she came in to do the stairs, running them was completely out of the question. Each time she passed by the gym, Drilora was looking over at her with a look that Cecilia figured was disappointment; it was completely different on zer than it looked on humans. On her father.

Doing the punching exercises on top of that wasn't nearly as bad as Cecilia had been expecting. She figured that was because her legs were already exhausted, but her arms were still well rested. That quickly changed, and she barely managed ten minutes of punches before Drilora had sent her up to her room. With how disappointed ze was in her performance, ze almost forgot to assign her the homework.

Almost.

With it already getting late, after the hours-long training session, Cecilia kept thinking that she needed to get out of the shower. That she needed to start working on the homework so that Drilora wasn't more disappointed in her. That ze didn't try to kick her out after only two days because she wasn't taking the work seriously.

Cecilia kept her hand solidly on the handle of the shower door as she reached over with her other hand to shut off the water. A shiver ran through her once the water was no longer flowing down her back, the heat trapped within the room not enough to keep her warm. She quickly pulled open the doors, grabbing her towel even as she stepped out of the shower. By the time she was heading back into the bedroom, the towel was properly wrapped around her body, hiding it in case Drilora was waiting for her out there.

There was no sign of the creature in her room, though there was another takeout container on the floor just inside the door. She hadn't turned the lights on in the room when she had come inside, so the fading light of dusk and her grumbling stomach told her the time better than that food. With the workout that she had that afternoon, all she wanted was to inhale that food and more. But the bigger concern was the pile of comic books on the table next to her bed.

Rather than giving her the entire collection, which was still spread throughout the tower, Drilora had only assigned her the first volume of Batgirl, which ran seventy or so issues. They were all stacked high on the nightstand, looking just as daunting as the run had been. Even with the comics being mostly pictures, she wasn't sure she would be able to read all of them that night, let alone know them on the level that Drilora was expecting. But then, with how he was talking about the superheroes in the comics, it had become clear to Cecilia that ze had a photographic memory.

Of course, this was another thing that all uvvelians had, and not some superpower that was exclusive to Drilora.

With her father's words about reading in the dark in her ear, Cecilia flipped on the light before scooping up the food. There was a fork already sticking out of the container, stressing the fold. She quickly ate a few bites, just enough to settle her grumbling stomach, before turning to her bed next to her. Cecilia all but collapsed onto her bed, which was a bit awkward with the food in her hands and only the towel on.

She managed to find a semi-comfortable position leaning against her headboard, with the container tucked into the crook over her elbow and her lap mostly empty. The towel threatened to come undone, but she flipped her covers over her, keeping herself warm in the cold and drafty tower.

Once she was situated there, she grabbed the first comic off the pile, starting to flip through it even as she ate her dinner.

The comic was a bit confusing at first, with Cecilia being just aware enough of Batgirl to feel completely lost by what was supposed to be the start of the story. There wasn't much depth to the material, despite what Drilora seemed to indicate, and she was able to catch up well enough by the end of the third issue. However, she was still lost in what she was supposed to be learning from reading it. As with most of the superhero tales, it was mostly fighting random bad guys and just normally being the hero, while dealing with her own issues. While Cecilia could definitely relate with all of that, none of it seemed all that relevant to her training.

She shook her head as she tossed the first few issues onto a pile next to the main one. It seemed like a drop in the bucket compared to what was assigned to her. She just stared at those two piles as she finished her food, not wanting to get the issues messed up as she snarfed up the last few bites. Drilora had made it clear that ze expected the issues back in the state that ze gave them to her.

Once the food was finished, she turned back to the reading. She had no idea how the geeks of her school could read so many of these comics at a go, as she was getting rather tired of it. With the full-sized books just two floors below her, Cecilia wished that Drilora had assigned her one of those. They were much more entertaining, and she always preferred the flow of the longer form works. But then, it was becoming clear to her that Drilora was just as much of a geek as the comic book dorks at school.

It had gotten quite dark out by the time Cecilia managed to get through the first ten issues. With so many more left to go, Cecilia tossed another issue onto the read pile with a heavy, annoyed sigh. She was about to grab another one when she heard something in the distance. With having her head in comic books for the past hour, Cecilia started thinking the worst. Thinking that someone was trying to break into the tower. They would soon regret that, of course, once they ran into Drilora. Still, Cecilia decided it was better to go look, rather than relying on the creature all the time.

Besides, what if they managed to slip past the creature and get to Cecilia?

Cecilia carefully placed the almost emptied takeout container back on the floor before tossing aside her covers. Her towel came away with it, and she found herself lying naked on the bed. Only then did she remember her state of undress. She quickly rolled off her bed, away from the takeout container and toward her drawers. Rather than going for her usual dress, she pulled on another set of her new workout clothes. They were black and would work well to hide her in the darkness of the rest of the tower.

Slowly, Cecilia creeped around her bed, heading over to the door to the hallway. She kept her shoes in her hand, not wanting to make a sound as she slipped through the tower. Not wanting to draw attention to herself until she needed to. It felt like exactly what Batgirl would be doing at that moment, and she started to wonder if that was the lesson all along as she slipped out into the hall.

The tower was as quiet as it always was as Cecilia snuck down the hall. Perhaps more quiet, with no sounds coming from the creature, hidden deep within the building. At first, Cecilia worried that the intruder had already gotten to zer. But with Drilora spending most of zer spare time in the garage with the spaceships, the intruder would have needed to get the jump on zer right there.

When she came up to the first window in the stairs, though, Cecilia instantly knew that she had gotten it all wrong.

That there was no intruder sneaking into the tower. No, Drilora had snuck out, and was already heading down the road toward the city, far too fast for Cecilia to ever hope to keep up with zer.

She stood there for a moment, staring out through the window in shock. The only time she had ever heard about the creature heading out of the tower was for a mission. This felt like the same to Cecilia. Like ze was heading out into the night on a mission, but sneaking out of the tower to keep Cecilia out of it. Not even using her exhaustion as an excuse to keep her in the tower. She was having none of that.

"Ugh," Cecilia groaned, when she knew that she had to at least try to catch up with zer. Try to see what it was that the creature was up to, sneaking out into the city at that time of night. "More running," she groaned, as she sat down on the stairs right there to get her shoes on.

Chapter Twenty-One
Sneaking Out

Cecilia's legs complained to her as she rushed down the stairs and out into the night. Drilora was just visible in the distance, more as a shadow playing across the city lights than as a form. At first, as she ran after the creature, Cecilia worried that Drilora would hear her. That ze would force her back to the tower. But then, as she quickly got out of breath again, she realized how unlikely that was. How unlikely it would be for Drilora to even hear her, because there was no way that she was catching up with zer.

Drilora was taking zer time, walking along the main road out of the park. The road turned and bended as it went along, so Cecilia kept to the grass in the park on the far side of the parking lot, hoping that a direct path out into the city would help her make up some time. The tall grass would help her hide from Drilora's eye, if ze ever looked in her direction. But when she broke into the bright lights of the city, she looked around, feeling completely lost. Worse was the fact that Drilora was nowhere in sight.

"Damn it," Cecilia muttered to herself, stamping her foot down on the sidewalk in frustration. Even that hurt her foot more than it should have, with having used them far too much that day already.

The city felt almost normal to Cecilia as she stood there, looking around her. There were pedestrians walking along the sidewalk across the street from her, though there were none along the park side of the street. No one wanted to get even that close to the park if they could avoid it. And yet, none of them seemed to sense that the creature was about to emerge from the park, heading out into the city.

As she stood there, looking around her, a strange patch of brown ran through the corner of her eye. It wasn't the shade of brown that she was looking for, but she turned at it all the same. There was someone standing on her side of the road, wearing what looked like a humongous, tan trench coat. Cecilia didn't think that Drilora was fooling anyone in that outfit, but it was the first time that she had seen the creature wearing anything close to clothes.

Drilora stood there at the end of the park road for a moment, looking around at the traffic heading past. The moment that the road was clear, ze rushed forward, heading across and into the city. Unlike how Cecilia had seen the creature walk before, ze was keeping low to the ground, rather than bouncing from step to step. It seemed like ze was trying to make it seem like ze was a human, despite how alien ze looked.

Cecilia stayed next to the park for just a few seconds longer, letting two more cars pass by her before heading forward after Drilora. Ze was half a block over from her, walking along Eighth Avenue. As Cecilia crossed the street, she looked over at Ninth just next to her, closer than Eighth was. She figured that it would be smarter to head over to that other street, to follow Drilora on the parallel street to avoid being spotted. That felt like something that Batgirl would do. However, Cecilia was too worried that she would lose the creature in the night. So, once she made the far side of the road, she turned left, heading back over to Eighth to follow behind Drilora.

By the time Cecilia made it over to Eighth, Drilora was only a block and a half down the road, slowly moving along with the rest of the foot traffic. Despite how obvious the creature was to Cecilia, the people around zer didn't seem to notice zer there. Cecilia rushed forward, meaning to keep up with Drilora as ze headed through the city. But by the time Cecilia got to the end of that first block, she realized that the creature wasn't running. That ze was walking as slowly as the rest of the foot traffic around zer.

Cecilia gave a sigh of relief at the thought that she wouldn't need to run to keep up with the creature. That she could head along at a pace that she could keep up, especially with how tired she was from the workout. She kept to the edge of the crowd, though, keeping her eyes on Drilora in the distance so that she didn't lose zer. But with zer following along with the crowd, much like Cecilia was, she hoped that wouldn't be likely.

Half a block further up Eighth Avenue, Drilora stopped suddenly. "Move it," someone shouted, as the people right behind Drilora were forced to move around zer. Drilora glanced over at the person, though zer face was hidden by the hood on the trench coat. If the person noticed the glare that Drilora would be giving him, he didn't say anything about it.

Once that first group headed around Drilora, the rest of the crowd shifted to flow around zer, leaving zer in a widening gap. Ze turned back to zer right, and Cecilia worried that ze could see her back there. That ze had spotted her and that was why ze had stopped. Cecilia quickly ducked into the next doorway, worried that it was already too late. That the damage was already done. However, Drilora wasn't calling out for her. Ze wasn't turning back to look at her. Ze just slowly walked over to the wall of the building next to zer.

With a glance around at the crowd passing by zer, Drilora reached out to that wall, seeming to pull something off of it. Cecilia was still too far away to see what it was. Drilora glared down at it for a moment before crumpling it into a ball. Cecilia had a feeling that it was another one of the flyers that she had been seeing around the city.

Drilora started off down the road again, falling into the crowd flowing around zer. Cecilia stayed in that doorway for a bit longer, trying to keep that block between them. Once she thought ze was far enough away, Cecilia headed back out into the crowd. The crowd seemed completely oblivious to her, which was normal for her. No one thought much of her, and most would just ignore her as they headed through the city together.

At the end of the block, Drilora tossed the crumbled flyer into a trash can as ze passed it. As Cecilia approached that trash can, she considered reaching into it, pulling the flyer out to make sure it was what she thought. However, before she came up next to it, someone dumped their coffee into it as they passed by, pouring the liquid into the trash before dropping the cup. Cecilia barely glanced at the trash, seeing several similar bits in there. She turned up her nose at the very idea of reaching in there at all, not slowing as she continued up the road.

Cecilia followed along with the crowd till the end of the block. She looked all around her, trying to find Drilora. With how tall and stocky ze was, it had been easy enough to follow zer. But when Cecilia came to the cross street, with still no sign of the creature anywhere, she suddenly worried that she had lost zer.

"What?" she asked herself, desperately looking around her. The crowd was continuing along Eighth Avenue in front of her, seeming oblivious to the two of them hidden among them. To her left, the cross street headed off into the distance, not quite as crowded as Eighth was, though enough so for it to take Cecilia a few seconds to be sure that Drilora hadn't gone that way. She quickly turned around, looking the other way down the cross street, but the crowd swarming past her hid her view of it. For once, she wished that she was as tall as Drilora so that she could see over those heads, but she knew that no one would ever underestimate a seven foot tall woman.

Cecilia pushed her way through the crowd, making for the other side of the cross street. No one seemed to care about her pushing past them, the complete opposite reaction from what Drilora had gotten just from stopping. Once she was through the crowd, she spotted Drilora off in the distance, already another block ahead of her. Cecilia quickly rushed after zer, desperate to catch up before ze disappeared on her again.

Soon after Cecilia spotted Drilora down that cross street, the creature stopped once more. This time, Cecilia continued forward, not bothering to hide out in the next doorway alcove. She was too far away, still hidden among the reduced crowd of the cross street, and just as likely to be confused for one of them. Cecilia thought for sure that Drilora wouldn't see her. And yet, when the creature turned her way, her heart skipped a beat. It seemed like ze was looking straight at her, rather than just around at the crowd. Seconds later, by the time Cecilia's heart started beating once more, Drilora was looking the other way.

Whatever Drilora was looking for, ze didn't seem to find it, as ze moved toward the building next to zer. For a moment, Cecilia thought that maybe ze had spotted another one of the flyers. But Drilora quickly disappeared over there, heading inside somewhere. And with how far away Cecilia was, she suddenly worried that she would lose zer. That she couldn't possibly figure out which building ze had headed into, let alone where in the building.

Cecilia ran faster, her already complaining muscles yelling at her. She stayed in the small gap between the foot traffic and the wall, risking running into someone heading out of one of the doors or accidentally bumping into the wall itself. Once she made it over to where she thought for sure she had spotted Drilora head inside, she came to a stop. Her hands went to her knees as she bent over, panting deeply, desperate to regain her breath. Even as she did so, she looked around her, trying to figure out where Drilora had gone.

The door in front of Cecilia had another one of those flyers staring back at her. After seeing Drilora pull one off a wall earlier, she figured that wasn't a good sign. That if the creature had headed past there, ze would have pulled that one down as well. However, unlike the flyers that Cecilia had seen before, this one had some writing on it in purple marker, written on the flyer by hand. It had an address, date, and time, though no other explanations. While Cecilia had no idea the time, she thought for certain that the date was that day.

And the number above the door matched the one on the address as well.

Cecilia looked around her for a moment, worried that she had gotten it all wrong. That Drilora had gone into another door, some other building there in the city. If this wasn't the right door, she knew that she would never find the creature out there in the city. That wherever ze had gone, she would never know. She would miss the mission. But none of the other buildings showed any interest to her, any reason for the creature to head in there. She just knew that this was it.

And that Drilora had gone in there to find out what was going on with the flyers and the people that put them up.

Chapter Twenty-Two
Earth for Humans

As Cecilia came into the lobby of the building, there were only two other people in there, giving Drilora no place to hide. There was also no one stopping Cecilia from heading over to the elevator. Several flyers were hanging up around the lobby, hinting at why it was so easy for her to head through. The flyers seemed to be an invitation to an open meeting of the group.

When the doors to the elevator opened, there was another flyer hanging inside. Again, the address, date, and time were written there, though it was in blue marker this time. Cecilia hit the button for the twelfth floor, to match the apartment number on the flyer. Just as the door was closing, someone was heading inside the building.

"Hold up," one of them called out.

Automatically, Cecilia reached her hand out through the elevator doors, triggering the sensor. As the two of them headed through the lobby, Cecilia looked at the two of them, a man and woman. The man was staying close by the woman's side, almost possessively in a way that made Cecilia think that they were together. But the woman seemed oblivious to him, just focused on the elevator in front of them.

"Thanks," the woman said, as they came in. She turned toward the controls, her finger halfway to the button before coming up short. "Oh, are you going to the meeting, too?" she asked, glancing back at Cecilia.

"Um..." Cecilia said.

"Oh, don't be nervous," the woman said. "We're really a great bunch. I've gone to about half a dozen of these things.

Haven't we, Matt?" She glanced back at her boyfriend, who just nodded at her.

"I, uh... I had been seeing the flyers around town," Cecilia said, shrugging. That was true enough, though she didn't know what else to say about it. How to convince the woman that she was just there for the meeting, rather than because she was looking for the creature. The alien that they seemed concerned with.

"Yeah, the movement isn't building all that quickly, but it's only been a few years," the woman said. "I'm just worried that it won't be enough. That the alien will show its true colors and all we'll be able to do about it is say 'We told you so'. Eddie seems to think we'll be able to do something more soon, though."

"Who-who is Eddie?" Cecilia asked. She would have thought that her boyfriend was Eddie, but she had already called him Matt.

"Oh, you'll meet him soon enough," she said, just as the elevator let out a ding. "Come on." The woman reached out, grabbing onto Cecilia's arm as she pulled her out of the elevator and down the hall.

The door to apartment 1209 was held open by a brick, and the general din of discussion was already spilling out into the hall. At first, Cecilia figured that the meeting had already started, and that they were late. But when she came inside, she spotted a clock in the corner that said it was still a few minutes before the time on the flyer. And yet, the place was already packed.

"Whoa," the woman said, seeming surprised by the crowd.

Matt stayed close behind them as the three headed inside the room. The only place that they could find large enough for the three of them to stand was over in the corner by the windows. Cecilia looked out into the dark evening, almost sensing Drilora's eye on her out there. However, all she could see was the reflection of the crowd in the apartment.

"Alright, I think we can get started," someone called out, and the crowd instantly went silent. "For those new here, I'm Eddie. I'm the leader of this group, but not of the movement. We'll get into that later on in the evening."

As the crowd settled down for the meeting, several people started sitting in chairs that were hidden from Cecilia's view. Once they were out of her way, she spotted a man standing opposite from her, over in the kitchen. He was leaning against the counter, practically sitting on it, as he looked out at the crowd.

"From how crowded the room is, I know that many of you are new here. So, I'll go over a few things to start. We are the Earth for Humans Coalition. Our goal, in case that wasn't obvious, is to get rid of the alien that is currently occupying the tower in Franklin Park."

He raised up a wrinkled, much abused copy of the flyer, holding it above his head so that people could see it. With how blurry the photo on it was, Cecilia wasn't sure how helpful that would be as a prop. However, everyone there, everyone in the world, would know exactly who he was talking about. After all, Drilora was the only alien on Earth, as far as anyone knew.

"The alien is often spotted jumping across the city, all but flying through the air," Eddie continued. "It can throw cars like they're nothing and can take bullets shot at it at close range. There is nothing known to man that could stop that thing without causing a lot of damage around it. Some have even suggested that it would be able to take a direct impact from a nuke."

A few people started muttering at that suggestion. From what little Cecilia could hear in the back of the crowd, she thought that many of them were worried what that would mean. That there would be no getting rid of Drilora, no matter what they did.

"Isn't it helping out the city, though?" someone asked, their voice cutting over the other comments.

"Yes," Eddie said, nodding. "For now. But it's all a ploy. A way for the alien to ingratiate itself into our society. We know that there's a bigger plan in place. What we don't know is what form it will take. If there's a larger invasion coming, or if the alien thinks that we would start worshipping it. Maybe turning control of the government over to it. All we know for sure is that something is coming, and it's going to be bad. We need to be ready for it when it comes."

Cecilia looked around the crowd, trying to get a sense of the people there. Trying to see if they were looking to do something or just spread that fear that Eddie was building in them. She wanted to say something, to question the man's take on Drilora's presence. As far as she was able to tell from her time in the tower, Drilora would like nothing more than to leave that place. To go back home. If either of the spaceships in the garage worked, ze would have already left.

"How do you know?" someone asked, saving Cecilia from having to.

Eddie looked around at the crowd, seeming to search for the person who asked the question. Several other people in the crowd were, too. The looks that Cecilia could see weren't favorable. Whoever it was, though, they were hiding, not volunteering anything.

"We know because of how it came here," Eddie said. "It came down in a warship, shot down by another alien. It killed that other alien right in front of people, showing its very nature to everyone there. The only reason why the army didn't kill it right then and there was because they didn't know how. And since then, they seemed to have forgotten the very real threat that it had shown. But I didn't forget. I was there when it got here. I saw the look in its ugly eye when it killed that other alien. It was like it was nothing to it. That it cared nothing about that other alien, about the humans that surrounded it. It could have just as easily killed the humans as well, but that would have ruined the plan. That would have made it impossible for what was to come next."

Several people let out sounds of agreement, nodding along to Eddie's words. Cecilia just looked around at the crowd, trying not to seem out of place there. Trying not to draw attention to herself. The woman that came in with her was looking her way, so she nodded as well, smiling over at her.

"There are plans in place to work with the mayor," Eddie continued, as those sounds of agreement died off. "To reach out to congress and the president if needed. But for now, we're just trying to get the word out. To spread this information around to anyone that will listen. Truth dies in silence, and this is a growing movement to get the alien off our planet. To make it so that Earth is for Humans again."

A cheer rang out through the room at that call, people raising fists into the air as they did so. It seemed like this was the response that Eddie was looking for. He stood there, silently smiling at the crowd, as he looked around them. Once the cheers wound down again, he nodded his head, waving his hands as if those cheers were only dying because he wanted them to.

"For now, let's break up here," he said. "Talk amongst yourselves. Share your own stories of the alien and how you came to worry about what it might do to us once it got the chance. I'll be up to speak more later."

"Exciting, isn't it?" the woman asked, as the low din that had filled the apartment when they got there quickly returned. "Eddie is really a great speaker. You should totally hang out for the later speech. It should be interesting."

"Right," Cecilia said, nodding her agreement. But the woman wasn't hanging around to wait for that, already disappearing into the crowd. Cecilia stood by the window for a bit longer, watching as the woman headed around the crowd, seeming to find people that she recognized. Matt remained next to Cecilia for a moment longer, his eyes still locked on the woman, before heading off himself.

The moment that Cecilia no longer had eyes on her, she slowly slipped along the back wall of the apartment, heading for the door. It was clear that Drilora wasn't in there, hidden among the humans. That the group wouldn't stand for the alien being hidden in their midst. Whatever was going on, whatever Drilora was doing sneaking out that night, it was clearly not to go to that meeting.

Once Cecilia managed to slip out into the hallway, she ducked off to the side, out of view of the people in there. She glanced back at the meeting, making sure that no one was watching her. That she had escaped from in there without being seen. However, as she turned back toward the elevators, she noticed that there were more people heading along the hallway, making for that door behind her. Late arrivals to the meeting that had missed the opening remarks. Many of them nodded at Cecilia, like they had recognized her, though she had never been to that meeting before. She just nodded back at them, not wanting to show how out of place she felt. But then, no one there would think much of her leaving the meeting early, if they even noticed it at all. That was how her power worked.

After the group headed inside, Cecilia went back along the hallway, heading over to the elevator. The display over the doors showed that the elevator was already heading down without her. That she would have to wait for it to get back. And with the group of late arrivals, she worried that there would be a similar group heading up. Cecilia dithered there, bouncing back and forth between her feet, worried that she would be caught. Worried that people would know that she had no right being there.

But before the elevator started to head back up, something large and brown jumped into the window next to her. Cecilia let out a light squeak as she turned to the window, her hand going to her heart to stay it.

Chapter Twenty-Three
Tending to Injuries

The cool, night air blew past Cecilia. Drilora's fur, so close to her side, protected her from some of it, keeping her warm. But the air blowing across her forehead felt nice, soothing her. With her body still spasming from the electricity that had been flowing through her, she needed that. She needed Drilora's comforting arms more, though. That reminder that ze had her, that she was in safe hands as they all but flew across the city skyline.

Cecilia lost all sense of where they were until Drilora came to a stop on top of the tower. The stars shined overhead, showing from over the water, beyond where the lights from the city could mute them. She wondered if Drilora would put her down there, if she would have to climb down the ladder herself and risk falling off of it when her body refused to move correctly. But after a moment of Drilora standing on the roof with Cecilia in zer arms, ze moved over to the edge of the tower, dropping down to the ground below.

If things had been different, that fall would have been scary to Cecilia. But she felt safe in Drilora's arms. With her body not moving for her, all she could do was stare up at Drilora's face, hidden in the darkness. But as they came inside, the lights of the tower lighting up that face for the first time since leaving the rooftop, Cecilia suddenly realized that she was picturing it differently. That she almost expected Drilora's face to have changed in that time in the dark. Changing into that of a human.

Cecilia wondered why Drilora hadn't gone through the trap door, which would have been so much closer to her

154

room. Instead, Drilora had to carry Cecilia back up through the tower. With each of Drilora's hops, Cecilia almost felt weightless, like gravity didn't have the same effect on her. Like it was some power of Drilora's that kept them from being weighed down.

The lights shifted around Cecilia, giving her an indication of when they moved from one floor to another. Each time, Drilora had to shift to the side, slipping Cecilia through the tight gap. Halfway up the tower, she thought about counting the lights by the stairs, giving her an indication of how close they were to her bedroom. But it was already too late by then. However, when Drilora jerked to the side for the fourth time, pulling her up onto the top floor of the tower, she realized that they were already there.

"It's alright," Drilora said, seeming to sense a discomfort in Cecilia. "You should be fine in a day or so. Once I get you up to your room, I can take a look at these burns."

That hadn't been what Cecilia had been thinking about until ze said something. In the excitement of the fight, she hadn't looked at her hands. She had no idea what touching the cable on the harpoon had done to her. If her hands were burned, or if the burns were somewhere else on her body. If in saving Drilora she had hopelessly disfigured herself. She kept picturing her face looking like Drilora's from all the burns, turning her into as much of a monster as the Earth for Humans people had thought that Drilora was.

Drilora shifted once more as ze came up in front of Cecilia's door, using zer foot to open it. The empty takeout container skittered across the floor, knocked aside as ze brought her over to the bed, lying her down gently on it. As Cecilia laid there, unable to move, she momentarily worried that Drilora would try something. That ze would take advantage of her state. She had no idea how ze might do that, though. What ze might do to Cecilia, or try to do anyway.

Once Cecilia was situated on the bed, Drilora picked up her hand, looking at it. That one eye seemed weirder than usual as it stared down at the burns there. Cecilia could almost see her hand in the reflection on it, though zer eye was too dark to see much of anything. When the look of concern slowly faded from zer face, Cecilia's own worry faded along with it.

"It doesn't look too bad," Drilora said. "Something must have kept the worst of the electricity from going through you. It was enough to dull it in me, though. Both times. Without you there, I... Well, I don't know what would have happened. If that electricity would have been enough to do any lasting harm to me. As it was, I think I'll manage to make it out of this whole thing without a scratch."

Drilora laughed a little before looking down at zer chest, ruffling zer own fur around where the harpoon had hit the first time. Already, the divot that had formed in zer fur was gone, the rest of the fur filling it to cover it. It reminded Cecilia of how zer fur on zer shoulders had been thicker as they were leaving the bank, like zer fur got tougher as it was damaged, healing like a scar. However, when ze reached up to the hole through zer fur at zer neck, there was still some damage there. It took some effort for zer to smooth that out, forming more of a divot than a hole.

"I should be fine by morning, I think," Drilora said. "Not-not that you were worried about me. I mean... I mean, you shouldn't be worried about me. I should... Oh, wait, your-your feet."

Drilora nodded at zerself before slipping down along Cecilia's legs. Confusion flitted through her at that, wondering what it was that ze was talking about. What ze was doing down there. And when ze pulled off zer sneakers, that confusion only deepened.

"Oh," ze said, looking between the sneakers and her feet. "Rubber soles. Clever. Did... No, you... You wouldn't have known... Are these types of shoes commonplace?" Ze looked at Cecilia's face, as if expecting an answer to come from her. She tried to say something, but she could barely feel her own jaw, let alone move it. "Well, this one looks a bit ruined. They probably saved your life, though, keeping the worst of the electricity from flowing through you like that. Things could have gone a lot differently today, it... Well... Anyway, I think I have some ointment for those hands of yours. Wait here."

"I'm not going anywhere," Cecilia thought at zer, though she couldn't move her mouth enough to say much of anything. She managed to grunt a little, which seemed like an improvement. A sign that she was going to be better soon enough. Drilora smiled over at her before heading out into the hall, disappearing deeper into the tower.

Cecilia could only lay there, waiting for Drilora to return. Her face was turned to the side, pointed at the door to the hall. Just in view above her was the pile of comic books on the bedside table. She managed to shift her eyes to look up at them, almost willing herself to reach out to them. To pull the top one off the stack so that she could read it while she waited for Drilora to return. Her hand moved the slightest bit closer to that stack, but Drilora came back before she could manage much more than that.

"Alright," Drilora said, as ze came back into the room. Cecilia looked back at zer, her eyes moving more smoothly than before. She just wished that she could move the rest of her body as well.

Drilora was carrying a chair in one hand and a first aid kit in the other. Once ze placed the chair in front of Cecilia, ze swung around it, sitting down gently in it before reaching out to take Cecilia's hand again. The same hand that she managed to move those few inches closer to the comic books. It felt like Drilora had taken what little progress she had been able to make.

The creature was gentle with Cecilia's hand as ze coated it with the ointment. After the fight on the rooftop, where Drilora had been so wild and dangerous that it had scared Cecilia, it was an odd comparison. It made her wish that the Earth for Humans group could see Drilora like that. Could see how comforting ze could be when tending to her. But even as Drilora worked on that hand, ze was shaking zer head.

"I should have gone after that one," Drilora muttered, seemingly more to zerself than to Cecilia. "That group is going to be a problem; I just know it. But... Well, that was why I went to the meeting tonight." Ze looked up at Cecilia's eyes, smiling a human smile at her before turning back to her hand. "I keep an eye on each of the... the hate groups, as you called them. Some are more active than others. More dangerous than others. That weapon tonight... I know that they specifically designed it for me. That isn't something that the army warned me about. I... We will have to be careful the next time we go on a mission. If they're expecting me... Well, maybe I'll take a page out of your playbook. Those shoes of yours saved your life, and they can probably protect me. I'll have to have Leanne get me a pair."

Drilora finished coating Cecilia's hand just as ze finished talking. Ze reached back into the first aid kit, returning the ointment and pulling out a bandage. No words passed between them as Drilora wrapped Cecilia's hand, keeping the ointment in place and protecting her covers from it. Once ze was done wrapping her hand, ze placed it back onto the bed next to her, patting it lightly.

"You just rest," ze said, before reaching over her to pull her covers around her. "Don't worry about getting up early for tomorrow's workout. You can sleep in a bit. You need to heal. I'll look in on you in the morning, but... Well, you're as safe here in this tower as you can be anywhere."

Drilora sat there next to Cecilia for a moment, just looking at her face. Cecilia managed to blink, but her eyelids threatened to stay closed. She wasn't sure if that was from being electrocuted or from being tired. Either way, she gave into it, letting herself fall to sleep with the creature looking over her. It was difficult for her to tell just when she managed to get to sleep, though she thought she kept hearing Drilora talking to her in the night.

"I should probably go back out there," ze said. "Chase down those humans before they come at us again. Before they try to attack the tower. But... Well, if they tried to come at us here, they would soon regret it. If they're not already dead." There was an odd tone in zer voice, like ze didn't know how ze felt about that. If ze would prefer the humans dead, prefer having killed them, or if ze would accept the continued risk that they would pose to keep zer hands clean.

Chapter Twenty-Four
Talking it Over
Drilora

The tower was quiet when Drilora woke up early the next morning. Ze liked the quiet; it reminded zer of space and the serenity that ze felt out there. But when ze remembered what had happened the night before, remembered how badly injured Cecilia was, ze quickly hopped out of bed.

"Ow," Drilora muttered, when zer head hit the ceiling. Ze was usually better at remembering not to put too much force into getting up from the bed, with the low gravity of that planet. But in zer eagerness to get across the hall, ze had forgotten. Once ze came back down to the floor, ze made an extra effort to be careful, trying not to wake Cecilia or injure zerself again.

The door made barely a sound as Drilora opened it. Ze took one step out into the hall, standing right in front of Cecilia's door. Drilora held zer breath, something that ze did often just to avoid having to smell the stink of that world, but this time it was to make as little sound as possible. Ze opened Cecilia's door just enough to peek in around it to make sure that Cecilia was still in there.

That she was still alive.

Drilora stood there, staring over at Cecilia, waiting for signs of life. When ze noticed her chest rising and falling with her breath, ze just nodded before backing up, closing the door quietly behind zer. Ze stood there just a moment longer, listening to Cecilia through the door. Waiting for some sign of distress. When nothing came, Drilora turned to zer right, heading for the stairs down.

As Drilora came up to the first window, the same window that Cecilia would have seen zer through the night before, ze spotted Leanne's car pulling into the parking lot below. With Cecilia still asleep above zer, Drilora rushed down the stairs, wanting to get down to the door before Leanne rang the doorbell. Before she could wake Cecilia.

Down was always easier than up when Drilora was trying to be careful. All ze had to do was push off the stairs, letting the light gravity keep zer from catastrophe. Zer hands went above zer head, feeling along the ceiling of the stairwell, keeping zer from hitting zerself again. Whenever zer feet hit the stone stairs, it was another shove forward, constantly falling around in that arc.

By the time ze landed on the ground floor, Leanne was just coming up to the door. Drilora quickly flitted through the door, closing it behind zer. Leanne came up short, her hand halfway toward the doorbell, just staring up at Drilora in confusion.

"What did you do?" she asked, suddenly, her confused expression still in place.

"Nothing," Drilora insisted.

"No, no," Leanne said, waggling her finger in front of zer face. "You tell me what you did. I can't fix anything if you don't tell me. Did you kidnap another girl?"

"I didn't kidnap the last one," Drilora said. "And, no. I didn't... It-it was the meeting last night."

"The meeting?" Leanne just stared up at Drilora, her confused expression slowly melting away, only to be replaced by a look of disappointment. "Didn't I tell you not to get involved with all of that?"

"Yes, but--" Drilora started.

"That I would take care of it and make sure that no harm came to you?" Leanne continued, ignoring zer words.

"Yes, but--" Drilora said again.

"And that you really shouldn't involve Cecilia in all of that mess," Leanne continued.

"Uh..." Drilora said.

Leanne's face fell when ze said that, seeming to sense exactly what was going on there. That something had gone so horribly wrong the night before. It didn't surprise Drilora in the least that she would immediately think the worst.

"Is Cecilia dead?" Leanne asked. "I mean, it certainly would fix your issues with her, but that wasn't the best way forward with that."

"No, no," Drilora said, shaking zer head. "No, Cecilia isn't dead. She's... She just came away with some electrical burns on her hand. That's all. Her shoes kept her from the worst of it. By the way, I'll be needing similar shoes. Think you can manage that?"

"Electrical burns?" Leanne asked, yelling the question.

"Shh," Drilora hissed. Ze looked back at the door behind zer, like ze could see Cecilia from all the way down there. But the door was closed behind zer, keeping Leanne's yell from flowing through the tower up to her. "She's still sleeping up there."

"Tell me exactly what happened," Leanne demanded.

Drilora explained what had happened the night before, both what ze had seen and done, along with what Cecilia had, based on what ze had figured out on the rooftop before the terrorists showed up. Ze left off the part about zer breaking through the window and pulling Cecilia out of there, saying simply that ze safely extracted her from the meeting once she would no longer be missed. When ze got to the part about the terrorists attacking them, ze stopped.

"Have you heard anything about this kind of weapon before?" Drilora asked.

"No," Leanne said. She tapped her chin lightly as she thought about it. "I mean, a harpoon gun is nothing new. But adding an electricity component to it? And that much voltage, to get through your thick fur? Did you see it plugged into anything?"

"I... Uh..." Drilora said, as ze tried to think back to the incident the night before. "If it was, it must have been behind Eddie. Once the fight was over, I was too preoccupied with getting Cecilia out of there to go after him. He made off with the weapon, just leaving the harpoon behind. Maybe... Maybe I should have looked, but--"

"No," Leanne said. "No, you did the right thing, getting Cecilia out of there like that. You should have brought her to a hospital, though. They probably would have been better at treating her than you were. Not-not that I'm saying you can't do fine on your own. But... Well, it's not like you have much experience with treating humans like that."

"You want to go up there and wake her?" Drilora asked, zer hand flipping out behind zer to point back at the door. "Drag her halfway across the city to some hospital, only to lie in a bed for four hours, waiting to be seen? I've seen how your healthcare system works."

"Watching General Hospital while working out doesn't count," Leanne said, knowing all too well what exposure Drilora had to human culture. "It's not as bad as they depict it sometimes."

"Ha," Drilora said, shaking zer head. "I wasn't even talking about General Hospital. I was talking about your own news. There was a report just the other day about issues at that hospital. It really is a disgrace. Uvvelians know how to tend to our own wounded."

"Yeah, well, humans are a lot more breakable than uvvelians," Leanne said. "And harder to repair, I imagine."

"I just didn't want her waiting around for some overworked doctor to spend all of three seconds looking at her when I knew that I could do better here," Drilora said. "Not after she almost died trying to save me. Not after..." Ze trailed off, only then remembering that ze didn't tell Leanne about that part.

"Not after what?" Leanne asked, noticing that slip. She knew Drilora all too well not to notice it. Not to know exactly what that was about. "What did you do, Drilora?"

"I just..." Drilora said hesitantly. "It-it was nothing. Just a misunderstanding."

"Misunderstanding?" Leanne asked. "Oh, you... Drilora."

Leanne rushed forward, pushing past Drilora and through the door. Drilora could have stopped her, but not without hurting her. Ze knew how stubborn Leanne could get sometimes, especially when she thought that she was defending Drilora from some of zer worst instincts.

Drilora followed behind Leanne as she rushed up the stairs. Ze knew exactly where she was going, and Leanne was being quiet enough about it. Her steps made barely a sound on the stairs as she headed up. Once they came up to the fourth floor, Drilora glanced off to the side, wondering about starting breakfast. About cooking something for Cecilia so that she could eat as soon as she was feeling up to it. But with Leanne storming up in front of zer, ze just followed her.

Leanne paused by Cecilia's door, seeming to brace herself to see what was going on inside. To see what Drilora had done. With one more motherly glare over at Drilora, Leanne pushed open the door, peeking around it to the sleeping form of Cecilia beyond. Drilora came up behind her, squeezing between Leanne and zer own bedroom door to look over her head into the room. The place hadn't changed in the few minutes since ze had last seen Cecilia in there.

Slowly, Leanne closed the door again. She backed up a step, only to bump into Drilora behind her. When she did, she let out a light squeak, her face turning up to look at Drilora looming over her. She shook her head at zer before turning toward the stairs, heading down toward the kitchen.

Drilora stayed by Cecilia's door for a moment longer, just looking at the wood. Ze wanted to reach out, to pull the door open once more and look in on Cecilia, but ze figured that they had disturbed her sleep enough. Zer hand still went out to that door, lightly touching the wood, before turning toward the stairs.

Leanne was waiting for zer at the door to the kitchen. Drilora slinked zer way over to her, slipping through the door with her. Once inside, Drilora closed the door, making it so that their words wouldn't carry through the tower to Cecilia.

"You lost your temper again, didn't you," Leanne said in a harsh whisper. "I told you--"

"I didn't hurt her," Drilora insisted. "I was careful. I remembered that humans are breakable, though I wanted to break her at that moment. She... I didn't know... All I saw was Cecilia in that meeting, and I thought the worst. She didn't know what the meeting was until she was in there. She just followed me out of the tower, thinking that it was a mission. Thinking that I was trying to leave her out of it."

"If it had been a mission, would you have?" Leanne asked.

Drilora thought about that for a moment, honestly thinking about it for the first time since it all went down the night before. Cecilia had seemed so useless during training the day before, beyond anything that ze could help with. Assigning the comic book reading for her seemed the best way to put Cecilia off the whole thing. Only Drilora didn't see Cecilia as Batgirl in that comic. Ze saw her as Oracle. As a cautionary tale of what could happen to a real superhero, even when they're prepared for the worst to happen to them.

"Cecilia is no superhero," Drilora said, simply, as if that was the only answer ze needed to give.

"Then you can't really blame her for chasing after you," Leanne said. "God knows, I'd want to chase after you myself if I were in her shoes. But she did save your ass last night. Even you have to admit that."

"I admit nothing," Drilora said, smiling over at Leanne. It was more joke than stubbornness, and even Drilora laughed at it, zer eye flicking all over. "She will make... an adequate sidekick... for someone that doesn't need one."

"Oh, sure," Leanne said, nodding like she really agreed with what Drilora was saying. "But then, maybe you're just underestimating her? That is the superpower she says she has, right? I've been looking into her since yesterday, and that seems to track. No one has thought much about the girl. But there is one weird thing about this whole mess."

"Only one weird thing?" Drilora asked.

"With everyone underestimating her, thinking her hopeless on her own, none of her neighbors, the families of her friends, none of them would take her in. She really is on her own right now. Or, she would be, if she didn't have us."

Chapter Twenty-Five
The Pain of Victory
Cecilia

Cecilia's hand hurt all night long. It made it difficult for her to sleep for more than a few minutes at a time. What little sleep she managed to get mostly came from her exhaustion from the training and felt more like passing out from the pain. All she wanted was to go home and forget about ever becoming a superhero. Ever being anything other than a scared, little girl that no one ever thought much of.

When she woke up for the hundredth time, she thought that she heard some voices coming from deeper in the tower. She knew that it was likely Drilora talking with someone. Perhaps Leanne, or some other helper that she hadn't met yet. Even if those voices told of a mission to come, Cecilia knew that she was in no state to go out on one. That she needed to heal up further before she could be of any use to anyone.

Slowly, Cecilia sat up in bed, slipping her legs off the edge next to her. Her whole body was stiff, though she didn't know if that was from the workout or from being electrocuted. She just sat there for a few minutes, slowly flexing her hands and rotating her shoulders. Trying to work out her stuff joints so that she could move without it hurting. But her right hand hurt every time she moved it.

"Well, it's better than it hurting constantly," Cecilia muttered to herself, as she stared down at that hand.

Once she thought that she could move without assistance, Cecilia reached down to the bed next to her, slowly pushing herself to her feet. The moment that her weight hit her right hand, though, it gave an odd spasm as pain lanced through it again. She let out a whimper before falling back onto the bed.

"Ugh," she grunted, as she pulled her injured hand to her chest. "You were the one that wanted to be a superhero. This is what you get for reaching for your dreams."

Cecilia shook her head before trying again, pushing herself up to her feet. Once she got there, she was a bit unsteady, her hands still on the bed behind her as she got her balance back. It took her a moment to be sure that she wasn't about to fall back onto the bed as soon as she pulled her hands away. She pulled her right hand away first, clutching it to her chest once more. Then, when she wasn't falling over, she pulled her left away. Only after standing there on her own two feet for a moment did she turn toward the door.

Her right hand was halfway to the handle before Cecilia thought better of it. She shook her head as she reached out with her left one. It was awkward, but it didn't hurt nearly as much as her right would have. As she headed out the door and into the hallway, Cecilia raised her right hand against her chest, holding it there to remind her not to try to use it. She kept it half open so as not to agitate the burn. Fortunately, the only other door between her and her destination was the one to the kitchen.

The voices immediately went silent when Cecilia opened the door. Leanne was standing over by the fridge, with Drilora right next to her. The way that they both went silent the moment that she came inside reminded her of something that her parents had done when she was growing up, before her mother had died. It made her feel like she walked in on something, though she wasn't sure if it was them talking about her or some hint that the two of them were in some kind of relationship. For some reason, Cecilia almost felt jealous about that.

"Good morning, Cecilia," Leanne said, once she got over the shock of her coming in there. "How are you feeling this morning?"

Oh, yeah, Cecilia thought to herself. They were talking about me.

"How's the hand?" Drilora asked, before Cecilia could answer the first question.

Cecilia pulled her hand away from her chest so that she could look down at it. The bandage was still in place, hiding her view of the burn itself. All she knew was that it still hurt, that it would likely hurt for a long time before she was properly healed up.

"It's fine," Cecilia said, simply, not wanting to make more of a deal about it than it needed to be.

"I'll be bringing you back into the city this morning for a real doctor to look at it," Leanne said. Her eyes flicked to Drilora, making it clear to Cecilia that that was part of the argument that she had walked in on.

Cecilia looked over at Drilora, who had gotten far worse than she had the night before. Ze seemed completely unharmed from the encounter, with zer fur as smooth and tough as always. It seemed like that fur was completely impenetrable and the thing that kept zer safe no matter the situation.

"It's fine," Cecilia insisted. While she knew that she wasn't as invulnerable as Drilora clearly was, she didn't think that it was bad enough to need to be looked at. She clenched her hand, trying to show that there was nothing to worry about, but she flinched away from the pain as it ran through her, belying her bravado.

"Uh huh," Leanne said, clearly seeing through Cecilia's facade.

"I'm sorry," Drilora said. "I should have done better to protect you last night."

"Yes, you should have," Leanne said. "You also shouldn't have gone out at all. It wasn't just Cecilia's life you were putting at risk unnecessarily."

"Well, I don't think it was unnecessary," Drilora muttered. Ze looked down at the floor in front of zer, clearly mollified by Leanne. Despite the creature being almost twice her height and three times her size, it seemed like Leanne was the boss there. That she was in charge, and Drilora knew it.

"Uh huh," Leanne muttered, not bothering to look back at Drilora. "In the meantime, you should grab some breakfast. My team will get back to me when they have your appointment booked. No sense in heading out on an empty stomach when we don't know where you're going."

"And you can tell us what you found out at the meeting while you're eating," Drilora said. "We were interrupted by those terrorists last night before we could get to that part."

"That part can wait until later," Leanne said. "Like I told you, many times, my team is working on monitoring the hate groups. I'll bring Cecilia by the office after she's been looked at."

"There really wasn't much to it," Cecilia said, as she headed over to the fridge. At the mention of breakfast, she realized that she was quite hungry.

As Cecilia opened the fridge, she quickly remembered that there wasn't anything in there for her. That it was mostly filled with Drilora's alien foods. However, when she looked inside, she was surprised to find a carton of eggs, some bacon, and a loaf of bread, mixed in with quite a lot of less identifiable foods. She grabbed the purely human food before heading over to the stove.

"I can do that for you," Drilora said, quickly taking the food from Cecilia. Ze was extra careful with the eggs, seeming to barely pinch them to avoid breaking their shells. "You sit. Tell us what happened." Ze nodded toward the small table in the corner of the room behind Cecilia.

"Like I said, there wasn't much," Cecilia said, as she reluctantly headed over to the table. "I got out of there after just a few minutes. Once I realized what was going on there and that you weren't in the room. It was just that Eddie guy talking about their group and what they wanted. There was supposed to be another speech later, but it turned into something of a meet and greet. The people there trying to seem more normal before showing how abnormal they were."

"And you weren't swayed by that?" Leanne asked.

"Not really," Cecilia said, shrugging. "I mean, they were just talking about getting rid of Drilora. Getting zer off the planet. If they knew that Drilora wanted off just as much as they wanted zer gone, they might have been singing a different tune. Perhaps even helping zer."

"Ha," Drilora said. "I fear that those ships downstairs are beyond anything anyone on this mudball of a planet can do anything about. It's to the point where I think my best bet is to get my sub-space communications system back up and running, but I don't know what state Uvvelia is in with the war. There's no telling if they would be able to send help."

"Uh, yeah, probably better not to do that," Cecilia said. "One of the reasons Eddie gave for them being against you is worrying about a bigger invasion to come. A big spaceship showing up over the tower would be a dead giveaway. Unless you have some way to make the ship invisible."

"Nope," Drilora said, shaking zer head. "Cloaking technology is beyond even the uvvelians, though I wouldn't put it past the krylonians."

Drilora shrugged zer shoulders, shaking out zer fur in a strange way. Cecilia wasn't quite sure what that movement meant, but Leanne looked at zer with a level of concern that suggested she understood it. She reached out a comforting hand, placing it on zer shoulders.

"Hey, you don't know what happened after you left," Leanne said. "Your people can still be out there. They might have won the war while you were stuck here and could be looking for you. There's still hope that you can go home."

"And, in the meantime, you can still train me to be a superhero," Cecilia said. She wanted to get Drilora's mind off zer troubles, but she also needed to make sure that she wasn't about to be put out of the tower. That heading off with Leanne after breakfast wasn't going to be zer getting rid of her finally. Not after everything that she had gone through to get there.

"Is that really the best of ideas?" Drilora asked, as ze plated Cecilia's breakfast. "After what happened last night--"

"Last night just proves that I can hold my own in a fight," Cecilia said. "You can't tell me that I didn't save you. You said that yourself last night."

"You... You heard that part?" Drilora asked. "I was just worried that you were going to die."

"Well, I didn't die. I'm still here. I'm still ready to go." Cecilia wasn't sure how accurate that boast was, but she wasn't about to let up about it all. Besides, it wasn't like they were about to head off on a mission right then.

"None of that needs to be decided just yet," Leanne said. "Right now, you just need to eat. Then we can get that hand looked at. After we make sure that you're not about to lose the hand, or worse, we can discuss you coming back here for further training."

"Ugh," Cecilia grunted. However, she had to admit to herself that she was more frustrated with the thought of further training than having to get a clean bill of health from some doctor.

Chapter Twenty-Six
Research

Cecilia was staring down at her hand as Leanne drove her back through the city. The doctor had removed the bandage during the appointment and had applied a fresh layer of ointment. It glistened on her skin as it slowly dried. Other than some scarring on her hand from where the electricity had run through her, there wasn't much damage done. The doctor had said that she would be back to normal in a few days, with just that scar to tell about her first time being electrocuted.

He seemed to think that being electrocuted was going to be a normal part of her life as a superhero.

"Stop picking at that," Leanne said.

"I'm not picking at it," Cecilia said, though she closed her hand around the ointment. Her hand didn't hurt as much as it had that morning, and she figured that she would be back to normal far sooner than a few days. That she would be ready to get back to training that night, if Drilora would let her. She thought about just doing the training from the day before again if ze didn't, but her legs were still sore from that endeavor.

Leanne turned off the road soon after that, heading into a small parking lot. The place was packed, but there was a spot near the back that she pulled into. She didn't explain anything about where they were, and Cecilia was looking around them as they both got out of the car. Leanne led her to a side door of that building, heading through to a small office just inside. The glass door to the place named the office the Leanne Mooney Agency.

"Morning, Leanne," someone called out, as they came inside the small office.

Cecilia stood just inside the door, looking around the place. There were three desks, one against each wall, with two of them occupied. Leanne headed over to the third one against the far wall, turning her chair around to look back at Cecilia. There wasn't much more to the office, not even a receptionist desk near the front to separate the three people in there from the people walking in.

"Oh, who's this?" someone asked. Cecilia looked between the other two women in there, surprised that it was a group of women. Her father always spoke down about the idea of women working together like that, making it seem like they were just as likely to tear each other apart than get any work done. Of course, that had never been something he discussed in front of her mother.

"Jerri, Lindsey, this is Cecilia," Leanne said, pointing around to the group as she said their names. Jerri was the one on Cecilia's left, the one that had greeted Leanne when she came in.

"Oh, I knew she looked familiar," Jerri said. "Nice to see you in person."

"Huh?" Cecilia asked.

"These are my coworkers," Leanne said. "The ones that I tasked to call around for you yesterday. They pretty much know everything there is to know about you by this point. Maybe more than you know yourself."

"Huh?" Cecilia asked again, this time in shock. Her face blanched a little at the thought of that. The idea that these three might know everything. Know things that she didn't want to get out. That she didn't want Drilora to know about. But she figured that, if they had found anything worth telling Drilora about, they would have already.

"We're also the main interface between Drilora and the city," Lindsey said. "When they need Drilora's help on a mission, they call us, and we call zer."

"After we've negotiated a proper fee," Jerri added. "Gotta keep the big one in that swanky tower of zers."

"Not to mention the research we do on the hate groups," Leanne added. "Which is why I brought Cecilia by this morning. I wanted to debrief her here so you guys would hear about the meeting she stumbled in on last night."

Jerri let out a gasp, her hand going to her chest. "You went to an alien hate group last night?"

"I didn't mean to," Cecilia said. Jerri and Lindsey both laughed at that, instantly putting Cecilia at ease.

"Which group?" Jerri asked, before spinning back around in her chair to face her desk. She started typing on the keyboard in front of her, bringing something up on her computer. Cecilia took three steps further into the room, coming up behind her.

"Uh, it was Earth for Humans," Cecilia said.

Jerri just nodded before clicking into the Earth for Humans file. Several faces popped up on the screen, including Eddie and Janine. There was also a blacked-out picture with a white question mark over it on the top of the display.

"I recognize these two," Cecilia said, pointing to Eddie and Janine. "But who's that?" She pointed at the blacked-out picture.

"That is their leader," Jerri said. "You can just tell they're evil from that picture alone."

"No one has seen their leader, Rene Marks," Leanne explained. "All we have is a name. Hell, he might have been at the meeting last night for all we know."

"You said Eddie was there?" Jerri asked. "Did he seem like he was deferring to someone else there?"

"I don't think so," Cecilia said, shrugging. She tried to think back to the meeting, but all she remembered was the incident on the roof. All the words of trying to do what was best for the humans seemed to be thrown out the window with what they had done up there.

"Drilora was watching it from the building across the street," Leanne said.

"Again?" Jerri asked. She rolled her eyes at the thought, seeming frustrated by the whole thing. Cecilia snickered at that, resulting in a smile from Jerri.

"Ze would have said something if ze had noticed someone new in a position of authority," Leanne continued, ignoring the comment. "There's another meeting at another location, which I'm hoping Drilora doesn't know about. Maybe we should try to get someone in there. Spy on them. See if Eddie will lead us to Rene."

"What about the new girl?" Lindsey asked, nodding toward Cecilia. "She's all about trying to be a superhero and all that, right? Spying should be right up her alley."

"She got burned last night," Leanne said, shaking her head.

"I'm right here," Cecilia said, pointing to herself. "But, yeah. They saw me with Drilora. Saw me help zer. None of them are going to trust me again. But... I mean, if you have this Rene Marks guy's name, can't you figure out something from that?"

"The guy is a ghost," Lindsey said. "We don't even know if that's his real name. It's just the name we managed to get from some online chatter."

"Oh," Cecilia said. "Right, I guess that makes sense. You can't very well use your real name when leading a hate group."

"Not when there's a terrorist cell within it," Leanne said. "But then domestic terrorism never gets the same attention that foreign terrorism gets. I don't even think the FBI is on to this group, so it falls to us to watch them."

"What about last night?" Cecilia asked. "Isn't that something that the FBI should be looking into? I mean, they attacked us."

"Drilora would need to press charges, and ze isn't about to do that," Leanne said. "Ze is a bit egotistical there, thinking ze can handle everything alone. It gets zer in a lot more trouble that way, but... Well, after what happened when ze arrived, it's understandable for zer to be a bit hesitant when it comes to trusting people."

"But... I mean, ze trusts me, right?" Cecilia asked. She had thought that they had bonded the night before, with her saving zer the way that she did. The encounter had made them quite the team, something that her coming to the tower wasn't enough to accomplish on its own.

"Ze barely trusts me," Leanne said. "Don't feel too badly about it. Drilora has been guarded for as long as I've known zer. But... Well, I think if anyone is going to get through to zer, it's going to be you. Someone who... while not quite being able to fight on zer level, is at least trying to do better than most humans out there. Just don't try to push the whole thing too far too quickly. You might end up losing all the progress you've made with zer."

"I feel like I almost did last night," Cecilia said. She went quiet as she thought about the look on Drilora's face when ze thought the worst of her. When ze thought that she had joined the enemy.

The phone on Lindsey's desk rang as she thought about all of that. Lindsey quickly reached out, scooping the phone up and sticking it to her ear. "Leanne Mooney Agency," she said, before going silent, listening to the other end of the line.

"I wouldn't worry about it," Leanne said. "You stick to Drilora's training, do what ze tells you to do, and you'll be on solid ground by the end of the week. It might even be enough for us to convince zer to keep you on longer. Continue your training so that you can be a proper superhero."

"Understood," Lindsey said. "Yup, same amount as last time. Ze'll be there. No, the... Drilora will be there. The alien. Yes, the same alien we've been talking about. Look, the longer you keep me on this line, the longer it's going to take for me to get zer over there. Zer. It's a non-binary pronoun. Yes, it's really a thing. No, it's not just some fad. Yes, sir. Thank you."

"What's going on?" Leanne asked, turning to Lindsey as she finally hung up the phone.

"Just more closed-minded crap," Lindsey said, rolling her eyes.

"No, I mean the call," Leanne said. "Another mission?"

"Huh? Oh, yeah, a fire downtown. It's about ten blocks from here, in fact. I'll call over to Drilora, get zer heading that way."

Cecilia perked up at the mention of a mission. She stood straighter, looking toward the door behind her, ready to head off. Even with her hand still hurting, all she wanted was to get back out there. To help Drilora as best as she could. However, when Lindsey mentioned a fire, she turned back to her. She couldn't keep the look of worry from her face.

"Don't worry," Leanne said. "Lindsey will get Drilora on the phone. I can drive you over there and you'll meet zer there. I'm not sure how useful you'll be with a fire, but it can't hurt to have you there to watch at least. Part of what we do is make sure that Drilora's skills are properly being utilized. You have your own skills that we'll take into consideration on these calls. Once you get far enough in your training to take your own calls, we'll start advertising what you're capable of. Although, at the moment, you're... well..."

"I'm not capable of much of anything," Cecilia said, knowing full well what Leanne wasn't saying. She wasn't sure that she agreed with that sentiment, but it was what she had heard all her life.

Chapter Twenty-Seven
The Second Mission
Cecilia

Cecilia heard the sirens when they came out into the parking lot. By the time they made it over to the fire, she wondered why they hadn't heard them sooner. How they hadn't seen the fire from Leanne's office.

The building was completely engulfed in flames, with fires raging all over and threatening to spread to the neighboring buildings. There were three fire trucks on the street, all shooting water at the buildings on either side of the one that was burning. No one seemed interested in stopping the main fire, though.

Leanne came to a stop near the back of the crowd that had built up around the area. Cecilia expected her to pull through the crowd, to start leaning on her horn. But instead, Leanne just sat there, looking over at Cecilia.

"Sorry, this is as close as I can get you," Leanne said. "We don't usually drive to these things, so I have no idea how to get you access. You'll have to figure it out on your own. But if you tell them that you're Drilora's sidekick, maybe they'll let you in."

"Ha, right," Cecilia laughed. "Leanne, look at me. Do I look like a sidekick to you?" She pointed down at her outfit, showing how unready she was for this.

After breakfast, Cecilia had gone up to change. She hadn't thought that she would be going on a mission that day, so she went with one of her usual dresses instead of the workout gear. With how often she figured that she would be wearing them, for training and for missions, she didn't want to be stuck in the workout gear all the time.

"But then, it's not like anyone will see me as a sidekick even if I was wearing a proper superhero costume," Cecilia muttered.

"It's called a uniform," Leanne said. "I gave up the battle to get Drilora wearing one long ago, but maybe I can get the team working on one for you. Even if people keep underestimating you, they'll respect a proper uniform."

"Ha, right," Cecilia laughed again. "Well, wish me luck." She quickly turned to the door next to her, not waiting for a response from Leanne.

"Good luck," Leanne called, leaning toward Cecilia to yell at her through the open door. After Cecilia slammed the door behind her, Leanne stayed there, looking around at the crowd that had been accumulating since they arrived. There were too many people around her for her to make much progress in pulling away.

Cecilia had to push her way through the crowd as she made for the center. A few people gave her sideways looks as she went past, but the moment that they saw her they all but forgot about her. No one seemed interested in stopping her, likely thinking that someone else would stop her further along. None of them ever thought that Cecilia would make it to the center of the crowd and past the perimeter.

Not even Cecilia.

A cop seemed to emerge from the crowd around Cecilia as she came up to the edge of it. At first, she wasn't sure if that really was the edge of the crowd, or if there had been a cop in uniform that came out to look at the fire. But as the space opened up in front of her, she could see more of the area around the closest fire truck. There were people scrambling all around there, desperate to do their part in putting out the blaze. She felt like she should be doing something as well, but she had no idea what that would be.

"Whoa, whoa, whoa," the cop called out, waving a hand at Cecilia when she came up in front of him. "No one is coming past here without a badge."

"Oh, uh, I-I don't have one," Cecilia said, looking down at her dress like she could have had a badge hidden somewhere in that. But she didn't think that Drilora had a badge, either. "I, uh, I'm Drilora's sidekick." A few people in the crowd around Cecilia laughed at her comment, but the cop just gave her a confused expression.

"Who?" he asked.

"Drilora?" Cecilia asked. "The... The alien. Ze's supposed to be coming to help."

"You don't look like no alien to me," the cop said, waving a finger up and down Cecilia's body.

"No, I'm... I'm just zer sidekick," Cecilia said. "I'm here to help."

"Yeah, uh huh," the cop said, nodding like he believed her, though it was clear that he didn't. "Maybe when the alien actually gets here, we'll let you through. For now, stay out."

Cecilia wasn't so sure about that. About the chances that Drilora would even agree that she should be let in to help. But as she stood there, waiting for Drilora to arrive, Cecilia got a better view of the activity over there. With the fire blazing hot in front of her, she wasn't sure what help she would be able to provide. And with it being a fire, the same type of incident as where she first met Drilora, she knew that she would only get in zer way if she went inside the building.

"Look, up there," someone shouted, causing many in the crowd to look up at the rooftops, gasping. Cecilia looked around her, searching for Drilora heading their way. But the moment that she spotted zer, ze was jumping off the building across the street from the fire.

Drilora

Drilora slammed through the windows on the top floor of the building. The moment that air had that added pathway to the blaze, the fire burst forth, consuming what oxygen it could. Drilora slid across the floor, coming to a stop just a few feet inside the building. It was hot, with the flames all around zer, threatening to light zer fur on fire. Drilora got a flash of memory from that battle with the krylonian, the same memory that ze always had when ze first entered a fire. Ze quickly put it aside, trying to focus on the job at hand.

"Hello?" Drilora shouted, trying to be heard over the roaring fire. All reports indicated that there was no one left in the building, but ze had gotten such reports before. The fire the week prior was meant to have no one left behind, but that was when ze saved Cecilia. Ze didn't take anything that the humans reported for granted.

Humans made mistakes all the time. Drilora couldn't afford to.

When no response came from Drilora's call, ze headed forward into the fire. There was a door right in front of zer, leading out into the hallway. Ze continued through the upper floor of the building, calling out for anyone that needed help. But that wasn't why Drilora was at that fire. Whenever a fire got out of hand like that, they would call Drilora to help bring the building down. The building was already a loss, the firefighters outside only containing it as the fire burned wildly. A well-placed show of force would bring the whole thing down safely, while saving the rest of the neighborhood.

It wasn't common for there to be two similar fires like that so close together, but Drilora didn't think much of it as ze headed for the center of the building. Fires were common on Uvvelia, and it was one of the few hazards that still claimed uvvelian lives, even with the technology that they had at their disposal. Uvvelian fur didn't regenerate as quickly after fires as it did after pretty much anything else that was thrown at it. Of course, that wasn't something that Drilora let on while on Earth. Ze knew that zer enemies would only use it against zer.

Once Drilora came to the center of the building, ze tapped zer shoulder, checking that zer fur was still cool to the touch. That the fire-retardant spray was still keeping zer protected against the blaze. The spray was one of the few things that the humans had gotten right, though it didn't work as well to keep the humans safe from the fire as it did with Drilora. Ze kept hoping that zer fur would absorb it and maintain the protections, but it always came off in the shower. It was easier to reapply the spray every time ze was called out for a fire than to go the entire time smelling like the fire that it saved zer from.

"Anyone up here?" Drilora called one last time, looking around the floor. When no one called out loud enough to be heard over the raging fire, Drilora balled up zer fist, reaching back over zer shoulder. Ze eyed the wall in front of zer, knowing from the layout of the floor that it was load bearing. Once it fell, it would trigger the chain reaction to take the rest of the building down. Ze just needed to get out of there before that happened.

"Hello?" someone shouted, seemingly out of nowhere.

Drilora was in mid-swing when ze pulled up short, zer fist barely tapping the wall in question. Ze looked around at the floor, searching for the source of the voice. When ze couldn't see anything, ze called out again.

"Hello?" ze called. "Is someone here?"

"Down here," the voice called.

Drilora looked all around, searching for the source of the voice. It was hard to hear over the roaring of the flames, but ze thought that it was coming from zer left. That it was further down that hall, deeper into the floor. Drilora looked between the wall next to zer and that hall for a moment before heading down there.

The flames were everywhere, making it difficult for Drilora to breathe in there. The smell of the fires at least blocked the worse smell that that planet always had, though ze thought ze preferred it to that of the smoke filling zer lungs. When ze came up to the first set of doors, ze kicked in the one on the left before turning to the right. Both apartments were already engulfed by the flames, with no sign of anyone in there.

"Hello?" Drilora called out again. "Where are you?"

"Down here," the voice came, and Drilora could tell that it was coming from deeper down that hallway. That it was close to the end of the hall, if not at it.

Drilora rushed down to the last set of doors. The flames were lower over there, not quite having spread that far into the floor, but ze knew that it was only a matter of time. That this would have to be the last survivor in the building. If there was anyone else in there, they weren't likely to make it out. Ze just hoped that ze wouldn't be blamed for it once they found the bodies in the rubble. But ze wasn't going to leave this one to the flames.

"Which apartment?" ze called out, hoping that the voice would come again.

"This one," the voice called out, coming from the last apartment on the right.

Drilora quickly turned to that door, kicking that one open as well. The flames rose up in front of zer as the air came through the open doorway. Ze stumbled back a step away from those flames, wanting no part of the inferno in there. But ze knew that ze needed to get inside. That the person needed help, and ze was the only one that could help them.

Ze just hoped that ze wouldn't be saddled with another life debt from this.

When the flames calmed down once more, Drilora could see inside the apartment, but there was no one in there. The place seemed as deserted as the rest of the floor. But then, the door behind Drilora erupted, blowing towards zer back. Drilora stumbled forward under the force of it, zer arm coming up in front of zer as ze spun around to look back at the door.

And the large weapon pointed zer way.

Chapter Twenty-Eight
Regretful Rescue
Drilora

Drilora instantly knew that ze was in trouble. The gun looked exactly like the one from the night before. Only this time, ze didn't have Cecilia to help zer. Ze still hadn't gotten those rubber soled shoes to take the worst of the electricity from zer. The most ze could hope for was that the fire would make the person's aim go wide.

A clicking sound came from the gun, and Drilora quickly dodged to the side. Ze put all zer strength behind the move, slamming into the wall next to zer. The wall broke open, sending debris to the ground below. It was the back of the building, overlooking an alley between it and the next building over. That other building would have been evacuated because of the fire. Ze could see water running down the outer wall of that building, keeping the flames from spreading to it.

Water that was raining all over Drilora's arm as ze stood there in the gap.

Drilora let out a stream of Uvvelian curses as ze pulled away from the water. It wasn't just the water threatening to clean away the fire-retardant spray, but the fact that the water would make the electricity from the gun hurt worse, flowing across zer fur instead of being focused at the point of impact. Ze turned back toward the hall, where the harpoon was already being retracted for another shot.

"Come out, come out, wherever you are, Mr. Alien," came a taunt from the hallway. The voice sounded different from what Drilora had heard earlier, but ze knew that they would have been the one to call out. To bait zer down there.

"Mister?" Drilora asked, bristling at the term. At the supposition that ze was male. That seemed the insult after the injury, though Drilora was hoping to avoid both.

The gun swept around the corner, the harpoon leading the way. Before the human could fire off a shot, Drilora rushed forward, angling to the side away from the inner wall of the apartment. The gun kept turning the other way, though the human turned his head to follow Drilora's darting form. As Drilora rushed toward the human, ze got zer first real look at them. The man was wearing a fire fighter's uniform. If ze didn't know better, ze would have thought that the fire fighters had been in on the whole thing. But with the gun there, ze knew that there was only one group that could be involved.

However, ze figured that some of the fire fighters could be in the Earth for Humans terrorist cell.

Drilora led zer charge at the human with zer fist. While ze tried to avoid killing the humans during zer missions, things were already getting complicated in there. Between zer fur threatening to light up from the blaze still burning around zer and that horrible weapon being in there, ze couldn't afford to take it easy on the human.

As zer fist came at the human, he twirled around, pulling the weapon back out in front of him. He seemed to overcompensate with the spin, falling backward into the inner wall behind him. The quarters were close enough that Drilora was still on top of him, zer fist still heading for him. Only, instead of hitting him in the head like ze intended, zer fist glanced off his shoulder, pounding into the wall behind him.

"Ow," he shouted, as he stumbled to the side under the force of the blow, closer to the hole leading outside. The wall next to the door was narrow, and the man came dangerously close to falling through the hole and down to the alley. His hand went out, coming off the weapon to grab onto the wall next to the gap, holding himself there. The weapon continued to swing, threatening to fall out into the alley.

Drilora turned toward the human, rushing forward. Ze meant to bash him through that hole, to have him fall into the alley. But before ze could make it to him, he had the weapon spinning around in front of him, aiming for Drilora. Ze had to jump to the side once more, this time running straight through the inner wall and into the hall.

The gun let out that same clicking sound as before, and Drilora braced zerself for the impact of the harpoon. Once ze was in the hall, ze spun around, looking back at the hole that ze had made. The wall around it started to crumple in, showing that the whole structure was already weakened from the fire. Drilora couldn't afford to stay in there much longer, not with zer fire protection already fading. Ze could feel zer fur heating up, threatening to ignite while still in there, surrounded by the flames.

Drilora knew that ze couldn't afford to keep up with the fight. That the human was more stuck in that inferno than ze was. As long as Drilora could make it back outside before the human could hit zer with that weapon, ze would be alright. That was more than ze could say about the human.

Rather than going back to the apartment, Drilora did something that ze always hated doing in situations like that. Ze ran away, heading away from the human that was trying to kill zer.

"Where are you going?" the human called out after zer. "Come back here, you filthy alien."

"Yeah, that's not happening," Drilora called back. Instead, ze ran faster, worried that the human would get the gun reloaded before ze could make it back to the elevators. Ze still needed to trigger the chain reaction, only it was more to destroy that gun than to complete the mission. Ze no longer cared if the human was killed in the process.

Just as Drilora came up to the apartment where ze first broke into the building, ze heard the familiar sound of the gun going off. Ze didn't think about it, didn't hesitate, before jumping to the side, right through that wall.

The harpoon came straight at zer, clipping zer on the shoulder. The same shoulder that the water had hit. Electricity ripped through zer arm, causing zer muscles to clench. However, the harpoon kept right on going, heading further down the hall. The cable pulled away from zer fur, and the electricity faded before doing any lasting damage. Before causing zer to lock up there, stuck at the whim of the human.

Drilora glanced back through the hole that ze had made, only to see the human chasing after zer. He was already starting to reel the harpoon back in. But the wall that ze had jumped through was starting to buckle. The ceiling let out a light groan that was steadily getting deeper. Ze wasn't at the best place to start the chain reaction, but with the fire already compromising the building's integrity, ze knew that the rest of the building would come down soon enough. That ze had done enough damage already to topple the rest of the building, just as ze was meant to.

Ze took three steps deeper into the apartment before coming to a stop. Zer eye was locked on the broken window where ze came in, but zer thoughts were on the human behind zer. On the regret that ze would have if ze didn't at least try to save his life, even as the man was threatening to take zers.

"Last chance not to die," Drilora called out, looking back toward the hole in the wall. "Just leave the gun behind and I can still save you."

"Save yourself," the man called out, right before sticking the gun through the door to the apartment. The gun went off the moment that it was pointed Drilora's way, the harpoon zooming straight at zer.

It felt like the night before, where Drilora couldn't jump out of the way of the harpoon fast enough. The projectile came straight at Drilora, with the gun too close for zer to react in time. When the harpoon slammed into Drilora's chest, ze stumbled backwards under the impact. Ze followed through with the movement, trying desperately to make it back out through the window before the shock caused zer muscles to lock up once more. With all zer strength, ze jumped upwards and away from the door. Away from the gun. Away from the terrorist.

However, there was enough force directed upward to have Drilora soaring up through the ceiling. Up through the roof of the building and into the open air.

People down on the ground shouted when they spotted Drilora over the rooftop. They all pointed up at zer like ze had been doing tricks up there, rather than trying desperately to escape the terrorist. Ze could feel a slight tingling running through zer fur, even as ze flew through the air, over the edge of the building. It was clear that the electricity was already flowing through the cable, but without Drilora standing on something, there was nowhere for the electricity to go. But ze needed to get the harpoon out before ze came down to the ground below.

As Drilora fell, ze reached down to zer chest, grabbing onto the harpoon once more. The harpoon resisted, clinging to zer fur like a burr. Like the harpoon had spikes on it, embedded in zer fur. All Drilora could do was pull as hard as ze could, desperate to get the harpoon out before ze hit the ground. But ze was only halfway down the side of the building when the cable snapped taught.

Several things occurred to Drilora when ze noticed that happen. First, the fire was still roaring thick all along the side of the building. With the harpoon still embedded in zer fur, ze would be heading for that inferno. Hitting the outer wall of the building would be just as bad as hitting the ground. The electricity would flow through zer and into the stone of the building itself.

Second, was the fact that the human, still trapped in the flames above, was likely still holding onto the gun.

The human let out an odd scream as he was pulled out through the window after Drilora. The moment that he left the building, Drilora started falling once more. The gun no longer seemed connected to anything, but ze didn't bank on that keeping the electricity from flowing through zer. Ze could still feel it running through zer fur.

Another blast of flame came out of the window after the human, as the building started to buckle. The top floor quickly crumbled in on itself. But with Drilora and the human freely falling through the air, they would hit the ground long before the building caught up with them.

And Drilora was quickly finding zer way there.

Just as Drilora passed the water cannon on the fire trucks, ze managed to pull the harpoon out of zer fur. Ze quickly raised the harpoon over zer head, tossing it away from zer and away from the fire trucks. In the few seconds that ze had before hitting the ground, ze shifted zer body, pushing zer legs down under zer. Zer feet slammed into the pavement first, but ze didn't quite have zer legs under zer. Ze leaned forward, zer fist slamming home on the pavement, breaking it apart under the impact. But zer fall was stayed, and ze came to a stop right there.

Then again, Earth's gravity wasn't going to be enough to do any real damage even if ze landed on zer head.

The human's scream got steadily louder as he fell. Drilora stood up, zer arm reaching out to the side. As the human came down for an impact, Drilora ducked back down, slowing the man's descent even as ze caught him. Catching him straight out would have been just as bad as him landing on the pavement. But Drilora's reflex was to save the man that had just been trying to kill zer.

Chapter Twenty-Nine
Entering the Fray
Cecilia

With the crowd focused on Drilora's spectacular entrance, Cecilia managed to push past the cop that was keeping her out of the area around the building. She rushed forward, heading over to Drilora's side, even as the building continued to collapse in front of her. Her arms went up to block the debris heading her way, but Drilora was close enough to the building that she was covered in dust by the time she got over to zer.

"What are you doing?" Cecilia called out over the noise of the collapsing building. "Who is that?"

"You tell me," Drilora said, shrugging. "He's some Earth for Humans guy. Do you recognize him from last night?" Ze hiked the man up a little, raising his head so that Cecilia could see it.

Cecilia looked into the man's face, trying to picture him without the fire fighter uniform. But the soot from the fire and the dust from the collapsing building covered his face, and she couldn't make much out. If she had seen him the night before, she didn't recognize him.

"I don't think so," Cecilia said, shrugging.

"What's going on here?" someone asked.

Cecilia looked back to the source of the voice, surprised to see one of the fire fighters coming over to talk with them. He was pointed at the man that Drilora was still holding, though he was glaring more pointedly at Cecilia.

"Tell that thing to put the man down," the fire fighter said.

"That thing?" Drilora asked. Zer fur stood up on end as ze glared over at the fire fighter.

"You were called here to help take the building down before the fire could spread, not take humans hostage," the fire fighter said.

"Drilora isn't taking the man hostage," Cecilia said. She tried to stand taller than her short stature would have normally allowed, straightening her back as she took on what she thought was an imposing posture. It clearly had no effect on the fire fighter, though Cecilia wasn't sure whether or not that was because of her superpower. "Clearly, he was in the building. And from the gun still in his hand, he attacked Drilora."

"Why would a fire fighter attack an alien?" the fire fighter asked. "That makes no sense. Clearly, it did something up there." He stressed the word "clearly", throwing it back in Cecilia's face.

"I was doing the job that I was called in here to do," Drilora said. "It sounded like someone was trapped, so I investigated. Then he started shooting at me. Nothing else happened, besides me doing my job and trying not to get killed in the process."

"Killed, ha," the fire fighter said. "Like anyone can kill you. Just put the man down. We'll get this all straightened out."

Drilora glared over at the fire fighter before slowly placing the man on his feet. Before the man could get away, though, Drilora reached over to grab onto the gun, pulling it from his hands. The man held onto it, trying desperately to keep it from Drilora, but the alien's strength quickly won out. Drilora raised the gun up above zer head, keeping it out of the man's reach.

"Hey," the fire fighter shouted. At first, Cecilia thought that he was going to argue with Drilora more. Order zer to return the gun. Instead, he was staring at the man, his fists going to his hips. "I ordered all units out of that building half an hour ago," he said. "What were you still doing in there?"

"I... uh... I got trapped," the man said, looking between the fire fighter and his weapon in Drilora's hand.

"Uh, huh," the fire fighter said. "Who's your supervisor? I was told that everyone was pulled out. We'll get to the bottom of this."

"I... uh..." the man said again.

The fire fighter reached out, grabbing the man around the shoulders and escorting him away from Drilora and Cecilia. Drilora's eyes stayed locked on the two of them, watching as they merged with the rest of the fire fighters that were still working around them. The building was down, but there were still spot fires to put out. The crowd at the edge of the area was slowly breaking away, with much of the entertainment portion of the incident over.

"That was..." Cecilia started, though she couldn't come up with the right word to finish that sentence.

"What were you doing here?" Drilora asked, glaring over at Cecilia.

"Oh, please, tell me we're not on this again," Cecilia said, rolling her eyes as she turned back to look at Drilora. "I was with Leanne when the call came in. She brought me over so I can try to help."

"And why weren't you helping? Why were you just coming through the crowd when I came back down."

"Ugh, because the cops wouldn't let me through. I don't have a badge, and it's not like I look like your sidekick." Cecilia waved her hands up and down, showing off her outfit, which was already covered with the dust from the building. It seemed quite ruined, which felt typical of her new life living with Drilora.

"I'm still not sure you should be my sidekick," Drilora said. "Not after how you handled the fire chief."

"I'm still learning," Cecilia shouted, frustrated. "Besides, it's not like you did much better. Who was that man you pulled out of the fire? I doubt he was a real fire fighter."

"Well, hopefully the chief will figure that out," Drilora said, zer eye flicking over Cecilia's head to search for the man, hidden in the crowd over there. "In the meantime, we at least managed to get the weapon away from them."

"Unless they have more than one of them," Cecilia said. "You don't think... I mean, what if every criminal in the city gets one of those? How are we going to handle that?"

"We?" Drilora asked, glaring back at Cecilia.

"Yes, we," Cecilia said. "You're stuck with me, at least for this week. Longer, if I have any say in it. Not that I have much say in anything in my life. But for now, I'm your sidekick. I'll try to help out where I can, but... Well, with a fire like that..."

"Yes, yes, you would have been quite useless in there," Drilora said. "It was better that you weren't in my way. That you weren't getting in the way of these fine fire fighters." Ze waved around at the fire fighters that were still working around them. A few looked their way, but none of those looks were favorable to the alien. Ze seemed oblivious to that fact, just smiling around at them.

The last of the fires died off soon after that, and the water stopped flowing from the trucks. The fire fighters still had more work to do to secure the scene, but Drilora and Cecilia were no longer needed there. With one final look around them, Drilora turned back to Cecilia.

"Did Leanne leave already?" Drilora asked.

"Uh, I think so," Cecilia said. She looked back at the crowd where she had last seen Leanne's car. As the crowd cleared her view, there was no sign of it. "I guess she had more important work to do back at the office."

"Great," Drilora muttered. "Well, I guess you're coming back with me. Can't very well leave you out here, now can I." Ze shook zer head in disappointment about that. "Hop up."

Drilora turned around, kneeling so that Cecilia could climb back up onto zer back. Ze held onto the gun, keeping it firmly in both hands so that ze wouldn't risk dropping it on the trip back. But even as ze crouched there, ze looked around them, seeming to search for something.

"Are you forgetting something?" Cecilia asked, even as she climbed onto Drilora's back. Her hands went to the same place on zer shoulders. The fur wasn't feeling nearly as thick there as it had the last time. Instead, it was a bit slick, like the water from the fire trucks had gone all over them. It somehow felt more slick than during the storm. She was a little worried that she might slip off on the trip back, though she trusted Drilora enough to keep her safe.

"I'm not sure where the harpoon went to in everything," Drilora said.

Ze raised the gun up over zer head so that Cecilia could see it. There was no sign of the harpoon, and even the cable that had connected the harpoon to the gun was missing. However, Cecilia figured that the gun was the important part of the whole thing. Even if they still had the harpoon, they would need to throw it at Drilora for it to be of any danger to zer. The real danger was the electricity flowing through it, but Cecilia figured that the gun had more to do with that than the harpoon.

"Could someone have run off with it?" Cecilia asked, when she didn't see the harpoon anywhere around there.

"That's what I'm worried about," Drilora said. "I have a feeling that the Earth for Humans guy wasn't working alone here. That one of the actual fire fighters was involved. This group is getting more powerful. More dangerous, for both of us. Maybe..." Ze trailed off, slowly shaking zer head.

"No," Cecilia said, guessing at what Drilora was thinking. "You're not going to throw me out of the tower for my own good. Besides, they've already seen me with you. They know that I'm working with you. I won't be safe until we can stop them."

"Ha," Drilora said. Ze glanced over zer shoulder back at Cecilia up there. "I thought that they were just a hate group."

"That was before all of this," Cecilia said. She reached a hand out past Drilora's head to wave around at the scene in front of her. "The group's terrorist cell is obviously more dangerous than either of us were giving them credit for."

"Wait... You don't think..." Drilora said, trailing off as ze thought about the ramifications of what Cecilia had said. "Could they have started the fire? No, of... Of course, they could, but... But would they?"

"Would a terrorist cell burn down a building to get rid of an alien?" Cecilia asked. "It depends on how much they want to get rid of you. I'm sure that, if they wanted it enough, there are people that would burn down the whole world for the sake of getting rid of you. Oh, uh... Sorry."

"No, you're probably right," Drilora said, shaking zer head at the very thought of that. "We can't afford to underestimate this group. Not anymore. Not with them possibly having more of these weapons. They might already be trying to get them out there so that anyone could use them. Come on. We need to get back to the tower. We need to take this thing apart and see how it works. See what we can do to counter it in the future."

"Right," Cecilia said, nodding her agreement. She smiled broadly at the fact that Drilora was using the word "we", knowing full well that Drilora wouldn't be able to see that smile. She just held on tightly as Drilora crouched back down, jumping off once more. The moment that ze left the ground, though, Cecilia clung tighter to Drilora's back, shielding her eyes against the sight of the world zooming past them.

Chapter Thirty
The Weapon
Cecilia

Cecilia paused just outside of her door, thinking about heading inside to change quickly. Drilora continued without her, the gun still in zer hands. After that brief pause there, Cecilia raced after zer, not wanting to miss anything of Drilora's work with the gun.

As Drilora practically floated zer way down the tower, Cecilia ran to keep up with zer, putting in at least some of the workout for her training for the day. By the time they made it down to the garage, though, she had a feeling that Drilora wouldn't count it. That ze would expect her to do more training than the day before. But that would have to wait until after they dealt with the weapon.

Drilora headed over to one of the tables against the wall of the garage. Ze held the gun up over zer head as ze pushed everything that was on that table onto the ground. Once the table was clear, ze placed the gun down in the center. It let out several clatters as it settled onto the table, making it sound heavier than Drilora made it look.

"So, now what?" Cecilia asked, as she stared down at the gun.

"Now, we take it apart," Drilora said. Ze picked the gun up gently, shifting it back and forth as ze inspected it. "There's a seam here, several screws along here. One moment."

Ze stuck a finger up in the air before heading over to another table, grabbing several tools. Some of them were recognizable to Cecilia, like the screwdriver and drill. Some weren't, like an odd, bladed device. She wasn't sure if the unrecognizable tools were ones that Drilora had brought with zer, or just human tools that Cecilia had never seen before. Drilora took zer time, examining the gun as ze unscrewed the screws and pried it open along the seam. Once it was all open, though, Cecilia was only more confused by what she was seeing.

The two halves of the gun folded open like it was meant to be taken apart like that. There were several wires stretching between the two sides, and a strange, metal box that took up much of the space in the handle. The barrel of the gun stayed on one side, with several brackets on the other where the two sides were joined around it. The weapon looked more like something out of Drilora's spaceship than anything that Cecilia had seen before.

"Is it... alien?" Cecilia asked.

"Not in the slightest," Drilora said, shaking zer head. "No, it is purely human, and sloppily done, too. I could make something far better than this with only using human technology. If I used uvvelian technology, it would be half this size. I could probably do the same thing with a round the size of a normal, nine-millimeter bullet that would be impossible to extract, even from my fur. However, this seems to be the biggest surprise in all of this."

Drilora tapped the strange, metal box as ze said that. Ze pulled the box out of the rest of the gun, placing it lightly on the table next to it. There were several more wires coming off of it, connecting it with the rest of the mess inside the gun. Drilora grabbed another one of the items that Cecilia didn't recognize, which had more wires coming off of it. Ze placed those wires onto the metal box, next to some of the wires that still connected it to the rest of the gun. The gauge on the device quickly ran up, the hand hitting the far side. Drilora turned something on the device, and the gauge went back down to the middle of the display.

"Well, there's that at least," Drilora said, pointing to the display like Cecilia would understand what was happening.

"Yes, quite," Cecilia said, nodding, though she couldn't keep the smile off her face. Drilora seemed to sense what was behind that smile, as ze soon explained what ze was looking at.

"This battery is storing more power than a battery of this size would normally store, using human technology," Drilora said, pointing to the metal box. "Last night, the thought was that the cable was somehow plugged into a socket somewhere in the building to pack that kind of punch. But to have that on a mobile unit, coming out of a battery this size... It's not even all that heavy."

"Not all that heavy?" Cecilia asked. She reached out, picking up the battery off the table with both hands. While it was quite heavy, Cecilia managed it herself. However, she knew that the combined weight of the gun would have been too much for her to lift. "Maybe for an alien," Cecilia said, as she placed the battery back down.

"The battery is about thirty pounds," Drilora said, pointing at it. "The rest of the gun, another twenty. Then there's the force of the harpoon being ejected from the barrel. All told, yes, not many humans will be able to hold and fire this thing. That will help limit the damage that it could do. Not just to me, but to any human out there. While it is immeasurably painful for me, almost lethal if it was run long enough, it most certainly would be lethal to a human."

"I survived it," Cecilia said, shrugging.

"Not the full force of the weapon," Drilora said, shaking zer head. "If you got shot by that harpoon last night instead of me... Well, depending on where the harpoon hit, that might have been lethal enough on its own. If you managed to survive the harpoon itself, the electricity flowing through you like that would be enough to kill you. Even with your rubber soled shoes. The electricity would find a way, and as soon as it did, the full force would flow through you. You would be cooked from the inside out within seconds of being hit. In less time than it would take for you to realize that the harpoon itself didn't kill you."

"So... that would be bad," Cecilia said.

"Yes... Quite..." Drilora said, simply. Ze then turned back to the battery in front of them. "This kind of battery technology, though... It's beyond what you humans should be capable of at this point. I fear that my presence here has had a bigger impact than I had thought. Just seeing what a more advanced civilization is capable of can sometimes be enough to cause huge advances in your own technology. But... Well, most of the materials that uvvelians use in our batteries aren't found naturally on Earth. Hmm... Maybe the battery's materials will tell us where the battery itself came from. That might lend us information on the source of the gun, and how many could still be out there."

"Well..." Cecilia said, before reaching out to pick up the battery again.

She had momentarily forgotten just how heavy the thing was and let out a light grunt of effort as she lifted it up from the table. Drilora smiled a little at the grunt, zer hand going up to hide it. Carefully, Cecilia rotated the battery around, trying to see if there was anything written on it. To see if there was a Made in China label.

"I don't see anything saying what it's made of or where it was made," Cecilia said, before putting the battery back down.

"I'm not that surprised," Drilora said, shrugging. "Were you expecting there to be a signature on it? The name of the inventor?"

"No," Cecilia said, shaking her head. "Of-of course not." She could feel a light blush of embarrassment running through her cheeks, so she turned away from Drilora, not wanting zer to see it. "So, how are you going to tell what it's made of, then?" she asked.

"Well, I am a member of a technologically superior race," Drilora said, with no hint of gloat in zer voice. "I have a device in my spaceship that can scan the contents of the battery and tell me the exact makeup of it."

"Really?" Cecilia asked. She turned back to Drilora with wide eyes, thinking about how they could use such a technology. It seemed quite fascinating, though not that useful when it came to being a superhero.

"However, it hasn't worked since the crash," Drilora said, shrugging. "You humans have ways of determining such things as well, though. I have an atomic emission spectrometer here." Ze pointed off to one of the several devices on the other table that Cecilia thought for sure was something alien. "However, I can't do that while you're here."

"Trying to keep the human in the dark about your alien secrets?" Cecilia asked. She folded her arms over her chest as she glared over at zer.

"No, it might be hazardous to your health," Drilora said. "It involves burning the substance. Even exposing the chemicals within the battery to air might be deadly. I'll need to use several safety measures that are more easily accomplished alone."

"Oh," Cecilia said, her arms falling to her side. That made perfect sense to her, and it was clear that she had nothing to be defensive about.

"Besides, if you're so far on the mend that you feel like you can come out on a mission, then clearly you're healthy enough for some training," Drilora said.

"Ugh," Cecilia muttered. She knew it was coming, but it still hurt to hear it. Of course, it would hurt a lot more to do it.

"I'll go easy on you this time, though," Drilora said. "Twenty laps around the tower, plus forty laps on the stairs. Once you're done with that, I'll have you doing an hour of fighting training."

"But... That's going easy on me?" Cecilia asked, her face going white. "That's the same thing I did yesterday."

"Exactly," Drilora said, nodding zer head. "I would have had you increase your training today. So, maintaining your previous training is going easy on you."

"Ugh," Cecilia said again, rolling her eyes at the whole mess.

"Just go up and change," Drilora said. "Unless you think that dress is ruined enough that you want to run in that."

Ze pointed up and down at her dress, reminding her that she was still filthy. Cecilia looked down at herself, wondering if she should shower before the workout. But knowing that she would be drenched in sweat by the time she was done, she figured it was better to just save it for later.

"Fine, fine," Cecilia said. "But as soon as you know what's going on with that battery, I expect you to tell me."

"Of course," Drilora said, nodding. "I won't be able to start working on it until you head outside, though. And knock before coming back in. I'll have to make sure that the tower is safe for humans again before you can do the stairs. No sense in kicking you out now if I'm just going to expose you to it right after."

"Especially with how deep I'll be breathing after that run," Cecilia said. She started to whimper as she turned away from the gun and the mysteries contained within, heading back up to her room. Even before she made it up there, she knew that she was going to be more sore than she ever was by the end of her training. That while the weapon hadn't killed her the night before, Drilora's training might very well do it.

Chapter Thirty-One
A Night between Friends
Cecilia

Once again, Cecilia was exhausted by the time she was done with her training. From Drilora's earlier comments about increasing the workout over time, it was clear to her that this was going to be a regular thing. Her new norm, working out until she collapsed. So, rather than hiding out in her room again, after her shower, Cecilia grabbed some of the comics that she hadn't gotten to yet and headed down to the kitchen.

Drilora was over by the stove as Cecilia came inside. Ze glanced her way for a moment before looking back at the food in front of zer. Whatever ze was cooking, it was sizzling like juicy steak, and smelled like it, too. However, Cecilia knew that it was some uvvelian dish that would probably kill her if she tried to eat it. Instead, she headed over to the fridge, placing the comics on the small table in the corner as she passed it. She was expecting a new takeout container in there and was hungry enough to eat the whole thing at a go.

"I didn't order anything today, if you're looking for another takeout container," Drilora said. "I'm not made of money."

Cecilia let out a light laugh at the comment. It was exactly what her father would have said at that moment. But after a quick perusal of the fridge, she spotted some chicken, and what looked like human potatoes. She grabbed both of them up, bringing them over to stand next to Drilora to wait her turn at the stove. When Drilora didn't say anything about the potatoes, she figured that they weren't zer thunder potatoes.

"Any word on the battery?" Cecilia asked, more to make conversation than that she thought there would be news already. Or that Drilora wouldn't tell her the moment that ze found out.

"Nothing yet," Drilora said, as expected. "Leanne and her team have more than enough on their plate, but I made it clear that this is a priority. We might have something back by tomorrow, but... Well, as long as we hear something before it becomes an issue."

Drilora reached over to take the chicken and potatoes from Cecilia's hands. There was suddenly a second pan on the stove, and ze tossed them into it, chopping and seasoning them even as they cooked. It seemed strange to Cecilia, but she figured that was the norm for Uvvelian cooking. As the sizzle started, the smell came up, making Cecilia hungrier than she already was.

"Is it that unique of a substance?" Cecilia asked. "Something that they can actually track?"

"Well..." Ze started, but ze trailed off, not finishing that thought. Instead, ze said something different. Something that Cecilia hadn't been expecting from the alien. "Why don't we not discuss work, shall we?"

"Not discuss work?" Cecilia asked. Ever since she first came to the tower, work was all that they had talked about. Her becoming a superhero like zer, or the training that ze assigned to her. Only the day before did it turn to the Earth for Humans terrorists. Without work, Cecilia wasn't sure what they had to talk about. What they had in common at all.

"Like I said, nothing is going to come from the investigation on the battery for a day or so," Drilora said, as ze pulled another plate out of the cabinet, plating her food. Ze grabbed zer own plate, holding the two of them, as ze turned around to look back at Cecilia. "It's been a while since

I had a normal conversation over a meal. Shall we?" Ze nodded over to the table behind Cecilia.

"Oh, uh, sure," Cecilia said.

Cecilia turned around, heading back over to the table. As she passed by the closer of the two chairs, she pulled it out for Drilora before heading around to the further chair. The comics were over there, but she quickly slid them off to the side, out of the way. Drilora placed the two plates down on the table as ze sat down in the offered chair. The two dishes looked similar, and Cecilia wasn't sure how Drilora could tell them apart. But she trusted zer not to kill her.

At least, not by accidentally giving her the wrong food.

The two of them sat in silence at first, slowly picking at their food. Cecilia was trying very hard not to inhale the whole thing at once, but the chicken was hot enough that she needed to let it cool down at first. That didn't stop her from eating half of it even as it cooled.

"So... What-what did you usually do for fun, before coming here?" Drilora asked. Ze seemed almost tongue tied as ze tried to come up with something to discuss. Some topic of conversation that didn't involve work.

"Not much," Cecilia said, shrugging. "Reading, mostly."

"Ah hah," Drilora said. Ze raised zer fork up in the air like a scepter, waving it around a little. "So, my comic book assignment yesterday wasn't that unusual for you?"

"I don't think being assigned comic books for homework is usual for anyone," Cecilia said, trying very hard not to laugh at Drilora. "But, no, I... I usually read novels. Not comic books."

"Ah," Drilora said, nodding, as ze went back to eating.

"My mom got me into it growing up," Cecilia said, shrugging to try and make it sound like less of a big deal for her. She wasn't looking to be vulnerable in front of the alien.

"I brought a few books with me, but they're not doing too well after the storm. I keep meaning to check out your library, but... Well, my boss is keeping me pretty busy these days."

"Wow, they sound horrible," Drilora said. Ze let out a very human laugh at the comment, sounding quite uncomfortable about it all. "Where is your mother in all of this? What does she think of you wanting to be a superhero."

"Oh, uh... She died," Cecilia said. She focused on her food in front of her, not wanting to see the look on Drilora's face. The same look that she always got whenever her mother came up in conversation.

"Oh, uh... I'm-I'm sorry," Drilora said.

"It's alright," Cecilia said, shrugging. "It happened a few years ago. Before you arrived on Earth, in fact. I remember more years since she's been gone than when she was alive. It's my dad I worry about most of the time."

"Oh?" Drilora asked, obviously prompting her to say more. She needed that prompting, though.

"Mom was the fun one in the pair. The one that could make anything exciting. When she died... I don't know. It felt like Dad was just lost. That probably had more to do with why he dumped me on your doorstep than anything about a life debt. Just trying to get rid of me. That's why..." She trailed off, not wanting to bring up her father's more recent disappearance. She didn't want to bring up the fact that she had no idea where he went, or even if he was still alright.

With all that was happening with the Earth for Humans terrorists, Cecilia could almost convince herself that her father's disappearance had something to do with that. That the terrorists had found out that he was her father and had done something to him. However, she knew that couldn't be the case. That her father had gone missing before the terrorists even knew about her. Still, she couldn't help but worry about him, out there alone like that.

Drilora reached out a hand, lightly touching Cecilia's where it rested on the table next to her plate. She glanced up at zer eye, surprised to recognize a look of concern there. It wasn't clear if that look was the same in aliens and humans, or if Drilora was intentionally scrunching up zer face like that, to properly convey the emotion.

"Anyway, what about you?" Cecilia asked, desperate to get the conversation off of herself. "Did you leave anyone behind on that planet of yours?"

"Oh, quite a few," Drilora said, nodding. "I mean, it was a pretty big planet, and all that."

"No, I mean, did you leave behind anyone special?" Cecilia asked, laughing at what she hoped was a joke.

"Uh, no, not really," Drilora said. "Uvvelians don't form family groups in the way that humans do. When we mate, it falls to the village to train the child to become a proper member of society. So, in a way, I left behind a few thousand family members. But I had never found a mate. The war did much to derail all of that."

"What started the war?" Cecilia asked. She remembered Drilora bringing it up a few times, and the story of zer arrival always included that other alien and how they had tried to kill each other. But she knew that there must have been more to the story.

"We don't know, really," Drilora said, shrugging. "Our best guess is simply... because the krylonians found us. They were the first sentient species that we had encountered, other than ourselves. It was the krylonians that had discovered interstellar travel. We discovered the drive on one of their crashed ships. My people had been working on a prototype, but they needed data from the unit that we had gotten. That was the purpose of my mission, before I got sidetracked and stranded here. It is one of many reasons why I am eager to return home, as soon as I can."

Cecilia stared at Drilora quietly for a moment, trying to read more into zer words than what ze was saying. It was clear that ze had a sense of duty, of responsibility for zer people. That ze hated being away from them when they needed zer most. She found it hard to believe that ze would be so ready to give up Earth as ze said, though a sense of duty to return made sense to her.

"There's nothing you're going to miss about Earth?" Cecilia asked. "Nothing you're going to feel like you're leaving behind?"

"Well..." Drilora said, trailing off as ze seemed to think about it. But after a few seconds of silence, ze shook zer head. "No, I don't think so."

"Ouch," Cecilia said, smiling over at zer. "I'm hurt."

"No, that... I mean, I've made some... friends here, I guess. For-for lack of a better word. English isn't exactly the best language to properly capture the relationships developed between a member of my species and one of a lesser one."

"Ouch," Cecilia said, again. This time, with more feeling. "Do you really think so little of humans? I mean, sure, we're... technologically inferior, or whatever." She dropped her voice when she used those words, trying to do an impression of Drilora, but it wasn't even close. "We do well enough on our own, though, don't we?"

"Do you?" Drilora asked. "I mean, if you were doing well enough on your own, would you even need someone like me to play superhero? The missions that I go out on, none of them would have happened on Uvvelia. We don't attack one another or try to steal from one another or burn down entire buildings to get the attention of someone that's just trying to help. If you were doing well enough on your own, your father wouldn't have just left you on my doorstep. You wouldn't be worried about where you're going to go after your week here is up. And no one would ever underestimate you."

"God, you're so... so..." Cecilia said, struggling for the right word to describe Drilora.

"Accurate?" Drilora asked.

"Egotistical," Cecilia snapped. "Self-righteous. Self-centered."

"Ha," Drilora said. "Self-centered? That's rich coming from the most self-centered species we've ever met."

"Ugh," Cecilia grunted, before sliding her plate away from her and standing up. The plate was mostly empty already, with her having eaten almost all of her food while they talked, but it was the principle of it all. She just shook her head at Drilora before storming off, leaving zer back there to clean up.

Chapter Thirty-Two
New Outfit
Cecilia

Cecilia didn't sleep all that well that night. She kept replaying the argument over in her head. It felt weird to feel the need to defend her entire race, especially since she had once argued on the other side of the issue. With most people, most humans, just seeing her as some useless girl, it was hard to put much faith in them. But having Drilora be the one to denigrate the humans was a bit much for her. Some alien that was relying on those same humans that ze had denigrated.

When the sunlight started to come through her window, Cecilia let off a low groan, knowing that she wasn't going to get any more sleep that morning. Knowing that Drilora would likely expect her out of bed soon. That ze might use the argument from the night before as an excuse to chase her out of the tower, or to give her a harder training session than she would have had otherwise. Hard enough that she might not survive it.

Slowly, Cecilia rolled over in bed, dropping her legs off the edge. As she sat up, it felt like every muscle in her body complained. Her hand no longer hurt from the electrical burn, though she knew that had more to do with the rest of her body being so sore. She looked down at her injured hand, which looked about the same as it had the day before. Suddenly, she was worried that her hand would never fully heal, that she would be left with a scar for her time with Drilora and nothing more to show for it.

"What am I doing?" she asked herself, slowly shaking her head as she looked down at the floor, a few inches below her dangling feet. It felt like she couldn't move at all, let alone stand up. The silence coming from the rest of the tower seemed to suggest that Drilora was still in bed. That she could get away with just rolling over and going back to sleep. However, that impression didn't last long.

Just a few seconds after Cecilia had decided to go back to bed, the doorbell rang out, seeming to echo in her head. She knew that it was likely Leanne. The woman seemed to come over every morning at the same time, suggesting that it was later in the day than Cecilia had originally thought. She glanced over at her bedside table, where her bedroom clock usually was. But the clock wasn't there because that wasn't her bedroom; she hadn't brought it with her from home. It didn't occur to her that morning that the clock wasn't back in her old bedroom, either.

Cecilia sat there in silence for a moment, just trying to get up. Or, at least, she was trying to try. She kept telling herself to move, to stand up, but her body just sat there. It took her far longer than it should have for her to notice that she was only thinking it, rather than actually doing it. Once that clicked in her mind, she shifted forward a little, slipping down those last few inches to finally stand up.

On her way out of the room, she slipped on her flats, though she stayed in her nightgown. Her hands shifted behind her back, reaching for a robe that wasn't there, even as she headed out into the hall. There was no sign of Drilora around there, though she figured that ze had already gone down to answer the door. That ze had likely not been in zer room, considering it was late enough for Leanne to be coming over. That assumption was soon confirmed, just as Cecilia came up to the stairs.

"Cecilia," Drilora called out from downstairs.

Another groan came from Cecilia, though it didn't go far. As she started down the stairs, she called out, "Coming."

The entire walk down the stairs, though, she was grumbling to herself, still annoyed at Drilora from the argument the night before and at her own body for being so sore.

Drilora and Leanne were both looking over at the stairs as Cecilia came out onto the ground floor of the tower. Their eyes followed her down that last flight of stairs, though she couldn't tell anything from the expressions on their faces. Clearly, something was going on, but Cecilia hadn't the faintest idea what it was.

"What's up?" Cecilia asked Leanne, as she made the ground floor. Her arms crossed over her chest protectively, shielding herself against the slight chill of the room. She pointedly didn't look in Drilora's direction as she came up to them.

"Well, we have a surprise," Leanne said. A slight smile was starting to form on her face, like she was trying to hide it. With her arms behind her back, Cecilia figured that whatever the surprise was, she was holding it back there.

"Uh oh," Cecilia said, suddenly suspecting that it was a bad surprise. That Leanne had found her somewhere to live or had located her father. Whatever it was, she worried that it would take her away from the tower. That her dreams of becoming a superhero would be gone.

"No, no," Leanne said, shaking her head. "This is a good surprise. Really. Come."

Leanne nodded her head to the side, motioning over to the table where the electricity gun was still sitting from the day before. Without another word of explanation, Leanne led the way over to that table. It made Cecilia think that it had something to do with that. That she had found something out about the gun or the battery and that it had something to do with Cecilia.

However, as the two of them came over to the table, Leanne pulled a long, black box out from behind her back, placing it on the table there. It looked like a boot box, though the sides were a sturdier cardboard than what Cecilia had usually seen. Once the box was in place, Leanne waved at it before taking a step to the side.

"Voila," she said.

"Uh... Thanks?" Cecilia asked, looking between Leanne and the box.

"Oh, just open it, silly," Leanne said, smiling at her. "Go on."

Cecilia rolled her eyes at the whole thing. She didn't often get presents growing up, not since her mother passed. But whatever was in the box, Cecilia knew that her day couldn't start until she opened it. So, she reached forward, grabbing the top of the box by the corner and flipping it open.

Inside was what looked like a brown shirt, folded so that the sleeves were tucked within it. When she looked closer, she noticed the soles of a pair of boots sticking out at one side of the box, suggesting that there was a whole outfit inside. Hesitantly, Cecilia reached out, picking up the shirt by the shoulders. As the whole thing fell open, she realized that it was more than just a shirt. That it was a jumpsuit with long sleeves. The entire thing was the same shade of brown as Drilora's fur.

"Oh," Cecilia said, as she looked at her sidekick uniform.

While Cecilia wasn't all that into fashion, her first thought of the uniform was that it was quite ugly. If she wore it to her high school, there would have been an endless stream of jokes made at her expense. However, as she looked closer at it, she realized that it wasn't normal stretch cotton and felt almost as hard as leather. Whatever it was made of, it would likely keep her safer than her workout gear would, no matter what came her way when she was out on a mission.

That seemed to suggest that she would be going out on more missions. That they weren't looking to kick her out of the tower, but to bring her into the fold of the whole endeavor. That she had managed to do exactly what she had set out to do there at that tower; become what she was always destined to become.

"Uh, thanks," Cecilia said.

"I know, I know, it's not exactly stylish," Leanne said. "It's the first draft of the outfit. If you stay on, get more missions of your own, maybe get some sponsorships, we'll adjust the outfit. Maybe get something that both protects you and looks nice. But, for now, protecting you was more important. Especially after what happened the other night. And yesterday. And... Well... Yeah, anyway, you should go up and try it on."

"You should wear it whenever you're out of the tower," Drilora added. "You never know when you'll be called to a mission, and you won't always have time to go home and change."

"Uh huh," Cecilia said, though she didn't look back at Drilora.

Leanne looked between Cecilia and Drilora for a moment, before turning back to Cecilia. "I've been trying to get Drilora to wear something like this since ze started taking on missions around the city," she said. "Ze absolutely refuses to wear clothes, though at least ze has seen the use of shoes now. And, yes, I have your new boots in the car as well. Fortunately, no one has noticed that ze's always naked on missions."

"Well, go on," Drilora said. "Go try it on. Leanne will be absolutely insufferable about the whole thing until she knows it fits you properly."

"Uh huh," Cecilia said again. "Uh, thanks, Leanne," she said, smiling over at her, before heading back over to the stairs. Even as she headed up, she heard Leanne start to talk with Drilora.

"What happened last night?" she asked.

"Nothing," Drilora said.

"Did you say something to her? Clearly, she's upset with you about something."

"Is she?" Drilora asked. "It didn't seem like it."

"Ugh, have you learned nothing about human emotions these past few years?"

Their voices dropped off behind Cecilia as she came into the gym. Rather than heading up the rest of the tower, she slipped off to the side right there. She placed the box down on one of the destroyed machines before pulling her nightgown off. Even as she was pulling on the uniform, she slipped the nightgown into the box, under the boots.

The uniform was tighter than she was expecting, and it was difficult to get on at times, slipping out of her hands as she pulled it up. It hugged her in several places, though it was never too tight, holding in her butt and breasts in a supportive but not painful way. There was a zipper in the back that was annoying to zip up herself, though she managed it. Once it was done, she reached into the box for the boots. With how well the whole thing fit her, she wondered at when Leanne could have gotten her measurements.

Just after she got the boots on, Leanne's voice started to get closer, showing that the two of them were heading up the stairs. It seemed like perfect timing, like they had been watching her that whole time. However, when they came into the room, they both looked over at her in surprise.

"Oh, good," Leanne said, her surprised expression replaced by a smile. "It looks perfect on you."

"Does it?" Cecilia asked, looking down at herself. There wasn't a mirror in the room, so she hadn't gotten a good look at herself. From what she could see, from how it fit her, she figured that it would work for what it needed to do. It still looked ugly, though.

"Well, perfect enough," Leanne said. "It's a good thing, too, considering what I have planned for you for today."

"Uh oh," Cecilia said. "What do you have planned?" She had this feeling that Leanne had her own kind of training in mind for her. That it was going to be far worse than Drilora's training. However, when Leanne answered her question, her spirits immediately lifted.

"A solo mission, actually," she said.

Chapter Thirty-Three
The Solo Mission
Cecilia

"Whoa, wait, what?" Drilora asked. "I didn't agree to this. She's not ready."

"She's ready for this," Leanne said.

"Yeah, Drilora," Cecilia said, glaring over at zer. "I'm ready. Of course, I'm ready. Ready for what, exactly?"

"I'll brief you on the way over," Leanne said, nodding her head back toward the stairs. "If you want to come and supervise, Drilora, that's fine, too. You probably won't fit in my car, though."

"I'll follow along," Drilora said, making it clear that ze wasn't about to let them go off alone like that. That ze wasn't ready to let Cecilia do a mission by herself just yet.

"Okay, but once we get there, it's all on Cecilia," Leanne said. "She needs to learn to stand on her own feet in these. Besides, you're not getting paid for it."

"Is she?" Drilora asked.

"Someone has to cover the cost of the uniform," Leanne said, pointing over at Cecilia.

Cecilia wondered just how much the uniform cost. It was clearly custom made and done within the two days that she was at the tower. But considering Drilora's own missions paid for the tower itself, and everything in it, she figured that ze was getting well paid for the missions. Money that ze wouldn't need once ze left Earth.

"But don't worry," Leanne said. "It's not anything too dangerous, and it's right up her alley. In fact, they specifically said not to send you."

"What?" Drilora asked. It was clear that ze was surprised, though it didn't taint zer voice like it would have in a human. "Why didn't they want me?"

"They mentioned a bull in a china shop," Leanne said.

"I am very careful on missions," Drilora said. "When was the last time I broke something."

"Uh..." Cecilia said, hesitantly.

"Accidentally," Drilora said. "Yesterday doesn't count."

"Anyway, we'd better go," Leanne said, pointing back to the stairs. "We're already late."

"Sure," Cecilia said. "Lead on." She glared over at Drilora as the two of them headed back down the stairs. Drilora stood there in the gym for a bit longer, watching them head off, before heading the other way. Cecilia figured that ze would head to the roof, jumping across the rooftops like always, following them through the city.

"So, what's the mission?" Cecilia asked in a low tone, as they headed out of the tower.

Leanne stayed quiet until they made it over to her car, climbing into the driver's seat. Once the doors were all closed and she was heading off down the driveway of the park, she started to explain what was involved.

"It's another hostage situation, actually," Leanne said. "From what you said the other day, I figured you're ready for one of those?"

"Uh, sure," Cecilia said. With the prospect of going into that kind of situation again, she wasn't as certain as she was before. "But why don't they want Drilora going in there, then? Ze seemed to handle the last one just fine."

"It's a smaller space, a more volatile perpetrator. They've been in there all night, with the cops holding the perimeter. They were afraid that sending in Drilora would only escalate the situation, but they had called, thinking they might need zer. I suggested you instead, thinking that you could handle this better. You can handle this, right?"

"Sure," Cecilia said, shrugging. "What do we know about the perp, though? I mean, not that I'm all that great on... Oh, what's it called. Profiling or whatever."

"Well, the guy is middle aged. The hostage is his ex-girlfriend who broke up with him a week ago. They're usually better at talking these kinds of people down, but he's resistant to any kind of logic at this point. He keeps insisting that the ex was cheating on him and insists on the new boyfriend coming down there. Of course, there's no one else. And even if there were, they wouldn't want to bring him into all of this."

"Okay, I think I can use that," Cecilia said, as she struck upon what she thought was a good plan.

"From what they've been able to see in the window from across the street, he has a gun and has been spending most of the night pacing across the living room. The blinds are all closed at this point, so the snipers don't have a line on him. All you need to do is get the girlfriend out of the apartment, and the cops can do the rest. No need to put yourself in more danger than you need to, alright?"

"Yeah," Cecilia said, nodding.

"Cecilia?" Leanne asked, glancing over at her as she watched where she was driving.

"I got this, Leanne," Cecilia said. "I know you don't have a reason to believe that, but I've got this. You just need to trust me."

"I do," Leanne said, shrugging. "Maybe your superpower doesn't work on me, but I believe you're ready for this. You've got this."

"Yeah," Cecilia said, nodding again. However, she wasn't as sure about all of that as Leanne seemed to be.

There were cop cars blocking off the road around the apartment building as they came up to it, reminding Cecilia of the previous two missions that she went on. However, the cop cars weren't alone, with a couple of news vans parked outside of the perimeter and reporters standing around, waiting to report on it all. Plus, this time, it was Cecilia that was going in, rather than Drilora.

Cecilia looked around as Leanne pulled up in front of the building, searching for Drilora. Part of her wanted zer to go in there with her. To throw away the fact that this was meant to be her first real mission, just for that extra protection. The guidance that ze could give her. But Cecilia knew that ze wouldn't be going in there even if ze arrived in time.

"Alright," Leanne said, as she pulled to the side of the road, right next to the cop cars. "It's in there. Sixth floor. The cops should be in position around the door, so you won't be able to miss it. Good luck. Or should I say break a leg?"

"Ha," Cecilia said, though there was no humor in her voice. There was only fear, and she could hear it just as easily as Leanne should have.

"Hey, you got this," Leanne said. She reached over to pat Cecilia's hand. "I wouldn't be sending you in there if I didn't think you had this."

"I've only been at the tower for two days," Cecilia said. "I have yet to help Drilora on any of zer missions."

"You helped zer on the roof," Leanne said. "Besides, this isn't a Drilora mission. This is a Cecilia mission. You don't need to beat anyone up or stop them. You just need to get the girl out. Right? Remember that. Get the girl out, and yourself, and let the cops do the rest."

"Right," Cecilia said, nodding. She sat there for a moment longer, just staring at the building, before finally reaching over to pull open the door.

As Cecilia stepped out of the car, the cops that were working the perimeter all turned toward her. At first, Cecilia expected them to block her from heading in there, like they had at the fire. But one by one, they turned away from her, looking back at the building and the road around it. Either they had been expecting her arrival, or her uniform was enough to tell them that she was there to help. That she was the superhero on duty. The sidekick without her hero.

A loud thump came up behind Cecilia as she came up to the stairs leading to the doors. She turned around to look at the building across from her. There didn't seem to be anything over there at first, but slowly, Cecilia looked up to the roof above her. Drilora was up there, looking down at her from that perch. Despite the argument from the night before, she felt better having Drilora there, watching over her like that. It felt like she was capable of anything, as long as she had Drilora there to help. She waved up at the alien, though it wasn't clear if ze would have seen her from so far up. Reluctantly, she turned away from the alien, heading up the stairs.

There were two cops standing on either side of the door. The one on the left took a step to the side, blocking the path to the doors. "You're Cecilia?" he asked.

"Um... Yes," Cecilia said, for a moment uncertain about her own name. She glanced behind her again, back up at Drilora, like the alien would know her name better than she would. When she looked back at the cop, he was looking up there as well.

"Right," the cop said, turning back to her after a moment. "That alien isn't coming in with you, is it?"

"Not unless I need zer," Cecilia said, more to herself than the cop. When the cop gave her a questioning look, she shook her head. "Ze should be staying out here. I'm running solo on this one."

"Good," the cop said, nodding. "Sixth floor. You'll need to take the stairs, just inside. They shut down the elevators in case he got past them."

"Right," Cecilia said, nodding like she expected that. "I'll be heading in there, then."

"Right," the cop said, nodding his agreement. But it took him a moment to realize that he was still blocking her way, and a moment longer for him to move. "Good luck."

"Ha, right," Cecilia said, before heading past him.

As she approached the door to the building, she realized that her hands were shaking. An odd combination of nerves, fear, and adrenaline. Her muscles no longer felt sore, and she figured that that was the trick to it all. That Drilora's training wasn't going to keep her away from missions; the missions had their own way of preparing her, no matter what she had been putting her body through. And as she headed inside, she got the sense that she was ready. Ready for her first solo mission. Ready to finally become a superhero.

Chapter Thirty-Four
Underestimated
Cecilia

By the time Cecilia made it up to the sixth floor, she was glad for Drilora's training. Normally, running up five flights of stairs would have winded her. She barely noticed it as she came out onto the floor. However, her nerves were so frayed, she had completely forgotten her earlier plan, and everything that Leanne had told her about what she was dealing with.

There were several cops standing in front of a door in the distance, and several more along the hall between them and the stairs, all wearing bulletproof vests. They all turned toward her the moment that she stepped out of the stairwell, watching as she headed their way. Most of them had guns at the ready, both pistols and long guns, just waiting for a chance to head in the apartment. The two cops closest to the door were holding battering rams, and they both looked like they wanted to swing them home immediately.

Cecilia heard the cops muttering under their breaths as she passed them. Most were commenting on how young she looked, on how she didn't look up to the job at hand. It was all normal for her; nothing that she hadn't heard before, about far simpler tasks. As she came up in front of the door, she hoped that the man inside would underestimate her just as much.

"You're who they sent up?" said the battering ram cop on the right, disbelief plain in his voice. "Sorry, it's just... Well, you don't look like much."

"I get that a lot," Cecilia said, nodding back at the cops behind her. "How am I getting in there?"

"Isn't that your job?" the cop asked, shrugging.

"Right," Cecilia said. She nodded to him before turning to face the door. Unfortunately, the door didn't seem to know either. On a whim, she reached out, trying the knob. As expected, it was quite locked. However, the move didn't go unnoticed inside.

"Go away," a man called out. "I told you, no cops. Just send the new boyfriend up."

"I'm not a cop," Cecilia called out. "Please, I'm just here to help."

"Ha, right," the man said.

A shadow played across the floor and a light creek came up as the man came up to the door. For a moment, she thought about telling the cops that. They could just shoot him through the door. But there must have been a reason why they hadn't tried that already. Without knowing where the ex-girlfriend was in the apartment, she realized that that shadow might be her instead of him.

"Who are you?" the man asked, his voice coming from right on the other side of the door.

The cop on Cecilia's right started waving his hands around, trying to draw the attention of the other officers. He flipped his free hand through several motions, seeming to be signaling them. Cecilia figured that he was telling them that the guy was right there, that they could end it if they just worked together. But before anyone could move against the man, the shadow drifted away from the door.

"I'm... My name is Cecilia," Cecilia said, when she realized that the man had asked her a question. That he would have been able to see her through the peep hole and likely noticed that she was distracted by the cops. "I was hoping to come in and talk with you a bit."

"Ha, right," the man said. "I open that door and the cops storm in."

"No cops," Cecilia said. She raised her hands up in front of her, showing that they were empty, though the man seemed to have backed away from the door and likely couldn't see her anymore. "Just me. I'll even have the cops back further down the hall." She waved her hands at the cops, but none of them were moving away from their positions.

"Not going to happen," the cop next to Cecilia mouthed at her, shaking his head emphatically.

"If you want to talk, then just talk," the man called out, his voice coming from deeper in the apartment.

"I just... We-we want to make sure that Felicia is alright," Cecilia said, remembering the girlfriend's name from Leanne's briefing earlier. "It's been a while since we heard from her, and people are getting a bit nervous."

"Tell them," the man said, his voice low.

"Ah," someone said. "I'm-I'm fine." Cecilia didn't recognize the voice, but it sounded like that would be Felicia. When she glanced at the cop next to her, he just nodded confirmation of that.

"Now, why don't you get us some breakfast," the man said.

"Well, that's why I'm here," Cecilia said. This wasn't part of her original plan, though it seemed like an approach. She needed to get inside that room before she could do anything to help. "I'm here to cook you both breakfast."

"Ha, right," the man said.

"What? Do I look like a cop to you?" Cecilia asked. She waved her hands up and down her body, though the shadow was still missing from beneath the door. "Do I look like someone that can do anything to hurt you?"

"You don't look like a cook, neither," the man said. "And what's with the outfit?"

"It's my uniform," Cecilia said, before she could think better of it. "Uh... for-for my cooking service. We're 'The Beast's Bistro'. The place just opened up down the street."

"You know anything about that?" the man asked, his voice low.

"I... Yeah-yeah, I think I went past there yesterday," Felicia said.

This took Cecilia aback. Was Felicia just playing along or was there really a place called The Beast's Bistro in that neighborhood. It seemed like an interesting name for a restaurant.

"And, what? You just decided to come over and cook us breakfast? I doubt the cops are paying you."

"Did you not notice my uniform?" Cecilia asked, laughing like it was all some big joke being played on her. "My boss is a bit weird."

"Should you really be lying like this?" the cop next to Cecilia mouthed at her. He glanced back at the door, like the man would be able to hear him through the door, even without voicing the words.

"My boss is weird," Cecilia muttered, shrugging. That was true enough.

"Fine, fine," the man called out. "But just you. You come in, cook, then leave. No funny business or I start shooting. And Felicia isn't going to be my first shot."

The cop perked up at the man's words, obviously surprised that the whole thing worked. Cecilia wasn't that surprised by it. One of her mother's coworkers had come by the apartment right after she died to cook for her father. It always seemed to Cecilia like something one does for people in distress.

The door let out a loud clunking sound as the deadbolt was flung wide. Several more clicks came soon after, as the other locks clicked open. Finally, the door opened a crack, bumping against the chain that was still in place. Rather than the man looking out through that crack, though, it was Felicia.

"Uh, no-no cops," she said. "Have them back away."

"Come on, guys," Cecilia said, looking around at the cops. "We girls have this. Don't we, Felicia?"

Felicia's eye flicked up and down Cecilia, obviously appraising her. Cecilia already knew what she would see, what everyone sees when they look at her. But it wasn't like they had much of a choice on the situation that they were stuck in. Felicia didn't say much of anything in response to the question before backing away from the door. The door slammed shut once more, with them waiting for the cops to move away.

"Come on, guys," Cecilia said again, looking all around her to the cops. "This is why I'm here, isn't it?"

"Is it?" the cop asked. He, too, looked Cecilia up and down, but the look on his face told her exactly what he thought of her chances of pulling the whole thing off were. That estimation was clearly far lower than what Cecilia gave herself. But they had just as few choices as Felicia did in everything. So, after a moment, he waved off the other cops.

Slowly, the cops started to back away from the door, clearing the hall around the apartment. That one cop stayed next to Cecilia, looking like he wasn't about to leave her there alone like that. Like he needed to.

"I got this," Cecilia mouthed at him, smiling broadly. Trying to seem braver than she was feeling. After a moment, the cop nodded at her before backing away from the door like the other cops. "Alright," Cecilia called out, once the man was far enough away. "We're alone here."

The door clicked open again, bumping against the chain. Felicia was still standing there, looking around the hall. Once she seemed satisfied, she nodded before closing the door again. This time, however, Cecilia could hear the chain coming off the door, before the door opened.

"Come in," Felicia said. "Just you."

Slowly, Cecilia moved forward, pushing the door open. She kept her hands up in front of her, trying to seem as harmless as she could. Given what the man would have already seen of her, though, that wasn't hard. She knew that he would only see a poor, innocent girl that had come to help out.

The man was standing behind Felicia, his gun pointed to the side of her head. Tears were flowing freely down Felicia's face, her own hands up in front of her. The man jammed the gun harder into the side of her head before saying, "Close the door."

"Alright," Cecilia said. "It was Logan, right?" she asked, trying to remember his name from the briefing. Felicia was easier to remember, as she had a friend growing up with that name.

Cecilia kept her hands raised in front of her as she faced the two of them and used her left foot to kick the door closed behind her. The moment that the door was closed, Logan rushed forward, heading around Cecilia to put the locks back in place. With where he was standing, the gun safely pointed away from both of them, Cecilia could have ended it right there. She could have punched him in the back of the head or tried to slam him into the door. But then, the game would be up, and the man would know what was going on. Her training wasn't far enough along that she would be able to keep him pinned there. Besides, that wasn't the plan.

"Alright," Logan said, after peeking through the peephole. He turned back toward the two women, his gun coming up again. This time, it was pointed at Cecilia, rather than Felicia. "Go. Cook us some breakfast."

"Right," Cecilia said, nodding, before heading into the kitchen.

One of the chairs from the kitchen was pulled away from the table, set out in the middle of the room. From the rope that was still draped over it, it seemed like Felicia had been tied up there for most of the night. Felicia headed back over there, sitting on the edge of the chair. It seemed almost automatic to her. Logan glanced over at her but kept his focus on Cecilia.

"What would you guys like?" Cecilia asked, as she pulled the fridge open.

"Wait, why didn't you bring food with you?" Logan asked. "Is this some kind of trick?"

"No trick," Cecilia said, shaking her head. "Do I look like someone that could trick you? I mean, I'm sure you're a pretty smart man."

"Damn right," Logan said.

"Ready to adapt to things coming your way."

"Very adaptable," Logan said.

"You could probably see that I'd make a better hostage than Felicia," Cecilia said.

"Wait, what?" Logan asked. He looked between Cecilia and Felicia, though his gun stayed on Cecilia the entire time.

"Well, think about it," Cecilia said. "Felicia has been in here all night. She's probably quite tired. The cops outside are worried about her. If you release her and keep me, I'm sure they'll just head off. No one really cares about me in all of this. I'm expendable, and the cops are less likely to make a fuss about me than this new boyfriend of Felicia's. What use am I to anyone?"

"No, that..." Logan said. "You're just trying to trick me."

"How?" Cecilia asked. "You have control over this whole thing. You're calling the shots."

"Damn right, I am," Logan said.

"Which is why you don't need Felicia here," Cecilia said. "You can use me as a hostage."

That was, of course, Cecilia's plan all along. Exchange herself for Felicia. It was what almost happened during the bank incident, though without getting anything for it. She was pretty sure that a hostage exchange might work there. That Logan wouldn't see her as a threat. As anything but a scared girl, just like Felicia. And as Logan looked at her, it seemed like he was considering it.

"But... No, I... I'm not here to take hostages," Logan said. "I'm here to get my girl back. To prove to her that I'm better than this new man of hers. Besides, Felicia wants to be here. Isn't that right, babe?"

"What?" Felicia asked. Her head flicked to the side, looking back at Logan before he noticed her eyeing the door. "Oh, uh... Of-of course, babe."

"See?" Logan said, pointing his gun back at Felicia. "I knew that she would come around to see things from my side. We-we belong together."

"Well... Of-of course you do," Cecilia said, nodding her agreement, though she thought that nothing could be further from the truth. Even without looking back at Felicia, she could hear the fear in her voice. She knew that Felicia just wanted out of there. To run away from the man that was terrorizing her. But that wasn't how Logan saw it. "You belong together. Which is why you should let her go."

"What?" Logan asked. "No, that... That doesn't make sense."

"What? Are you going to hold her at gunpoint for the rest of your lives?" Cecilia asked. "What kind of relationship is that? But if you let Felicia go, and keep me here, we can get the police to calm down. Felicia can tell them to let you go. And we can all go home, right?"

"That..." Logan said. He looked between Cecilia and Felicia, struggling to come up with some counter to Cecilia's words.

But the thing about people underestimating Cecilia wasn't just that they didn't see what she was capable of. It also meant that people trusted her more. They didn't think that she could lie convincingly. That she could trick them so easily. So, when Logan started nodding his agreement, Cecilia knew that it was all going to work out. That her superpower was going to save the day. That she was becoming the superhero that she was meant to be.

"Yeah, yeah," Logan said, nodding. "You're right. I'm... I'm sorry, Felicia, babe. I shouldn't have... Why-why don't you go out and talk with the police. We can get this whole mess squared away."

"Uh... Sure," Felicia said. "Is... Are-are you going to be alright?"

"I'll be fine, babe," Logan said.

"I meant her," Felicia snapped.

"Hey, hey," Cecilia said. She stepped between the two of them, trying to stop the whole situation from escalating again. "I'm sure that Felicia is just tired. We're all tired, right? Felicia, why don't you head out. Logan and I can talk in here. I can... I can make that breakfast that I promised you both."

"Sure," Felicia said, nodding.

Slowly, Felicia headed over to the door. She kept her hands up like Logan was still holding her hostage. But the gun was safely on Cecilia, not threatening to turn her way. His eyes stayed on the woman, though, and Cecilia tracked her progress over to the door by them.

The moment that Felicia made it over to the door, she grabbed hold of the knob, pulling the door open and rushing out into the hall. And the cops came sweeping in after her, guns at the ready.

Chapter Thirty-Five
Success

The cops had Logan on the ground within seconds, pinning him there as they recovered the gun. Cecilia backed away from them, letting the cops do their job. Once she was sure that Logan was no longer a problem, she turned away from the scene, heading back into the hall.

Felicia was standing out there, leaning against the wall with her eyes on the door. When Cecilia came out, her eyes went wide with shock. It seemed like she wasn't expecting her to make it out of there.

"Hey," Cecilia said, before coming over to stand next to Felicia. The woman jumped forward, her arms wrapping around Cecilia, hugging her tightly. "Hey," Cecilia said again, as she hugged the woman back. "Everything is fine. You're safe now. Logan will get the help that he needs."

"Help?" she asked. There was a hint of a sniffle in that word, though Cecilia couldn't tell if that was from humor or tears. "He should go to prison for the rest of his life. You hear me in there? I want you locked up."

"You don't mean that, babe," Logan called out, sounding closer than he should have.

Cecilia moved aside, pulling Felicia out of the way of the cops as they headed outside, dragging Logan with them. He was struggling against their grip, moving toward Felicia as he came up to her. But the handcuffs and the strong grips of the cops on his arms kept him from moving in their direction.

"I love you, babe, and I know you love me too. Please, tell me you love me," Logan said.

"I despise you with every inch of my being," Felicia yelled back at him. Cecilia felt like she was more holding her back than comforting her at that point, with Felicia pushing against her, desperate to get at Logan.

"Despise is a strong emotion," Logan said. "Just like love. I'll see you soon, babe."

"Ugh," Felicia grunted, waving a hand dismissively at the man as she shook her head in annoyance. "I'm never going to get rid of him, am I."

"Of course, you will," Cecilia said. "You get a restraining order, and he'll go to prison. And if you need me to come back here and kick his ass, I will totally do it, too."

"Ha, right," Felicia said, laughing. "No, but... Thank you. I... I didn't know what you were trying to do in there, but... Well, I guess it worked."

"Of course, it worked," Cecilia said, trying to put on more bravado than she felt. Trying to sound like Drilora at zer braggiest. "It was a perfect plan, and it worked flawlessly."

"Uh huh," Felicia said.

Before either of them could say anything further, a woman came up to them and introduced herself as the social worker on the case. Cecilia left Felicia in her capable hands.

"Not bad, kid," the cop from earlier said, as he came out of the apartment. With the incident over, he was pulling his vest off, and Cecilia saw his nametag for the first time. The name Barnett sounded familiar to her, though it was a common enough name for the city. "Let me walk you out," he said, nodding toward the stairs. Cecilia just nodded at him, smiling a little, as they headed off.

Not much had changed while Cecilia was inside the building, though Leanne's car was no longer parked nearby. Automatically, Cecilia looked up to Drilora on the roof across from her. Ze was still standing there, looking down at her, but ze was too far away for her to make out anything of zer expression. To see how ze was feeling about the whole thing. About her first solo mission going off without a hitch.

"Anyway, thanks for your work in there," Barnett said, reaching his hand over to her to shake. "I don't think that would have gone down as smoothly without you."

"Thanks," Cecilia said, smiling as she shook the man's hand. "That was certainly an interesting experience. It was my first solo mission."

"Really? I couldn't tell. You certainly don't look the part, but you're an excellent superhero. Probably a better one than that alien. Oh... Uh... Don't-don't tell it I said that, will you? I don't want it going after me."

"Don't worry," Cecilia said, though her eyes flicked up toward where Drilora had been a moment ago, figuring that the alien could hear him just fine. However, there was no sign of zer up there anymore. Cecilia wasn't sure if ze had stepped away from the ledge, letting her take the victory with the cops by herself, or if ze had started on his trip back to the tower. "I don't think ze'll be interested in going after you, even if I told zer."

"Oh?" he asked, sounding surprised by that. "Well, good, I guess. Anyway. Take care."

"You, too," Cecilia said, looking back at him just long enough to smile his way.

Cecilia stood there a moment longer, just looking around at the cops as they started clearing away. After the previous missions, Drilora had just taken off, not bothering to wait around for anyone to ask zer questions. But then, no one would have thought to stop zer, either. As she looked around her, she wondered if anyone would be asking her questions. If anyone was going to try to debrief her. The cops were all preoccupied with their own jobs, though. The only one that seemed to show any interest in her at all were the reporters across the street.

Once the cops started to clear out, dropping the perimeter, the reporters moved forward. At first, it looked like they wanted to interview Cecilia. But once they got a proper look at her, Cecilia's superpower seemed to hit them. She could practically see it coming over them, the point when they lost interest in her, thinking that she couldn't have had anything to do with what happened in there. That she wouldn't have been worth interviewing anyway.

A car horn honked off to the side, pulling Cecilia's attention away from the reporters. Leanne was just pulling up to the edge of where the perimeter had been, though she didn't pull through it. She turned, like the cops were still there directing traffic away from the building.

"Hey, superhero," Leanne called out through her window. "Come on. I'll drive you back to the tower."

Cecilia stood there for a moment, looking between Leanne and the reporters. Part of her wanted to rush over to the reporters, tell them everything that happened in there. But that wasn't how she was raised. She was told to stay in the background, not to draw attention to herself. With her superpower, that was easy enough to do.

"Yeah, thanks," Cecilia said, finally turning away from those reporters. Away from the fame that she knew would come soon enough, once people started to hear about her own missions. Once she managed to get out from Drilora's shadow.

"So, from what I've heard so far, sounds like everything worked out great," Leanne said, as she pulled away from the scene. "Better than anything that Drilora would have been able to do."

"I guess," Cecilia said, hesitantly. "Ze was there, but ze never came down from the roof across the street."

"Well, it sounds like you didn't need the help. Ze wasn't invited, anyway. You know Dril well enough by now to know that ze doesn't like the limelight. Maybe you do? I could call a press conference or something if you'd like. Get started on getting you those sponsorships and all."

"No, that's alright," Cecilia said, shaking her head. "I don't... I don't think I'm quite ready for all of that."

"Oh?" Leanne said. "Am I sensing some hesitance here? Are you starting to underestimate yourself?"

"It doesn't work that way. Or it hasn't for a while, anyway. I think... Well, growing up with this power, I think I believed people's assessment of me for longer than I should have. But when everyone around you tells you that you can't do anything, you tend to believe them. This? This was huge for me. Thank you so much for setting this up."

"Hey, it's what I'm here for," Leanne said. "It's my job, and I love what I do."

"But... Well... Don't-don't tell Drilora this, but... Well, there was a moment in there that I could have ended the whole thing sooner. With a little more training from Drilora, I could be a better superhero. As much as I loved my solo mission back there, I... I'm not quite ready to go solo full time."

"Good," Leanne said, nodding. "You're not about to pull in a Dril level of money just yet, so you're not going to afford your own tower. Or whatever your fortress of solitude is going to be. The longer you spend training with Dril, the better. And as much as ze doesn't like to admit it, Dril isn't going anywhere anytime soon."

"Right," Cecilia said, nodding her understanding. "Not unless the Earth for Humans people get their way. Any news on that battery?"

"Nothing yet, but I don't expect anything for a few days," Leanne said. "These things take time. Once I have something, I'll bring it to both of you. With this success under your belt, it might be better if you track down who's behind it all, rather than Dril. Ze would likely go in there swinging and get zerself killed in the process."

"Maybe," Cecilia said, shrugging.

Everything seemed normal as they came up the driveway toward the tower. Even with Drilora having a head start on the trip back, Cecilia still expected to see zer jumping across the park as they came up to the parking lot. But the tower was quiet as they hopped out of the car, making it feel exactly like the first day that she had come there. Like she wasn't coming back from her first successful solo mission, but rather coming there for the first time, begging to stay.

When Cecilia noticed Leanne hopping out of the car with her, she gave her a questioning look. Leanne just shrugged at her before saying, "I have to talk some things over with Dril. Now that both of you will be doing missions, together or separately, we'll need to come up with some kind of system. Like if you're getting a solo mission, should I just call you, or would ze want to hear about it, too? You not having your own phone at the moment makes that difficult, too."

"Oh, right," Cecilia said.

Leanne quickly swept past Cecilia as they headed for the door, looking like she was all but running for the tower ahead of her. Rather than ringing the bell like she usually did, Leanne barged forward, slipping through the door. Cecilia skipped forward a step, almost feeling like Leanne was about to slam the door in her face. And when she came inside, she suddenly realized why Leanne had been in a hurry.

"Surprise," Jeri called out.

Jeri, Lindsey, and Drilora were all standing in front of the spaceships, with Jeri and Lindsey holding their hands above their heads. There were a few decorations hanging up around the room, though most of it seemed hastily put in place while they were out. Cecilia wondered if they had been putting that up while she was on the mission, or if they had started when she left the apartment building. Either way, it was the first time in a long time that someone had put that kind of effort in place to celebrate something that Cecilia had done.

Chapter Thirty-Six
Bitterness
Drilora

Drilora spent the entire time that Cecilia was inside the building on the roof across the street, watching and waiting for signs that she needed zer help. It had only been a couple of days since Cecilia came to live with Drilora, and there was nothing that ze had seen during that time that made zer think she was ready for any of it. Not to stand by and watch Drilora work, let alone do the work herself. And yet, she was in there, doing just that.

Nothing seemed right to Drilora from the very beginning. From the moment that Cecilia showed up at the building, the humans seemed different. Ze had been working with these same humans for five of their years, and they had never gotten used to zer. They had never gone past their bitter, reluctant acceptance of zer help. And yet, the officers at the door barely gave Cecilia a second glance before waving her inside.

Ze heard the officer telling Cecilia the floor number, and ze spent the next few minutes looking around at that floor. There were three windows with the blinds pulled, and ze figured that one of them was where everything was going down. Ze spotted some snipers set up on the next building over, all with rifles pointed at one of those windows, which seemed to confirm that guess. It meant that ze wouldn't be able to see anything of what was going on in there. That ze wouldn't be able to come to her rescue if Cecilia needed it.

As ze waited, Drilora realized something. Ze actually cared if Cecilia got hurt in there. Part of it was a feeling of responsibility, knowing that ze had trained her and had made it so that she could get missions like that. However, ze knew that wasn't everything. That ze actually cared about Cecilia as a friend.

And perhaps as more.

Every minute that passed with Cecilia in there, Drilora got more nervous. More worried that something had happened. That Cecilia was going to be pulled out of there in a body bag. And when the blinds were suddenly being pressed against the window in that apartment, ze thought for sure that this was it. That Cecilia was being attacked. It was all that Drilora could do not to jump across that road and into that window.

"Bull in a china shop," Drilora muttered to zerself, those words from earlier staying zer movement. Keeping zer standing on that rooftop and not rushing after Cecilia. Fortunately, just a few minutes later, ze spotted Cecilia coming back out of the building, alive and well.

"Anyway, thanks for your work in there," one of the cops said, his voice easily reaching Drilora from across the street. The man reached out a hand, shaking Cecilia's, before heading off with the rest of the cops that were clearing away from the area.

"Thanks for your work?" Drilora muttered to zerself. In the five years that ze had been working with these humans, not one of them had thanked zer. At least, no one besides Leanne, and she didn't really count. Not in the same way.

Drilora bristled as ze stared down at Cecilia below zer. There were several reporters out there as well, and they all looked at Cecilia with interest. For a moment, it looked like they were going to go over to her, trying to interview Cecilia. Interview the supposed hero in the saga. However, they stopped just halfway across the street, seeming to think better of that.

"Yeah," Drilora muttered. "Can't have the truth from the person that actually did the work." Ze knew all too well how those same reporters were likely to spin the whole thing, to make it seem like Cecilia hadn't done anything important there. But then, ze realized that they probably didn't think Cecilia had done anything at all. That she was just there, not involved in the encounter. Ze realized that the reporters had underestimated Cecilia, just like everyone else in her life had.

Just like Drilora had been doing.

Drilora looked back down at Cecilia, momentarily wondering if she would need a ride back to the tower. However, ze quickly spotted Leanne's car heading back up the road. With the mission over and Cecilia having an easier trip home, Drilora turned away from that other building, heading off across the rooftops.

It all seemed inside out to Drilora. Ze was easily the more accomplished hero of the two, the one that had pulled off more saves, the bigger saves. And yet, Cecilia was thanked, was seen as the hero. Halfway back across the city, Drilora realized why that was. Ze realized that Cecilia was human and was being treated well because of that. That the humans didn't fear her or what she was capable of, worry that she was going to hurt anyone, accidentally or otherwise. Cecilia was considered safe, not because of her so-called power, but because of the simple fact that she was already one of them.

And Drilora never would be.

By the time Drilora made it back to the tower, ze was quite bitter about the whole thing. About the unfairness that was systematic in the culture there on Earth. More than ever before, ze wanted to be out of there, to get one of the ships working again so that ze could just head home already.

When Drilora slipped through the trap door, ze heard something deeper in the tower. Immediately, ze thought the worst. Thought that the humans had spotted zer heading over the rooftops and just assumed the tower was unprotected. Ze was feeling miserable enough already, and ze wasn't about to put up with the humans infringing upon zer solitude. So, ze was quick to rush down the stairs, or as quick as ze ever was sliding down that stairwell, stuck slowly floating down them because of the horrible Terran gravity. That felt like the planet itself conspiring with the humans against zer.

The noise was coming from the ground floor, but Drilora paused at each floor along the way, searching for the trespassers. Ze kept expecting to see people poking through zer stuff. However, once ze made it past the gym, ze spotted the two women hanging decorations around the garage.

"What is the meaning of this?" Drilora shouted, zer voice booming around the room.

"See? I told you ze would be mad," one of the women said to the other. "Sorry, Drilora. I'm Jeri. We work with Leanne. We wanted to surprise Cecilia with a celebration, and we needed to get the decorations up before she got here. Leanne was going to delay the return, but we only had so much time before Cecilia realized something was going on. Don't worry; we'll clean it up afterwards. You don't have to do a thing."

"You don't even have to attend, if you don't want to," the other woman muttered, her focus still on the banner that they were hanging.

Drilora grumbled to zerself as ze slowly came the rest of the way down into the garage. There was plenty of stuff that ze would rather be doing at that moment than celebrating such a small achievement as Cecilia's first solo mission. However, ze really did want to see Cecilia. To congratulate her on not being completely useless like ze had been thinking she would be. Reluctantly, ze headed over next to zer computer, zer arms crossed as ze stared around at the decorations, all of which were quite in the way of zer work down there. Fortunately, neither of the women asked Drilora to help out, so that ze didn't have to tell them off.

After all, no one had ever thrown a party for Drilora.

Before the women could finish decorating, the doors to the tower opened. Drilora glanced over there, unsurprised to see Cecilia there, heading in after Leanne. The women both dropped what they were doing before rushing back over to stand next to Drilora.

"Surprise," Jeri called out, her arms going wide and almost hitting Drilora in the process.

The three women started congratulating Cecilia, and again it was feeling like it had back at the apartment building. That the humans were celebrating the human and would be better off without zer infringing on the whole thing. Never mind that it was zer tower. Never mind that ze had plenty of work to do right there, like making sure that no one had video of zer waiting outside of the apartment building. However, as one of the humans started up the music, Drilora figured that the one thing that ze could do while the humans were doing their own thing was head up to get zer workout in.

And yet, with how much they were celebrating such a mediocre achievement, Drilora almost thought that ze shouldn't bother. The humans had their own hero, finally, and it wasn't like ze was any closer to getting the stupid ships fixed. If ze was stuck on Earth, what was the point in maintaining zer muscle and bone mass?

Ze spent the entire workout watching the humans on the surveillance system, making sure that they kept to the garage and outside. Even having them among the ships was more than Drilora wanted to allow, but they fortunately headed outside soon after the party started. And yet, the one thing that ze was feeling the entire time, watching those humans from afar, was a desire to join them. Not join them as ze was, but as a stupid, ugly, stinky human.

"Can't get back to my own people," Drilora muttered to zerself, in Uvvelian as usual. "Can't be one of them. All I am is the stupid monster, stuck in the tower, wishing for something more."

Only Drilora wasn't sure what that something more would have been, nor whether or not ze wanted that something more with Cecilia.

Chapter Thirty-Seven
Celebration
Cecilia

"Congratulations, Cecilia," Leanne said. She reached over, wrapping her arm around Cecilia's shoulders to pull her into a side hug. "Really, this was amazing. I don't think any of us expected you to pull this off so well, so early on in your training. Oh... Uh... Sorry."

"It's fine," Cecilia said, shrugging as she pulled away from the hug. "It's... Well, I'm used to it. My superpower, and all that."

"Right, right," Leanne said, nodding.

"Hey, Cici," Jeri said, as she and Lindsey came over to join them. Cecilia never liked that nickname, but she didn't say anything about it. "Sorry we couldn't put a better party together on such short notice and all."

"It's fine," Cecilia said. "I know you guys weren't expecting success. This... This is great. Really."

As the three of them surrounded Cecilia, talking about the mission and what it would likely bring down the road, Cecilia looked over at Drilora. Ze was standing over by the spaceships, zer arms crossed over zer chest. She could tell that something was going on with zer, though she wasn't sure what that was. If ze was somehow jealous of her one victory, when ze already had so many others.

"I just wish that we could have gotten in touch with your dad," Leanne said, seemingly out of nowhere.

"Huh?" Cecilia asked, looking back at her.

"Well, I think he would be proud of what you managed to accomplish here," she said. "He should be here celebrating your victory with you. But we still don't have word on where he disappeared to."

"Oh, I wouldn't worry too much about Dad," Cecilia said, waving off her concern. "I'm sure he's fine, just busy... Uh... Wherever he is."

From the looks on the women's faces, Cecilia realized that she said something that she probably shouldn't have. That she hadn't shown the right level of concern for her father. She worried that they might read too much into that, notice something that she hadn't wanted them to. That she hadn't meant to suggest. Her mind struggled to come up with something to say to back that off, but she couldn't think of anything.

"Well, he is an adult," Leanne said, seeming to fill in that excuse where Cecilia couldn't.

"Right," Jerri said, nodding her own agreement. "And, seriously, if my dad just dumped me on someone's doorstep and left me there, never to be heard from again, I'd stop caring about him, too."

"I don't... It's not..." Cecilia started. "I just don't want to think about Dad right now."

"Say no more," Leanne said. "Your father doesn't exist at this party. Speaking of parties, let's get this one started, yeah? Where's the music?"

Cecilia let out a relieved laugh as Leanne thankfully dropped the subject. Jerri pulled out her phone, placing it on the table next to the weird gun. Cecilia could hear music playing from the phone, just loud enough to be heard at first before Jerri cranked it up enough to fill the garage. Jerri and Lindsey started to dance together to the music, but Cecilia just went over to stand against the wall next to the table. She had always been a wallflower at the few dances that she had gone to.

As she stood there, listening to the music and watching the others dance, Cecilia saw Drilora heading out of the room. Ze barely looked back at her as ze went up the stairs to the gym above. With how much ze needed to work out to maintain zer muscle and bone mass, Cecilia just figured that ze was heading up to do that. That the music and sounds of revelry would reach zer up there, so ze wasn't entirely missing out on the celebration.

"Everything alright with you?" Leanne asked, as she came over to stand next to Cecilia.

"Huh?" Cecilia asked, turning away from Drilora's fading form to look back at her. "Oh, yeah, it's fine. I just... I think it's still all just sinking in. I mean... I'm a superhero now. A proper one."

"The first real superhero that Earth has ever had," Jerri called out. Lindsey gave a cheer to that, raising her hand like she was toasting with a drink that wasn't there.

"Drinks," Leanne said, her hand going to her forehead. "Wait-wait here. I forgot the drinks in the car."

Cecilia stayed against the wall, watching as Leanne headed back over to the door. The door stayed open as she headed out toward the car, but the wall blocked Cecilia's view of her. Once Leanne disappeared around the corner, Cecilia turned back to Jerri and Lindsey.

"When did she have time to get drinks?" Cecilia asked. "We didn't stop on the way back from the mission."

"I think she was getting them while you were in there," Jerri said. "The moment that you went inside, she called us up and told us to get over here to set up for the party. If I had gotten more notice, I would have done a better job of it. Maybe get it catered, at least. Some proper decorations. We just hit a Party Town on the way over."

"We probably would have booked a venue, too," Lindsey added. "We can't very well invite press to the tower, and Drilora wasn't all that excited to celebrate. Ze practically bit our heads off when we showed up like this." She laughed a little, like it was an exaggeration, though Cecilia knew that it likely wasn't. That Drilora probably hated having them in the tower like that.

With that thought on her mind, Cecilia glanced back over to the stairs, wondering if that was the real reason why Drilora had left. That ze was hiding out from the party that ze didn't want in the tower. Seeing as how ze still didn't want her in the tower either, Cecilia figured that it would be better to move the party elsewhere. To let Drilora have at least some of zer privacy back.

"Hey, why don't we move this party outside?" Cecilia asked. She reached over to pick up Jerri's phone, handing it to her. "We have that whole, big park outside that no one ever uses anymore. It's a sunny, beautiful day out today. Who needs hastily bought decorations when we're surrounded by nature."

"Absolutely," Jerri said, nodding her agreement as she took her phone back. She just smiled over at Cecilia before heading for the door, Lindsey right behind her. Cecilia stood there for a moment longer, unsure if they sensed the real reason why she wanted to move the party, or if they were just agreeing with her because it was supposed to be her party.

Leanne was still heading back from the car when the three of them headed outside. She had a bottle of wine in one hand, and a large box of beer tucked under her other arm. There was no sign of any non-alcoholic beverages.

"Come on," Jerri said, as she grabbed the wine from Leanne. "We're moving the party outside."

"Woot," Lindsey called out.

"Everything alright?" Leanne asked, as Cecilia came up to her.

"Fine," Cecilia said, not mentioning any of the dozens of thoughts that were swirling around in her head at that moment.

Jerri led the group past the parking lot and over to the other side of the park. The trees between the park and the city came up into their view, blocking out the sight of the buildings and making it seem like they really were out in nature. With the park being as empty as it usually was, they had the entire place to themselves. The music from Jerri's phone was loud enough for them all to hear, though it wasn't quite loud enough to fill the entire area.

Cecilia glanced over her shoulder, back toward the tower. They were far enough away that the music wouldn't be pumped through there. Suddenly, she was having second thoughts about moving the party. Of leaving Drilora out of the celebration. It was one thing if ze had left because ze didn't want to be a part of it, but quite another if ze wanted to just be on the fringes of it. A wallflower, like Cecilia was, only not against the wall itself.

"Here," Leanne said. She tapped something against Cecilia's arm, pulling her attention back away from Drilora. When Cecilia looked back, she noticed the beer can that Leann was offering her.

"Oh, uh, no thanks," Cecilia said, waving her hand at the offered can. "I'm underage."

"Oh, right," Leanne said, sounding like she really had forgotten that. "Wow. How did I miss that? Of course, you're... Well, after what you accomplished today, I think you've earned one if you want." Despite her words, she placed the can back into the box, sitting on the ground between them.

"That's right," Jerri called out, pointing toward Cecilia with one hand as she took a swing from the wine bottle in her other one. "The first superhero this planet has ever seen and she's only a teenager. Now that is quite the success, right?"

"Except, well... Drilora really is still the first superhero, right?" Cecilia asked. She felt like they were just ignoring Drilora in everything, ignoring zer contribution to her success that day.

"Drilora never thought of zerself as a superhero," Leanne said. "What ze does is just natural to zer species. You... Well, you go above and beyond what most humans can do. That's special, Cecilia. Something to be celebrated."

"Hear, hear," Jerri called out, before taking another swig from the wine.

"Alright, that's enough for you," Lindsey said. She reached out to grab the wine bottle from Jerri, though she took her own sip once she got it away from her.

"Hey, if you want to go do something else, somewhere else, we can do that, too," Leanne said. "This is your celebration, after all. We can go back to your old neighborhood. See if we can find some of your old friends."

"No, this is fine," Cecilia said, shaking her head. "My old friends have probably all moved on by now. My life is here, at least for the rest of the week. Beyond that... Well, I don't know beyond that."

"Ah hah," Leanne called out, like she thought she had struck upon something. "That's where this mood is coming from. You're just worried about what comes next. Well, don't you worry about that. By the time Dril is kicking you out of the tower, we'll have something set up for you. Besides, now that you're a superhero in your own right, maybe Dril will see you as something more than just an interloper. You'll see. Week's end, you might not be going anywhere."

"Sure," Cecilia said, nodding her agreement, though she didn't quite feel like that was the case. She still felt like Drilora wouldn't see her as anything more than a scared little girl, out on her own for the first time, and never as what she could be with the right training.

As the others continued to celebrate Cecilia's victory, she kept looking back over her shoulder at the tower behind her, trying to see Drilora back there. Trying to see her future coming for her.

Chapter Thirty-Eight
The Future

The party ran right up until dusk, when Jerri and Lindsey had to head off to get more work done. Cecilia stayed out a bit longer, watching the sunset until the sun dropped behind the trees in the distance. Leanne spent that time cleaning up the few beer cans that littered the ground and collecting what was left of the pizzas that they ordered at lunch. Once the park was back to its normal state, the two of them started to head back over to the tower together.

"Well, I'll be reaching out first thing in the morning," Leanne said. "Like I said earlier, plenty of things to arrange with Dril, now that the both of you will be taking missions. At least, while you're still living in the tower. But we can talk over all of that in the morning. You have a nice night, yeah?"

"Yeah, thanks, Leanne," Cecilia said. "Take care. Drive safe, and all that."

Leanne just nodded to Cecilia before heading for her car. Cecilia waited next to the parking lot, watching Leanne heading off into the night. She seemed sober enough to drive at that point, and her car was steady as it headed down the driveway toward the city. Once the car was out of view, disappearing into the deepening night, Cecilia headed back toward the tower.

"About time you showed up," Drilora said, once Cecilia came inside. She jumped a little at zer voice, spinning around to look back at zer. Drilora was standing on the stairs, glaring down at Cecilia with zer arms crossed. "You completely missed your training for today."

"Ugh," Cecilia groaned at the mention of training. "I'll..."

She was about to suggest that she do double the training the next day, when she remembered that one training session was more than her body could handle most of the time. But it was still early, and she figured that she could get some of it in that evening. However, with her uniform still new, and having worn it for most of the day, she shifted her comment.

"...change and get at least some of it done tonight," she finished. "Don't you celebrate things on Uvvelia? My first solo mission. Successful, solo mission."

"Yes, yes, we're all impressed," Drilora said. "I guess that means that you don't need me anymore, right? That you'll be moving on soon enough?"

Cecilia just stood there quietly for a moment, digesting the questions. Trying to guess if Drilora was kicking her out or just seeing if she wanted to leave. But she already knew that leaving that tower so soon wasn't an option, for so many reasons.

"I... I still need you, Drilora," Cecilia said. "Of course, I need your training. Today was... It was the perfect mission for my first time out. Exactly what I had been saying I could do since I arrived here. It wasn't fighting or rushing into a burning building or shrugging off bullets like they're nothing. Well... I don't think I'll ever be able to do that last one, but... But I still need you to teach me how to fight. How to cover so many types of missions that don't involve people underestimating me. That was the whole reason why I came to you in the first place."

"No, the whole reason why you came to me was because your father wanted to pawn you off on someone else," Drilora snapped. Ze came down the stairs slowly, looming over Cecilia. "I wouldn't be surprised if he tried it on several other people before coming to my doorstep. Life debt, bah."

"No, that..." Cecilia started. She wanted to defend her father. But given his disappearance, and her own feelings of abandonment about the man, she couldn't help but agree with zer on part of that. She just didn't like zer anger directed at her. "I wanted to come here," she said. "I wanted to be a superhero. And, yeah, that life debt thing was mostly an excuse. Dad didn't think you would agree to it any other way."

"Oh," Drilora said, most of zer bluster dispelled by Cecilia agreeing with zer. "Well... I have heard of such things before you came here. And... And I must admit, your assistance on the roof the other night very much fulfilled that debt."

"Huh?" Cecilia asked.

They hadn't discussed the life debt since the incident on the roof. But when Drilora said that, Cecilia knew that ze was right. That she really had saved zer life, the way that ze had saved hers. If that had been the only reason why she was in the tower to begin with, she would have already returned home. However, there had been plenty of other reasons for her to be there. Reasons that were still in play.

"But... I mean, you're-you're not going to kick me out of here, are you?" Cecilia asked. That was her biggest fear at that point. That Drilora would just chase her off, get rid of her before she was ready to stand on her own. Especially without her father's help.

"Well..." Drilora said, seeming to actually think about it for a moment. "No, I guess not," ze said, shaking zer head. "I agreed that you could stay for the week, and I'll stick to that."

"Just the week?" Cecilia asked. While that was what they had agreed to originally, it didn't seem nearly long enough for her to learn everything that she needed to learn from Drilora. There was plenty of training that she would need in order to be able to do what Drilora could. To fill in for zer once ze got one of the spaceships working again.

If ze got it working. If ze ever managed to leave the planet.

"You're not going to be squatting in my tower for the rest of your life," Drilora said, a low growl coming out with zer voice. "I'm sure that Leanne will find you something more appropriate soon enough."

"That's not... I mean, yes, I don't want to be out on the street, but... Well, what-what about you training me? I just... I know that I have so much to learn from you."

"Well, yes, obviously," Drilora said, a smile starting to form on zer face. "But... Well, you can get your training here without needing to live here. Plus, as I said, I would find you a better trainer in the city. A human trainer. One that specializes on a fighting style that suits you. I still feel that is the better approach, over you coming here every day. You're not that great at the training that I can provide to you, because... Well, because you're not an uvvelian. You'll never be an uvvelian, despite... Well, anyway."

Ze went silent, shaking zer head like ze wanted to say something but decided against it. From how ze clammed up, Cecilia had a feeling that it was something embarrassing. Something that ze didn't want to admit to thinking. She wasn't about to pry, to risk giving zer another reason to chase her off.

"Right," Cecilia said, nodding her agreement. After all, it was nothing more than she had been expecting. Drilora just wanted the human gone so that ze could get zer space back. "But... But you're not going to kick me out before Leanne finds better arrangements for me? And you're not going to stop training me until you find me a better teacher?"

"Sure," Drilora said. "I can agree to that."

"What about the rest of it?" Cecilia asked.

"What rest of it? Isn't that enough?"

"I mean the rest of the training," Cecilia said. "Yes, I need to learn how to fight, in a way that's better for me, but... Well, there are other things about being a superhero that I still need to learn. Things that you can still teach me."

"Again, I'm not a--"

"Not a superhero, I know," Cecilia said. "Except, you're still a hero. People consider Batman and Batgirl superheroes, despite not having powers. You might not have powers for an uvvelian, but you're still stronger and faster than any human. And you've been doing this work for far longer than I have. When are you going to teach me about all of that?"

"Well, that had been on the schedule for today," Drilora said, surprising Cecilia. "I have all the recordings from my previous missions. The... What do you humans call it? The CCTV footage? I was going to start taking you through all of that, before your day got taken up by all this nonsense. First successful solo mission or not, you still need to put in the work if you want your next solo mission to be a success. If you even have another one."

"Oh," Cecilia said. "Wait, was that... Was that why you were so upset earlier?"

"I don't get upset," Drilora said, the growl coming back to zer voice, showing that ze was quite upset indeed.

"Alright," Cecilia said. "Of course, you don't get upset. It's just... Well, I thought that you might have been feeling like we invaded your space, which was why we took the party outside. But if you were feeling left out... I mean, I know you had your workout to do, but I wasn't sure if the party was disturbing you or not. You could have come out to join us if you wanted."

"I had more important things to do today," Drilora said, pointedly. "As did you. Speaking of which, you should get to it, if you're going to be doing anything. Plenty of that pizza to burn off."

"Yes, Drilora," Cecilia said, snapping to attention and saluting zer. Though her smile quickly found its way onto her face.

Cecilia slipped past Drilora, starting up the stairs. Halfway up the first flight, she thought she realized why Drilora was so upset about everything. She turned around to look back at zer.

"If you do need to talk about anything, I hope you know that I'm here for you," she said. "Whatever it is."

"Ha," Drilora said. "You're only a human. What could you possibly understand about anything that might be bothering me? I'm an uvvelian, and quite above the concerns of the people of this planet."

"You might be surprised," Cecilia said. "I know that you probably feel lonely, stuck here on Earth, surrounded by us humans. But you're not as alone as you might think. Like I said, you could have joined the party. We could celebrate your next mission, if you want. Celebrate it in whatever way you want to. Just think about it, alright? As long as you're stuck here, as long as you're stuck with me... Well, you have me for as long as you want me, in whatever way you want."

Cecilia suddenly realized that her words might have been misconstrued the way that she said them and blushed deeply. She turned away from Drilora, hoping that ze wouldn't have seen it. But the uvvelian just shook zer head, waving her off toward the higher levels of the tower.

"Go up and change before I have you doing a double training session today," ze said.

Chapter Thirty-Nine
Results

Over the next few days, Cecilia and Drilora settled into more of a routine in the tower. After that first evening physical training, that became the new norm. Mornings were taken up by Drilora working out in the gym while Cecilia watched the old missions in the library. On occasion, she would come down to ask zer questions on it, but mostly she left zer to zer peace in the gym as ze had asked for.

However, it soon became clear to Cecilia that Drilora's original request that she clear out of the gym while ze was working out had nothing to do with wanting privacy, and everything to do with her own safety. The equipment that Drilora was using was still designed for human use, rather than uvvelian use, and it didn't hold up all that well. When one of those machines broke down, it could be quite dangerous to anyone that was in the room at the time. This became quite obvious one morning, when the sound of a window breaking could be heard up in the library.

"Sorry," Drilora called up. "Everything's fine."

"What happened?" Cecilia asked. She stayed up in the library, just peeking around the edge of the stairs into the gym below. Drilora was standing next to one of the machines, holding one handle that was no longer attached to the rest of it.

"Damn thing broke again," ze muttered, shaking zer head at the thing. "I don't know why I bother with these stupid machines. No, I do know why; it's because I can't get enough weight on the free weights to work some of my muscle groups. This damn low gravity is going to kill me one day."

Once she was sure that it was safe, Cecilia slowly made her way down the stairs. She came over to stand next to Drilora, the two of them staring at the machine as they tried to figure out how to fix it. Or if it even could be fixed. One of the broken machines from when Cecilia first arrived had been swapped out just the day before, with the technicians hanging around to fix the rest of them. The newly broken machine had been fine at the time.

The two of them stood there, staring at the machine, trying to come up with a fix for it. Not that Cecilia knew much about such things. Before either could come up with anything, the doorbell rang. With her thoughts on the machine in front of them, Cecilia almost thought that it was another technician, coming to replace the machine despite it only just happening. But then, Cecilia heard the door open, marking it as Leanne arriving.

In the days that Cecilia had been in the tower, Leanne was the only regular guest there. The only one that felt comfortable enough around Drilora to barge in like that. Their main, and sometimes only, contact with the outside world. However, unlike how it seemed at first, Leanne didn't come over every day. It seemed like that had only happened because Cecilia was there.

"Hey, guys," Leanne called out, as the two of them headed down the stairs into the garage. Leanne was just inside the door, looking up at them with a huge smile on her face. Normally, Cecilia wouldn't have thought much of that smile; Leanne had always seemed like a happy person to her. But since it was later in the day than her usual visits, almost noon, Cecilia got the sense that there was something more to the visit than normal.

"Do you have another solo mission for me?" Cecilia asked. It was her first guess, with that smile reminding her of the other day. There hadn't been a mission for either of them since the hostage situation with Logan.

"No," Leanne said, her smile disappearing. "Did you want a new mission? I might be able to find something in a different city. Catastrophes don't happen every day, you know."

"That's fine," Cecilia said, shaking her head. "What's up, then?"

"Does something need to be up?" Drilora asked.

The smile came back to Leanne's face, and she seemed to blush a little, looking away from Drilora. But then she pulled a leather binder out of her bag, holding it up in front of her like a prize.

"I come bearing results," she said. "Sorry that it took so long."

"Results?" Cecilia asked, confused.

"Oh, the research," Drilora said. "On the battery materials."

"Exactly," Leanne said, pointing to Drilora. "I was able to track it down to the manufacturer, which was surprisingly hard to do without a label on the battery itself."

"Yes, yes, you're quite amazing," Drilora said. Ze held out zer hand toward Leanne, silently asking for the binder, which she happily handed over.

"Then how do you know you found the right manufacturer without a label to confirm it?" Cecilia asked.

"Because there are only two manufacturers that are working with potassium ion batteries," Leanne said. "One of them only works with larger batteries, for use in electric vehicles, while the other, Potion Industries, is the one that created the battery we're looking for. At least, I think it's Potion Industries. It might be Pot-Ion Industries, a play on what they make."

"That's great," Drilora said, as ze flipped through the papers in the folder. "So, you know how many of these guns are out there? Who ordered them?"

"Well, the who part was easy," Leanne said. "It's our Rene Marks, the unknown leader of Earth for Humans. Jerri managed to get into Potion Industry's system and pull an old invoice. It's probably for the prototype, as it was from a couple of weeks ago. As for the number, that's where we hit a snag. The info we got from their system suggests that they're starting to mass produce those batteries, but before we could get anything more, they kicked us out of their system. Their security has been beefed up since, and we're not getting back in there. You'd have to go on-site for more info on all that."

"Ooh, breaking in," Drilora said. Zer eye seemed to light up at the prospect of it, though that might have just been a trick of the light. "It's been a while since I've done that."

"I didn't hear that," Leanne said, putting her hands over her ears.

"I said--" Drilora started, speaking louder.

"Do we need to know how many there are, though?" Cecilia asked. "The fact that they're mass producing these things is bad enough, isn't it?"

"Which is why I'm here this morning, and not trying to get more information on all of this," Leanne said. "I held off a little to get more details, not wanting Dril to... Well, to try to break into their factory." She waved her hand over at Drilora, drawing attention to the fact that that had been zer plan just a moment ago.

"It's more important that we find out where the batteries are going," Cecilia said, nodding her head. "That would be where the guns are being manufactured."

"Or, better yet, where Rene Marks is hiding," Drilora said. "Nothing like biting the head off the snake to take down a dangerous organization."

"Do they have snakes on Uvvelia?" Leanne asked.

"Wait, snakes are real?" Drilora asked. "I thought that was just an expression."

"Weren't there any snakes in those comic books you keep reading?" Cecilia asked. While she had read through the Batgirl series, and a few other female led series that Drilora suggested for her, Cecilia hadn't gotten through nearly as many as Drilora read during zer time in the tower.

"Comic books aren't real, Cecilia," Drilora said, like ze was talking to a child.

"Yes, but snakes are," Cecilia said in the same tone.

"Anyway, we do have the address on the original invoice," Leanne said. She reached into the folder in Drilora's hand, flipping the pages until she came up to the invoice. "It's an old, abandoned factory down by the docks. That was another dead end; no one has been there in years."

"Maybe not on paper, but that's where most of the criminal enterprises set up shop," Drilora said.

"Sure, in comic books," Cecilia added. "Didn't we just go over all of that?"

"I sent Sargent Barnett from the hostage situation down to check it out," Leanne said. "He seemed eager to help the cause the other day, so I reached out to him."

"Eager to help Cecilia, maybe," Drilora muttered, zer earlier bitterness coming to his voice.

"The place was as cleared out as it is on paper," Leanne said. "The one lead that I haven't been able to follow up on is where the first shipment of batteries is going to go. From what little we got from Potion Industries's system before we got cut off, it looks like that shipment is going out tomorrow night. I'm thinking that Dril could stake out the factory, follow the truck when it goes off."

"That... sounds sensible," Drilora said. Ze sounded almost disappointed by the plan, or by the fact that ze couldn't come up with a more dangerous one. "What about the money? Can we track that back to Rene Marks?"

"The first unit was bought in cash," Leanne said, shaking her head. "If they paid for the new shipment, it wasn't anywhere in the system."

"Well, alright, then," Drilora said. "It sounds like we have a plan. And it fits perfectly within our own schedule for the next few days."

"Huh?" Cecilia asked. She didn't think they had a schedule, beyond their normal training activities. "What are you talking about?"

"I'm talking about the fact that tonight is a special occasion," Drilora said.

Cecilia thought about that for a moment, struggling to think what Drilora could be talking about. She knew that it wasn't Drilora's anniversary; the anniversary of the crash was three months earlier. It wasn't her birthday, though it could have been Leanne's or Drilora's for all she knew. Drilora seemed to sense her confusion, as ze soon explained.

"It's the end of your first week here," ze said. "The time when we all agreed that you'd be moving on. We already know that jiu jitsu is the best fighting style for your form, and there's a few dojos in the city for it. And..." Ze trailed off, turning to look at Leanne.

"And we have an apartment available for you in the city," Leanne said. "I'm still working to line you up a day job to fill in some of the costs that your missions won't cover, one that will allow you to cut out at a moment's notice. Those aren't easy to come by when you have no work experience.

Short of joining the police force, or something similar, which all requires you to be eighteen, it's mostly service industry placements and gig apps."

"Oh," Cecilia said. "Well, I guess it was only a matter of time before this all happened, I guess. I just... Well, I thought things were going alright around here. We were getting in a nice groove, not getting in each other's way. Wouldn't it be cheaper for me to stay here? Just for a bit longer, anyway."

"I would have thought that you would be eager to be out on your own," Drilora said. "Not stuck with the creature for the rest of your life."

It had been a while since Cecilia had thought of Drilora as a creature, and she didn't think that she had called zer that in front of zer before. However, she quickly remembered that she had used that term just outside of the door that first morning she was there. She blushed deeply at the reminder of that.

"I'm sorry that I ever thought of you that way," Cecilia said. "And I don't feel like I'm stuck here. It's been... Well, not exactly great, but..."

"Either way, we should celebrate," Leanne said. "A night out on the town, or something."

"I think we should do 'or something'," Cecilia said. "Something that Drilora would feel comfortable joining in on. I don't want to celebrate without zer again. I wouldn't be where I am now without zer."

"That would be nice," Drilora said, nodding zer agreement.

"Alright," Leanne said. "I'll set something up for tonight. You two, go back to your normal day, and let me handle everything."

Chapter Forty
The Weekaversary

With the pending celebration, Cecilia was hoping that she would be able to get away with not having her training session that evening. Drilora made it clear that she wasn't about to get out of it so easily. Drilora assigned the same workout from the day before, but it didn't leave her nearly as worn out or sore. It made her think that maybe it had more to do with her growing into the role than Drilora being nice. As Cecilia came out of the shower, she was all smiles, feeling refreshed and renewed rather than sore and drained.

"Warning, you're not alone," Leanne called out, as Cecilia opened the bathroom door.

"What?" Cecilia asked. She looked over at Leanne, standing by her bedroom door with her eyes averted. Cecilia clung to the towel that was still wrapped safely around her body, hiding everything sensitive. "Oh, hey, Leanne. I'm mostly decent."

"Ah, good," Leanne said. "Anyway, I came by with another gift." She pointed over at Cecilia's bed.

Cecilia moved forward into the room, coming around the footboard. Laid out on the bed was a yellow dress that looked more formal than she had been expecting the party to be. She carefully reached out to pick up the dress, holding it in front of her as she looked over at Leanne. Leanne was still wearing her suit from earlier, not having changed for the party.

"Uh, what's going on?" Cecilia asked, feeling like she had missed something.

"Hey, do you trust me?" Leanne asked. She reached her hand out to lightly tap Cecilia's arm as she smiled at her. "I have something special planned for tonight, and it requires you to dress up a little."

"Dress up? For a party in the park? Isn't that a bit much?"

"Sometimes, we can use a bit much in our lives," Leanne said. She patted Cecilia's arm a few more times before turning around and heading for the door. "Get dressed. I'll be sending Lindsey in for hair and makeup shortly."

"Hair and makeup?" Cecilia called after her. "Is this a celebration or a..." She trailed off, not sure what it could have been other than what Leanne had suggested.

At first, Cecilia tried to pull the dress over her head, like she usually did with dresses. It took her a bit to realize that it wasn't designed like that. That there was a zipper on the back that was done up, and she needed to unzip that in order to get the dress on. Once she was done fighting with the dress and got it on, the zipper was in too awkward of a place for her to get it up on her own. As she stood there struggling to reach it, the door opened once more.

"Here, let me help," Lindsey said. There was a hint of a laugh in her voice, though she didn't let it out.

"Thanks," Cecilia said, as Lindsey came up behind her, zipping her up.

Once the dress was zipped, Cecilia realized why it was so hard for her to do it on her own. The dress was quite tight, tighter than she was expecting. Tight enough that she thought that it might be the wrong size. But when she turned to look in the mirror, she realized that the dress looked perfect on her, making her look older and more sophisticated than she usually looked.

"Perfect," Lindsey said, looking at Cecilia in the mirror over her shoulder. Cecilia smiled at her in the mirror, at that word that seemed to echo her own thoughts on it. "Now, come over here. Let me handle the rest of you."

"Alright, what's going on?" Cecilia asked, even as she headed over to sit in front of the desk. There was no mirror there, so she couldn't see anything as Lindsey started working on her.

"I am not at liberty to say," Lindsey said. "Leanne threatened to fire me if I hinted at what is planned."

"Oh, this is so silly," Cecilia said. But she didn't fuss, didn't move around or fidget, as Lindsey straightened her hair and did her makeup. Cecilia hadn't bothered with makeup over the years, knowing that no one would care much about such things. It went right up there with all the other side effects of her superpower. No one could see her as anything but a child to be taken care of.

"There," Lindsey said, after what felt like an hour of her working on her. "What do you think?"

"What do I think about what?" Cecilia asked, as she opened her eyes.

Lindsey was holding up a huge mirror, letting Cecilia see her work all at once. Her hair wasn't just straight but done up in a way that showed off her neck and perfectly framed her face. The makeup was subtle in a way, but made her look like an adult for the first time in her life.

"Whoa," Cecilia said, as she stared at herself in the mirror. "What is going on? Why do you have me made up so..."

"Amazingly?" Lindsey asked. "I know. I'm awesome. You don't need to stoke my ego. But, as I said, it's a surprise. Don't worry about it. It'll all make sense soon enough."

"Uh huh," Cecilia said. She wasn't so convinced of that, though. "What about you? Why aren't you all dressed up?" She pointed at Lindsey's outfit, which wasn't far off from what she was wearing the last time that Cecilia had seen her. Not too far off from what Leanne had been wearing before.

"Oh, don't worry about me," Lindsey said, waving off Cecilia's words. "It'll all make sense soon enough."

"So you say," Cecilia said. But the longer she sat there like that, the more it all seemed like a huge trick.

"Just wait here for a bit," Lindsey said. "I need to check if everyone else is ready."

"And get ready yourself?" Cecilia asked.

Lindsey didn't answer as she headed for the door. She lingered over there for just a moment longer, looking back at Cecilia, before heading out into the hall.

Cecilia stayed in her chair for a moment, just staring out that open door into the hall. At first, she thought about running for that door. Going out into the evening to find out just what was going on. But when she stood up from her chair, she noticed movement off to the side. Instantly, she leapt forward, her hands up defensively in front of her, ready to take on any threat. Just as Drilora's training was meant to work. The dress resisted a little, but her legs and arms moved freely. However, it only took her a moment to notice what it was that she had seen.

Her own reflection in the main mirror across from her.

Cecilia stood there, still crouched in her defensive position, as she stared at herself in that mirror. The first time that she got a look at the whole product, not just the dress alone or the makeup and hair. It made her think of her mother in a way, back when her parents would go out for special occasions. She wondered if that was what was happening that night. If the others had thought her weekaversary something special to commemorate, rather than to mourn. To Cecilia, it was just the last night that she would be spending in the tower. The last night for her to accomplish what she had come there to do.

Slowly, Cecilia moved from her defensive stance, walking over to stand in front of the mirror. She just stood there, staring at herself, as she waited for the others to return. As she waited for them to tell her what was going on. She could have rushed outside, could have seen it for herself, but she no longer felt so anxious. No, she felt nervous. Nervous about what they were planning. Nervous about ruining whatever surprise they had put together for her.

"Ready?" Leanne asked, pulling Cecilia's attention away from that mirror and back over to the door. Leanne had changed since she had left earlier, wearing something a little more dressy, though not as formal as Cecilia's dress was. Her own hair was done up, her makeup on point, though it was clear that she hadn't had Lindsey's help. She was holding a pair of wedge shoes in her hands that matched Cecilia's dress, completing the look. They were taller than she would normally wear, but perfect for walking in the grass in.

"Ready for what exactly?" Cecilia asked, as she walked over to her. She took the wedges from her, slipping them on. "What is going on? Is this some kind of trick?"

"I told you, you have to trust me," Leanne said. "Now, come along." She reached out, grabbing onto Cecilia's hand to pull her out through the door.

The hallway looked normal as they came outside, giving Cecilia no hints at what was going on. The window next to the stairs had a blanket over it, blocking her view of the park. That was her first hint that something big was happening out there, rather than them taking her out into the city somewhere. She hoped that that meant that Drilora would be joining in on everything this time. That the uvvelian wouldn't be left out.

"It's a shame that the only way up onto the roof is that stupid ladder," Leanne said, as they headed through the tower. "The roof would have been an amazing place to set up everything, just the right size for the five of us, with the view of the ocean and everything. But, well, with our dresses, it just wouldn't work, right?"

"Uh, right," Cecilia said, knowing that was the response that she was looking for. However, Cecilia wondered why they needed the dresses at all. If the roof would have been the better venue for whatever celebration that they had planned, it would have been worth wearing her usual clothes for it.

Drilora was standing by the door to the tower as Cecilia and Leanne came into the garage. It might have taken Cecilia a moment to recognize the uvvelian, if ze hadn't been seven foot tall and had such a distinctive face. For the first time since Cecilia had met zer, Drilora was wearing clothes; a brown suit that wasn't too far off from zer own fur, though it was a completely different cloth that was easily distinguishable from it. The suit wasn't too masculine, and seemed to suit the alien perfectly, if human clothes could do such a thing. However, even as ze stared up at the two women heading zer way, ze was picking at the collar of the suit, pulling it away from zer fur.

"Wow," Drilora said. "You two look amazing."

"Thanks," Cecilia said, blushing. "Maybe now you two can tell me what the heck is going on?"

"Oh, I would have thought it was obvious," Drilora said. "We're celebrating you. Celebrating your success here, and what is in store for you in the next few months."

"Yeah, sure, but... All this?" Cecilia asked, pointing down at her dress.

"It's also a celebration of you coming of age, of sorts," Leanne explained. She continued over to the door, pushing it open to reveal the park outside all at once. "You might have missed the timing of it all, but tonight is your senior prom, back at your high school."

"Oh," Cecilia said, as she looked out at the park, all lit up.

Chapter Forty-One
Starlight in the Park
Cecilia

A tunnel of lights came up in front of Cecilia, leading out from the tower door. In the distance, she could make out a tan dance floor at the end of the path, with more lights spread all around it. With the dark night, it looked like stars surrounding them as they headed out into space. It felt like a cross between magic and space themes, like they had designed it not only for Cecilia, but for Drilora as well.

None of the decorations had been there during Cecilia's laps around the tower, which meant that Lindsey, Jerri, and Leanne must have been working on all of that in the three hours since she had come inside. It seemed like so much work to her, and she felt quite embarrassed about it all. She didn't have the heart to tell them that, if she had stayed back home with her father and kept going to high school, she never would have gone to prom.

Instead, all she said was, "You guys. This is... Wow."

"Hey, nothing but the best for our two heroes, right?" Leanne said. She nudged Cecilia a little, pushing her closer to Drilora as they started down the path of lights.

Cecilia looked up at Drilora, who was looking down at her. When she noticed that, she blushed a little, looking around them. Looking anywhere but at Drilora.

"Shall we?" Drilora asked. Ze raised zer arm up between them, offering it to Cecilia.

At first, Cecilia was a little taken aback. It was only then that she realized that Drilora was her date to this impromptu prom of theirs. It wasn't often that Cecilia had a date to anything, let alone to something like that. And yet, it seemed perfect in a way. Not someone that was only looking to take care of her, to protect her, but someone that saw her for who she was. What she could do, what she could be.

"Sure," Cecilia said, smiling up at Drilora, as she took zer arm. Drilora smiled down at her like ze was feeling relief that she hadn't rejected zer. It was the first time that the alien looked even remotely vulnerable to her, and it was almost endearing.

The others seemed to drop off into the darkness of the night as the two of them walked toward the dance floor in the distance. Just as they came out of the tunnel, the music started to rise up around them. Rather than sounding like the music was just coming out of a single phone, like at the picnic, the music was everywhere, with speakers framing the dance floor, though hidden beyond the lights. It was a slow song, something almost classical, though it didn't sound familiar in any way. Cecilia couldn't quite tell what instruments were being played, but none of them sounded human.

"Ah," Drilora said. Ze looked up at the sky, like the music was playing down from above. "This is a song from my planet," ze explained. "I had a few songs with me when... Well... Can-can I have this dance?"

"Of course," Cecilia said, smiling up at zer.

While the music was fully alien, Drilora quickly swept Cecilia into a purely human dance. Something that she could easily follow along with. Cecilia wasn't much of a dancer, but with Drilora taking the lead, they were sweeping all over the dance floor like they were professionals. It almost felt like she had been dancing all of her life. She couldn't tell how much of that was from Drilora's strength, pulling away from the gravity, and how much was just Drilora.

As they floated around that dance floor, Cecilia felt like they were the only people in the universe. There was no sign of the others, hidden out there in the night. All she could see as she was taken all over the floor were the lights and Drilora. Drilora's eye seemed to capture the lights, throwing them all over like stars. It looked like there was another universe in there, hidden from the world.

"So, were you in on all of this?" Cecilia asked, as the song slowed and Drilora pulled them to a stop.

"I guess that depends," Drilora said. "I knew they were planning something ,and that I would have a part in it, but... No, I... I wasn't expecting all of this. But, you'll learn soon enough, once Leanne is set on something, she doesn't easily give up on it. Sometimes, it's best to just follow along; she rarely leads you astray."

"That's good advice, I guess," Cecilia said. "I just wish that I'd be hanging around here longer. That you could look out for me, too."

"I..." Drilora started, but then ze just shook zer head.

Before either of them could say something more, another song started up. This one was clearly human, something that Cecilia remembered from her childhood, though she had long forgotten who it was by. Without another word, Drilora pulled Cecilia into another dance, and they just lost themselves in the music. In flowing through the steps of the dance, like they were the only important things in the world at that moment. And in that small portion of the park, they were.

But the doubts and fears weren't far from Cecilia's mind. She kept looking around them, searching for the others. Searching for answers that weren't out there. Searching for what her future would bring her. However, every time Drilora would spin her around, twirling her through more elaborate dance moves, her eyes always returned to zer. And each time, Drilora would smile at her, zer eye lighting up, like ze was only doing that to get her attention again. That to zer, all that was there at that moment was her.

As another song wound down, Drilora pulled Cecilia to a stop. It took her a moment to notice that they were right by the tunnel of lights. That ze had managed to bring her all the way around the dance floor several times, only to return to the beginning. That felt like a metaphor to her somehow, but she wasn't sure how. She wasn't sure what it all meant. All she knew was that she felt safe there, in Drilora's arms, looking up at zer face in the night.

"Maybe you..." Drilora started, but then ze shook zer head like ze was shaking an errant thought out.

"Yes?" Cecilia asked, trying to draw it out of zer. Trying to find out just what it was that ze was thinking. There were times when Drilora felt like just a normal person to her, but then there were times when zer alienness came out in full force. Standing there in zer arms, it felt like those two sides were at war with each other.

"I just thought that... Well, maybe..."

"Maybe what?" Cecilia asked.

Cecilia knew what she wanted that maybe to be. She wanted Drilora to agree to let her stay in the tower. It wasn't just that she had so much to learn from zer. There was still more for her to do there. More for her to accomplish. It felt like her mission, her goals, were so close at hand, but just out of reach. Zer "maybe" seemed to suggest that they weren't as far as she had thought. But she worried about pushing Drilora, about asking for something that ze wasn't quite ready to offer her.

"Maybe you don't have to leave the tower," Drilora said, finally. "I kind of... like having you here. Is-is that silly?"

"No," Cecilia said. She smiled up at zer, though she tried to keep that smile light and innocent. Not to hint at the victory that she had won there. "It's not silly at all. I like it here. I like... spending time with you. Even when you're yelling at me and making me run laps around the tower." She laughed as she said that, though her arms started to hurt at the memory of her fighting training.

"Good," Drilora said, smiling down at her. "Good."

Ze didn't say anything further as another song started up. This time, as ze pulled her around the dance floor, Cecilia's eyes stayed locked on zer face. On that one eye staring right back at her. She still wondered about the others, why they were hiding out in the shadows rather than joining them out there on the dance floor. But perhaps they were just giving the two of them that time alone.

The more that she thought about that, though, the more she wondered at the reasons. Wondered if the others thought that there was more going on between them than Cecilia did. And with the way that Drilora was looking at her, the way that ze seemed so nervous, and how ze was her date to that whole thing, it seemed like ze agreed with them. That ze wanted something more between them. More than just master and apprentice. More than teacher and student.

It meant that Drilora didn't see her as less than zer anymore. That ze wasn't underestimating her, like everyone else did. It meant that her superpower didn't work against zer. And considering everything, that could be quite dangerous for her.

Drilora seemed to sense something in her, as ze pulled them to a stop in the middle of the dance floor. The music continued on, ignorant of the storm brewing between them. Zer smile stayed in place for a moment longer before slowly slipping away. Before the grimace that was more often found there returned.

"What?" Cecilia asked. "Is... Is something wrong?" She was nervous, worried that ze would say that there was. That ze would yell at her and chase her out of the tower right then and there.

"I... I don't know," Drilora said. There was a tone in zer voice that Cecilia didn't recognize. Something that almost sounded like fear, though she knew that couldn't be the case. That it was another difference between uvvelian and human voices. There was no way that Drilora could be afraid of her.

"What is it?" Cecilia asked. She gave zer a strained smile, desperate to get zer off of whatever ze was thinking. Desperate to get them back to dancing, if for no other reason than to make it seem like they were happy together.

"I..." Drilora started, before shaking zer head. "I have to..." ze said, before pulling away from Cecilia.

Cecilia just stood there in the center of the dance floor, watching as Drilora headed off. Rather than returning to the tower, ze was heading out into the night, out into the darkness of the park. Once ze disappeared out there, Cecilia looked around her. She looked for answers to the mystery that was Drilora.

"What happened?" Leanne asked, seeming to materialize out of nowhere.

"I... I don't know," Cecilia said, shaking her head. As she did so, she felt tears forming in her eyes.

"Oh, honey," Leanne said. She quickly came over to stand next to Cecilia, reaching her arms out to pull her into a hug. "I'm sorry. I know you two weren't ready for this. But... Well, with you possibly moving out of the tower, I just had to push a little."

"Push?" Cecilia asked. "Push what? What exactly did you think was going to happen here?"

"Well...," Leanne started. She pulled away from the hug to look at Cecilia. "I saw how the two of you were. You're both alone in the world. Both heroes, in your own right. I just... You don't see the way that ze looks at you sometimes. The way that you look at zer. It seems like you two belong together, and you just can't see it."

"Oh," Cecilia said. She turned back toward the night, back toward where she last saw Drilora disappearing out there, as she thought about that, really thought about that for the first time.

Chapter Forty-Two
Talking under the Stars
Cecilia

Cecilia stood at the edge of the lights, looking out into the darkness of the park. She could just see Drilora's form, backlit by the low glow from the city. Her hand went to one of the polls that were holding up the lights, holding onto it as she thought. Thought about everything that she had been through since arriving at the tower. How Drilora had been there by her side through it all.

With the two of them off the dance floor, the others had emerged from the night to take it up. Jerri and Lindsey were dancing together, with Jerri's head on Lindsey's shoulder. It seemed like the two of them were together, something that Cecilia hadn't picked up earlier. But then, she had apparently been missing a lot lately.

Standing there on the edge of the dance floor, between the lit up space and the darkness of the night, it felt like she was on the edge of something else. That she was about to make a leap into something that she hadn't thought that she was ready for. That she might not be ready for. And yet, she knew that she had to take that leap. She didn't want to look back on her life in a few years and regret that she hadn't given it a try.

Slowly, Cecilia started out away from the safety of the dance floor, embracing the night. Embracing the future that she might be finding there. Her wedge shoes worked well in the grass, which had been cut low for their celebration, giving her a steady footing as she headed for Drilora.

Drilora stayed still as Cecilia came up behind zer. Ze was looking up at the stars, far enough away from the lights behind zer and the city in front of zer, that ze might be able to see some of them. But as Cecilia came up next to zer, she looked up to see nothing but a dark sky overhead.

"I'm sorry," Cecilia said, simply.

Drilora let out a purely human sounding snicker, but ze didn't look over at her. "What do you have to be sorry for?" ze asked. "If you don't... I don't mean... I'm-I'm sorry. I shouldn't have pushed the issue."

"It's not that... It-it just took me by surprise, is all," Cecilia said. "I hadn't thought about it."

"You mean you don't think of me like--"

"No, that's not..." Cecilia said, quickly. "I hadn't really thought about it... ever... With anyone. It's never come up before. No one has ever seen me like that, and whenever... It-it just gets... messy. My superpower gets in the way."

"I... I don't get it?" Drilora said. "How does--"

"People don't see me as... well, as me. They'll see me as a child, or as someone to protect. But you... I mean, you, Leanne, Jerri, Lindsey. You all see me as an adult, as a hero. It's... I've never had that before. I guess... I guess I just didn't think of everything that that could lead to."

"Well... I still see you as someone that needs my protection," Drilora said. Ze turned to look at Cecilia, and she thought that ze was smiling at her, but it was hard to see in the darkness. "But no more than any human out there. You're fully capable of handling yourself in many situations, just not as many as I can. Nor as well as I can. But I've seen you in action, I know what you can do."

"What do you mean you've seen me?" Cecilia asked. At first, she thought about her one solo mission the other day, but Drilora had stayed outside for that whole thing. Ze couldn't have seen her in the apartment building.

"Oh, I thought... Well, I hacked into the body cam footage of the cops that were at the door to the apartment," Drilora admitted. Ze turned away from Cecilia to look out at the city in front of them, hidden behind the trees there. "I could hear how you manipulated that man. Got him to trust you and use that to your advantage. It's not the way that I would have approached the incident, but... Well, bulls and china shops."

"We each have our strengths and weaknesses," Cecilia said. She looked back out at the city as well, trying to hide her face in her hair. When her hair didn't sweep out in front of her face, she reached her hand up to it. She had forgotten that her hair was up.

"You know, you haven't done that in the past few days," Drilora said, pointing at her. "Not since your solo mission. I've seen your confidence growing. It's like... It's like your superpower always worked on you as well, but it's losing its hold on you."

"Is it that it's losing its hold on me, or that it's going away?" Cecilia asked.

She had always hated her superpower growing up. Hated being underestimated by everyone. Not seen like someone that could do anything on their own. It wasn't until a few years earlier that she realized how powerful it was. That she noticed that she could use it to her advantage. That it was a superpower, and not just some character flaw.

"Would it be so bad if it did?" Drilora asked. "You can still be a superhero without it. Like Batgirl."

"But not like you," Cecilia said. "Would you still see me as an equal without my superpower?"

"Of course," Drilora said. "You'll always be my sidekick, even when you grow up and go out on your own." Ze reached over to ruffle Cecilia's hair a little, but the updo held against it, keeping her hair in place.

"And if I don't want to go out on my own?" Cecilia asked.

"Then that's alright, too," Drilora said. "You'll always have room in my tower."

Cecilia nodded, liking that thought. The idea that she could stay there at the tower, forget ever going out on her own. That she could forget why she was really there. But even if she stayed in the tower, even if she was always there, always the sidekick, it wasn't the same for Drilora. Ze could always leave, could always head home.

"In the tower," Cecilia said. "Not with you."

"Right," Drilora said, nodding. "Cecilia, I... I'll always be trying to get home. This world, this planet, it... It's never been my home. But you can't come with me. You would never be able to survive on my planet."

"But you could stay here," Cecilia said. "You don't have to keep up your workouts just on the slim chance that you'll get one of those ships working again. You could just... stay. You could acclimate to this mudball of a planet that we have. Would that be so bad? To stay here... with me?"

"Yes," Drilora said. Ze kept the anger from zer voice, though Cecilia could still sense it there. The low growl under the words. "I'm sorry, Cecilia. I wish that we could be together, but... You're right. I need to go home. It's not just a matter of choice. My people need me."

"My people need you," Cecilia said. She pointed out at the city, hidden by the trees in front of them, but they both knew it was out there. "They need a hero. One that's better than me. Better than I could ever be."

"Maybe they do," Drilora said. "But they don't see that. They can't. Whenever they look at me, whenever I come out for a mission, it... All they see when they look at me is an alien. When they look at you... No, you-you think I'm this great superhero. But to the humans, to your people, I'm just a monster. You're the superhero. You're already more of a superhero to them than I'll ever be. More than they'll ever let me be."

Cecilia didn't say anything to that at first. She didn't have to. They both knew that it was true. That when she came out of that apartment building, everyone was congratulating her. When Drilora left the fire, everyone was blaming zer. Trying to make zer actions worse than they were. Something more sinister than just trying to help. And it wasn't just at the fire. It was at every mission that ze had done. She had seen that in the old mission files as well.

"I wish that I could change that," Cecilia said, once the growing silence between them became too much for her. "I wish that I could fix the world. I wish that I could make them see you for who you really are, just like you helped them see me the way that I really am. I may be a superhero to them now, but you made me into that. You did far more for me than my father ever did."

"But I don't want to be a father to you," Drilora said. "I don't want to be some protector that has to watch over you. You're not a child, Cecilia. Not to me. You wouldn't be to my people, either. Once you can stand on your own two feet, can contribute to society, you're an adult."

"And to my people, I'll be an adult in three months," Cecilia said, laughing a little at how stupid it all seemed to her. The differences between the two peoples, between earning adulthood and it being thrust upon you once you reached a certain age. Just like Drilora was saying, she felt more adult than ever before. She felt like she could take on the world, if she needed to.

That she could stand between the world and Drilora if it came to it. That she could protect zer from the rising mobs aligned against zer.

"So, maybe we discuss it again in three months," Drilora said. "You don't have to make any big decisions right away. Neither of us do. I'm not going anywhere, much to my dismay. There's plenty of time, plenty of things for us to get to before either one of us is safe from the Earth for Humans, or any number of hate groups out there." Ze went silent again, thinking about that, as they stared out at the trees in front of them. "Before any of the humans would allow us to be together."

"Not all humans are like that," Cecilia said, defensively. "Leanne isn't."

"Leanne is the dearest of friends," Drilora said. "All three of them are. They see me for who I really am, just as we all see you clearly. But, you're right. Not all humans are like that. And the more work I do for your people, the more I hope that they change their minds about me. That they see me clearly. Until then... Well, until then, maybe we shouldn't worry too much about us."

"Or maybe we just don't worry too much about what they think," Cecilia said. "Let's just see where the next few weeks bring us."

"I like that thought," Drilora said, nodding. "Come on. Let's go back and enjoy our time together."

"I like the sound of that," Cecilia said. She reached over to take Drilora's hand, pulling zer back toward the lights. Back toward the celebration, already in progress.

Chapter Forty-Three
A Shared Night
Drilora

Despite the friction between them at the start of the evening, Drilora and Cecilia spent most of the night together, just dancing the night away. It felt almost magical to Drilora, the best night that ze had had since arriving on that mudball of a planet. What surprised zer most of all, though, was that it had more to do with Cecilia being there than ze had expected.

When the music wrapped up around midnight, Drilora looked around them. Ze was hoping for more music, more dancing. But when ze noticed that Leanne, Jerri, and Lindsey had disappeared, their cars already gone from the parking lot, ze realized that they were alone. That the party was over, leaving only the two of them behind.

"Uh, should we clean up?" Drilora asked, looking around them.

"Probably not," Cecilia said. She stifled a yawn, showing just how tired she had gotten from all the dancing, and the workout from earlier in the day. Or, perhaps more accurately, just how late it had gotten.

Drilora wasn't quite ready for the day to be over. The Terran day always felt short for zer, especially since it was three hours shorter than the Uvvelian day. It wasn't usually a problem, with zer staying up later when ze wasn't tired. However, if ze got closer to Cecilia, if ze spent more time with her, that was going to come up more often.

And ze very much wanted to spend more time with her.

"Alright, alright," Drilora said, nodding zer agreement. "Cleanup can save for another day. I don't think it's going to rain tonight, with all these stars."

"What stars?" Cecilia asked. She looked up at the sky above them, a scowl in place. "I can't see anything up there with all the lights."

"Ah, you and your human eyesight," Drilora said, smiling over at her. "I can see them perfectly fine. If I couldn't, well... Those stars do keep me from feeling too homesick."

"Sometimes..." Cecilia started. She turned away from the stars, looking at Drilora's face instead. "Sometimes, I can almost forget that you're an alien. That you're not from this planet. Is... Is that bad?"

"No," Drilora said, smiling at her. "I imagine, if I get stuck here too long, I might start forgetting my own homeworld. I might start thinking the same, that I was just some weird human. The question would be, would you think more of me at that point, or less?"

"I don't think that it is possible for me to think less of you," Cecilia said. After a moment, there was a flash of red flowing through her face. "Oh, I didn't mean... I just meant, I don't think it's possible for you to disappoint me."

"I understand," Drilora said, nodding. It was only then that ze realized that Cecilia had noticed a possible insult in her words. That she was trying to be careful of zer feelings, trying not to anger zer. Ze didn't understand what possible insult she could have been trying to avoid, though. "Come on. Let's head inside. Clearly, you need some sleep."

"No," Cecilia said, a slight whine in her voice. "I want to stay out here all night. It's far too magical of a night for it to be over." A yawn soon followed her words, belying them. Drilora just chuckled at it all.

"There will be plenty of other nights like this one," Drilora promised. "Maybe we can keep the decorations up and do it again tomorrow night. Just don't start expecting this sort of thing every night. We need to stay on our guard for when the next mission comes along."

"Yup," Cecilia said. "Gotta pay them bills somehow." She laughed a little before turning toward the tower.

Drilora raised zer arm between them, offering it to Cecilia again. She clung to it readily as they started off across the park. The moment that her feet hit the grass on the edge of the dance floor, her weight shifted to the side. At first, Drilora worried that she had broken something; humans always seemed so fragile to zer. But as they walked, Cecilia reached down, taking off her shoes. She held them in her off hand as they continued along, but she suddenly seemed half a foot shorter. With the height difference between them, that made Cecilia look that much more like a child. Like a human.

But no less amazing.

When they came up to the door, Drilora reached out, opening it for Cecilia. She smiled up at zer, holding her shoes out to the side as she curtseyed to zer. "My prince," she said. "Or is there a non-binary version of that, too?"

"Not that I'm aware of," Drilora said.

"I'll have to remember to look that up," she said, as she slipped through the door and into the tower.

Just inside, Cecilia lost her balance. Her hand went out, reaching for the railing to the stairs, but it was too far away for her to grab. Her shoes fell to the ground next to her, and she almost went with them. Drilora quickly scooped her up off her feet before she fell.

"Careful there," Drilora said.

"Wow," Cecilia said. She gazed up in Drilora's eye as her arms wrapped around zer neck. "I kind of meant it as a joke before, but... You really are my prince, Drilora. My princez."

Drilora smiled down at her in zer arms. Ze liked the sound of that, the word, the idea, the connection between them. All ze could think of was how close she was to zer. How close her lips were. But ze didn't know if she was ready for more, not so soon after their earlier discussion. So, ze didn't try anything, didn't force the issue.

"Come on," Drilora said, as ze turned to the stairs, carrying Cecilia up them. "Time to get you to bed."

Cecilia seemed to dip in and out of consciousness as Drilora carried her up the stairs. She felt light in zer arms, the added weight doing little to keep zer from bouncing with each step. Whenever ze landed on the steps, Cecilia's head would jerk to the side, seeming like she woke up again. But it was only when her eyes locked on zer eye, lighting up with her smile, that ze knew that she was awake. And as they got to the top of the stairs, that smile instantly returned.

"No, wait," Cecilia said. She clung tightly to Drilora's neck, though Drilora knew that ze could pull free of her grip if ze needed to. "Don't leave me."

"I'll be right in the other room," Drilora said, nodding backward at zer door as they passed it. "I'll hear it if you call out for me."

Cecilia seemed to nod off again, as she didn't say anything about it. Drilora shifted her slightly, putting her legs in the crook of zer elbow, to reach out and open her door. Ze swept inside, lightly placing Cecilia down on the bed.

"Stay," she mumbled, low enough that she might have been talking in her sleep. But when Drilora tried to pull away from her, her arms only got tighter around zer neck. "Stay with me."

"I don't think that's a good idea," Drilora said, but ze didn't pull away from Cecilia. Ze didn't want to accidentally hurt her when breaking that death grip on zer. "You might think differently when waking up next to me."

"I won't," Cecilia said, though one of her arms fell away from zer neck. It was easy for zer to spin around, turning out of the other arm. Ze stayed there next to her, just looking down at her in the low light of the room. "I want to be with you, Drilora," she said, sleepily. "I love..." She trailed off, not quite finishing that sentence.

Drilora's heart soared at that word, nonetheless. The idea that Cecilia cared for zer back. That the week together had changed her just as it had changed zer. All ze wanted was to stay. To just lie down in that bed next to her and be there, even if nothing else happened. Even if nothing else ever happened. Just being close to her felt like enough for that night. And it was only that feeling that made Drilora agree.

"Alright," ze said to Cecilia's sleepy form. Ze wasn't sure if she heard it, but she didn't deny zer. She didn't change her mind and push zer out of there.

Drilora took zer time walking around the bed, zer eye locked on Cecilia, waiting for her to say something. To tell zer that it was all a mistake and that ze should head back to zer room. It was clear that Cecilia was already asleep, though. That ze should just leave. It wasn't until ze made it to the other side of the bed that ze realized ze didn't want to.

Ze pulled the extra pillow off the bed, slipping it next to Cecilia before sliding into the bed next to her. Even with the longer than normal bed, Drilora's legs still stuck up over the foot board when ze was lying straight out. It took some effort to slip zer feet into the space between that foot board and Cecilia's feet, sleeping diagonally across the bed like ze had to do in zer own room. But Cecilia didn't stir at zer movement, and ze quickly settled into the bed next to her.

At first, ze just laid there, staring at the back of Cecilia's head as she slept. The pillow between them acted as a wall, keeping Drilora's arms to zerself, though ze had plenty of self-restraint to do that without it. Gradually, Drilora managed to drift off to sleep as well. It was comforting to have Cecilia there, to share that space with her. Ze still wanted more, wanted everything, but that shared bed was enough for that night.

When the day dawned around them, something felt off for Drilora. At first, ze thought that it might have been the difference in the light, with being on the opposite side of the tower. That instead of seeing the rising sun in the window, ze was catching the first rays of dawn as they spread around the tower. It took zer a moment to realize that that wasn't it. That there was something else off.

Sleepily, ze reached an arm out, touching the open bed space next to zer. That felt normal for zer; zer bed was usually empty besides zerself. But as ze remembered that ze was in Cecilia's room, that the woman had slept next to zer, ze slowly sat up in the bed, looking around the room. When ze noticed that zer arm wasn't brown anymore, that it was closer to the pale pink of the humans, for one split second zer waking mind thought that maybe ze had gotten zer wish after all. That ze had suddenly changed into a human. Once that moment passed, though, ze looked around zer, searching for Cecilia once more.

"Cecilia?" ze called out, sleepily.

A light laugh came from the bathroom. The laugh seemed just as off as the morning did. It wasn't playful or happy. If anything, it was malicious.

"Ah, I see you're finally awake," Cecilia said, as she came around the corner. Instead of coming over to the bed, coming over to Drilora, she just stood there, leaning against the doorframe. There was a small, black object in her hand, but

Drilora couldn't see it properly from across the room. "That tranquilizer really did its work."

"Tranquilizer?" Drilora asked, zer brain slow to catch up with what was going on there. With the mood coming off of Cecilia.

"You didn't wake up once while I was doing all that," Cecilia said, pointing to Drilora with the black object. It was then that ze noticed the silver tip to the object. A moment later, ze realized what the object was: electric clippers.

And what Cecilia had done with them.

Chapter Forty-Four
The Truth
Drilora

As Drilora sat up in the bed, zer fur spilled off of zer in droves, falling to the bed around zer. While an uvvelian's fur is a dark brown, their skin was closer to a light tan. It wasn't often that one would see that skin, as most uvvelians are born with their fur already growing in, though not nearly as thick as on an adult. But when ze looked down at zerself, that light tan skin was all that ze could see.

"What-what's going on?" Drilora asked. Zer mind was slow to wake that morning, slow to catch up with the horror that ze was seeing.

"Isn't it obvious?" Cecilia asked. "I shaved you while you were sleeping. It wasn't nearly as hard as they said it was going to be. Shaving you, that is. Your fur really was tough stuff, and it took forever for me to find the right approach to start on it all. But, once I got that first patch off, the rest of it was rather easy. It came off in droves. I had been hoping to keep it as a rug or something, maybe hang it on my wall? But, well..." She just pointed at the fur around zer. While it was falling off in clumps, none of it would hold together.

Drilora reached down to pick up some of that fur, trying to press it together like a snowball. Like ze was hoping to get it to reattach if ze pressed on it hard enough. But ze knew that ze would need to wait for zer fur to regrow, if it ever did. There were old folk tales back on Uvvelia that spoke of uvvelians losing their fur permanently. With how smooth and fur-free zer skin felt, ze was worried that was going to happen to zer. The fact that the fur wasn't burned off of zer was little consolation. That would have been far worse, but it didn't seem like that was Cecilia's intent.

"Why-why did you do this?" Drilora asked, zer eyes still locked on the fur around zer.

"Why do you think?" Cecilia asked. "Is it really so hard for you to figure out what's going on here?"

Slowly, Drilora looked up at Cecilia, looking at her properly for the first time since ze woke up. Instead of the sweet and innocent look that she usually had early in the morning, she was glaring over at zer with disgust. She was wearing her superhero uniform, but it had been dyed black since ze had last seen it. Sticking up over her shoulders were the handles of two weapons that hadn't been there before, looking like they were in scabbards attached to the back of the uniform. Ze wasn't sure if she had done that while ze was sleeping as well, or if that had happened earlier. If she had planned the whole thing out.

But the one thing that ze didn't see over there was any affection for zer at all.

"You... You mean you don't love me?" Drilora asked. That, more than anything, seemed the obvious truth. The one thing that was instantly clear. But ze still needed to hear that from her. To confirm the worst, as zer brain struggled to wake up that morning.

"Of course, not," Cecilia said, practically spitting the words at zer. "Who could ever love a freak, a creature, a thing like you? You disgust me. Every minute of every day that I had to suffer in your presence was torture. I only wish that I could have the pleasure of killing you myself. To end my suffering by ending you. But no. My father has plans for you."

"You're father?" Drilora asked. "But..."

"Oh, no, he didn't abandon me here. I'm not some scared, little girl, unaware of the world around me. This isn't

Beauty and the Beast. This is Samson and Delilah. I was sent here to find your greatest weakness. And I did. So, now, you're weak as a newborn baby."

"Ha," Drilora scoffed. "I'm not so weak that I can't wring your scrawny neck." Anger started to fill Drilora, but zer tiredness kept it in check. Ze reached out a hand toward Cecilia, but it barely went past zer waist.

"Aren't you, though?" Cecilia asked.

"I don't... My strength doesn't come from my fur," Drilora said, as ze struggled to understand just what Cecilia had done to zer.

"No, but your protection does," Cecilia said, laughing. "I could shoot you right now, and nothing would stop the bullet. You'd die, just like any human in your position."

"But then, why... Why can't I move?" Drilora asked. Ze hated to have to ask that, to reveal just how vulnerable ze was at that point.

"Why do you think?" Cecilia asked. "Really, you just opened your home to me so completely, it was hardly difficult at all. Finding just the right bits to use against you. Drawing you out of the tower when we needed to. I played you like a fiddle the whole time that I was living here, and you didn't even know it. Because, just like everyone else I've ever met, you underestimated me."

"I... I didn't..." Drilora said. "I see you for who you are. This... This isn't you, Cecilia."

"And even now, with the truth laid bare, staring you in the face, you still don't see me," Cecilia said. "No one ever could."

A hint of sadness played across Cecilia's face, something that Drilora had seen there often enough in the time that they had spent together. But before ze could say anything about it, Cecilia's face shifted once more. The conniving smile returned, and Drilora realized the mistake that ze had made. Just how easily Cecilia had manipulated zer.

"But... But how... What did you do to me?" Drilora asked again. Ze wanted to demand an answer, but there wasn't enough force left in zer voice.

"I've been drugging your food this whole week," Cecilia said. "We needed to get the sedative dosage just right so that I could inject you while you were sleeping. It'll be enough to keep you down until we can move you to the holding facility. Then, we just need to keep you sedated until we're ready to kill you. It's really that simple."

"But... Human sedatives won't work on me," Drilora finally managed to get out. It was the thing that most confused zer in everything. How could they have gotten a sedative that would work on zer? Ze hadn't brought any from Uvvelia.

"Human sedatives won't, but uvvelian sedatives do," Cecilia said. "God, even now, you just think of me as some idiot child. I found your food replicator the first day here, after you let it slip that you have to use it to create your food. Hell, you used it while I was in the tower. It was easy enough to figure out from there. It doesn't just create food, you know. It creates medical supplies, like sedatives. I made enough of them to last us weeks, and you didn't even notice."

Drilora tried to think about the food replicator, about the levels that were in it. Ze had enough resources in the replicator to last a few decades with normal use, but ze felt like that amount of sedatives should have drained it enough for zer to notice. Ze wasn't a doctor, though, and had never used the replicator to create such things. Even how much sedative was needed for all of that went beyond zer training.

As ze struggled to think of how ze could have been so foolish, to think of ways that ze could have seen that coming, the doorbell rang. Ze turned to look over at the door, as if whoever rang the bell was just outside the bedroom door, rather than four floors down. It took zer longer than it should to think about who would likely be out there. That Leanne would be arriving for another visit.

"No," Drilora said, zer voice low and without strength. "No, run away."

"Are you talking to yourself?" Cecilia asked, laughing a little. "Wow, you're worse off than I thought. Or are you trying to warn off Leanne out there? Maybe I should invite her in here. Invite her to join our little party, eh? She was even easier to manipulate than you were. Ha." She laughed as she started through the room, heading past the bed and over to the door.

"No, wait," Drilora said. Ze put all of zer strength into zer arms, but it was barely enough to move zer across the bed. Zer hand reached toward Cecilia again, flowing through the air right behind her, just as she made it to the door.

"Don't worry," Cecilia said, laughing. "I'll be gentle. At least you'll both be together when you die." Her laughter echoed through the hallway as she headed through the tower, slowly fading as she descended.

Drilora knew that ze had to do something. That ze had to fight off the drugs in zer system. That ze needed to save Leanne. All ze could think about was saving zer friend. The only friend that ze had managed to make there on Earth. Without Leanne, ze would have been lost.

For one brief moment, Drilora wondered about that. Wondered if Leanne was somehow in on it. That she had helped Cecilia trick zer. Leanne had been the one to push the whole situation on zer, when all Drilora wanted was to kick Cecilia to the curb. But ze remembered those first few days, when Leanne had helped zer settle the tower, having it built.

There was far too much help that she had given zer, help that would have made things more difficult for Cecilia's work.

Drilora managed to pull zerself forward, zer arms extending off the edge of the bed and down to the floor while the rest of zer stayed in place. The open door was right in front of zer, but ze knew that ze couldn't make it down the tower with the sedatives still in zer. Ze wasn't floating off the ground with every push of zer muscles. Ze was as weak as a human, perhaps even weaker, and would be an easy target once Cecilia returned.

"Must... Save... Leanne," Drilora muttered to zerself, pushing against the bed with each word. Slowly, ze slipped off the edge, falling back down to the floor much faster than ze should have. Only gravity wasn't working harder on zer; zer muscles just weren't pushing against it as much. Zer perception of that gravity, of zer falling back to the ground, was off.

Zer legs slammed hard into the floor as they fell off the bed. Without the padding and protection of zer fur, it almost hurt, though not enough to stop zer. Ze pushed zerself up to zer hands and knees, starting to crawl toward the door. But just as ze came out into the hall, Cecilia's face appeared around the corner, over by the stairs.

"Wow," Cecilia said, sounding almost impressed by Drilora's movement while she was gone. But the smirk quickly returned to her face, her voice thick with sarcasm. "You almost had me there, didn't you. Oh, wait, no, you're still just as weak." She came over to stand next to Drilora, raising her foot high enough to kick zer in the side, knocking zer over.

"Leanne, run," Drilora managed to get out.

"Oh, my Drilora," someone said, using a falsetto voice to make it sound feminine. But Drilora wasn't fooled by it.

Especially not when Cecilia's father came into view. "Oh, look what we have here," he said, in his normal voice. "An alien, all set for delivery. It's almost a shame that you managed to pull this off, Cici. I have so many other plans in play against this one. A shame to have them all go to waste."

"Well, you can still test out that gun of yours on it," Cecilia said. She wrapped her arm around her father's shoulders, the two of them smiling down at Drilora from above. "The prototype is still downstairs. I can go get it for you if you'd like."

"Naw," Cecilia's father said. "I got plenty more where it came from. Besides, I think I'll enjoy torturing this one over the next few days. It'll be interesting to see what happens first: it surrenders and gives us all the knowledge we want, or it dies."

Chapter Forty-Five
The Invasion

Drilora laid there on the floor, staring up at the two of them. It took zer far too long to realize that Cecilia's father was the leader of the Earth for Humans terrorist organization, the Rene Marks that they had been hearing about. Longer than it would have without the sedative running through zer body. But as that revelation hit zer, the anger only grew hotter, stronger. Strong enough to chase off the sedative.

"Uh oh," Rene said. He pointed at Drilora as ze slowly pushed zerself back up to zer feet. "Got another dose ready?" He looked over at his daughter, Cecilia.

"Oh, not you, too," Cecilia muttered, rolling her eyes at her father. "Of course, I have another dose."

Before Drilora could properly get to zer feet, Cecilia pulled something out of her pocket. She took two steps toward Drilora before jabbing it into zer side, right below zer arm. The pain of the impact barely registered before Drilora's body started to get heavy once more, another dose of the sedative running through zer. Ze tried to put a hand on the object, but Cecilia retracted it before ze could move. Zer legs became wobbly under zer, and ze tried to catch zerself against the wall next to zer. But zer hands were still reaching for the object that was no longer in reach.

Even as Cecilia took a step away from Drilora, ze fell down to the floor between them. Zer hands were nowhere close to being in position to catch zer, so ze landed hard on zer face. Again, without zer fur, it hurt like hell, but with the sedative flowing through zer, ze barely noticed.

"I have enough doses on hand to keep it out for the rest of the day," Cecilia said, turning back to look at her father.

It. That word rang in Drilora's head as ze laid there, unable to move. Ze couldn't understand how ze could have been so wrong about Cecilia. About the woman that ze had grown to love. Only the woman that ze had loved didn't really exist. The woman standing next to her father, staring down at zer prone form, was a completely different woman. One that was hiding who they were the entire time that ze knew her.

"Where are we?" someone called out. The voice sounded familiar to Drilora, but ze couldn't place it. Ze kept worrying that Leanne would show up that morning. That she would fall into the same trap that Drilora had found zerself in. But when the woman came up next to Cecilia and her father, Drilora recognized her.

"Janine, Matt, so nice of you two to finally show up," Cecilia said. "Do we have more hands? I think it's going to take about twenty to drag this thing out of here."

"Oh, are we on the same side again?" Janine asked. She folded her arms across her chest, glaring over at her. "I wasn't sure after you helped beat the crap out of me the other day."

"Oh, can it," Rene yelled at her. "Save it for when we're not standing over the body of the alien. We don't want to give it any more ammunition against us than we have to."

"I don't know why we don't just kill the thing," Matt said. "But, fine, whatever. I'll get some of the others."

"Others?" Drilora managed to get out, before ze could think better of it. Before ze could think to keep zer mouth shut, staying out of their attention.

"Do you need to dose it again?" Rene asked.

"No," Cecilia said. There was a hint of concern in her voice that Drilora didn't think was fake. "If we give it too much, it might die on us before we can get anything out of it. Or it might start developing a resistance to it. Either would be bad. I'll only inject it again when it starts to move."

When it starts to move. Drilora figured that was the key. The trick to getting out of there. To escaping from the Earth for Humans. Just don't move until ze knew that ze could escape. Until ze knew that zer body was back to full strength.

The hallway quickly became crowded as several people came up around Drilora. They all reached down, grabbing a leg, an arm, a foot, zer head. Drilora couldn't tell just how many people crowded around zer, how many they needed to carry the one uvvelian. Considering ze had carried Cecilia up those same stairs just the night before, it felt almost ironic that so many needed to carry zer back down.

The stairwell was worse than the hallway, with the humans having to raise Drilora high over their heads to make it through the close quarters. As they passed through the fourth floor, Drilora noticed several more humans rushing around the place. One was coming out of the far, right door, holding the food replicator in his hands. It was the only device that Drilora ever went into that room to use; the washer and dryer were completely useless to zer. Unfortunately, the replicator needed the same level of power as the dryer.

The library was harder for Drilora to watch, with the humans pawing through zer comic book collection. There were several boxes on the floor, suggesting that they were meant to be packing all of that stuff up to bring it out of the tower. That they were planning on stealing everything from Drilora, not just zer freedom and possibly zer life. But instead, the humans were just standing there as they flipped through the comics, tossing some on the floor.

Drilora barely noticed it as they passed through the second floor. The gym was only ever a way for ze to keep zer muscles and bone mass, and not something that ze cared much about. Ze was starting to nod off again as they came out of there. But then, rather than carrying zer down the last flight of stairs, the humans flipped Drilora over the railing and down onto the floor of the garage.

The trampled, dead grass of the garage floor was softer than the stone floors of the higher levels. So, it didn't hurt nearly as much as ze hit the ground. Ze rolled with the momentum, coming to a stop facing away from the stairs. This room had the most activity of the tower, with dozens of humans working on the two spaceships. Or, at least, trying to, anyway.

Drilora figured that these humans were meant to be taking the ships apart, pulling them through the doors piece by piece. It had always been something that Drilora worried about, if there ever came a time when ze needed to do just that to fly them out of there. If taking them apart in the wrong way would just break them further. But as the humans poked around the ships, most of them were just staring at them, scratching their heads, unable to figure out just how to take them apart. Or to even start with that. Drilora pictured a bunch of monkeys slamming rocks and clubs against the ships; they would have made as much progress as the humans were making.

"Great," Cecilia said, her voice coming from the stairs behind Drilora. "Now, pick the thing back up. We need to be out of this tower before people figure out what we're doing here."

Ze wanted to roll over, to look back at her, but ze couldn't. It wasn't just zer trying not to move to make it seem like ze was still under the sedative. The sedative really was keeping zer too weak to move at all. It was all that ze could do to not fall asleep. That seemed more dangerous than not being able to move.

"Who cares?" Matt asked, as he and the rest of the humans came back over to Drilora, picking zer back up off the ground. "People would be thanking us for taking out the trash."

Several of the humans laughed at the comment, but Cecilia didn't. It was easy for Drilora to convince zerself that there was something to that. That Cecilia wasn't as committed to the Earth for Humans' cause as she seemed. That maybe there was still some room to get her back from them. But when Cecilia came back into zer view, the look of complete disgust on her face clearly showed how foolish that thought was.

Once the humans picked Drilora up again, Cecilia headed through the open door, out into the park. That open door felt like a wound in Drilora's heart that could never be mended. It was bad enough having those humans invading zer space, but to see the door opened wide, not broken down or destroyed by the invaders, felt like a betrayal to zer. Ze knew that Cecilia would have opened it for her people. That she was the one that betrayed zer so completely. Still, it felt like the very tower itself had conspired with her.

After all, the tower had always been a work of humans, based on a human concept, and not something that would ever have been found on Uvvelia.

As the humans carried Drilora out through the door and into the park, Drilora wondered just how they were planning on getting zer out of there. There weren't many vehicles that could handle zer weight, and fewer still that could do it without being noticed. Ze tried to lift zer head to look ahead of them, to see what type of vehicle they were heading toward. The human carrying zer head kept too tight of a grip on it for zer to move it in the state that ze was in. But then, ze didn't need to wait long for an answer.

"Just get it in the truck," Cecilia said. "You guys know where to meet up. We'll need to get over there before anyone notices that it's gone. Before another god forsaken mission comes in. The assistant isn't going to be preoccupied for much longer, and she'll put up a huge stink once she notices. Not to mention the stupid decorations from last night. I almost threw up when I found out what they had planned. Ugh."

"I'm telling you, no one will care," Matt said again. "Even if the assistant tells everyone in the world, no one is going to do a thing about it. We're just taking out the trash. Why else would we be using this kind of truck?"

"Uh oh," Drilora muttered, when ze realized what Matt was talking about.

Soon after that, the humans started to swing Drilora back and forth. The momentum helped lift zer higher off the ground and keep zer up. One by one, the humans dropped off from either side, revealing the back of the garbage truck right next to zer. Once ze was high enough, the last few humans let go, letting zer fly up and over the lip. Zer arm hit the side of the hopper, but zer momentum kept zer moving, flipping over it and into the truck.

Worse was when the scraper plate started moving toward zer. Ze was worried that the truck was going to crush zer, making zer into so much garbage. The humans had already said that they wouldn't care if they accidentally killed zer in taking zer out of the tower. But the plate stopped just above zer, blocking the light from coming in and hiding zer from the world around them.

Ze held zer breath, trying to hear something from the world outside the truck. To hear if the humans were still out there. All ze could hear, though, was the low grunt of the truck as it started up, bringing zer away from the only home that ze had had in the past five years. Away from zer only chance of getting back to zer real home, still out there among the stars.

Chapter Forty-Six
The Cell

With how dark the back of the garbage truck was, it was hard for Drilora to notice when ze nodded off. When the effects of the sedative became too much for zer. Ze felt heavy for much of the trip, heavier than ze had felt since arriving on that planet. The only thing keeping zer awake at all were the worry, stress, and fear surrounding what was to come. What the Earth for Humans terrorists were going to do to zer, and what they would manage to get from zer.

In the dark of the hopper, the low rumble coming from the truck sounded more like the engine of zer ship than a truck. As Drilora slowly woke back up, ze almost had zerself convinced that ze was still up there. That ze never came to Earth in the first place and was just waiting for the go ahead from the Uvvelian Space Agency to start the test. It was only the lack of stars that confirmed the worst. Drilora could always see the stars, no matter how bright the night got.

Suddenly, the truck came to a stop, jarring Drilora out of zer thoughts. Ze slammed into the metal side of the hopper, zer head hitting home. The pain radiating through zer was enough to keep zer awake against the sedative, though ze could still feel it there, trying to pull zer back down. However, with the truck stopping like that, ze figured that they had gotten to their destination. That zer next chance of escape was coming on quickly.

Just a few seconds after the truck came to a stop, it started to make a different sound. One that Drilora hadn't heard on the way over. One ze couldn't remember ever hearing. Zer first thought was that the truck was about to crush zer after all. But when the hopper shifted underneath zer, ze realized that they were about to dump zer out of the truck. Zer hands went up in front of zer as ze braced zerself against the fall.

Light came up all around Drilora as ze found zerself tumbling onto the floor. Ze almost expected to find trash under zer, with the humans bringing zer to the dump. But the floor was solid stone, a concrete floor unlike anything in zer tower. Without even trying, ze already knew that it would be too solid to punch through, even for zer. Ze quickly pushed against it, coming up to zer feet, looking to run from them.

Drilora was unstable standing there, but ze managed to remain standing. Zer fists came up in front of zer, ready to fight for zer freedom. Ze spun around, searching for the humans, searching for an escape, but that only made zer balance worse. Zer vision swam a little, and ze was worried that ze would fall again before ze could escape. Only, there was no path to escape that ze could see. No humans standing there, looking for a fight.

Stone walls rose up all around Drilora, with a stone ceiling overhead. There were lights spread all over the space, making it brighter than day, though none of them hinted at weak points in the cell. They were all attached along the seam between the wall and ceiling, shining down from above.

The stone walls came up to either side of the back of the garbage truck, with barely a crack between the metal and the stone. The hopper kept rising like the driver wasn't sure that ze was out. But once the hopper was fully extended, a metal wall came slamming down across that space, blocking any escape through there. Ze could see the slot where the metal wall had come down, where it was attached to the cement on either side. As technologically inferior as the humans were, construction wasn't easy to screw up, even on that level. Ze knew that the room, the cell, would be enough to contain zer, even once the sedative wore off.

"Ah, but then what?" ze muttered to zerself. "Once the sedative wears off, they'll have to face me with my strength returned. Unless..."

Ze didn't finish that thought, but the fears still flowed through zer. The worries that the humans would just leave zer in there, locked up in that unbeatable cage. In a few days, without food or water, Drilora wouldn't be able to stand up to them anymore. They wouldn't need the sedative to get what they want from zer, or to do the kind of damage that ze knew they would want to do.

With no obvious target to punch, Drilora slowly lowered zer fists. Ze stood there for a moment, just staring at that metal door, as the depression slowly flowed over zer. As much as ze didn't want to admit it, even to zerself, ze knew that ze had been defeated. That the humans had managed to do the one thing that they had always wanted to, what ze had always tried to keep from happening. They got past zer defenses, and made zer trust them. Ze promised zerself that ze would never make that mistake again, that ze would never trust another human.

Once the shock of zer arrival in the cell finally wore off, Drilora started to walk around. The cell was small for Drilora, barely twenty feet to a wall, so pacing the perimeter wasn't much exercise. But Drilora needed to burn through the rest of the sedative. If ze hoped to escape from that place, ze needed to be at zer best. Zer metabolism was going to be the only ally that ze was going to have there.

However, it was also going to be zer biggest detriment. Ze doubted that ze would be getting food anytime soon. Without having breakfast that morning, ze was already getting hungry. Hungry enough to suggest that it was much later in the day than ze had thought. With Cecilia sedating zer sometime in the night, it could be any time. The more that Drilora walked, the more zer body woke up, and the more zer stomachs demanded food.

As ze walked, ze got a closer look at the lights overhead. As expected, they were attached perfectly, with no sign of places to pull them away. The lights themselves were LEDs, making destroying them difficult without tools, and they were too close together to get any leverage.

On zer third trip around the room, ze realized that the lights didn't extend to the corners. Instead, there were black blocks there, connecting with the lights on either wall next to them. Drilora came up in front of one of them, staring up at it as ze tried to figure out just what it was. There was a glasslike sheen to it that made zer think of a camera. And considering the humans would need to be watching their prize, ze figured that was exactly what they were.

"Enjoying the show?" ze shouted at the camera. Ze raised zer arms to either side like ze was presenting zer body to the humans on the other side of that camera. As zer arms came back down, there was less drag than ze was expecting. It only reminded zer that zer fur was gone. That ze was standing there, quite literally naked, in front of the humans. It only made zer madder, more vulnerable in front of them.

Drilora continued to pace around the room, taking all of it in. Not that there was much to the place. Ze was just glad for the small bathroom in the corner opposite from the camera, though the camera would be on zer whenever ze used it. It was unclear if the humans would turn away from that sight, or if they would care either way. But with zer fur gone, with no clothes to replace it, it wasn't like the humans would see anything that they couldn't already.

As the day wound on, and Drilora only got hungrier, ze wished that there was a clock in the cell. That ze could tell just how long ze was in there, how much that ze would be missed in the world outside. For all ze knew, even Leanne had no idea that ze was gone. If Leanne didn't have business with zer, she could go a few days without visiting. But ze didn't for one moment think that any of them would come for zer once they knew ze was missing. Ze didn't think that anyone would care if ze starved there in that cell. Or if the feed from the camera was limited to the Earth for Humans terrorists. It could just as easily be sent all around the world for all the humans to watch.

Ze was about to try punching the camera, trying to destroy it so that they couldn't watch zer pace, when a weird, metal on metal sound rang through the cell. Drilora turned all around, searching for the source. But there was only the one metal wall in the cell, so ze should have known exactly where it was coming from. Before ze could spot the small slot in the base of the metal wall, the slot was already sliding closed once more.

On the floor, right in front of the slot, was a metal plate. On the plate was what looked like an uncooked thunder potato. At first, Drilora thought that it was just a regular, human potato. That the humans were just playing with zer. Ze couldn't eat a human potato. But as ze slowly came closer to the plate, ze realized that it really was a thunder potato. That the coloring was just yellow enough to mark it as one.

Thunder potatoes aren't meant to be eaten raw. They're meant to be cooked until right after turning black. But as Drilora's stomach growled once more, ze knew that ze didn't have much of a choice. That it was better to eat it raw than to starve. Worse was the thought that that thunder potato might likely be zer last meal. That the humans would only give zer the one, or use the promise of more of them to get zer to cooperate. All ze knew for sure was that they clearly knew how to use the food replicator, though that was clear from the sedative that Cecilia had created with it.

Drilora glanced back at the camera behind zer, taking zer time as ze went over to the potato. Ze couldn't let on just how hungry ze was getting. How much ze needed the food. If the humans ever learned how well they could manipulate zer, ze would lose any leverage ze might have to get out of there. With zer eyes locked on that camera, ze reached down, picking the plate up.

Instead of eating on camera, ze came over to that back corner, sitting down on the floor beneath it. However, as ze looked around the room, ze realized that the camera in the other corner could still see zer. That there was full coverage over the cell, with no spot not being watched by the humans. Ze glared up at that other camera as ze picked up the thunder potato, biting into it.

Drilora had never eaten a raw thunder potato before. It had an odd taste to it, and ze was worried that it would make zer sick. That ze wouldn't be able to get any nutrition from it at all, and that ze would be stuck relying on the humans' ability to cook it. Cecilia had seen zer cook it enough to do it, though ze doubted that she would bother. When ze managed to swallow that first bite, ze sat there, waiting for zer stomach to react to it. Waiting for some sign of whether or not it would stay down. When it didn't threaten to come up, zer stomachs starting to settle from the food given to them, ze took another bite. It was all that ze could do not to inhale the entire thing while the humans were watching.

However, soon after ze finished the potato, ze felt lightheaded once more. It took zer a moment to realize why that would be. What the humans could have done to zer.

Cecilia had already admitted to drugging zer food before. It seemed like the humans had done it again, and that they would likely continue doing it while ze was in their custody.

"Ah, crap," Drilora said, in Uvvelian, a purely human curse in zer native language. Darkness flooded zer vision as the sedative did its work once more, reclaiming zer to unconsciousness right there on the floor.

Chapter Forty-Seven
Victory
Cecilia

"What did it say?" Janine asked, staring at the screens in front of her. The two screens were on a desk against the corner, showing the two camera feeds coming from the cell. In the wall behind her was a window looking out on the main floor of the factory, the cell visible in the distance.

"Who cares?" Matt asked. He was standing behind Janine, his hand on the back of her chair, watching the feeds with her. "The sedative still works on the thing. We can keep it under control for as long as we want. That's the important part, right?"

"Right," Rene said. "Contained and under control. At least, until we can figure out how to kill the thing."

"We already know how to kill it," Cecilia said. She rolled her eyes at her father, annoyed that they were stuck babysitting the alien when they should be killing it. "I told you, the fur is the only protection that thing has. Just put a bullet in its brain and be done with it."

"Does it even have a brain?" Janine asked, scoffing at the thought.

"Cici, you know why we can't just kill it," Rene said. "We need it to get what we want. That was the deal we made. We capture the thing, and we get the advanced technology."

"Easy for you to say," Cecilia muttered. "You haven't had to put up with living with it for a week. And that smell... I mean, seriously, I'm sure that it was showering, but that smell never went away. At least now, it will have to put up with its own stick, stuck in there like that."

"Can it breathe?" Janine asked. "I mean... Not-not that we care."

"The cell isn't airtight, if that's what you're asking," Matt said.

"Can you two give us a moment?" Rene asked. "My daughter and I need some time alone to catch up."

"What about watching the monitors?" Matt asked. "You said--"

"He doesn't need to be reminded about what he said," Janine said. "I'm sure these two have it. Come on, Matt. Maybe I'll let you make it up to me."

"Make what up to you?" Matt asked, clearly oblivious to her mood. But the two of them headed off together anyway, ducking into the next room. Cecilia watched them go, heading over to close the door once they were gone.

"I don't know why you trust those two," Cecilia said, shaking her head as she walked back across the small room. She flopped back down on the couch next to the desk, her feet going up on the arm.

"Who said that I trust them?" Rene asked. He came over to stand next to the couch, reaching a hand down to lightly touch Cecilia's forehead, sliding her hair out of the way. "I don't trust any of them, but they are useful. You're the only one that I trust in this whole mess, a trust that even you had to earn."

Cecilia didn't say anything to that. She knew all too well what she had to do to earn that trust. But with her father saying how little he trusted the minions in the group, she was beginning to wonder if she should trust him anymore. After all, it wasn't like he had earned any trust from her.

"Well, this whole thing will be over soon enough," Cecilia said. She shook her head, sliding it out from under her father's hand. Her own hand went up to straighten her hair, undoing what her father had been doing. "Once we get what we deserve, we'll be rid of the aliens once and for all."

"Oh, now, I hope you're not referring to me," came a low, guttural voice from the back door to the room.

The hairs stood up on the back of Cecilia's arm as she sat up on the couch, her eyes flicking over to that door. The door was across from the one leading out to the factory floor, but it was visible through the windows. Cecilia wanted to check that none of the minions outside were watching, but she always hated turning her back on the alien. On any alien.

"Especially you," Cecilia said, scowling over at the alien.

Vortax leaned against the doorway, smiling over at Cecilia. Or, at least, Cecilia thought that it was smiling. Its face was elongated like an insect, the mouth dropping down from its nose rather than being a separate part of its face. The green carapace shined in the overhead lights, making it hard to look at the thing. Harder than its ugly form already made it.

"Like our group always says, Earth should be for humans, and humans alone," Cecilia said.

"Don't listen to my daughter," Rene said. "She's just overly sensitive, being stuck with the... the other alien all this time."

"Don't apologize for me," Cecilia said, glaring back at her father. However, turning away from the alien unsettled her too much for her to do it for long, and her glare went right back to it soon enough.

"Ha," Vortax said, its mouth clattering as it laughed in its alien way. "Children can be so ungrateful. Usually, we eat our young when they get too uppity before they're old enough to stand on their own feet. But then, this one looks too gangly to be much food."

"Come over here and you'll see just how uppity I can be," Cecilia said, shuddering at the thought of that thing eating its young.

"Now, now," Rene said, stepping forward to stand between Cecilia and Vortax. "As agreed, we've captured the uvvelian." He pointed toward the monitors across from them. Drilora was curled up on the bottom of the display, safely asleep once more. "It's in that cell out there, ready for you to take it away. But not before you give us what you promised us."

"Yes, yes," Vortax said, waving off Rene's words. Its claw ran through the air between them, just barely missing Rene's arm. If it had hit it, the claw was hard and sharp enough that it would have taken off his arm, but Rene seemed oblivious of that. Cecilia would have liked nothing more than an excuse to kill the thing right where it stood. However, she might miss her father if he died from the blood loss. Possibly.

Vortax headed over to stand in front of the monitors, its pincers rattling the entire way. With its back to Cecilia, she was able to glance over at the window, making sure that the minions were all preoccupied outside. They were busy setting up the rest of the factory for the delivery of the batteries that was scheduled to arrive that evening. With the uvvelian safely contained, they no longer needed the energy guns. They were a useful technology, just a taste of what Vortax had offered them, and would be worth a lot of money on the black market. Almost enough to make the whole effort worth it.

But then, that wasn't all that Vortax had promised them.

"The creature is asleep," Vortax said. It was hard to tell if that was just a statement or a complaint, its voice not shifting in the least when it said it.

"Yes," Cecilia said. "How else were we to control the thing?"

"It's of no use to me asleep," Vortax said. "I need it awake. I need it to give me the information."

"You'll get the information soon enough," Cecilia snapped. "It will wake up in a few hours. You're going to want to go in there soon beforehand, so that it's still under when you start questioning it. The thing is quite stupid when coming out of the sedation."

"Stupid by your standard or by its?" Vortax asked. "If by yours, I'm sure that I'll be able to get everything from it just by promising to let it go after." It started chitter-laughing again before it managed to finish that sentence, clearly thinking very little of human intelligence.

"We're smart enough to rescue you," Cecilia muttered.

"From your own people," Vortax said. It turned its head around to look back at Cecilia, its body still facing the monitors. Cecilia shuddered at that sight; she never liked it when the thing did that. "That is little proof of any intellect on your side. It is obvious that I was the one you should be aligned with. These... things... They're not even worth the planet that they call theirs. They are as technologically inferior to our people as you are to theirs."

Several retorts flowed through Cecilia's mind at that remark, but she didn't voice them. She needed to keep her temper around the thing, lest she accidentally kill it before it could give them what they wanted. A dead alien was no use to them. However, she couldn't help but wonder, if the krylonians were against the uvvelians simply because they thought them inferior, what exactly would happen once Vortax returned to its people.

If it returned.

When Vortax turned back to the monitors in front of it, Cecilia glanced over at her father. While they had never discussed the plans for after Vortax handed over the technology that it promised, she always hoped that he was planning on double crossing Vortax. That she would have her chance to kill the thing, to kill both of the aliens, before they could return to their people. She didn't trust either of them not to return to Earth with an invasion, though they both knew that no invasion was coming from them just yet. That was just a lie that they used to get more humans on their side. To see the dangers that these aliens presented.

"Fine, fine," Vortax said, sighing in a weird way. It was clear to Cecilia that the krylonians didn't actually sigh, but that it was something that it did to convey the sentiment to the humans. "I'll return once the thing is coming out of the sedation. But don't have the... humans around when I return." It waved a claw back toward the window behind it, and the minions outside. "I'll want some privacy with the thing. The answers I want from it weren't part of our deal."

"Agreed," Rene said. "But we expect the technology once you have your answers. You've had these past five years to transfer it all onto our technology. Blueprints, science behind it, everything, as agreed."

"Yes, yes," Vortax said. "Everything short of the slip drive. You... humans are to stay in your system until we are quite ready to deal with you."

"Is that what happened with the uvvelians?" Rene asked. "They left their system?"

"No," Vortax said. "We were just ready to deal with them."

That comment landed like a punch to Cecilia's stomach. The first real confirmation that they had of Vortax's plans for the human race, once it returned to its people. She glanced over at her father, hoping for some sign that he heard it too. That he understood the threat for what it was. But he was just smiling over at Vortax, clearly thinking only of the power, influence, and money that he would get from it all.

Cecilia wondered if the problem wasn't her. That it wasn't that everyone underestimated her, but that they underestimated everyone. Or, perhaps, she had gotten the superpower from Vortax somehow. That everyone was underestimating him just like they always did for her.

The alien glanced back at her again, turning its head while keeping its body steady. It seemed like it was silently asking her if she noticed that as well, but it was hard to know for certain with those alien features that turned her stomach.

Chapter Forty-Eight
Gloating
Drilora

Something felt different to Drilora as ze slowly came back to consciousness. The hard floor beneath zer was cold and uncomfortable, grounding zer against the continued weight of the sedatives. Zer hand reached out, searching for a blanket that wasn't there. Only, there was something else there instead.

Pain lanced through that reaching hand, and Drilora instantly jerked awake. Ze looked at zer hand, at the foot that was standing on it, before following the leg up to the person, the alien, that it belonged to. But that only confused Drilora more as zer brain struggled to shrug off the sedative.

"What?" ze asked. "You... You're supposed to be dead."

As ze struggled to explain why there was a krylonian standing on zer hand, zer first thought was that it was a different krylonian. That the one that ze killed when ze arrived there on Earth was long dead, only to be replaced by another one that came looking for it. But when the krylonian spoke, in perfect English, it was clear that this was the same krylonian.

"You tried," it said. "We krylonians are harder to kill than you pitiful uvvelians seemed to think. It's no wonder why your people lost the war."

Drilora's heart fell as ze feared the worst. Stuck there on Earth like ze was, ze never heard anything of the war. But with the krylonian there, obviously working with the Earth for Humans terrorists, it could have had access to some form of communication system that would reach its homeworld. Something that it had put together itself, while Drilora was stuck working with the two damaged spaceships. For all ze knew, a krylonian fleet was on its way to Earth, ready to destroy the planet just like they had tried with Uvvelia.

"Things like you are so easy to contain. To defeat. You are like humans, only there to help us win, even against yourselves. You should make everything easy on yourself, on everyone, and just tell me what I want to know," Vortax said. It pressed harder on Drilora's hand, grinding its foot down. Drilora hissed at the pain, but ze clenched zer teeth, trying to keep from screaming out. To avoid giving the krylonian the pleasure of seeing zer squirm.

"What you want to know?" Drilora asked. Ze wanted to sit up at least, but with zer hand pinned on the floor like that, it was impossible for zer to move. All ze could do was glare up at the krylonian as ze tried to extract zer hand. "What could you possibly want to know from me? Something that you couldn't figure out already. That would still be important if your people really won the war."

"Where is the slip drive navigation system?" Vortax asked.

"What?" Drilora asked. Despite the precarious position that ze was in, ze had to laugh at that. At the idea that ze was only alive because of one component to Vortax's ship. Only if Vortax had contacted its people, they could have easily sent a ship. And if it hadn't, then it couldn't know what had happened with the war.

"The humans have searched your entire tower, packed everything that they recognized and left the rest behind for me," Vortax said. "I have both ships, and I can tell why you've been stuck here all these years. While you had the ships, you are clearly too incompetent to repair them."

"Not incompetent enough not to hide the navigation system," Drilora said, smiling back at the creature. As ugly as the thing was, ze was getting some enjoyment out of its annoyance with zer. "You'll never find it."

"Oh, I'll find it soon enough," Vortax promised. "It's only a question of which will happen first; I torture the location out of you, I find it on my own, or you die from the torture."

"Except, how can you keep searching for it if you're in here torturing me?" Drilora asked.

Vortax just stood there, staring down at Drilora. It wasn't clear if it was struggling to come up with a proper retort to that, or if it just hadn't thought about that wrinkle. While it was clearly siding with the terrorists, it didn't seem to trust them any more than Drilora would have. Any more than Drilora trusted any of the humans at that point.

"Torture me all you want," Drilora said. "You won't get anything out of me." Ze smiled up at Vortax, pleased as punch that ze was getting something over on the creature. Vortax pressed its foot down harder, grinding into zer hand more. The skin, no longer protected by fur, peeled away. A light white blood seeped through the growing wound. Drilora tried to keep the pain to zerself, but a hiss came out of zer against zer wishes.

"Tell me, and this can all end," Vortax said. "The pain. Your fight for freedom. Your people. There's no sense in prolonging this."

"You know nothing of my people," Drilora said. "Or their fate. You're as trapped here on this mudball as I am. If you knew anything of the war, you would have already sent for rescue. You wouldn't need the navigation system, or the ships in my tower."

"The ships aren't in your tower anymore," Vortax said. "Those ships are mine, property of the Krylonian Empire. As is the navigation system."

"Well, then, you're all set," Drilora said. Ze wasn't trying to be snarky, but any way of delaying Vortax's victory could only help zer people. While ze had no idea the status of the war, ze knew that Vortax was only guessing that it was over. It had no way of knowing, either.

Vortax let out several annoyed sounding chitters, waving its pincers back and forth in front of Drilora's face. It threw its hands up over its head as it backed away from Drilora, heading around the rest of the cell. The moment that Drilora's hand was free, ze took it back, cradling it against zer chest as ze sat up on the floor. The blood quickly stopped flowing, forming a patch over the broken skin as ze held it back in place. Even as ze watched it, the skin reattached like nothing had happened.

"You will tell me," Vortax shouted.

Its claws waved closer to Drilora as it came back at zer. It swung its left claw straight at Drilora's face, but ze quickly dodged the attack. The claw slammed into the cement wall behind zer, and several bits of cement dust rained down. The wall showed a slight divot, making Drilora think that maybe the krylonian was stronger than ze was. Strong enough to help zer break out of that cell if ze could trick it into helping.

Drilora hopped up to zer feet, backing away from the raging krylonian. It was glaring back at zer, obviously frustrated and annoyed, if the creature was capable of feeling such emotions. Or any emotions at all. All that Drilora had ever seen from krylonians before was anger and rage.

Vortax rushed at Drilora once more, but Drilora was quick to back away from it, staying clear of its swinging claws. As ze backed away from the wall, ze looked up at the cameras in the corners. Ze figured that the humans were all clustered around those displays, watching the fight to come. The last thing that ze wanted was to give them a show, but ze was fighting for zer life. For zer people. For freedom.

Drilora stayed close to the walls as ze walked around the perimeter of the cell. Each time Vortax swung a claw, it flowed through the space where Drilora had just left, never coming close to hitting the wall again. There was no sign of damage on the claw that had hit the wall before, suggesting that the claw was unharmed by the impact. That Vortax wasn't worried about hurting itself, but was making an effort not to destroy the cell. Not to do the very thing that Drilora was hoping for.

And that meant that Drilora wasn't going to be able to escape with Vortax's help. That zer dance around the cell was only wasting time. So, Drilora took a different approach.

Vortax swung its right claw straight at Drilora. If ze had continued around the wall, it would have slammed right into zer face. However, Drilora stopped in zer circling, pivoting around that swing. The training that ze was bringing Cecilia through earlier was fresh in zer mind, and ze lined up one of those moves. Zer arm wrapped beneath the still swinging claw, grabbing Vortax by the arm and using the force of its own swing against it.

Drilora pulled on that arm in the same direction as the swing, dropping zer shoulder below the arm and pushing it straight into Vortax's side. The momentum had Vortax flipping up and over Drilora, allowing zer to throw it across the room. It slammed into the metal wall, bouncing off of it to fall to the cement floor. But Vortax didn't stay there for long.

"You fool," Vortax said. "You're only delaying the inevitable. You are no match for me; your people are no match for mine. The krylonians are impervious to harm, invulnerable in a way that your people never could be."

"No?" Drilora asked. "How about I take that carapace off of you? I'll bet you're just as vulnerable beneath it as I am without my fur. I'll shove that claw of yours right up your--"

"Don't make me laugh," Vortax yelled, before giving a purely human sounding laugh that didn't sound the least bit natural. "You could never penetrate my carapace. You're too weak to even stand on your own."

"Look at me, krylonian," Drilora said, raising zer arms out to the side. "I'm standing. The sedative has already worn off. If I had my fur, we would be on even ground here. Only the humans are keeping us contained."

"No, they're keeping you contained," Vortax said. "I can walk out of here anytime I want. The humans are on my side."

"The humans are on the humans' side, no one else's," Drilora said. "I learned that the hard way. You'll learn that yourself soon enough. Once they get from you what they want, they'll have you in a cell just like mine. Just you wait."

"That is where you went wrong," Vortax said. "I have no intention of giving these things anything. Once I have the navigation system, I can leave this dirtball of a planet and return to my people. And then, after your people have been exterminated, like the insects that they are, I will return here to annihilate the humans as well."

"Look who you are calling an insect," Drilora said. "You're the insect. The cockroach, just looking to be squashed. If only we discovered a sedative that would work on your people, the humans would have everything that they needed to take you down."

"Ah, but you didn't," Vortax said. "They don't. They only have what I have given them."

Just as it said that, the metal wall behind it burst forward. It slammed into Vortax from behind as it was dislodged from the frame, knocking him forward a step. Drilora stared at that wall, at the gaping hole that was forming in front of zer. The wall fell onto Vortax, tackling it to the floor. Once the metal was out of the way, Drilora could see a huge truck, the front of which was sticking into the opening where the metal wall once stood. Staring back at zer from the driver's seat was Leanne, her wide eyes locked on the metal wall.

"That... and a truck," Drilora said, as ze stared openly at Leanne. At the woman who had finally come to zer rescue.

Chapter Forty-Nine
Rescue
Drilora

At first, Drilora was thrilled to see Leanne there. But that feeling quickly soured as the questions started to flow through zer mind. Forefront of those questions was just how Leanne had found zer in the first place. It only suggested that Drilora was a bigger fool than ze already thought.

"What are you doing here, Leanne?" Drilora asked, zer voice tainted by the paranoia that ze was feeling.

"Gee, Leanne," Leanne said. "Thank you so much for rescuing me from these terrorists. How can I ever repay you?"

Drilora wasn't amused. Ze folded zer arms across zer chest, staring Leanne down. It wasn't nearly as intimidating with zer standing in front of the huge truck, which could just as easily crush Drilora as it had Vortax. But ze wasn't about to go anywhere with Leanne until ze knew that ze could trust her.

"How did you find me?" Drilora asked.

"Seriously?" Leanne asked. "Don't you trust me? We've been working together for--"

"I trusted Cecilia," Drilora shouted. Ze pointed up toward the cameras behind zer, figuring that Cecilia would be watching them through that feed. "She's one of them."

"Wait, what?" Leanne said, sounding honestly surprised by that revelation. "No, that... That's not... How? Why?"

"Her father is their leader," Drilora said. "Maybe if you had done your job and gotten me his information sooner... Gotten a photo at least. I had seen her father when they came knocking on my door."

"Look, we can argue about this later," Leanne said. She looked into her side view mirror, seeming to be able to see the building behind the truck through it. With where it was, jammed against the lip of the cement section of that wall, Drilora figured that the mirror was broken, but ze couldn't see anything of it. "We need to escape while we still can."

"Escape?" Drilora asked. "Or is this just some trick to get me to show you where the navigation system is."

"The navigation system?" Leanne asked. "That's why they kidnapped you?"

"No, they kidnapped me because they're terrorists," Drilora shouted at her. "The krylonian was threatening to kill me if I didn't tell it where the navigation system was. Of course, as far as I knew, it was still in the ship."

"You know what, fine, you're right," Leanne said, exasperatedly. "I took the navigation system."

"Ah, hah," Drilora said, pointing an accusatory finger at her. It didn't make zer feel any better that ze was right about Leanne. That ze couldn't trust her any more than ze could trust Cecilia.

"I brought it to an astrophysicist," Leanne continued.

"What?" Drilora asked, suddenly not sure what to think. What could she possibly have gotten out of taking the navigation system to an astrophysicist? Perhaps the coordinates of Uvvelia? But then, ze couldn't figure that out either. That was the whole issue with the navigation system to begin with. "Why-why would you do that?"

"To help you, you moron," Leanne said, saying the words slowly and enunciating each one. "You needed the thing reprogrammed so you could get home. Why else would I do it?"

"Oh," Drilora said, thoroughly defeated. But then, ze realized that maybe Leanne wasn't trying to trick zer. That she really was there to help. To save zer from the humans. From the terrorists. "But then..." ze started, still unsure how Leanne could have found zer in the first place.

"Ugh," Leanne grunted. "How do you think I found you? I told you last night, there was a shipment coming out of the battery manufacturer. When you didn't show at my office, and there was no answer at the tower, I went looking for you. The tower was cleared out, completely. Even the ships were missing. So, I had to go on the mission myself. It was very scary, by the way. But it led me here. The place was abandoned, making sneaking in rather easy, and I saw you and that thing on the camera feeds. There's only the one cement box in the middle of the factory floor, so I stole the truck and rammed it into the metal wall. Then, you continued to accuse me of working against you this whole time, wasting precious escape time, by the way, and risking us getting caught when the terrorists returned."

"But... Where are the terrorists?" Drilora asked. Ze figured that they would all have been watching the fight with the krylonian.

"How the hell would I know?" Leanne yelled at zer. "Now, come on if you're coming, or I'll be getting out of here on my own. I'm sure these batteries would get me a pretty penny on the black market, and Jerri knows all about selling stuff on the dark web. It might make coming here and trying to rescue you worth it, even if you get yourself killed by being stubborn."

"Fine," Drilora yelled at Leanne.

"Fine," Leanne yelled back. She quickly turned away from Drilora, looking around the cab of the truck as if searching for something. Perhaps searching for how to back the truck up.

"No, wait, wait," Drilora shouted, quickly rushing forward before Leanne could leave without zer. The passenger side door was jammed against the cement, but Drilora hopped up onto the hood of the truck, holding on for dear life. With the sedative gone from zer system, zer strength was back on in full force. Ze was ready to get out of there, even if ze had to carry the truck zerself, rather than the other way around.

The truck let out a low grumble and a grinding sound before it backed away from the hole in the cell. As the rest of the building fell into view, Drilora saw a huge, empty, abandoned looking factory. It seemed like such a cliché to zer, exactly like they always showed in the comic books. Only, just as Leanne had said before, there was no sign of the bad guys anywhere.

Just a few feet out from the cell door, the truck came to a stop. Drilora stayed there, holding onto the hood of the truck, zer head swiveling around to take in everything around them. To zer left, there was a huge opening in the far wall, showing the night sky beyond it. To zer right, ze saw a huge window overlooking an office. Standing in that window, staring out at them with a stunned look, mouth agape, was none other than Cecilia.

"Oh," Leanne said, when she spotted her over there. "I guess the bitch is with them."

"Just get us out of here," Drilora said.

Drilora quickly hopped down from the hood of the truck, rushing over to the passenger side door. As ze came up to it, ze realized that the door was too small. That ze would need to squish down to get through it, and it was unlikely that the cab would be much better. Without zer fur to protect zer, ze would feel like a raw nerve, either inside or outside of that cab. Ze settled for grabbing onto the door, staying close to it as they escaped.

Once Drilora was positioned over there, Leanne continued to back the truck up. She spun the wheel, trying to turn the truck in the close quarters of the factory. But then a loud crash rang out and the truck jerked a little before stopping. Drilora was jostled in zer position on the door, but ze was able to hold on well enough.

"Uh... What happened?" Leanne asked.

"You're asking me?" Drilora asked. Ze looked back toward the rear of the truck, but ze couldn't see anything over there.

Leanne fiddled around with the controls for a moment before driving the truck forward. It came closer to the cell, threatening to head in there again. She slammed on the brakes, which let out a loud screeching sound. Then she turned the controls once more, taking the truck backwards. Again, the truck let out a loud bang as it came to a stop.

"What the..." Leanne started.

Drilora quickly hopped down from the truck, racing around to the other side of it. That was when ze saw the issue, where the back of the truck was bashing against the edge of the door. It looked like Leanne didn't have the truck angled just right to get outside.

"Let's just hoof it," Drilora said.

Ze glanced back over zer shoulder at the window to the office, expecting to see Cecilia still over there. But there was no sign of the woman back there. After underestimating her for much of that week, Drilora was worried just what that would mean for their escape.

"Come on," Drilora said, turning back to look at Leanne.

"I'm coming, I'm coming," Leanne said. She was already climbing out of the passenger side door, hopping down to the floor. Once down, she ran toward zer, grabbing onto Drilora's hand before ze could offer it.

Together, the two of them started around the truck, heading for the open doors beyond it. Drilora just got a few steps past the side door when ze noticed something off to the left, beyond the cell. Or, more accurately, two somethings. The two spaceships were sitting there, in the space between the cell and the far doors. Neither of them looked worse for the wear, though the gaping hole that had been in the side of the krylonian ship was repaired. With how Vortax had been talking before, Drilora had a feeling that the krylonian had repaired the ship. That the ship was just waiting for the navigation system to be replaced so that it could navigate its way back to Krylonian space.

Or Uvvelian space.

"Wait, wait," Drilora called out. Ze pulled Leanne to a stop as ze looked over at the ships.

"There's no time, Drilora," Leanne said. "I'm sorry, but we can get the ships back from them later. Once your fur has regrown, you can take on the terrorists on your own."

"That could take months," Drilora said, looking back at Leanne. "Years, maybe. I could be home in minutes."

"Yes, but--" Leanne started.

But then, a loud bang rang out through the space, echoing around the open room. Drilora turned back toward the window into the office, unsurprised to see that Cecilia had returned. That she wasn't alone.

Drilora didn't recognize the man that was holding the gun, but it was aimed right at zer heart. Without zer fur, there would be nothing stopping that bullet from ending zer life. The humans were all slowly stalking their way forward, giving the man with the gun a wide berth and staying out of his shot. As they closed in around the two of them, Drilora looked over at Leanne, about to tell her to run for it. After everything that she had done for zer, ze needed to keep her safe.

Only, it was already too late.

Leanne wasn't looking at the humans closing in around them. She wasn't looking up at Drilora's eye. Her hand was in front of her face, and she was staring at it. Staring at the splotch of red that was on it. It took Drilora far longer than it should have to recognize that splotch of red, and the hole in her chest that it was coming from.

Just seconds after Drilora looked back at her, Leanne's legs quit, falling out from beneath her. She toppled backwards, her head falling toward the cement floor. Before she could fall far, though, Drilora turned to the side, reaching out to grab onto her. Zer arms cradled her, gently placing her down on the floor, as her life's blood flowed out of her.

Chapter Fifty
The Cost
Drilora

"Drilora, I... I have to tell..." Leanne started. A cough came up before she could finish the sentence, and blood flowed out from her lips, hitting Drilora in the face. Ze didn't notice it. All ze saw was zer friend dying in zer arms.

"Shh," ze said. "Don't try to talk. We... We need to get you out of here. We need to get you some help."

"I don't think you can help me," Leanne managed to get out, before another few coughs came up. Her hand reached up to cover her mouth, blocking the blood. When the coughing stopped again, Drilora grabbed that hand, holding it tightly to zer chest. "I need to tell you, the navigation system--"

"Don't worry about that," Drilora said, shaking zer head. "I'm not mad about that anymore."

"No, it... It's in my... My car." She lifted her free arm, trying to point, but there was no strength in that arm. It quickly fell back to the cement floor next to her.

"Don't worry about that," Drilora said again. "Let's just get you out of here."

"Get out of here, Drilora," Leanne said. "Get out while you still can. Forget about me. I... I'm just glad that... That they didn't hurt you."

"Nah, you know me," Drilora said. "I'm invulnerable. They can't hurt me. But... But you, I... We need to get you some help."

"Oh, but your fur," Leanne said. Her free hand managed to reach up, touching Drilora's face below zer eye. "It is a shame that I'll never see it again. It was spectacular. You are spectacular. I just wish that I had told you sooner. I... I love..."

"No, no," Drilora said, shaking zer head. "You just hold on. I'll get you to some help."

Drilora looked around zer, trying to find somewhere that ze could take Leanne. Ze had no idea where ze was, where the closest hospital was. Without signs around to direct zer, all ze could do was carry Leanne out of the factory and into the city. Ze already knew that Leanne would be dead before ze found anywhere to bring her. Before ze could find anyone to save her.

Except, they weren't alone there in the factory. The humans were already streaming out of the office, guns at the ready, all pointed toward Drilora. Ze braced zerself, waiting for those humans to shoot zer. Waiting for the end to come. Without zer fur, the bullets would rip right through zer, much like that first one had to Leanne. However, no one was shooting just yet. They just closed in around Drilora and Leanne. Despite the bluster of the group, none of them seemed interested in being the one to end Drilora.

Drilora clutched Leanne to zer chest, shielding her from the terrorists around them. Ze could feel Leanne's hands clenching zer shoulders, pulling at the bare skin there. There wasn't much strength in her hands, but whatever strength she had, she was using it to hold Drilora close. To hug zer as she died in zer arms. But Drilora was too distracted by those humans around them to notice just when that happened.

"Aw, isn't that a shame?" Cecilia said, with only a slight bit of sarcasm in her voice. "I kind of liked Leanne. She was nice enough. You know, for a traitor to the human race."

Drilora glared over at her, hidden at the back of the crowd. She was smiling over at them from behind the terrorists, her people. Drilora wanted to go for her, to push through the terrorists and wring the girl's neck. Everything that had happened that past week, from the fires to Leanne's death, it all went back to her. Ze knew that it was all her doing, her fault. And she got away with it, too, because everyone underestimated the girl, including Drilora.

Including Leanne, who had died for it.

"Why?" Drilora asked, zer eye still locked on Cecilia. Demanding an answer from the woman. An answer that ze knew wouldn't come. At least, not one that ze would ever understand. That would ever explain why they had done what they did. "Why come after me when all I ever wanted to do was leave? To help the humans while I'm here and earn my way off this planet. I wanted to leave just as much as you wanted me gone, more so perhaps. Why come after me at all?"

"Why do you think?" Cecilia asked. A sneer played across her face as she slowly strode forward, slipping through the crowd between them. The terrorists slipped to the side, letting her pass, but quickly folded in behind her. They all wanted to watch the final battle to come. "You're an alien, Drilora. You're not human. You don't look like us. You don't think like us. You don't act like us. We have no idea what you might do if pushed in just the right way. If you would destroy the world just to leave it. Or if you would kill us just for knowing that your people exist."

"I feel like I've already proven that I wouldn't," Drilora said. Slowly, ze placed Leanne's body onto the floor at zer feet before standing up, turning to face Cecilia head on. "I've done nothing but help. I've shown no sign that I'm a danger to anyone. But that krylonian in there?" Ze pointed back toward the cell, where ze had last seen Vortax. "From the moment that that thing landed on this planet, it had shown exactly what it was. It had tried to kill those soldiers at the site of the crash. It had killed some of them. It was only because I stopped it that any are still alive now. That they lived to arrest me. And you are working with that thing?"

A few of the terrorists looked between Drilora and Cecilia, confused expressions coming onto their faces. Some of them started to squirm, seeming uncomfortable with their hypocrisy laid bare like that. It quickly became clear to Drilora that their involvement with the krylonian had not been common knowledge, and that those that did know about it weren't comfortable with it.

"Oh, you didn't tell them?" Drilora asked, pointing to a few of the terrorists that were showing their obliviousness. "Didn't think your sycophants could take the truth? That they might turn on you if they knew that you were inviting the very invasion that you warned about? The krylonians are the danger here, the ones that have shown to be the danger from the beginning. And yet, you work with them. Them, not me. Not the uvvelians. If the uvvelians ever chose to come to your planet, it wouldn't be as conquerors. It would be as friends. Even now, even after what you did to me, what you did to Leanne, we would never come here to kill. We would sooner leave you to your own demise, one that would likely be brought on not by us, but yourselves. Or the krylonians."

Drilora shrugged, not quite sure which was more likely at that point. Ze didn't for one moment think that Vortax was dead. All ze wanted was to get out of there before it came back at zer. Before it was too late for zer to escape. But with the terrorists all still having their guns aimed zer way, ze knew that they would shoot zer the moment that ze made any movements against them, or to flee.

"The krylonian is as big of a fool as you are," Cecilia said, as she came out of the crowd. She barely looked at them, seeming completely unperturbed by their discomfort. "We wouldn't have let that thing leave Earth any more than we were going to let you leave. At least, not in the way that it would have wanted." She laughed at that comment, clearly thinking of how she wanted to kill Vortax and Drilora both. "We were just going to take its technology and kill it as soon as we got the chance. Of course, it looks like you beat us to that. Now, we just have to get rid of you and we'll be safe from you aliens again. No impending invasions. No dangerous aliens living in our midst, ready to go off at a moment's notice. At the first perceived insult to its honor, or whatever excuse you came up with."

"You lived with me for a week," Drilora shouted at her. "Do you really think that I would be so dangerous? That I would kill anyone at the slightest provocation? You would have been dead the day you moved in if that had been the case. You're still alive, though I probably should have killed you while I had the chance."

"See?" Cecilia said, pointing toward Drilora as she looked around at the terrorists. "Even this high and mighty warrior, claiming virtues that it never showed, would stoop to killing a poor, innocent, defenseless girl."

"Oh, give it up, Cecilia," Drilora spat at her. "Despite how you presented yourself to me that first day, I know the truth. You've never been poor or innocent. You're just a viper, looking for something to bite. If I had never come to this planet, it would have been something else. Someone else. Some other person who never earned your ire and doesn't deserve it. Someone that did nothing against you besides exist. Someone... Someone like Leanne."

Ze glanced back over zer shoulder at Leanne's body, wishing that ze could have done more for her. That ze could have kept her safe, like ze had promised. Or at least that ze could give her a proper burial, whether by zer people's standards or the human's. But standing there, all but surrounded by those terrorists, and escape too far away to get it, ze needed to focus on getting zerself out safely. And that meant dealing with Cecilia and her people.

Before the terrorists could try anything against zer, Drilora turned back to look at them. Ze squared off against them, getting ready to take them all on if ze needed to. It wasn't going to be easy with all their guns and without zer fur to protect zer, but ze didn't have a choice in the matter. The terrorists weren't giving zer a choice in the matter. That was what made them terrorists.

The only things ze had going for zer were zer strength and the fact that Cecilia was standing between zer and those guns. From the smirk on Cecilia's face, though, Drilora got the sense that she wanted to take zer down herself.

"Leanne did far more than exist," Cecilia said. She slowly sank into a defensive posture, one that Drilora had taught her zerself, reminding zer of that training. Of the fact that ze had created the very monster that ze was up against, and that the fight was much more even than ze was thinking. "She betrayed her people to the aliens that had come here. You claim innocence. You claim that all you wanted to do was leave. But no one invited you here in the first place. You didn't have to come here. All you had to do was stay away. And you didn't."

"I had no choice," Drilora said. Ze felt like ze had told that story to everyone that ever asked, but no one seemed to be listening. "The krylonian attacked me. I was only trying to survive. It shot me down and I crashed on this mudball of a planet. I've been trying to leave ever since. All that you and your people have done was make my life more miserable than it already was, make me want to leave more, and make it impossible to do so. So... thank you for that. Maybe now you'll actually let me leave?" Even as ze said that, ze knew that they wouldn't. That they would attack the moment that they were allowed to. It was only Cecilia there, showing that she wanted to fight zer, that kept them from shooting zer dead right there and then.

"Oh, you'll leave alright," Cecilia said, nodding at Drilora. "In a body bag."

"Are we really going to waste a perfectly good body bag on that thing?" one of the terrorists asked, causing several of them to laugh.

Chapter Fifty-One
The Confrontation
Drilora

Cecilia gave no other warnings before she attacked, striking out at Drilora. She raised her leg up, swinging it down at Drilora. Her sidekick uniform had metal tipped boots, and they glinted in the light as they came at zer. While Cecilia's form was better than during their training sessions, it was still sloppy. Drilora was easily able to deflect the strike, putting zer arm up to block it. However, when the boot tip slammed home, it hurt zer arm more than ze was expecting.

"Erg," ze grunted, taking a step backward under the blow and pulling the offended arm against zer chest. When ze looked down at the arm, ze quickly realized why it had hurt more. That ze was still expecting zer fur to take the damage, keeping zer safe. Ze reminded zerself that ze needed to be more careful, to approach the fight differently.

Even as Drilora was distracted by that pain, Cecilia was following through with that first strike. Rather than going for another kick, she punched out, hitting Drilora on the shoulder as it turned toward her. Cecilia let out her own grunt of pain from the impact, though it didn't hurt Drilora at all. From what Drilora could see of her punch, it looked perfectly done, as ze would have expected from her after their training. It was just the impact with zer bone as it was coming at her that hurt her hand. That gave Drilora a slight comfort, knowing that ze wasn't as defenseless without zer fur as ze feared.

Before Drilora could come at Cecilia again, a gunshot went off. The sound echoed around the room, making it sound like all of the terrorists were shooting. Drilora jumped to the side, putting zer back against the truck next to zer.

When ze didn't feel pain from bullets hitting zer, ze glanced down at zer body for barely a moment. There was no sign of blood anywhere, but ze knew that ze wouldn't be that lucky the next time the terrorists started shooting.

With Drilora distracted by the gunshot, Cecilia was able to get back into position, coming at Drilora again. This time, she reached up behind her, pulling the batons off her back. It was the first time that ze had seen more than the handles sticking up behind her back, the first time that ze noticed that they weren't just normal batons. The top of the baton showed several ridges, and let out an electrical sound as Cecilia swung them. Stun batons had shown up in enough of Drilora's comic books for zer to recognize them when ze saw them.

Cecilia quickly wound up her next swing, pulling the baton up over her head. Rather than going to block the baton with zer arm, Drilora dodged the attack, taking a step to the side out of range. The baton came through in zer wake, hitting the side of the truck. The truck's door let out a thud at the impact, a dent forming right where Drilora had been standing. However, the energy from the baton didn't seem to do much of anything as it dissipated across the metal.

Before Cecilia could line up her next attack, Drilora punched outward. Zer fist slammed right into Cecilia's shoulder. Unlike when Cecilia had punched Drilora's shoulder, the impact did a lot more damage. Cecilia was knocked backward under the blow, and she slammed into the first few terrorists standing over there. An odd, cracking sound went out at the same time, and Cecilia let out a light yip of pain before she could stop herself.

Several more of the terrorists brandished their guns at Drilora, taking aim at zer once more. With Cecilia's yip in the air, Drilora had no doubt that they would shoot. Before they could, ze dropped to the ground, ducking beneath the truck.

The shots went out anyway, the bullets hitting the side of the truck and the floor beneath it. The truck rocked a little under the force of the bullets before settling back down again.

"No," Cecilia shouted. "No shooting. That thing is mine. I'll be the one to kill it."

"It," Drilora scoffed, bristling at that word. At the audacity of Cecilia thinking that she was any match for Drilora one on one. Without those other terrorists ready to shoot zer, Drilora knew that ze could take Cecilia in a fair fight. Except, there was no such thing as a fair fight between a human and an uvvelian.

Once the shooting stopped again, Drilora came rolling back out from beneath the truck. Cecilia was waiting for zer there, standing over zer prone form. Before ze could stand up, ze felt the stun batons slamming into zer back. The energy flowed through zer, hurting just as much as when the harpoon was sticking in zer fur. It seemed like the batons were using a similar battery as the guns did. Without zer fur to absorb most of the current, Drilora worried that ze wouldn't survive many of those blows. Fortunately, Cecilia followed through with the blow, like ze had taught her. The baton slid off zer back and onto the floor.

The moment that the current left Drilora, ze was jumping back to zer feet. With Cecilia standing close to zer side, ze slammed zer shoulder into her. She was still bent over from her swing, and her face took the shoulder slam, right next to her nose. The force knocked her backwards and away from Drilora. Her left hand went up to her face, but there was no sign of blood there. She kept hold of both of her batons, and the one in her left hand came dangerously close to electrifying her.

Rather than chasing after Cecilia, Drilora glanced over at the terrorists, expecting them to be lining up their next shots.

Many of them were glaring at Drilora, but their guns were all lowered in front of them. No one was ready to go against Cecilia's orders just yet, but Drilora knew that wouldn't hold up for long. Not once Cecilia was defeated. The moment that Cecilia was knocked out, Drilora would need to get out of the line of fire.

That momentary distraction might have cost Drilora everything. Before ze could square off against Cecilia again, she was coming at zer, swinging. The first baton narrowly missed zer face as ze ducked to the side under it. The second stabbed forward, and Drilora had to hop to the side to avoid it. The two dodges had zer hopelessly off balanced, and the next strike would likely hit home. Before Cecilia could send another swing zer way, Drilora reached out, pushing Cecilia backward and away from zer.

Cecilia wasn't expecting the move. She stumbled backward several steps until she hit something behind her, toppling over. Her hands went out to either side, desperate to hold onto the batons while not hitting herself. Her rear slammed home on the cement of the floor, but her legs were draped over something else. Something that neither of them had noticed was right behind Cecilia.

Drilora's rage rose up in zer when ze noticed Leanne's body there. Ze charged forward, zer hand already reaching down to grab onto Cecilia long before ze was in range. Cecilia didn't seem to notice as Drilora came to loom over her. Ze grabbed onto the front of her uniform, pulling at the collar. The rest of the uniform had no give to it, holding against Cecilia's body even as ze pulled her up by it. Ze lifted Cecilia over zer head, turning back to look at the terrorists.

"Stay away from her," Drilora shouted, as ze threw Cecilia across the room.

Cecilia sailed through the air, slamming into the crowd and knocking several of them to the floor. The few terrorists that weren't knocked over all turned to look down at those that were, with a few of them reaching down to help Cecilia up to her feet. But Drilora barely noticed that before turning back toward Leanne behind zer.

"I'm so sorry, Leanne," Drilora said. Ze reached down to pick up Leanne's body, cradling it against zer chest. "I'm so sorry." Ze looked around zer again, trying to find somewhere to put Leanne's body so that it was out of the way of the fight. All ze could see were the open doors behind the truck, and the open space beyond them. With a quick glance back over zer shoulder, ze started off, running toward those doors. Running toward freedom.

"Oh, no you don't," Cecilia shouted out. When Drilora glanced back at her, she was just getting to her feet, still too far away from zer to stop zer escape. But instead of chasing after zer, Cecilia reached over to grab a gun from one of the terrorists next to her. She quickly took aim at Drilora's back.

Just before the gun went off, Drilora jumped to the side, ducking behind the back of the truck. A light ping went out as the bullet hit the back corner of the truck. The sound of glass shattering drew Drilora's attention over to a car that was parked back there, out of view of the doors. Ze had seen that car enough times to know that it was Leanne's.

Leanne's dying words came back to Drilora's mind upon seeing that. Ze knew that the navigation system was in there somewhere. That zer escape, not just from the terrorists but from Earth, was close at hand. With one last glance toward the back corner of the truck, Drilora rushed toward that car, still holding Leanne's body close.

The moment that Drilora got over to the car, ze quickly pulled open the door. Ze lightly placed Leanne's body into the driver's seat before looking around the rest of the car. The navigation system, a large, black box with a few wires poking out of it, was just sitting on the back seat, visible for all to see. If the krylonian had come out there, had seen the car, it would have already known where the navigation system had been. It would have left Earth, rather than coming in to torture Drilora.

"Not so fast," Cecilia called out. Drilora didn't need to look her way to know that Cecilia was standing by the door to the factory. That her gun was already pointed at Drilora, ready to end zer life. Ready to end the fight right then and there. "You're not getting away from me that easily."

"You thought that was easy?" Drilora asked.

Drilora looked down at the car in front of zer, the only protection ze had from the gun, and the only weapon ze had available to stop Cecilia. Only with Leanne's body sitting there, and the navigation system still in the back seat, ze couldn't afford to use it as either. If the navigation system took the bullet, ze would be stuck there forever. It was krylonian technology, and far beyond zer capabilities to repair with human technology.

So, instead of going for the car or the navigation system, Drilora slowly came back out from that protection. Zer hands went up in front of zer in surrender, hoping that Cecilia wouldn't just shoot zer. That she might consider trying to fight zer again. Just as Drilora stepped into the open, gunshots started going off once more. Drilora closed zer eyes, bracing for the inevitable. Bracing for zer death.

Only zer death wasn't coming. Ze didn't feel any pain from bullets hitting zer. After a moment, ze opened zer eyes once more, making sure that ze was still alive.

Cecilia was no longer looking at zer. Her eyes were wide as she stared back at the factory doors, and whatever was happening in there. It was only then that Drilora noticed the echoing of the gunshots. That it was the terrorists shooting at something inside the factory, rather than Cecilia shooting at zer.

And there was only one thing back in the factory that would have had the terrorists shooting at it.

Chapter Fifty-Two
The Final Fight

The gunshots gradually grew quiet, as the terrorists either ran out of bullets or died to the krylonian. With Cecilia distracted by whatever was happening over there, Drilora rushed forward, quickly grabbing the gun from her hands. Her eyes snapped back toward zer, but she didn't do anything before Drilora pushed her backward. She fell back onto her rear, over in the grass at the edge of the parking lot. There was a fence over there, and she clung to it as she stared up at Drilora, her eyes wide with fright. Just from the look on her face, Drilora knew that she was expecting zer to kill her.

"Just stay out of my way," Drilora shouted at her, pointing in her direction, before turning to look through the doors to the factory.

Vortax was standing just outside of Drilora's cell. It was holding one of the terrorists in one of its claws, and the terrorist's gun in the other. Several terrorists were shooting at the krylonian, the bullets ricocheting off of its carapace, though enough of those bullets were going into the terrorist that it was holding for him to be quite dead already. Vortax roared at those terrorists, sounding like he was mad that they had killed the human, preventing him from doing just that. Then, he threw the corpse of the terrorist at the others, knocking several over once more. The gunshots kept going off, and blood started to splatter around there, showing that several of the terrorists were shooting each other in the confusion.

"Krylonian," Drilora shouted out, drawing Vortax's attention.

"Dead thing," Vortax called back, turning away from the terrorists that were still shooting it to look at Drilora.

Vortax ran at Drilora, coming up along the truck. Rather than rushing toward the krylonian, Drilora came over to the corner of the truck. Ze reached out, pushing the truck with all zer strength. The tires squeaked as the truck turned in place, swinging around to hit Vortax. An odd clicking sound went out, but Drilora didn't see what happened. All ze knew was that the truck must have hit the krylonian head on, though ze doubted that it would be enough to kill it.

Rather than bringing the fight to Vortax, Drilora turned away from the truck, rushing back toward Leanne's car. Ze already knew that, with the krylonian's carapace still in place and without zer fur, ze would be no match against it. It would still be protected from most of zer attacks, and ze would be vulnerable to its attacks. Zer only hope would be to get the navigation system and take off in one of the ships. Ze wouldn't need the navigation system installed until ze used the slipstream drive to get back to Uvvelian space.

Of course, Drilora thought about leaving the krylonian there on Earth. The damage that it would do without zer there to stop it. Part of zer wanted to do something about that. To protect the humans, even after everything that they had done to zer. But ze knew that there was nothing that ze could do if ze was dead. That ze needed to get away, to live to fight another day. However, as usual, Drilora was soon to realize that ze wasn't going to have a choice in the matter.

Drilora was halfway back toward the spaceships when the truck jerked to the side. Ze wasn't prepared for the move, but ze was far enough away from the truck to dodge out of the way. The truck swung back through the doorway, slamming into the side over by Leanne's car. But it didn't stop there, continuing to slide forward along that edge of the doorway to slam into the car, right where Drilora had been a moment before.

Ze looked over at the car with wide eye, watching as zer friend's body was destroyed further by the truck crashing into it. Drilora couldn't see what happened to what was left of Leanne, but ze knew that it wouldn't be pretty. That when the first responders found her body, they might not be able to identify her right away.

With how distracted Drilora was, Vortax could have ended zer right then and there. But Vortax had its own distraction. It stayed over by the cell, staring at Drilora with a level of rage that was beyond anything that Drilora had seen from it.

"I knew you had it," it shouted, calling Drilora's attention back to it. "Give me the navigation system."

Drilora looked between Vortax, the navigation system, still held in zer hand, and the spaceships right inside the factory. Ze was closer to the ships than Vortax was, still able to get in one of them and take off before the krylonian could get to zer. It was the first thing that ze could think of, the only real chance that ze was going to have to get away. So, the moment that ze got over that initial shock, ze ran for the closer ship. The krylonian ship.

"Oh, no, you don't," Vortax shouted, as it ran that way as well.

As Drilora came closer to the krylonian ship, ze saw the gap in the hull where the navigation system was meant to be inserted. It was right next to the hatch, and ze thought for sure that ze could get the system inserted and get inside the ship before the krylonian would be on zer. Ze came to a halt just in front of the ship, lining the navigation system up to the hole as ze did so. The momentum helped get the system in place, and a satisfying clicking sound came from within it, followed by a whirring sound that told that the system was coming online. That the krylonian ship was ready to bring zer back to Uvvelian space, once ze got inside.

Drilora quickly headed for the hatch. Just as ze threw zer arms through the hatch, though, Drilora felt an arm grab zer around the waist. It felt like zer stomachs were left behind in the ship as the rest of Drilora's body was wrenched backward, away from the hatch. Ze fell to the cement floor, sliding away from the ship. Away from zer escape.

"Not so fast, dead thing," Vortax said, as it loomed over Drilora's prone body, glaring down at zer. "That ship is mine. But don't worry. You'll see it again soon enough, at the point of the armada that is coming to destroy this puny little dirtball of a planet."

Drilora was at a loss for what to do. How to defend zerself against the krylonian standing over zer. The only thing that ze could think of was to kick out at the creature, hoping that zer strength could overpower it. With where Vortax was positioned over Drilora, the only target that ze could hit was right between its legs. So, that was exactly what ze did, kicking upwards with all zer strength.

Vortax let out an odd, chittering sound when Drilora's kick hit home. Its eyes grew wide, the anger there only intensifying. But the one thing that Drilora had been hoping to happen, knocking Vortax out of the way so that ze could stand up, simply didn't. Vortax kept his feet planted on either side of Drilora. Worse, with his rising anger, the rage powering its next strike, Drilora knew that zer life would soon end.

All because of what Cecilia and her people had done to zer.

As Vortax wound up the killing blow, Drilora could only think of how that fight would have been different if ze had still had zer fur. If ze wasn't so flat-footed, being captured by the Earth for Human terrorists. Had Drilora known that Vortax was still out there, still alive, ze would have tracked it down sooner. It wouldn't have come down to such an uneven fight as that one. But while Drilora's presence in the city had been known to all, Vortax had done well at hiding among the humans.

The looming form of the insect-like creature seemed to belie that. To suggest that something else had happened there. Certainly, the creature couldn't have hidden among the humans without help. It wouldn't have been able to escape from the same facility that ze had been held in while ze was learning the local languages. The Earth for Humans terrorists must have been hiding it that whole time, working with one alien while condemning the other. It didn't seem fair to Drilora. None of it seemed fair. But then, Drilora's life had never been fair since the krylonians had entered it.

Drilora closed zer eye as the death blow came at zer. Ze didn't want to see that. Didn't want to see zer life ending, there on that mudball of a planet. So, ze didn't see it when the harpoon hit home, straight in the middle of Vortax's chest. Only after hearing the buzzing sound of the electricity flowing through that harpoon, electrifying the krylonian, did Drilora open zer eye once more.

Vortax still loomed over Drilora, but its back was arching backward in pain. Its mouth was clenched tightly together, keeping it from sounding the scream that it should have been making at that moment. As the electricity flowed through it, an odd smoke started to billow out from the cracks in its carapace. It took Drilora a while to realize that the creature was being cooked from the inside. That the carapace was keeping the heat from the electricity contained, working against the creature where no other weapon had managed to kill it before.

Once Drilora realized that ze wasn't about to be killed by the creature anymore, ze slowly slid out from under the krylonian's legs. Ze sat up next to the hatch of the krylonian spaceship, zer eye following the cable connecting that harpoon to the gun that had fired it. Cecilia was standing over there, at the back of the truck, holding the gun that had saved Drilora's life. The same gun that had been invented to kill zer in the first place.

"What?" Drilora asked. "Where? How?" So many questions were flowing through zer head at that moment, but none could form as ze struggled to think of what to say.

"The guns were in the same shipment," Cecilia said. "We were just putting them together here. There's plenty more in here, so don't even think of trying anything against me right now. I am not in the mood for any alien shenanigans."

"No shenanigans here," Drilora said. Ze raised zer hands up in surrender, not wanting to risk antagonizing Cecilia further. All ze wanted was to climb into that ship and get out of there. Only with Cecilia's glare locked on zer, ze wasn't sure if she would consider that a shenanigan or not.

After a moment, Cecilia turned from Drilora, staring over at Vortax. The electricity flowing through it was keeping its body vertical, but it seemed like nothing else was. Drilora figured that, once she shut off that electricity, the krylonian would just crumple in a ball there. It seemed vindictive to keep that electricity flowing like that, but ze had long since stopped putting anything past the woman. Ze was done underestimating anyone.

Chapter Fifty-Three
The Ultimate Escape
Drilora

When it became clear that Cecilia wasn't going to shoot Drilora, ze slipped back toward the ship. Ze was close enough to reach up through the hatch, pulling zerself through it. The inside was small, barely enough space to stand up in, with equipment all around zer. Drilora had spent enough time poking around the insides of that ship over the years, trying to get either of them to work, to know what all of it did. A cursory glance of the equipment told Drilora what ze already knew, that the krylonian ship was ready to leave Earth behind.

As was Drilora.

Drilora would have preferred to take zer own ship out of there. To return in the ship that ze had left in. But with Cecilia still out there, still looking to end the alien infestation of Earth, ze didn't have the time to spare to pull the equipment from the krylonian ship and put it into zers. Not enough of it would be easy to swap out, with many of the components needing to be retrofitted, like the scientists on Uvvelia had done with the slipstream drive.

Once ze was sure that the ship would fly, ze slid into the cockpit. Vortax's body was just starting to crumple into that ball that Drilora had been expecting, its carapace falling off the cooked flesh within it. Cecilia came over to stand next to the krylonian, her foot kicking the pieces apart like she was searching for something. For some part of the krylonian that was still alive, perhaps. It made Drilora wonder if that was how the creature had survived zer shooting it on the day of the crash. If ze had to worry about leaving that creature behind there on that planet.

The instruments of the cockpit turned on one by one the moment that Drilora was sitting in the chair. It was the first time some of them had turned on for zer, and it took zer a moment to figure out what some of them were, and others remained a complete mystery to zer. But all ze needed to get out of there were the flight controls and the slipstream drive controls. The latter were the same between the two ships, with the slipstream having been stolen from the krylonians in the first place.

Drilora activated the retrorockets, slowly lifting the ship off the ground. Cecilia turned away from the pile of meat that was the krylonian to look up at Drilora in the cockpit. She placed her hand over her eyes, blocking the light so that she could see zer through the front screen. To Drilora, it almost looked like she was saluting zer, though ze knew that wasn't the case. That Cecilia would sooner shoot zer than salute zer.

With Cecilia so close to the ship, Drilora was careful as ze brought it through the doorway and out of the factory. Leanne's car came into view behind the truck, and ze could see her body over there. It was knocked over, lying on the console between the front seats, but didn't show any other signs of damage beyond the bullet in her chest. Drilora wished that ze could stay long enough for the funeral, but after five years of being stuck on that planet, ze worried that any delay would cost zer that one escape.

However, Drilora wasn't quite ready to leave that planet just yet.

Once ze was clear of the factory, ze spun the ship around, aiming right back at it. Cecilia came back into view, her eyes still locked on the ship. Her hand slowly fell away from her eyes as she realized what Drilora's plan was. Why ze wasn't just flying away from there.

"Oh, f--" Cecilia managed to get out, before turning away from the krylonian ship and running deeper into the factory.

Cecilia wasn't Drilora's target, though. Ze locked onto zer own ship, the Uvvelian ship that ze was forced to leave behind, firing three blasts from the krylonian ship's cannon. All three blasts hit the ship straight on, destroying it completely. Fires started up where the ship once stood, threatening to spread to the rest of the factory. Drilora barely spared a single thought for that fire, and that Cecilia might once again be stuck inside of one.

It wasn't that Drilora didn't care if Cecilia made it out of there or not; just that ze figured she could take care of herself just fine without zer.

With no sign left of the Uvvelian ship, Drilora figured that the humans would have no new technology beyond what they figured out themselves. That the technological contamination from the arrival of the two aliens would be limited to that electricity gun, which would no longer be necessary for them to have. Ze thought about shooting the truck while ze was at it, but ze knew that would take out the rest of the factory. That while Cecilia might be able to escape the one fire, she wouldn't survive an explosion.

Of course, ze figured that she deserved that anyway, for what she had done to zer. For her hand in Leanne's death. But Drilora had never been a threat to the humans, had never been a threat to anyone or anything that didn't threaten zer first. So, ze left it at that, turning the ship away from the factory.

Drilora looked back at Leanne's body one last time before increasing the power on the retrorockets, bringing the ship higher into the air. Once ze was high enough, ze pulled back on the controls, lifting the nose of the ship toward the sky. The stars came into view all at once, inviting Drilora back to them. Ze didn't once look back before hitting the throttle and launching back into space.

Despite the ship being krylonian technology, the ship left no trace of its passing in Earth's atmosphere as it left the world behind. Only those close to the factory would have noticed the streak of light playing across the night sky. For the rest of the city, and the world, their only hint at Drilora's departure was zer absence from the tower.

Soon after the ship left the atmosphere, Drilora pulled back on the throttle. The ship was already heading away from the planet at a decent rate, and ze only needed to be far enough away to activate the slipstream drive. Still, ze couldn't help but to look back at the planet behind zer, the one that ze had been eager to leave ever since ze arrived.

With a slight flick of the controls, Drilora spun the ship around to look back at Earth. It still looked like a mudball to zer, perhaps even more so after living on it for five years. There was no interest in going back, nothing that ze felt like ze left behind. The only regret as ze left that place was not leaving sooner, not leaving before zer presence there cost Leanne her life.

Drilora was still watching the planet fade away when a light on the navigation display flicked on. Ze didn't need to look over there to know that ze was far enough away from the planet, or any other source of gravity, to activate the slipstream drive. That ze could finally go home. Ze took in a steadying breath, taking a huge whiff of the krylonian air. It didn't smell any better than the air on Earth had, but ze had gotten used to that. With one last glance toward the planet, Drilora hit the button to activate the slipstream drive.

The hole in space popped up behind the ship, rather than in front of it, further away from the closest source of gravity. So, Drilora didn't see it before the ship was falling into it once more. Seconds later, ze was coming back into Uvvelian space.

With what was left of Uvvelia in front of zer.

As much as Earth had looked like a mudball, Uvvelia looked like a burnt ember. The planet used to be nothing but green, with a few cities that were visible from space. Instead, it was all red, with what looked like fires still burning across the surface. Ze couldn't tell just how long the fires had been burning, when the uvvelians had lost the war with the krylonians. All ze knew was that zer home was gone. That there was nowhere left for zer to turn to.

Drilora stared at that sight for what felt like hours, at the horror that ze had escaped merely by accident. For all ze knew, ze was the last uvvelian still out there. That zer race was all but extinct save zer. Ze couldn't see anywhere on the planet that was untouched by the destruction.

But then, another light lit up on the display in front of Drilora. It was one of the displays that ze hadn't figured out. All ze knew was that it couldn't be a good thing. Not with the planet in front of zer in such destruction. Part of zer just wanted to give up there and then. To surrender to whatever came next and let the last of the uvvelians meet the same fate as the others. After fighting the humans, fighting Vortax, ze wasn't ready for another fight. Not if there was nothing left to fight for.

So, ze turned the ship again, turning away from zer home to look back out at the stars. That's when ze saw it. Saw the huge ship heading zer way, with guns already locked on the krylonian ship. However, the ship wasn't krylonian. It was uvvelian. Zer people had survived after all, even if it was without a homeworld.

And yet, Drilora had no way of contacting them. No way of telling them that ze was on the ship. No way of getting them to not kill zer. All ze could do was stand tall in the window and wave at the ship.

Cecilia

Cecilia managed to escape from the warehouse through a back door before the fires started up in earnest. She kept her distance from the blaze, watching the uvvelian escape into space above. The place seemed like a complete loss, the technology that both aliens would have provided them gone. The only saving grace in the whole mess was that her father was still out there, but he felt just as lost to her as he was when she was living in the tower.

By the time Cecilia made it around to the front of the warehouse, there was an odd ringing coming from over there. At first, she just thought it was the guns letting off that sound as the fire got to them, but the truck was sticking out the main doors of the building and the fires still hadn't gotten to it. It took her a moment to realize that the sound was coming from further away, over by Leanne's car, and a moment more for her to head that way.

When Cecilia got over to the car, she reached in, stretching over Leanne's body to grab the phone lying on the seat next to her. The display showed "Leanne Mooney Agency", and she quickly answered the phone.

"He... Hello?" she asked, hesitantly. With how destroyed she was feeling over the loss of the alien technology, her voice already sounded like she was close to tears.

"Cecilia?" Jeri asked, her voice coming through the phone. "Where's Leanne? What happened?"

"She's... She's dead... They're-they're all dead," she said, the tears already coming. She wasn't sure how much of those tears were real, and how much was her playing it all up for Jeri's sake. "You should probably send the fire fighters here. There's a raging fire. Drilora, ze..."

"Oh, god," Jeri said, her voice low. "Well... At least we still have you."

Enjoy the book? Remember to rate and review
on Good Reads:

www.ingramcontent.com/pod-product-compliance
Lightning Source LLC
Chambersburg PA
CBHW061501120726
48001CB00004B/1175